THE CAT'S EYE CHRONICLES #5

KRAIT'S REDEMPTION

T. L. SHREFFLER

Cover and interior design by the professional team at the Runaway Pen. For rights inquiries, contact therunawaypen@gmail.com.

ISBN 978-0-9993102-3-6

THE CAT'S EYE CHRONICLES

Books in this Series

CONTENTS

PROLOGUE

C rash watched the bonfires in the distance.

Each day, more devotees swelled the Shade's ranks. Shadow portals transported them from cities, from fields and mountains—from anywhere—to this forsaken desert. Nameless warriors pooled beneath a red plateau that towered in the twilight, blocking the moon.

An army of the lost, Crash thought. Their burning pyres beckoned to him like lighthouses on a foreign shore. But he had left those fires behind, walking miles into the flat desert to sit among the sand.

The Shade's encampment might be in the Desert of Ester, but he wasn't sure. His sense of certainty had fled long ago. He wondered at this unprecedented gathering. He wondered at the royal city's evacuation, so close to winter solstice night.

He watched the fires glint against the darkness. He watched, and sat, and pondered. At first, Cerastes' army had puzzled him. He didn't know why a Grandmaster, typically a solitary figure concerned with martial discipline and meditation, would want to gather so many numbers. But now, as Crash became more firmly entrenched in the Shade's activities, he knew what they were about. He had thought Cerastes meant to wage war against the human kingdom, but he was wrong.

Cerastes wanted the Hive.

Crash had realized the Grandmaster's ambition when the assassin Cobra had issued his last dying words. It had all become suddenly, perfectly clear. *Stop him.* Cobra's death had returned the arrow to Crash's compass, and perhaps for the first time, he knew true north. He knew what he had to do.

He stood and walked away from the crimson fires on the horizon, behind an outcropping of rocks. There, he emptied a bag onto the ground. Ingredients for his spell, including a sheaf of yellowed parchment and fresh salamander ink, fell to the sand. He wrote the spell, then built a small fire out of venomgrass and willow bark. He drew symbols in the sand, and the flames turned indigo blue. Then he burned the paper with its written message. A wandering wind brushed the top of the dunes, carrying wafts of sand and smoke up to the stars.

He doused the fire when he was finished. Then, his black hood pulled low over his face, he sat on his heels to wait.

Redemption. A returning, a renewal. Would the Hive help him now, or would they hold him to his trespasses? *Someone must answer,* he thought. Someone must answer his call, his message burned on the wind, and someone must answer for his Grandmaster's mistakes.

He thought back to Sora and the rest of his companions in the City of Crowns, and he felt ashamed. Under the influence of Cerastes' power, he had wavered. His demon had sensed his Grandmaster's dark aura, had sensed a home, and for a while, he had lost himself. But Sora's touch—more than that, her words, her spirit—had brought him back.

He couldn't fight Cerastes alone. He couldn't trust his darker half to re-sist the Shade's pull, because he, too, was a discarded outcast of the Hive. His Grandmaster's demonic presence was irresistible, drawing close all those scattered savants with nowhere to belong. Crash had felt his own will tremble. Even now, he couldn't quite steady his hands. He couldn't show Sora his weakness. More importantly, he couldn't show it to his own kind.

Someone had to do the right thing. *The right thing*, he thought ironically. Someone had to warn the Hive. *Anyone who can read the Wind can read this message,* he thought. He only hoped Cerastes was too distracted to see it.

Hours passed as he waited. The silence of the desert stretched, as spacious and echoing as a tomb. The stars and moon circled overhead, trailing across the heav-ens. He found the constellation of Kaelyn the Wanderer and asked, begrudgingly, for luck. Then his eyes picked out other celestial formations known to his race. He recounted their stories in his head: Sibilant, the assassin so stealthy and quiet, she could walk between this realm and the world of ghosts; Dartmouth, who replaced his teeth with knives; Marrow, so cunning he outsmarted the gods and stole the Dark God's weapons in eons past. Crash found it ironic that, despite all that had transpired, a story could still lend him courage. And each star was a story, a light in the dark, a dream in the abyss.

The wind picked up without warning. A whirl of sand twisted up from the ground, building, growing. Then a figure stepped from the dust.

Crash stood up. He didn't know what to expect.

The sand settled. A woman dressed in black stood before him. She was insidiously tall. Her hair fell in plaited rows down her back. He noted the chakrams at her belt: circular blades that could remove a man's head with a single powerful throw. Her eyes glowed the shocking green of aloe.

Memory stirred, and he recognized her. He searched for her name. It came to him.

"Grandmaster Natrix," he bowed.

"Viper," she returned, and waited for him to straighten. "I have listened long for word of my brother. Tell me, what has Cerastes done?"

CHAPTER 1

S ora stood on an open expanse of meadowland behind her stepfather's manor. Instead of green grass cushioning her feet, a layer of snow and ice caked her boots. Winter had overtaken the Fallcrest estate. The trees were licorice-limbed and sugar-coated, and the sky was a white, woolen quilt.

She glanced behind her. A rose bush grew against a low stone wall, its limbs naked, its thorns menacing, its branches arced like claws against the sky.

A chill wind blew her blond hair over her shoulder. She shuddered, wrapping her arms around herself. She didn't wear a cloak. Her skin felt as cold and stiff as marble.

She remembered this place. She had traveled here before in guided meditations. But the snow was new. The season had changed.

She trudged up the icy hill. Before long, a gated corral came into view, ringed by thick metal poles. Her stomach tightened, and she unconsciously reached for the Cat's-Eye stone at her neck, which sent only a little warmth to her hand.

A monster waited beyond the corral's closed gate, a monster whose strength she needed to harness. But every time she neared the *garrolithe*, it attacked her with terrifying rage. It stood on four legs, a great beast taller and broader than a bull. Its mane of bristling quills could pierce her skin. Its gaping jaws could swallow her in two wolfing bites. How could she tame a beast of such ferocity? The creature wasn't flesh and blood, but formed of magical energy centuries before her time. How could she control it?

Here, in the dreamscape of her mind, she must try.

She walked across the snowy meadow to the corral. As she neared, her sense of unease grew. The corral's gates dangled off their hinges like broken iron wings, the metal twisted and warped beyond use. Inside was empty.

A sudden, low growl erupted behind her.

Sora turned, numb with fear. She stared into the blue-fire eyes of the monster. Its teeth stretched as long as her forearm. A mane of bristling quills stiffened along its neck. It stood on four legs with shoulders as powerful as a bear.

Sora tried to find her courage, but she could only summon thoughts of Crash. *He's gone*, she thought, her fists curling at her sides. *He's left my side. How am I supposed to be strong?*

Her sense of hopelessness grew. The struggle seemed pointless. She couldn't win against the *garrolithe*—she couldn't win against herself. She knew, this time, she would be devoured.

The rumbling growl, deep in the *garrolithe's* throat, continued.

Sora took a shaky breath. A small cloud of mist formed between herself and the monster. The beast breathed with her as one. Within its fiery eyes, she saw her own reflection. She saw someone small, her face too pale and thin, her brows too low and gaze too focused.

Then the *garrolithe* widened its lionlike jaws. She closed her eyes and succumbed to its strength, to its dominion. She knew this moment was inevitable. A sense of relief filled her. *This is the only way.*

She felt like a deer in its final moments, after a long and harrowing run from the wolves.

The dank cave of the *garrolithe's* mouth enveloped her, its hot breath on her hair, her face. Her fists tightened as she braced herself. The first prick of the beast's fangs pierced her neck.

Ferran slammed his hand down on the desk.

"She's lying," he asserted.

"She's not lying," Caprion said.

The red stone at Ferran's wrist glowed in response to the Harpy's voice. *Magic.*

"A spell to sooth my temper? You arrogant bastard."

"Force of habit," Caprion didn't sound sorry.

"Bells!" Ferran swore. "Winter solstice is only three nights away. At this rate, we'll all be celebrating the end of the Kingdom, if not the human race. We need answers—we need this book."

"I realize that."

"Krait is lying, she has to be," Ferran repeated. "Of course she can read *The Book of the Named*. She's a Named assassin!"

"I showed her the pages, and she said they were blank."

"And you believe her?"

"She can't lie under my voice's influence," Caprion reminded him. "Only one explanation makes sense: she isn't truly Named at all. She's an imposter. Viper suspected as much during our initial interrogation."

"So it's possible?" Ferran asked.

"Of course," Caprion said. "Other races lie about their names; they just don't hold as much significance."

"Then we need Crash."

Caprion folded his arms. "He has joined the Shade."

Ferran kicked a footstool across the room, where it smashed into the wall next to a wide stone hearth. He glared at the stool. He had meant it to sail into the roaring flames.

He and Caprion stood in a small library on the second floor of the Ebonaire manor. Mahogany bookshelves lined the walls. A row of windows to Ferran's back revealed a night sky thick with falling snow.

Ferran shook his head, even more frustrated. Only a few days ago, he had managed to steal *The Book of the Named* from the Shade, but the pages were blank, and remained blank no matter who tried to read them. His Cat's Eye detected an enchantment on the book—an ancient spell soaked into the binding like old liquor—but his stone couldn't remove it. The magic seemed impossible to pry from the book's unassuming pages.

Only a Named assassin could read *The Book of the Named*. Semantically, it made sense. Crash could have read it, but he had vanished almost a week ago, when they had first arrived at the City of Crowns.

"She said her Name was Krait," Ferran repeated, his voice tight and controlled. "Under the influence of your voice, she swore it."

"Her mind is broken. Cerastes has manipulated her for years. He must have tricked her into thinking she was Named. Perhaps she isn't the only one of the Shade to carry a false title."

"If Crash were here..."

"Would you really trust his word, after what happened to Sora?"

"We don't know if he was involved."

Caprion looked like he wanted to argue, but he shut his mouth. He turned away and paced the room, his feet an inch above the floorboards. Silence fell as heavily as the snow outside the window.

"Has she improved at all?" Caprion finally asked.

"No."

Ferran stared blindly at the falling snow. No one knew what had happened to Sora, exactly. A hired coach had arrived at the Ebonaire manor the morning after the winter solstice parade, with little explanation from the driver, except that a cloaked figure had placed the girl in his carriage and given him this address.

For the last two days, she had laid unconscious in her bedroom, pale as a ghost, as her mother slowly cleansed the poison from her system. The wound at her neck was minimal, hardly a needle's prick, and yet the poison in her veins was powerful indeed. The herbs Lori needed were difficult to find this time of year, and the tonic took a master's hand to brew. They didn't know when Sora's fever might break, or when she would return to consciousness. Lori had left yesterday to the Healer's seminary, to purchase more herbs to treat Sora's condition. Doubtlessly the storm had detained her.

Ferran blamed himself. He should have searched for Sora when she didn't return from the winter solstice parade, but a fierce blizzard had made the city streets impassable.

"Only an experienced assassin could have brewed that poison," Caprion pointed out.

"That doesn't implicate Crash. There's an entire cult of assassins in this city."

"It doesn't prove his innocence, either."

Ferran glared at the Harpy. "Right then. We know the enemy poisoned her, but how did she escape on her own? She had help. The driver said a 'cloaked man' put her in that carriage. Perhaps Crash saved her life."

"A mystery left unsolved," Caprion said flatly.

Ferran pulled out *The Book of the Named* from his pocket and turned it over in his hands. It looked like a leather-bound journal, though obviously ancient. He flipped through a few of the blank pages. The parchment carried no stains, no rips, no creases. Unlike the book's binding, it looked hardly a day old.

The creak of floorboards distracted him. Ferran glanced at the closed door, listening. Who else would be awake at such an early hour? A strange scent filled his nose: sharp and brisk, like clear mountain air. His Cat's Eye glimmered at his wrist, indicating magic. Ferran tried to place the smell. The Sixth Race's magic carried the scent of mildew, like a pool of stagnant water, while the First Race was sharper and more metallic. Dracian magic always carried a burnt flavor, like campfire ashes or heavy incense.

The midnight hour had long since passed. No one in the manor should be awake....

"What is it?" Caprion asked, watching him warily.

Ferran crossed to the door, cracked it open and peered out into the hall. He checked left and right, but saw only darkness, no candles, no lanterns. At night, the Ebonaire manor became a maze of shadows and solemn doors. Walking about without a light came at the risk of breaking one's neck.

He sniffed the air, but the scent was gone. He touched the Cat's-Eye stone on his wrist cuff, but it remained dormant. He finally closed the library door and turned back to Caprion with a troubled frown.

"Nothing," he said. His red Cat's Eye had turned dark and quiet. He rubbed a hand over his jaw. He needed a shave.

"The hour grows late," Caprion said, perhaps in response to the weary look on Ferran's face. "I will return to our prisoner."

"Ask her again about the book, would you?"

Caprion's lips tightened. The Harpy always had an arrogant look about him, but his expression intensified it.

"Cerastes is winning," Ferran pressed. "I don't know what else we can do."

"Sleep, perhaps."

Ferran knew he was right. They had been burning the midnight oil since the parade, and nothing had come of it except more frustration. He was too tired to do anything now, even think clearly. Perhaps new ideas would come in the morning.

"I pray sleep finds me." He bid Caprion goodnight. The Harpy glided from the room like a ghost, his feet hovering just above the carpet.

Ferran rummaged in his pocket and withdrew a cinnamon stick, which he rolled back and forth between his fingers, thinking. His eyes turned to the falling snow outside the window. Then he moved across the room to an armchair and sat down heavily, allowing his head to loll back against the cushions. Perhaps tomorrow, they would find some other way to interpret *The Book of the Named* and discover Cerastes's plan. Until then, they were at an impasse.

CHAPTER 2

Sora traveled down a corridor in the Ebonaire manor. She could see quite clearly, despite having no candle to pierce the darkness. She felt rejuvenated and energized. Her feet sprang against the wooden floorboards. She smelled frost on the windows, and dust, and pine. Every sound seemed magnified: a clock ticking behind a closed door, a skittering mouse in the walls, a restless sleeper turning. The night was alive with endless movement.

Just minutes ago, she had awakened in her bedroom with a fire burning in her chest. She didn't remember how she had come to be in the Ebonaire manor. Delusions and dreams laced her midnight world. She only knew one thing—the enemy hunted her, the same enemy who had threatened her life and hounded her steps since her arrival in the City of Crowns.

I am not prey.

A memory flickered. She glimpsed, in shards and remnants, a great jaw enveloping her head. A stab of pain ended the image. She returned to the warm scent of the moment. A sense of purpose filled her, an aching need to hunt. She was tired of being controlled, caged.

The hallway ended abruptly at a tall window. Dead end. Sora stretched up, inspecting the window sill. She pressed her hands against the panes. The glass was so cold, it numbed her fingers at a simple touch. She pressed experimentally—the window wouldn't open. Then she noticed the latch.

With little thought, she unlatched the window and opened it. A fierce wind blew into the house, and snow immediately began piling onto the wooden floor.

Sora climbed out onto the roof. She didn't worry about the frozen tiles beneath her bare, pink feet. She tightened the knot on her robe, bent to all fours, and crawled to the side of the roof like a cat, where she found a trellis covered in frozen vines. She used the trellis to scale down the side of the manor, climbing almost forty feet to the ground. She ignored the icicles and thorns that cut her hands.

She needed to find a way into the sewers. From there, she would hunt down Cerastes and chew off his head.

Snowdrifts covered the manor grounds, some taller than her waist, but Sora kept to the main drive where a tunnel of giant oak trees shielded her against the storm. The snow wasn't as deep here, and she ran down the drive with minimal effort, interchanging between two legs and all fours.

Burn stood in the overhang of the stables, facing the weather, listening.

Lori would disapprove. He was still healing from a particularly nasty head wound inflicted by the Shade. But his insomnia didn't leave him much choice. Since his escape from the underground sewers and arrival at the Ebonaire manor, he couldn't sleep at night. He felt a growing pressure in his chest, a gathering sense of unease. So he left the cozy attic in the stables, where he and the rest of the Dracian crew hid from the Ebonaire staff, and faced the violence of the storm. He went to see, and he went to listen.

His ears were unusually long and pointed, and no other race could hear with such depth and precision. To Wulven ears, the wind spoke its own language, not always loud, not always clear. It carried knowledge. It whispered secrets. He listened now, as he had for years, sinking deep into himself and opening to the storm's voice.

Something about his escape from the Shade nagged at him, and he thought he knew why. When he had escaped through the underground tunnels, he hadn't run across any other assassins. The city's sewers had been empty, when just a week ago, hidden eyes had filled every alcove, every corner. It unnerved him, with winter solstice eve only a few nights away. What were they planning?

The wind howled, telling him of silent streets, darkened windows and smoking chimneys. He sifted through whining dogs and crying infants, horses jostling in their stables, spinning weathervanes and rushing water—but he heard no answer.

Then, muffled by snow and cracking ice, he heard something unusual, something he didn't expect.

Burn stood up. His nostrils flared sharply at a strong scent. Sora. Yet something unusual tainted her sweat. Something he couldn't name.

He launched into the tall snow drifts, then waded toward the column of oak trees that sheltered the front drive. He didn't quite believe his nose until he discovered footprints along the driveway, fast filling with snow. Soon, they'd be invisible, and her scent buried completely. He glanced back at the manor, wondering if he should get help, but there was no time. If he went back now, her trail would disappear.

He pulled up the hood of his cloak to protect himself against the cold wind, then started running down the front drive, following Sora's trail through the snow.

The Ebonaire front drive led Sora to a street, which she followed into The Regency proper. The snow hid much of the city, the road marked only by snowdrifts and icy lamp posts. Walls and fences were at times indiscernible from each other.

Eventually she turned down an alley and approached the great Regency wall, which separated the nobility from the rest of the City of Crowns. There, her nose alerted her to a metal grate in the ground that led to the sewers.

She searched the base of the wall, but her limbs felt stiff and heavy, and her heart labored in her chest. She took another step, and stumbled in the snow. She tried to regain her feet, but fell again. *What's wrong with me?* she thought in frustration. Why wouldn't her body obey? Her instincts told her she was stronger than this.

She crawled forward determinedly, looking for the grate, but it was covered in snow. She would have to dig. She studied her small pale hands. The tips of her fingers were turning blue. Why didn't she have paws? Paws were so much better for digging.

Then her nostrils flared. A scent reached her on the wind, and she turned, her eyes piercing the night. A bulky figure approached her from behind. She recognized the man's steps.

"Sora?" said a grumbly, baritone voice. "Sora, what are you doing?"

A growl started low in her throat, but it wasn't deep enough, not as fierce as she wanted.

"Go away," she said.

"I will, if you come with me."

"You shouldn't be here."

"*I* shouldn't be here?" said the Wolfy, surprised. He stood over her, almost seven feet tall. "What are you doing?"

"Hunting."

Burn gave that a moment of serious consideration. "We should hunt together then, in the morning, after the storm passes."

"No. I'm tired of waiting."

He peered down at her. Light from a nearby window half-illuminated his face, enough for her to see the concern in his whiskey-gold eyes.

She bared her teeth up at him.

"I suppose you've waited a long time," he said. His long ears twitched.

"You won't put me back." Her heart quickened and a note of desperation entered her voice. No, she wouldn't go back to her cage. "You won't. You can't."

"No, I won't put you back, but you shouldn't hunt alone. You have allies to help you, and against the Shade, you need your pack."

Sora snarled. "I won't be prey any longer."

Burn studied her. She watched his hand travel to his belt where he kept a knife. She prepared herself to fight. She crouched, facing him, her fingers arced into claw-like shapes.

Somewhere behind them, a tree branch cracked under the weight of its white burden. Burn turned. This could be her chance to escape. She leapt forward, past him...but her body was weak, not as it should be, and too affected by the cold. She fell face-first into a snow drift. She tried to push herself up, but the cold sapped what was left of her strength, and blackness flooded her senses.

Burn lifted Sora gently into his arms and turned back to the Ebonaire manor. Worry creased his brow. He didn't think her behavior was caused by a fever. When he touched her cheeks, they were icy cold.

No. He knew the Cat's-Eye stone at her neck was to blame. The entire time Sora had faced him, the necklace had shone with a piercing blue light, different than the green color it usually emanated.

He didn't know how to help her, but when he thought of his options, the only person who came to mind was Ferran. The treasure hunter also wore a Cat's Eye. Sora had studied under him before. Perhaps he would know what had caused this.

Burn started back to the Ebonaire house, carrying Sora through the heavy snow drifts. It seemed to take twice as long to return to the estate, perhaps because the snow was twice as deep.

Almost an hour later, he sat next to Ferran in Sora's room. They shared two armchairs in front of a roaring fire. She slept soundly in her four-poster bed, and hadn't stirred since her collapse in the snow. Her cheeks were pale, but she didn't seem to have a fever. Burn wished they could consult Lori, but the healer had left yesterday to collect more herbs for Sora's condition from the seminary.

Ferran sat next to him, chewing a cinnamon stick in deep thought. Burn watched the man out of the corner of his eye. He was reedy and tall, and had always reminded Burn a bit of a scarecrow. Streaks of gray shot through his mussed brown hair. He looked tired, his brow lined with worry. Firelight reflected from his dark eyes.

"She wasn't herself. She acted like an animal, and her Cat's Eye glowed a different color. Have you heard of anything like this?"

"Yes and no," Ferran said. "I won't know until she wakes up."

"Could it be the poison? A delirium, mayhap?"

Ferran sighed and ran a tired hand over his face. "Lori would know better than I. But no, I don't think so." He stood up from his chair. "I have an idea of what it might be, but I need to reference a few old journals of mine. They're in my room. Will you watch her?"

Burn nodded. "Gladly. I find it hard enough to sleep as it is."

"You and I both." Ferran turned to leave. He walked stiffly, like a man twice his age.

Burn understood Ferran's slouched shoulders. Since the winter solstice parade, the Shade's trail had turned cold, and his comrades were growing discouraged. *The Book of the Named* couldn't be read. Sora was poisoned. The weather had made traveling all but impossible. They knew Cerastes was collecting the three sacred weapons, but the final weapon had eluded all of them.

Burn's thoughts turned to Crash. The assassin was missing as well. He wished he could speak to the man; his five senses would tell him of Crash's intentions. He had given the two sacred weapons to Cerastes in exchange for Burn's life, but Burn couldn't say that was his only motivation. He didn't want to believe his old friend would betray them, but he couldn't deny the possibility—or perhaps, the inevitability—of it. He had shared the assassin's fire for years, but Crash had always kept a firm barrier between them. Every expression, every word, a deflectison. Beneath it all, a stranger remained.

Sora had changed that, at least for a brief time. She had found a way through the assassin's walls to whatever lay beneath. But was his true self worth all the trouble? Burn wasn't sure. He didn't think it was worth her life.

The Wulven mercenary pulled his armchair next to the bed and propped up his feet. He had spent countless nights on watch. He knew how to ease his body back into the chair while keeping his eyes partway open, his ears cocked for any unnatural sound. He kept his eyes trained on Sora, watching the light rise and fall of her chest, while his mind and senses drifted.

CHAPTER 3

Caprion wandered the halls of the Ebonaire manor, full of restless energy. For the last several days, he had remained here, stagnant, wasting time. With winter solstice approaching, an ominous feeling was growing in his gut. He knew the others felt it too.

His footsteps took him to Sora's bedroom. He hesitated by her door, one hand outstretched to turn the knob. Then his hand fell back to his side. Not even Sora, with all her warmth and acceptance, understood him. Who could blame her? Who could blame any of them? Human lives were finite compared to Harpies. Humans didn't spend hundreds of years on the earth, observing the passage of time. They didn't see the great threads of destiny that bound the races together. Even if he told Sora of his purpose, his calling, she would never truly comprehend it.

The burden of his task weighed down his shoulders, bringing his feet to the ground. He had been born a seraph, a powerful Harpy with six mighty wings. The birth of a seraph usually heralded a great danger to the races—an imbalance in the Elements that must be righted. He knew, as clearly as he knew his own name, that he must protect this world. The Dark God could not be allowed to rise.

Caprion had always found his people arrogant, but he was coming to realize their beliefs were not entirely based on myth. The seraphim were real. His duty, his calling, was real. He couldn't deny that he had been brought here, to the City of Crowns, to face down a darkness that threatened the world, just as the One Star foretold.

Sora thought he had turned against his own people by accompanying her, when really, he had followed his highest duty, his Song. The reason for his birth lay here in the City of Crowns. He knew the price he would have to pay to fulfill his destiny. He knew it, had prepared for it, and yet this far from his homeland, surrounded by the turmoil of humanity, he felt utterly alone. He yearned for something—for some other way, perhaps. Some other life.

He turned from Sora's room and headed for a flight of stairs. Even among his own people, even among the friends he wanted to protect, he was still an outcast.

Only another outcast would understand.

The natural glow of Caprion's skin gave him enough light to see by, and he traversed the staircase to the attic with some familiarity. The attic of the Ebonaire manor was sectioned into four quadrants, each filled with old furniture, paintings and family heirlooms covered in cobwebs and white dusty sheets. The attic spanned the length and width of the entire house, and by the undisturbed carpet of dust on the floor, Caprion figured it wasn't used often.

At the far eastern end of the attic, a girl sat chained to a blackened chimney pipe, her form illuminated from the dimmest glow of a lantern. The way she curled halfway onto her side looked eerily familiar to him, even through the deep shadows. He thought he remembered, from a lifetime ago, how her long black hair trailed over her shoulders.

He approached her silently. His magic carried him above the floorboards, his feet hovering an inch above the ground.

A mound of blankets covered her form. A plate of untouched food rested next to her, where several rats were feasting. They scurried away at Caprion's light.

She stirred as he approached.

He paused next to her. Then, without a word, he sat by her side.

After a minute or so, she sat up. She kept the blankets wrapped around her. Even still, she was shivering. The chimney next to her carried hot smoke out of a bedroom fireplace downstairs, but in this weather, it didn't make much difference.

"To what do I owe this pleasure?" She meant to sound snide, but her voice cracked. Burns, only half healed, marked her throat from a sunstone.

Caprion stared at her. She had a thin, angular face with piercing green eyes, narrowed with suspicion. Matted black hair fell around her shoulders. Still, the familiarity of her face unnerved him. His gaze fell to her throat, where the sunstone had inflicted its damage. He regretted using that stone, regretted ever causing her pain, despite her loyalty to the Shade.

Speaking of which....

"They haven't come for you," Caprion said softly. "If Cerastes wanted to, he could open a shadow portal to this very attic and take you back. He could end your suffering. But he doesn't."

Krait's lips tightened. "He can't open a portal if he doesn't know where I am. Or perhaps he is waiting for you to let your guard down. Watch your back, Harpy. I would gladly suffer for the Dark God."

Her words grated on his ears. "Have you ever considered *not* suffering?"

Krait gave him a look of loathing. "What other choice do I have? You could release me back to my people, but you don't. I've known nothing but pain since we met. Don't preach to me, Harpy."

Caprion nodded. A fair point.

She turned her head so her hair shielded her eyes. "Is that why you've come here? To taunt me?"

Caprion sighed. He didn't truly understand his own reasons. He had carried Krait away from the burning remains of the Dawn Seeker, rescuing her from Cerastes the same night Sora was poisoned. For the past several days, he had spent hours with her in this dark room, not always talking, sometimes just studying her. Exhaustion had worn down her defenses. Perhaps now, after so much time, they could have an honest conversation.

"I want to understand you," he said.

A hoarse laugh escaped her throat. "There's nothing to understand. I follow Cerastes. You can't change my loyalty."

"What brought you to the Dark God?"

"His will."

"Perhaps, but who were you before?"

Krait hesitated. Caprion didn't think she could answer his question, but then, "I woke up on a beach. I was dying. Cerastes saved my life. No. He gave me a *new* life." She shrugged. "I was no one before the Shade. I didn't exist."

"You don't remember anything?"

"No, I...." She halted. "Why should I even tell you?"

"I want to understand."

"No," she said sharply. "No, you're trying to get inside me, make me doubt myself. This is a trick."

"Do I make you doubt yourself?"

The question seemed to infuriate her. "This isn't about me," she spat. "You're looking for that girl, the one I remind you of, but that girl is dead, you told me yourself. You're looking for a ghost, Harpy. You won't find her here."

Caprion sat rigidly. Her words stung, far too insightful.

"Perhaps," he said. "I never knew what became of her. Perhaps we all must live with ghosts from the past, mistakes we cannot make right. Perhaps your memory loss is a blessing. You don't have to look back over years and years, and wonder if you made the right choices."

Krait didn't reply, and a brooding silence fell between them. Caprion eased back against the wall and folded his arms, his eyes roaming the dusty room with its ancient family relics and furniture. Cold air seeped through the roof above, but heat grew between their two bodies, trapped by the walls and the floor, until they sat in a small pocket of warmth.

Finally, she said, "Tell me about her."

Caprion released a slow breath. "About the girl?"

"Yes."

"You really want to know?"

"I asked, didn't I?"

He had never told the story to anyone. Part of him felt like it was too private to share, and yet strangely, he felt closer to Krait in this moment than he did his other companions. Krait saw him for what he was: tangled, dishonest, conflicted. Like herself.

"She didn't have a name, so I called her Moss." For a moment, that was all he could say. Then, "She was captured by my people and brought to our island, very young. I met her in the prisons. She helped me find my wings. She was a child then, but full of courage. She trusted me. I promised I would get her safely off the island, but when I gained my wings and became a seraph, the Matriarch took a special interest in me. Everything changed."

"Moss is a pathetic name," Krait said.

Caprion gave her a sidelong glance. "It suited her. She was gentler than others of your kind. I thought it was poetic."

Krait picked at her nails, feigning disinterest, then asked, "Did you free her?"

"I did, many times, but she could never escape the island. I tried to keep her safe instead. For a time, I kept her in a separate cell, away from the main prisons, and let her out at night. Then she lived in the ruins of the city, where my kind seldom went. I tried to give her the best life I could, I tried to protect her from the evils of my race. We became friends. She was my closest friend." He felt a dull ache begin in his throat, and paused for a moment. "I failed her. The Matriarch saw our friendship as a threat. She took her, and I never saw her again. They told me she was dead." Pain swelled in his chest. "I couldn't protect her. I couldn't fulfill my promise."

"And here you are, years later, still going on about her. Stop simpering about it. She wouldn't have survived long among her own kind. Only a spineless traitor would befriend a Harpy. Just look at where it got her in the end."

Caprion's fists clenched. "She survived for years on an island surrounded by my people, who wanted to kill her."

"Huh!" Krait scoffed. "But the moment you weren't looking, they snatched her away. Doesn't say much of either of you."

Anger surged. Caprion spoke harshly, "You speak so boldly, but you are nothing without the Shade. You say you're loyal to Cerastes, but all I see is fear. You haven't made a single choice that is yours and yours alone. Moss survived for as long as she could, however she could, against all odds. You wouldn't be able to survive without the Shade. You would need your own mind for that."

"We're not meant to survive alone," she said. "Even you travel with friends, Harpy."

"Yes, *with friends*," he enunciated. "You've abandoned yourself, gladly, to a god that makes you suffer. Beneath your facade, you are a terrified child. You are far from the woman Moss would have become. I can see that now."

She glared at him as though personally affronted. "Then you know nothing!"

"I know many things, Krait. I know your face, and now I know your story. I see where the pieces fit. Perhaps there's a chance that, many years ago, you were that little girl trapped on the Lost Isles...but she's dead now. Nothing of her exists in you. You're a typical specimen of your kind, brainwashed and now abandoned by your own."

"I am not abandoned."

"Then where is your master? Why hasn't he rescued you?" Caprion stood up. His wings gleamed on his back. A song tremored in his bones, a silent melody crying out for justice. "He doesn't care about what's best for you. He demands your loyalty, but how does he return it?"

Krait twisted away from Caprion, as though shielding herself from physical blows. "I am the Dark God's hands and feet. His will is my will. I am His child."

Caprion's song grew louder. "Who saved you from the fire on the ship? Cerastes didn't fight for you then, he won't fight for you now."

"My only duty is to obey."

"He didn't give you a Name. Everything he told you was a lie. He means to end this world, Krait. Even the Hive—your own race—won't condone his evil. You don't have to obey him." Caprion paused, hoping his words would reach her.

She spoke as though reciting from a textbook: "The Hive is blind. Their traditions are tainted, impure. Cerastes found the first scrolls of our race; he's unlocked secrets lost since before the War of the Races. He is the greatest Grandmaster ever to live, and I am his student, his *loyal* student! His will is the Dark God's will."

"Cerastes is not a god, Krait."

She stared at him, momentarily silent. At least she didn't argue. Perhaps he had finally pierced through the mess of her mind.

"I know," she recovered.

"But at times you forget, don't you? You worship the Dark God, you follow Cerastes, and sometimes the two get tangled."

Her jaw stiffened.

"You're not meant to suffer," he pressed.

"Then what is my life?" she almost screamed. "Why am I here? Why am I this way?"

Silence fell, again, between them.

Caprion knew he must tread softly. Push too hard past this point, and he might lose her.

"I don't know why you woke up on that beach all alone," he said, "but you chose this, Krait. You chose more suffering, and you can choose differently."

"No." She placed her hands over her ears.

He reached out to touch her, but she scooted away.

"Cerastes will come for me," she whispered.

"He won't."

"Be gone, Harpy. Your words are poison. Leave me."

"You are already poisoned. I am offering you the antidote. No matter how bitter it tastes."

Krait curled against the wall, her shackles scraping the floor, as far away from him as she could get.

Caprion considered her. Perhaps he had pushed too hard, but perhaps his words had taken root in her mind like seeds. It was his duty to her, whether she believed it or not.

"Leave," she murmured. She repeated the single word under her breath. "Leave. Leave. Leave."

He waited another few minutes, then rose to his feet. Perhaps she needed time to think, and perhaps he needed time as well. Sometimes solitude was the best teacher. As he crossed to the attic door, he listened to the strangled noises she made, the dry sobs, tears that weren't tears. He thought of Moss, and he thought of the words he couldn't say: *I need you to know who you are.*

Perhaps Krait wasn't Moss. Perhaps all their physical similarities were a coincidence. But reason—and his gut—told him differently.

He needed to find a way to restore her mind. He would wrestle Krait from her prison, even if he couldn't be gentle, even if she hated him for it. He wouldn't abandon her, no matter how many times she ran, no matter how hard she fought, no matter if one day, she led him to his death.

Fool, he thought. *She will be my undoing.* The Matriarch's warning had turned into prophecy. *The old witch was right all along.*

He should be hunting down Cerastes before winter solstice eve. He should be helping Ferran read *The Book of the Named.* But he didn't care about that anymore. His great destiny seemed very far away, and a new life, like springtime, teased his fingertips. The dream of Moss had reawakened.

He hesitated at the attic door, wishing to reach out to her in some way, to reassure her, but he didn't think he could.

"I'll return."

He stepped through the door into the dark stairwell beyond. She did not call him back.

His thoughts ran before him, surging ahead. He could think of a way to restore Krait's memories. It might not work, but it stood a chance of reaching her, of reminding her of what they shared. *Fool*, he thought again. He should have never dropped the sunstone into the forest near the Little Rain. But he couldn't blame himself. He had been as conflicted then as he was now, except he hadn't thought he'd find her again.

It still might not be her.

But he wouldn't know until he brought back that stone.

CHAPTER 4

Mistmire Hive was not as Crash remembered, but after so many years, he wondered how much of his memory relied on imagination. The gray rocks of the beach were smaller, harder. Their sharp edges bit into his heels through the soles of his boots. Iron waters broke along the cliffs, too stark, too real.

They passed the giant's mouth: a great, gaping cove where Cerastes had once tutored him in the ways of the Hive. The outcropping seemed much smaller, and the echoing waves more like murmurs.

They entered the pine forest beyond the shore. Sterile trees, garbed in white snow, braced themselves against the cold wind. Crash found the woods unnervingly vacant—but this was winter, and the world was dying.

Natrix led him down a path invisible beneath the snow. Their steps passed silently. Each turn, each new grove, brought back unexpected memories as sharp as the cold air. Here, he had snared his first rabbit. There, he had carved a bow from an ashwood sapling. And there, where the birch trees converged, he had hid during games of 'knife and rider.' His fellow savants never found him, and his knife always won.

He and Grandmaster Natrix did not partake in idle talk. To members of his race, particularly those who outranked him, a useless word was akin to profanity. Out of respect, he allowed the silence to rest between them, and kept his thoughts to himself.

Despite Natrix's help, he did not trust her. He was an exile of the Hive, and he need not be reminded of the Hive's law. By returning here, he was potentially forfeiting his life. He hoped the circle of elders would forgive his trespasses and allow him to leave again, but he couldn't predict what they would do. They had every right to kill him. They had tried to before.

Yet he couldn't turn back. He knew with certainty that this was the only path left to him. He would not succumb to the Shade, or flee to the countryside to hide as the world burned. He was done running.

Cerastes intended to wage war against the Hive, which meant far more than waging war against a city or a country. The Hive was a place, perhaps, but also a teaching, a tradition. It was a way of life, passed down by countless generations of assassins. Cerastes wanted to destroy the only thing that stood in his way, the only argument against his new doctrine, and Crash couldn't allow that.

Once, the Hive had bound their race together, but that had slowly dissolved over the centuries. The Sixth Race had become too scattered, too independent. Their villages were now smaller hives, each claiming to be the most legitimate, the most loyal to their kind's heritage, but all were isolated and distrusting of their neighbors. Some feuds between their colonies had lasted centuries. If the greater Hive remained in such a fractured state, Cerastes would win, and any remnant of it would be destroyed.

To be replaced by the Shade? Crash did not know. Perhaps that was Cerastes' original intent, before the Dark God's corruption took hold of his mind, before his demon had grown too strong. Now, Crash couldn't say where his Grandmaster's road led. To destruction, no doubt. But whose?

Would the elders listen to him, to the Viper, a Named assassin who had broken the code of his people? The elders had pronounced him dead, and had forced him into exile. They didn't want him here, alive.

Natrix and Crash came to a halt simultaneously. Someone approached. His hand hovered close to his dagger, though he knew the stranger did not mean to attack him. The underbrush rustled out of pure courtesy.

A man dressed in black leathers stepped through the trees. A cowl hid half of his face. Still, Crash noted his heavy brow and unusually pale eyes. He wore his long black hair tied in a knot at the back of his head.

"Grandmaster Simatus," Natrix acknowledged.

"The elders received your message," he said, his voice like the snow beneath them, soft. "They are ready to meet with you."

"So soon?"

He didn't answer, but turned back toward their hidden colony. Natrix fell into step behind him, and Crash was left to the rear.

Mistmire Hive was just around a bend in the trail. They passed through a grove of willow trees, naked now, and entered the hidden village.

Mistmire, too, was smaller than he remembered. A rough circle had been cut out of the forest. Simple stone huts with grass roofs dotted the clearing. The roads were dirt and mud. Savants walked back and forth, clothed in mottled gray and black robes. Hardly a voice spoke, hardly an eye met his. No markings differentiated one savant from the other, just as they lacked names, just as they lacked wives or husbands, mothers or fathers.

All were brothers and sisters in the Hive, or so they were taught. *A lie,* Crash now knew. Hierarchies existed here, circles of influence, bands of friends, just as they did anywhere else. Lovers, too. And yet all of it was curbed—*oppressed?*—by the Hive's law. He wondered if Cerastes was not so wrong. Perhaps he had opened his eyes one day and declared *no more.* Even the Shade had emotions. They had ardor and anger and zealotry. But his own brethren were like stone.

He thought of the human cities, of the Dracians, of the docks in Delbar and even the red-roofed town of Mayville. And he thought of Sora.

Simatus led them through the village and out the other side, back into the forest. Crash remembered the path as though summoning it from a dream. A line of black stones led them through the winter underbrush until they reached a hollow opening in the woods.

There, eleven granite statues, each twice the height of a man, stood in a circle. Dead ivy draped their shoulders and entangled their feet. Long ago, the statues had been carved to depict the first leaders of the Hive, but centuries of wind and rain had worn them into faceless sentinels. A bird's nest, long abandoned, rested in the crook of one's elbow.

Crash knew that beneath the snow, the statues encircled a sand-filled pit. This was the sacred arena where he had earned his Name. When they had sentenced him to death, they had held his trial here. The floor was dug down in stages to create an amphitheater. This was the circle of the elders.

Simatus left them and took his place at the entrance of the circle, facing away, as was tradition. Natrix bent to one knee before the statues. After a moment, Crash followed suit.

"Sacred elders of the Hive," Natrix began, "we humble ourselves in your shadow."

"Rise," a voice spoke, clear and resonant. Female.

Crash stood. The statues remained the same, but the Hive's elders spoke through them. This way, their true identities were never revealed, and the leaders of the eleven colonies remained anonymous.

"Grandmaster Natrix," the voice spoke again. "You've brought a traitor into our midst, a man sentenced to die many years ago."

It was not a question, but an opening statement.

"True," Natrix followed the protocols of speech, acknowledging the elder. "For years, I have been waiting for word from Cerastes. I caught his Name burned on the wind. I followed the smoke to Viper's fire."

"You observed something of importance."

"True. I saw a vast army gathering in the desert."

"An army of humans," a second voice stated, this one deep and masculine.

"Dissonant," Natrix said, which in this circle meant *no*. "An army of our own kind gathers in the desert. An army of exiles. They call themselves the Shade."

The circle fell silent for several minutes. Crash wondered if all of the elders sat together in some conference chamber far away, and deliberated. Or perhaps they each sat in the heart of a separate hive and spoke through the wind.

"Cerastes has left the Hive and broken his vows," said the female.

"True."

Crash cleared his throat. "Cerastes has resurrected the Shade to wage war on the Hive. He seeks the three sacred weapons of the Dark God. He means to attack you."

The air thickened around him.

"The dead man shall not speak."

"There isn't time," Crash said. "A plague is spreading across the land. The Dark God's essence is bleeding into the world. Should Cerastes succeed in awakening the god...."

Another voice interrupted, this time a young boy's. Crash knew it didn't signify the elder's actual age. His kind could cloak their identities easily.

"*Dissonant*. Many have tried before, and many will try again. Cerastes can't succeed at such a task. The Dark God is locked behind the seventh gate, and the seventh gate cannot be opened."

Crash frowned. The boy's words brought a niggling sensation to the back of his mind. An annoying memory wormed its way to the front of his thoughts.... Something Cerastes had said....

"But perhaps he found a key?" Crash asked.

Natrix turned to look at him. "Has he?"

"I...."

"The seventh gate has no key," the boy said.

"True," answered a woman's voice, another elder. "The gate is not a gate. Where the Dark God sleeps, there is no door, there is no temple."

Natrix bowed her head in submission.

Crash's neck grew hot. Did these old fools not understand?

"*Dissonant*," he snapped. "Cerastes is smarter than you think. The Dark God's essence is bleeding into the world. A plague is spreading across the land. Cerastes has already gathered two of the sacred weapons, and he plans to attack the Hive."

"Why would he?"

"Because he fears you, because only the Hive understands what he is doing, and only the Hive can act against him. We must act against Cerastes before he acts against us. He has an army, it grows larger every day, and he will attack with full knowledge of all the hidden colonies. A war would destroy us. We are fractured as it is."

The statues were silent.

"True," the woman's voice finally said.

"Dissonant," another said.

"True," a masculine voice interrupted.

The child remained quiet. Silence descended again.

Then, "We have decided."

Crash sensed the statues focus down on them. They seemed to grow taller in the gray winter light.

"Grandmaster Natrix," the boy spoke, "using the Viper's knowledge and accepting his aid, you will hunt down Grandmaster Cerastes and assassinate him. Put an end to this threat."

"Cut off the snake's head," the woman's voice echoed, "and its body will die."

"Viper," the boy continued, "you will aid Grandmaster Natrix in this task."

"What of the Dark God's sacred weapons?" Crash asked.

"Return them to us, if you can."

Crash didn't like the sound of that. He didn't think such objects of power belonged in the hands of mortals. There must be a way to hide them again, to return them to the underworld, or some unknown space between.

The boy continued, "When you return to our circle, you will pay the debt that is owed."

Crash hesitated, unsure that he had heard correctly.

"Elders," Grandmaster Natrix spoke before he could, "if the Viper seeks to serve and protect the Hive, surely he has earned back his place...?"

The light grew dim through the trees.

"If he wishes to return to the Hive, it will be in exchange for the price that is owed. He will answer for his trespasses."

Natrix looked like she wanted to protest again, but Crash held out his hand, stopping her.

"No," he said. "I knew what it meant to return here. I won't run from my fate."

The statues regarded him with empty, indifferent eyes.

"My life is owed to you, and you shall have it," Crash said, resigned.

"Mark him," said the boy.

Crash half-turned, but Natrix moved too quickly. Her hand struck the back of his neck, and for a moment, his vision flashed. His flesh stung, and when he touched the nape of his neck, he saw blood. A deathmark.

"I told you, I will not run from my fate!" he yelled, furious. A deathmark was a dishonorable symbol in the Hive. An insult. Crash glared up at the elders, but they might as well have been stones. He sensed their presence leave the circle. The faceless statues seemed duller now, unremarkable.

Natrix turned to where Grandmaster Simatus stood, his back to the circle. They left in single file, Crash's neck stinging. A human might have offered words of comfort or encouragement, but not his own kind. They neither acknowledged him or commiserated.

"Honors to you," Simatus said as they walked, speaking to Natrix alone. "A worthy task, assassinating our traitor brother. Your Name shall be written in the books."

"We shall find Cerastes and put an end to this madness," Natrix replied.

"Shadow's blessing, sister," the other grandmaster intoned. "I shall await word of your victory."

Natrix passed back through the village, stopping only to collect her weapons and a pack of supplies from her hut. Crash waited at the open doorway. Then, in front of her own hearth, she opened a shadow portal. She vanished into the swirling darkness without a glance over her shoulder.

Crash didn't follow her immediately, but took a moment to gaze out at the hive and the milky, overcast sky. He realized, now, that his mind had distorted this place like a dream. He had spent too many nights gazing at campfires, lingering on other fires, on other roads and other rooftops. Why had he made this place so expansive in his mind? It was so small, so gray and cold.

He didn't want to linger on these thoughts anymore; lingering meant he had traveled away, and he was done running.

He crossed to the hearth and followed Natrix through the portal.

CHAPTER 5

S ora woke up under the weight of many blankets. She opened her eyes. At first, she didn't recognize the four poster bed where she lay. When she looked to her left, she saw a grand, glowing fireplace, and beyond that, a window that revealed a fragile dawn outside, wrought with waves of falling snow.

She put a hand to her head. *Where am I?* She tried to think back, and summoned fragments of the winter solstice parade and her fight with Cobra in the alley. Then a haze of fever dreams confused her memory. Had she fallen ill? Had she spent the night with Crash in an abandoned apartment, or had she imagined all of it? Most importantly, how had she come to be here, in the Ebonaire manor?

Despite feeling somewhat disoriented, she was furiously hungry. She wrestled the blankets off and slid her feet to the edge of the bed.

"Hello?" she called, wondering if a maid might be waiting nearby.

Heavy footsteps thudded across the floor. She turned, and her heart caught in her throat.

"Burn?"

The Wolfy crossed the room to her side. She hadn't seen him standing near the window. He was so tall, he made her feel like a child, and he bent double to embrace her in a gentle hug. She wrapped her arms around him, tears stinging her eyes.

Last she remembered, he had been taken captive by the Shade. The assassin Krait had taunted her with his death. Since Burn's disappearance, his life had weighed heavily on her conscience, making her feel utterly inadequate and help-less, unable to confirm that he was even still alive.

She still couldn't believe her eyes.

"Burn," she repeated. Solid. Real. *It's not a dream,* she thought. "You're alive."

"Of course I am," he said. "A few crotchety assassins won't do me in."

She choked out a laugh. "How did you escape? How did you come to the manor?"

"I waited for the right moment. It appears The Shade have abandoned the sewers. Ferran found me and brought me here."

"The Shade have abandoned the sewers? Are they still in the city?" Sora pulled back and searched his face. "How long have I been asleep?"

"About two days," he said.

She scrunched up her nose in thought. "Then winter solstice eve is only a few nights away?"

"Aye."

Questions filled her, swelling her chest. "What about *The Book of the Named?* Or the third weapon? Why has the Shade left the city? Where is Crash?"

Burn answered her questions concisely, filling her in on what had transpired over the last few days. When he finished, he said, "Now let me summon Ferran. Something strange happened last night and we need to speak to you about it."

Sora gawked at him. *Stranger than waking up in the Ebonaire manor with no memory of the last two days?*

Burn released her and left the room. He returned about ten minutes later with Ferran in tow. Now that Sora could see them both in the morning light, she noticed their haggard appearances. Ferran needed a shave. His cravat was undone and his clothes rumpled.

They each pulled a chair to the side of her bed. Then Burn took her hand gently.

"Sora, last night you left the manor and ran out into the snow."

She almost laughed. "What is this nonsense?"

"At first we thought it was a delirium, perhaps brought on by the poison or your fever," Ferran said. "You've been unconscious for days, Sora. You suddenly took off in the middle of the night and ran out into the storm. Luckily, Burn saw you leave and brought you back."

"Oh," she said, a bit more sober.

Ferran folded his hands. "Do you remember anything at all from last night? Any dreams?"

She looked at him, suddenly doubtful.

"No, I don't...." But as she thought back, her head grew hot and cloudy. She saw the *garrolithe* standing before her once again, its massive jaws opening, lowering around her head, and an inevitable sense of surrender.

"I think your necklace was controlling you," Ferran said. "The blue light that Burn described from your Cat's Eye, I saw it once before. Do you remember the village on the Little Rain river?"

She did, when the *garrolithe* materialized in an explosion of blue light.

"What would the *garrolithe* have to do with all this?" Burn asked, looking back and forth between Ferran and Sora.

"It's a mecha-animist, a war spell from the time of the races," Ferran explained. "Sora has been struggling with it for some time now. It hasn't been reacting well to the Cat's Eye."

"He tried to help me to control it, but I couldn't." Her voice sounded weak, even timid, in her own ears. The memory was at the edge of her vision. She turned her head, but she couldn't quite see it. What was she forgetting? Unnerved, Sora pushed back the mountain of blankets and tried to stand up. Thoughts of the *garrolithe* flooded her mind, making her feel anxious and overwhelmed. She needed open air, open spaces. She needed to run.

"This is nonsense," she repeated. "Whoever ran out into the snow last night, it couldn't have been me. I don't need to be fussed over."

Ferran reached out and took her arm. His Cat's Eye glowed with a soft red light at his wrist.

Sora glanced down at it.

"It's influencing you," he said, searching her eyes. "You need to rein it in."

"I don't know how."

"Block it out. Don't think of it."

She tried, but *not* thinking about the *garrolithe* had the opposite effect. Its image only became clearer, and that claustrophobic feeling returned.

"I can't."

"Then think of your mother's cabin and your time spent there," Burn suggested. "Think of your childhood. Think of when we first met you."

Sora did so, taking herself away from the City of Crowns, away from the Ebonaire manor and its tight, confined walls. She was small again, stealing honey tarts from the kitchens with Lily. She was playing a flute in the music room before the wide bay windows. In her distraction, she didn't notice the blue light fade from the necklace.

Ferran stared at her Cat's-Eye stone. He looked alarmed, perhaps a shade fearful, but the expression passed quickly from his face.

"We need to release it," he said, partly to himself.

"Is that possible?" Burn asked.

"I don't know." He looked at the red stone at his wrist. "I don't have all the answers, only what I've experienced for myself. The Cat's Eye can contain powerful spells, but where mecha-animists are concerned, sometimes more than just magic is afoot. These are strange and ancient creatures that can't be disseminated and absorbed like smoke...."

"How do you feel, Sora?" Burn asked.

"Much better," she said, doing her best not to remember anything about the *garrolithe* or the corral. "Hungry, though. Very hungry. Is it not the breakfast hour?"

Burn and Ferran shared a glance.

"Are you sure you feel well enough? We can have breakfast brought up to you."

"No," Sora said simply. She didn't like the way they hovered around her, as though she might break at any moment. Hadn't she proved her strength over and over again? She swung her legs out of bed and planted both feet on the floor. "I feel fine. I don't want to waste any more time in bed. And I'm ravenous!"

Burn's ears twitched doubtfully. He looked like he might speak, but then a soft knock came to the door. Ferran went to answer it. Sora overheard a maid's voice.

"Lord Ebonaire invites you to join him and Lady Danica for breakfast."

Ferran hesitated. He seemed uncertain. "Perhaps tomorrow morning...."

"I'm fine, really!" Sora called, ignoring him. "Maid, please bring me a dressing gown. I am so hungry, I could eat the bed sheets!"

The maid held a hand to her mouth, suppressing a laugh, then bowed and disappeared down the hall.

Ferran shut the door. He didn't look happy, but Sora didn't feel sorry, either.

"You should rest until we can learn more about this poison and its effect on your necklace..."

"What effect? Truly, I feel fine, *better* than healthy. And what about Lady Danica?" she asked. "Martin's daughter? Wasn't she also sick?"

"She recovered the same day you were poisoned," Ferran said. "Ironically, she's been asking after you all this time. I think she's excited to have a cousin."

Sora remembered their guise with a start. How could she have forgotten? She was an Ebonaire now, yes, and so was her mother. Where was her mother? She would have to ask Burn, after she bathed and dressed for the day.

"Martin still doesn't know anything about our quest. He thinks you caught a chill," Ferran said. "He hasn't met Burn yet either. I'd keep any conversation simple."

"Of course," Sora agreed.

Another knock came to the door. The maid entered with a soft pink morning gown and a second maid in tow, who carried a basin of water and a vial of scented oil.

"I'll be down in a bit," Sora said, dismissing Burn and Ferran with a wave of her hand. "Please, I can't very well bathe and dress with you two here. I won't keep you waiting long." All she could think about was food.

Ferran and Burn still looked reluctant to leave her alone, but as the maid set up a dressing station next to the bed, they both stood and headed to the door.

"We'll be waiting for you," Ferran said.

Burn looked like he would be guarding the door.

Contrary to Ferran and Burn's misgivings, Sora joined them downstairs a little over a half-hour later.

Lord Martin's breakfast room was smaller than the manor's grand dining hall, and overlooked a rose garden through a series of wide windows. At the moment, the rose garden was covered in several inches of snow. A maid led Sora into the room, then quickly retreated.

Sora stood for a moment, a cheery fire to her back, and surveyed the breakfast table laden with silver plates, trenches of eggs, loaves of toasted bread. A girl with a fountain of black, luscious curls spilling to her waist stood up when she walked in. Sora could only assume this was Lady Danica. Her cousin wore a soft green morning gown and a velvet robe lined with white fox fur. Her eyes were the remarkable color of cinnamon, and her nose was cat-like and pointed. Her mouth was wide, entrancing, and framed with two deep dimples.

Lady Danica's beauty was intimidating, but perhaps even more so was her height. She towered over Sora, close to six feet tall. She did not slouch, but stood with an exceptionally straight spine, as though trying to out-tower the men as well.

Danica came around the table and embraced Sora in a hug.

"You must be my new cousin," she said, taking the words from Sora's mouth. "We are so glad to see you've recovered. Please, sit next to me."

"Oh," Sora said. It was not the welcome she had expected from a daughter of the Ebonaire house. Then she remembered her manners. "It's an honor to finally meet you."

"Please, no need for formality!" Danica grinned, and her expression reminded her oddly of Ferran. "I am told your mother brought me back from the threshold of death's door. I am eternally grateful to her...to all of you."

"I...well, of course my mother is a Healer and pleased by your recovery...." Sora wanted to say something sophisticated, but her nose was filled with the smell of bacon, and her thoughts were suddenly difficult to compose.

"Come now, Danica, give the girl time to find her strength," Lord Martin called, mistaking Sora's hesitation for feebleness. "She's been up and about for only an hour. Let her find her footing."

"Agreed," Ferran said around a mouthful of toast and eggs.

The breakfast had an informal air about it. Danica led Sora to the other side of the table, where she pulled out Sora's chair, and a servant started filling her plate with eggs and bacon. Danica sat by her side, her own plate only half touched. A tall stack of letters was piled before, which she was opening and reading through between sips of tea.

"I must apologize," she said to Sora as she picked up yet another small, square letter, addressed in swirling purple ink. "I've been ill for quite some time and unable to answer my mail. I'm dying to hear any news of the season! My friends have been very worried. I've counted at least a hundred missed invitations and twice as many inquiries. Can you imagine?"

"I can't," Sora said, flatter than she had intended. She had already swallowed a piece of toast and three strips of bacon, and she was much more focused on eating than talking. She wondered if she was behaving strangely, because Ferran kept shooting worried glances in her direction. Perhaps it was his attempt at fatherly concern?

Martin, thankfully, seemed oblivious.

"Good to see you've recovered your appetite," he remarked as Sora moved to another piece of toast. "Danica, as well, has made a full recover. I'm very pleased." Martin turned to Ferran as he cracked open a soft boiled egg. "Of course, I must find some way to thank Lorianne properly. Your wife's coming here was a blessing from the Goddess."

"Lori is most skilled," Ferran agreed.

"Where is my mother?" Sora asked, noticing the empty seat next to him.

"She's gone to the Healer's seminary to fetch more herbs," Martin said. "If she had waited one more day, she could have spared herself the trouble. She will be very relieved to hear that you've recovered."

Danica chimed in, "It's a shame we both fell ill so close to winter solstice. We've missed all the festivities! Surely, my dear cousin, you're attending First Winter's Ball? Do you have a gown yet? You must attend the masquerade!"

Sora avoided Ferran's pointed glance. First Winter's Ball was on winter solstice night, and seemed like a frivolous affair next to their true reason for being in the city. They still needed to interpret *The Book of the Named* before winter solstice. The masquerade would be a huge distraction.

Then, with a start, Sora remembered Lord Gracen's invitation to the ball. Her chewing slowed, and she had to sip her tea to help her swallow.

"Actually, I will be attending...I think," she said uneasily. "Lord Gracen Seabourne asked me to accompany him."

To Ferran's credit, he didn't spit out his food, though he made a small choking sound.

Danica dropped her teaspoon. "Did you accept?" she asked breathlessly.

"I did."

The table stared at her. Sora fidgeted.

"Well," Danica recovered, "*do* you have a dress?"

"Olivia ordered one made for me." Memories were rushing back, and Sora felt all the threads of her previous adventure coming together. "We went to the Flower

District and she had me fitted for a costume. I left most of the decisions up to her."
Sora remembered her premature flight from the tailor's shop. The dress remained
in an unopened package inside her room.

Danica seemed satisfied. "Then you are well-prepared. Olivia has impeccable
taste, I can attest! That means you must accompany me to the theatre this afternoon, if you feel well enough for it. It's better I introduce you to society as my
cousin, and not Lord Gracen's companion."

Sora thought that was a rather strange remark.

"I'm not sure I understand."

Lord Martin spoke. "Now Danica, don't be rude. Gossip is unbecoming of a
woman."

Danica quirked an eyebrow, undeterred. "And allow my innocent cousin to be
swept up by some rake? Gracen is a good man but you know his reputation. Our
family name will protect her reputation." Danica stood up, her back straighter
than ever. "My absence from The Regency has been long enough. This afternoon,
A Tale of the Four Winds is showing at the Troubadour Theatre in Diadem Park.
I shall go mad if I cannot attend. And Sora shall go mad with me."

Sora blinked. Then Danica took her hand and pulled her up next to her.
"Won't you, cousin?"

"I...yes, if you say so."

Lord Martin looked conflicted.

"Danica, you've barely recovered from your pneumonia, I don't think—"

"Father, I missed the parade! Please, I *must* attend the play before the season is
over. And Sora has barely experienced the winter solstice festival."

Martin considered them both. Sora saw how difficult it was for him to refuse
his own daughter. Somehow, she couldn't fault him for that. The look of paternal
anguish on his face was almost endearing.

"You've only just regained your health," he repeated. "I don't like the idea of
you traveling in this weather. We should wait for Lorianne's approval...."

"I feel right as rain, father," Danica said. "I've been up and about for days now.
Oh, please! Lady Sora will most enjoy it!"

Sora admitted that she was full of energy and felt right as rain as well. She was
intrigued by the idea of attending a play, but even more so, it would give her an
excuse to leave the manor. *Outside,* she thought. *Out of the cage.* A primal surge
of energy overtook her, and she suddenly couldn't wait to be outside.

Without her noticing, the Cat's-Eye stone under her dress shimmered blue, a mere reflection of light. Only Ferran might have picked it up, but he was turned away, his attention on Lord Martin and Danica.

"Danica has a point," Sora spoke up. "I would like to meet her friends, and I would be delighted to attend a play at the Troubadour Theatre. If I may say so, Lord Ebonaire, my mother has taught me some of the Healing arts. I think Danica and I will both survive an afternoon outside, granted we do not stress ourselves."

"Father, please," Danica pressed. "It isn't snowing anymore."

Martin glanced out the window. Indeed, there was a lull in the storm. Bits of blue sky broke through the heavy cloud cover, and fragile rays of sunlight sparkled upon the frozen rose bushes in the garden. He grunted when he saw that. Then he turned back to the breakfast table and regarded them both with discerning eyes. Danica held her ground.

Finally, he sagged in defeat. "Alright," he relented. "But I am giving strict instructions to the driver to bring you home after the play. No gallivanting about with your friends all evening. Do I have your word?"

"Yes, father, of course."

"Then it appears you are both going to the play."

Danica sat back down with a satisfied smile. Sora sat down as well and reached for more bacon.

Sora caught Ferran's suspicious look, but she couldn't quite meet his eyes.

CHAPTER 6

Lori stood impatiently as her carriage was readied. They had arrived at the seminary yesterday evening, but the storm had only just now lapsed long enough for them to attempt the journey home.

In the meantime, the Healers' seminary had been gracious enough to lend her and Lily--Sora's handmaid and Lori's traveling companion--a place to sleep overnight in the stables. All of their rooms were taken twice-over by the sick. Truth be told, Lori didn't know how all the seminary's Healers and priestesses hadn't been infected already. She regretted bringing Lily, and the chance that she might have exposed her to the plague. *This entire area really should be quarantined,* she thought.

Her gaze traveled past the seminary gates to the long dirt road that cut through the forest. To each side of the road, for the next half-mile, a makeshift city of tents and wooden lean-to's filled the spaces between the trees. Blue-robed Healers passed back and forth among the ill and dying. Impoverished farmers and peasants from the countryside squatted next to smoking fires, where they roasted squirrels or pigeons for supper.

Lori couldn't stomach looking at them for long. She knew the Healers were helpless to cure the plague or stop its spread. She had come here for a different reason. Back in the Ebonaire manor, Sora lay in the grip of fever dreams and hallucinations. Lori had successfully treated the poison so far, but the herbs she needed were rare this time of year, and her trip to the seminary was necessary to replenish her stores. Luckily, the seminary carried the herbs she needed, though at a much higher price per ounce than she had imagined. Lord Martin Ebonaire had sent her with a heavy coin purse, which she had taken reluctantly, but was now thankful for. She had been able to procure some of what she needed. Not all, but enough.

Lori clutched the bag of herbs in hand. Whenever she thought of The Shade's poison, she also thought of Viper. She had never liked the man, but now his betrayal curdled her stomach. At one time, Sora's trust in him had swayed Lori's opinion, but her own intuition had proven true in the end. The Viper was a menace, and now Sora was paying the price. Lori wished they had left him behind at the Lost Isles. He was poisoning her daughter's mind along with her body. Sora needed to be separated from him.

I should have protected her, she thought. Her knuckles turned white on the bag. Despite all Sora had endured, she was still a young girl, her heart open and vulnerable. *I should never have let her out of my sight.*

"Bad business, what happened at the winter solstice parade," Lily said next to her. "Setting fire to the king's float and all, can you imagine? The entire city is talking about it, even all the way out here. I wonder who was behind it."

"Who knows," Lori said, turning her thoughts forcefully away from Sora's condition.

"Did you hear they're planning to close the city gates?" Lily asked, missing Lori's wish for silence. "One of the Healers told me so. King Royce signed the order last night. Can't have the plague *and* these revolters running about the city unchecked. I guess the attack finally persuaded him."

"He has to protect his family, just like any other man," Lori said, at first dismissively, but then Lily's words sunk in. The king was closing the city gates. What about all of the other families who would be separated during Winter Solstice? The ones trying to come to the city for the celebration, or for help or shelter...? With all the sickness and suffering around her, she wished there was another way. Certainly there was another way?

"Some people are saying the king staged the attack so he wouldn't lose face in front of his courtiers when he closed the gates," Lily continued.

"I'd rather not feed into these rumors, Lily. That doesn't sound like something King Royce would do willingly. That kind of talk often impedes the truth."

"Or it *is* the truth..." Lily's voice wavered. "Maybe someone close to the royal family pulled it off. Who else would want the king dead?"

"These are fearful times," Lori said steadily. "I imagine quite a few people blame the king for what's happened to their families with the plague. But our king isn't responsible for the plague or the tragedies it's caused."

"Maybe not the king," Lily relented, "but the First Tier is certainly set against us peasants. They've been trying to lock us out of our city for months. And now they finally have the leverage to close the gates. I think it's rather rotten what the upper tiers are calling for, don't you?"

"What?"

"The nobility are trying to banish all those sick people from the city. Where will they go? Turning them out in the dead of winter won't stop the plague. Make it much worse, I imagine."

Lori felt even more unsettled. "I didn't realize they were turning people out."

"Not yet, but rumors abound and I believe them. They're trying to get the king to purge the city. If such a thing were to happen, it would bring about a civil war, let me tell you!"

"Hush your voice," Lori said. "It's treason to speak of such things."

Lily snorted.

A carriage approached through the seminary gates, distracting Lori from their conversation. Its cab was painted powder blue with an intricate crest of a falcon upon the door. Lori recognized it at once.

She grabbed Lily's arm, dragged her off the seminary steps, and forced her behind a low wall.

"Oh! What's all this?"

"Quiet," Lori hushed. "That's Lord Daniellian's carriage."

"I take it you don't like him?"

"Not at all."

Lorianne held her breath as the carriage rolled to a stop before the seminary gates. The coachman leapt down and opened the door. Then, much to her surprise, Lord Daniellian did not step out, but Prince Peric.

At her side, Lily squeaked softly, then covered her mouth with a gloved hand. Lorianne understood her reaction. Most commoners never stood this close to the royal family, whether separated by a stone wall or not.

Prince Peric was shorter than Lori had imagined, and thinly built. He looked more like an adolescent than a man over thirty, until he turned toward her and she saw the dark circles under his brown eyes and the gray flecks along his sideburns. He wore a long fur cloak over a purple doublet, with a silver circlet upon his head.

The royal family wore their crowns only when attending official business, never out casually, but the prince was an exception. Peric was past the age most rulers inherited the throne. Some people mockingly called him *the spinster apparent* or *the princely old maid*. And so he wore his crown everywhere. Lorianne found it hard to imagine an insecure prince, but Peric was a fine example: he did everything he could to remind the kingdom of his right to the throne.

After him, from the coach, came Lord Cedric Daniellian wearing the pastel colors of his house. Now Lorianne began to quiver—from rage or fear, she didn't know which. She hated Lord Cedric. The scars he had wrought upon her body and mind would never heal. He had forced her to flee from the seminary years ago, but she would never escape her own nightmares.

Headmaster Duncan appeared on the front steps to welcome them. Lorianne only caught snatches of his greeting. He led Prince Peric and Lord Daniellian inside.

"The Prince!" Lily gushed the moment they had disappeared. "He's quite dashing—though shorter than I thought, don't you think? I wonder why he's here. He should keep away from the plague and all that."

"Yes," Lorianne murmured, lost in thought. Then she made a decision. "I'm going to find out."

"What?"

"Stay here and wait for the carriage," she said, then she stepped out from behind the wall and ran up the seminary's front steps.

"No!" Lily outright refused. "I'm coming with you."

Lorianne didn't have time to argue. The two women hurried through the front doors of the seminary. Once inside, two hallways split off to her left and right. Both were full of pallets, cots and sick, moaning patients. Directly before her, a spiral staircase led up to the seminary's central tower. At the top of the tower was Headmaster Duncan's office where he had no doubt taken the prince. Cautiously, she started up the staircase. She didn't want to run heedlessly into Lord Cedric's back.

By the time Lori and Lily reached the top of the stairs, the men had entered the headmaster's quarters. The door to Duncan's study was closed. She could hear their voices from inside, but not very well, and standing next to the door was bound to draw attention from anyone passing by.

Lorianne glanced around, looking for options. She had lived in this seminary many years ago, and she knew there were dozens of small, pocket-like rooms where one might crouch and eavesdrop. Her eyes found the door next to Headmaster Duncan's study.

"This way," she whispered, and tugged Lily into the room next to the headmaster's quarters. It was the same size as the tiny cabins on Silas's ship. A single cot, empty, stood next to a shuttered window. Carefully, they both set their ears against the wall and listened.

The voices from Headmaster Duncan's office were still muffled, but audible.

"The plague is growing worse, gentlemen," old Duncan's voice traveled, reed-thin, through the cracking mortar of the wall. "But I still am not sure this is the answer."

"Well it's a bit late for that, isn't it?" said a fluid tenor. Lorianne thought it was Prince Peric. "Simply tell my father, persuasively, how much worse the plague will get as winter deepens. Tell him of the threat to his own family. The peasants are getting restless. He has traitors and turncoats in his midst. Soon, they'll do much worse than fire a few arrows. A rebellion is at hand. We must control it before it grows beyond our reach."

Lord Cedric spoke next. Lorianne knew his voice immediately. It made her feel physically ill.

"The prince's request is most reasonable, Duncan. What happens to the kingdom if the plague spreads to The Regency? Lord Ebonaire's wife has already succumbed to the illness. If the First Tier falls, the kingdom falls. We must preserve it. We must purge the city of the infected."

Lorianne glanced at Lily. As it turned out, the rumors she had overheard were right. The lower tiers were smarter and better informed than she had first thought.

Duncan's voice was full of misgiving. "I can't possibly persuade him to act against his own people. Not in good conscience. We are Healers here, gentlemen. The Goddess bids us to tend to all peoples, of all creeds, from every walk of life. I will not break my vows."

"Sometimes lives must be sacrificed for our greater survival," the prince said.

"Then I will leave that decision in the hands of the king. It would seem he has already made his choice."

"Have you considered what would happen to your funding, then?" Cedric said icily.

Lorianne and Lily shared yet another glance.

"How dare you," Duncan rebuked. Lori heard the scrape of a chair being pushed back. She imagined Duncan standing up in anger. "If this goes much further, Lord Cedric, I will go straight to the king and tell him exactly what you've been up to. I will not be bullied in my own seminary."

"Let me put this plainly," the prince said. "If you won't convince my father to purge the city, then I will see to it that you are thrown off the royal council and that the seminary is dissolved. I have many powerful friends among the First Tier, and more supporters than you could know. This is a far greater matter than your pride, Headmaster. This is for the good of the kingdom."

"My loyalty lies to the Goddess and Her people, and it always will."

Lorianne could sense Prince Peric's smile. His words were just as cold. "We shall see where that gets you."

More scraping of wood against wood as the men stood to leave. Then the door to Duncan's office opened and closed. Lily and Lorianne crouched, breathless, and waited as the two men walked back down the stairs. Lori didn't move until their footsteps had ceased to echo.

"Well, that was exhilarating," Lily said. "Told you they were trying to purge the city."

"There's something more. There has to be." A terrible feeling had settled in Lorianne's gut, one that she couldn't shake. She had to investigate further.

Without another word to Lily, Lorianne took off after the two men. She raced down the staircase to the front steps of the seminary, but Daniellian and the prince were not there. She backtracked into the seminary and ran down the left hallway to a rear door that led out into the gardens. Despite a layer of snow covering the ground, the seminary's garden was still bright with winter flowers, hardy squashes and frail green herbs. She saw two sets of footprints leading through the garden to a stone wall, where a second gate stood open.

Lori crept up to the low wall. Sure enough, she heard voices on the other side.

"My good friend assures me that your family name--and its reputation--will remain obscure. I take care of my supporters, Daniellian, and I have not forgotten your sacrifices," she overheard. "The dissenters will enter through the lower floors. It will look like a proper attempt at a rebellion."

"Yes, and then you will have your throne...and I will have a place on the royal council."

"I have not forgotten my promise."

Lori stifled her gasp. Had she heard correctly? Were they plotting against the king?

"Your friend, can we trust him?" Daniellian asked. "He has always struck me as a little odd...."

"A bit eccentric, perhaps, but true to his word," the prince said. "He would not betray us. Don't forget, he needs us as well."

"This has been a long time coming," Cedric said. "Years of planning, all culminating on winter solstice. A sign of good luck, I think. Auspicious timing."

"We planned it this way. No luck about it," the prince said. "Let's return to the city, before we lose our pricks to this cold."

Lori realized they were heading toward her. She had been so focused on the conversation, she had forgotten to pay attention to her surroundings. She stepped back, looking for a place to hide, only to run into a very hard, very metal, chestplate.

She fell to her hands and knees in the snow. She looked up. Two men in armor—the royal guard—stood above her.

"Spying on the prince, then?" one said.

"Too nosy for her own good, methinks," the second agreed.

Lori held up her hands, showing she was unarmed. "No, a misunderstanding, I simply...."

"What do we have here?" Prince Peric called. He and Cedric rounded the hedges, their boots crunching in the snow.

"This woman was listening to your conversation, your highness," the first guard said.

Lori opened her mouth, then shut it. She met Cedric's eyes, which had grown narrow with malice. Terror laced her thoughts. She saw the recognition in his gaze, and the evil little gears churning behind his eyes.

"Arrest her," he said. "She's one of the insurgents who attacked the parade, I'm sure of it."

"Let her alone!" Lily's voice cried. "She's just excited to see the prince, is all! She doesn't mean no harm!"

Lily marched across the garden, her skirts hiked up so she didn't trip in the snow.

Lorianne wanted to tell her to run home.

"Please, your majesty, take pity on us. We are simply awed by your presence," the maid said, and fell into a deep curtsy. She knelt in the snow at Lorianne's side, half-shielding her with her wide skirts. "Please, milord, we are but harmless women."

Prince Peric glanced over Lily once, then twice. His gaze lingered on her bosom.

"Here's a comely wench who knows her place. Fine then. Release them."

"Peric, they might have overheard..." Daniellian started.

"Are you questioning my orders, Daniellian?" Peric snapped. "I am to be king soon. My subjects should know I am a forgiving man."

Lorianne bowed, planting her hands in the snow. "My liege," she said, playing to his pride, "you shall make a fine king, the best our kingdom has ever seen."

Prince Peric's expression hardened, then abruptly dispersed from his face. After another long look at Olivia's bosom, he seemed to grow bored with both of them, and turned away.

"Harmless wenches," he said dismissively. "I have no time for this. I have much more important matters to attend to in the city. Come along, Daniellian. No need to dirty our hands with these two."

The soldiers saluted smartly and fell into step behind the prince. Peric walked past Lorianne and Lily with an aloof air. Lord Daniellian seemed more reluctant to follow, and he stared at Lori with a look that said he hadn't dismissed her at all. He spit at them as he passed, but he, too, followed the prince out of the garden.

Lorianne held her breath until the prince and Cedric had disappeared around the front of the seminary. Then she climbed back to her feet. Her hands were shaking, her fingers numb from the cold ground. She couldn't believe how close she had come to being arrested. And then what would have become of her?

"Well," Lily said at her side, "now I know where Sora gets it from."

"Get what?"

"Her tenacity."

"You wouldn't say that if you'd met her father," Lorianne said, still staring after the prince in distraction. Then she paused, realizing what she had said. She had spoken with Dane in mind, her lover who had died so long ago, but now she didn't know Sora's true parentage. Ferran had robbed her of that clarity. It was infuriating. Ferran had thought he was being helpful, but really, he was turning her world upside down.

She was so focused on her thoughts that she missed Lily's confused glance.

"You mean Lord Fallcrest?" the maid prompted as they walked back to the seminary's driveway. "You must not remember him well. He was a grumpy old scrooge. Obsessed with his riches and his accounts. No sensitivity. Not the type to raise a daughter. I must disagree with you there, miss Lorianne...respectfully, of course. Sora is really nothing like her father. It's a wonder she has so much compassion for people, after how that old miser treated her, and with you running off when she was a babe...."

Lorianne didn't want to continue this conversation. There were too many pitfalls. Too many lies to keep covered.

"Come." Lorianne started through the snow. "We should return to the city."

"Are we going to tell Lord Ebonaire about the threat to the king?"

"Not yet. Prince Peric mentioned he had many supporters among the First Tier. I wouldn't trust any of the nobility with this news."

"But we have to tell *someone* about the threat to the king!"

Lori worried her lower lip. As they neared the seminary's front drive, she saw the familiar black sheen of the Ebonaire carriage, and some of the tension left her shoulders. She had half-expected to see Lord Daniellian waiting for her, ready to silence her for good. Perhaps the Goddess had protected her after all. Daniellian and the prince--and their carriage--were nowhere in sight.

Lorianne and Lily walked toward the Ebonaire coach and the four dark stallions that pulled it. Who knew how many nobility supported Prince Peric? The promise of power in a new regime would entice many. She couldn't trust Lord Martin, not yet--money and corruption tended to go hand in hand. She couldn't run to Headmaster Duncan. He knew of her tarnished reputation, and besides that, he had already failed to act. She wasn't even sure about Lord Gracen Seabourne. He was sworn to protect the royal family, but the prince might have the king's soldiers under his thumb. Even if Lord Seabourne remained loyal, what about his men?

She could only think of one person the prince couldn't touch, one mind he couldn't influence.

"We're going to the Temple of the North Wind," she said, her mind made up. "The priestesses will help us." Of that, she was certain.

CHAPTER 7

Caprion flew as fast as he could for many hours without rest, following the Crown's Rush back to the Little Rain tributary. From this height, frozen under so much snow, the Little Rain river looked more like one of The Regency's many roads than an actual river. A white vein led through acres of trees, up hills and through ravines, away from the Crown's Rush and the royal city. Caprion followed it deep into the wilderness. He moved at speeds that would put a falcon to shame. He searched the endless acres of misty, snow-laden pines for the isolated village where he had first encountered the plague. Somewhere just outside of that village, he had dropped a rock that he now needed desperately back.

He must make her remember who she was. He had promised her that much.

He saw a stormhead looming on the horizon, and before long, the wind picked up and snow began to fall, fast and furious, through the sky. Heavy, wet clots pelted his wings with and soaked his clothes. The snow chilled his skin and near-blinded him. He continued on, and eventually he flew out from under the storm into an iron-gray afternoon, far away from the City of Crowns. A depressing light illuminated the forest below him, but he recognized the curve of the river. The Little Rain wandered beneath him, just like he remembered, just as it should. Chunks of broken ice floated down its length. Beneath it, he saw black, icy water.

Caprion suddenly banked his wings and hovered, still, in the air. Endless acres of sugar-white forest stretched below him, until suddenly, they stopped. The white forest abruptly ended and black, murky, naked pines began. Their barren trunks thrust up from the ground like sharp needles. It reminded him of the charred remains of a forest fire, except there could be no flames in this weather, and the foul stench that drifted on the wind was not smoky, but dank and rotten.

He flew closer. The earth, transformed into a gaseous swamp, radiated a dank, humid heat. The sulfuric heat melted the snow and stopped any ice from forming. He didn't see any wildlife, no bird nests or deer or wolves. No foxes or winter quails.

The plague, he thought. His eyes traveled up to the horizon and then in the direction of the coast. As far as he could see to the west, the forest was rotting. Even the air took on a smoky, grayish cast.

He wondered, with a sense of foreboding, if this was the terrain of the underworld, if somehow the two were bleeding into one another, merging, and if the Dark God's presence would turn everything it touched into a wasteland.

He clenched his fists, hovering in indecision. The sight made him want to turn back to the city, back to his purpose, and warn Sora and his friends. He couldn't let the world perish. Someone must be warned of this.

But what of Krait? Could he let *her* perish? He had made it this far. He remembered the approximate location where he had dropped the stone. He could call to it, activate it, and recover it. It wouldn't take long...but the plague was digesting the forest. He wasn't immune to the Dark God's essence, no matter how powerful his wings or the One Star's song within him.

But he had to rescue Krait.

He traveled slowly over the rotten acres, keeping the Little Rain river to his left. He hummed low in his throat, casting a vibration out and listening for the stone's answer. The ground was mostly swampland, with pools of stagnant water and noxious plants. He brought himself lower, just above the skeletal trees, where swarms of mosquitos, gnats and giant black flies created a haze above the ground.

A sharp vibration disrupted his thoughts, and he felt a chill move down his neck. *Yes, the stone.* He followed its call: a pure tone that tickled the roof of his mouth. He swooped into the forest and glided between the rotten tree trunks. The ground was like thick molasses, teeming with all manner of twisting black worms, leeches and slugs. He didn't dare land.

But the stone's vibration was clear and strong. It wasn't buried in the mud. Perhaps it had caught in a tree branch? Was he so lucky? Perhaps some curious bird or squirrel had hidden it in a nest, before the plague had forced the wildlife to flee?

The vibration grew stronger to his left. He turned, banking his wings. Yes, this felt right. A thorny grove of dead bramble blocked his path, and he flapped upward, gliding over the debris. He held his breath. On the other side, surely nearby, he would find it.

Then Caprion came to a sudden stop.

He hesitated, shocked, trying to regain his composure, trying to think.

"Hello again."

Before him, as though molded from the blackness of the trees, stood a familiar cloaked figure. His wide hood fell dramatically over his face, but just by his aura, Caprion knew him: Grandmaster Cerastes, one of the Sixth Race and leader of the Shade. They had faced off once before on the Dawn Seeker, when Caprion had rescued Krait from the demon's clutches.

Cerastes smiled at him. His papery skin stretched, tearing at the corners of his mouth.

Pinched between his thumb and forefinger, he held a sunstone. Unlike others of the Sixth Race, he didn't seem bothered by its light. In fact, as Caprion watched, the stone lost some of its glow and began to turn gray. The vibration dimmed.

No.

"Give that to me," Caprion commanded, summoning his voice magic. "Give it to me *now!*"

His command seemed to have little effect on the Grandmaster, just like the sunstone. And in fact, after spending so much time in the diseased forest, Caprion was also feeling gray.

"I've thought long and hard about our last confrontation, Harpy," Cerastes said. From his wet black hair to his mud-spattered robes, he might have been born from the rotten molasses of the bog.

"You followed me here," Caprion said.

"Followed? No. I waited for you."

Caprion didn't want to play the Grandmaster's game, but....

"How?" he asked. "I told no one where I was going, not even your servant, Krait."

"Her eyes are my eyes, and I have seen much in the last few days."

Caprion tried not to feel a little self-conscious. *Her eyes are my eyes.* Of course Cerastes would exert some sort of power over Krait, even when she wasn't in his presence. So everything Caprion had said to her, all of his passion and hope, had been laid bare in front of this monster? It was almost enough to make his cheeks flush, but he didn't allow them too. Instead, he fixed Cerastes with an angry glare. Somehow, though Caprion didn't know exactly, this demon had known about the sunstone.

"Why are you here, serpent?" Caprion's voice was soft. "Why did you come here to meet me? What about Sora and her Cat's-Eye necklace? Or has she lost your attention?"

"You mean that pitiful child Viper tries to protect? I haven't forgotten. She will still prove useful to me. No, I have come here to stop a greater threat to my plans."

"Then you realize what I am," Caprion said, feeling more confident. He had killed demons before. Cerastes was powerful, but he would succumb to the One Star's light in the end.

"Don't look so smug, Harpy. The Dark God has asked for you. I am simply here to follow his bidding."

Caprion reached for his sword at his waist.

Cerastes tossed the sunstone into the air, above the murky quicksand of the bog. If it landed, it would be swallowed forever by the black earth.

Caprion lunged for it, his sword half drawn from its sheath, his balance off-kilter. He fumbled for his blade, then fumbled for the stone. One of them fell in the mud.

Cerastes appeared behind him and dealt a powerful blow to his back. With a gasp, Caprion fell forward. His wings flickered, then brightened as he tried to fly up and away. He felt Cerastes's shadow grow around him, a cloud that threatened to engulf him, imprison him. Tendrils of shadow snagged his ankles and dragged him back down to the wet earth.

"Stop!" Caprion commanded with a burst of light from his wings. His song, his power, vibrated through his voice. It cut through the black shadow, peeling it back, and he darted up to the sky.

But the swamp chased after him. A tendril of black tar shot out and grabbed his ankle.

Cerastes's laughter rang in his ears as the Harpy was dragged violently downward. The ground bubbled like a slow-boiling stew. Caprion summoned four of his wings, their light blinding, but without his sword, he couldn't stop the black tendrils from wrapping around his body—one at his knee, one at his arm, another at his waist. They wrapped him in a suffocating grip, trying to drag him down beneath the swampwater.

It took a minute for him to realize that Cerastes stood only a few feet away. They were practically face-to-face. He watched the seraph's struggle with a look of cold indifference.

Then the Grandmaster spoke. "What you said about Krait is true. She is Moss, and she is from the Lost Isles. I am the one who blocked her memories, not the Matriarch, as I know you suspected. She cried for you when I found her. She wanted to go back to the island, to recover what your kind stole from her--her demon. When I forbid it, she fought me, but I would not let her leave my side. She promised to wait for you, and she did, for a time. But the Dark God chose her to be His servant, and I could not refuse."

A roar of fury began in Caprion's throat. It was choked off by a black, slimy tentacle. The swamp held him bound and immobile. He could not fight back.

Cerastes looked satisfied. "Of course, what Krait doesn't know, is that she has performed an invaluable service by remaining your prisoner. How else could I have trapped a seraph?" He moved closer, and ran one long, paper-dry finger down Caprion's cheek. "I would give her this sunstone as a reward, but that would just confuse her even more, don't you think? Besides, there are so many better uses for such a thing."

Cerastes raised the stone in his hand. It had turned completely black, like the swamp-mulch and the trees. Its vibration had changed as well, now jarring and offensive to the ears.

"Arrogant bird," the Grandmaster said. "You can't comprehend the Dark God's power. Oh, but you will serve us well. That is your purpose, isn't it? Seraph. To serve."

Cerastes shoved the stone into Caprion's mouth. It tasted of filth, of sewage. He retched and tried to spit it out, but the stone slid determinedly down his throat, to lodge somewhere above his windpipe. Caprion opened his mouth to speak, but the words would not come. His breath would not come. In horror, he realized that Cerastes had blocked his voice.

"Take him," Cerastes said to the swamp. "An offering to the Unnamed God of this new land. I pray He makes good use of you, seraph."

More black tentacles rose from the swamp, more and more, wrapping Caprion's body in a cocoon. He couldn't see, he couldn't speak, but in his thoughts, he screamed.

Cerastes hung the black cocoon amidst the pine trees and waited for it to ripen. He sat heavily on a rotten tree stump to rest. Summoning the plague's power--living with it inside of his bones--had taken a toll on his own body. Organic life was not meant to withstand the Dark God's taint, yet by His shadowed will, Cerastes remained alive.

In thought, Cerastes peeled a strip of skin from his hand and flicked it into the marsh. This body was turning to dust, and he was running out of time. This trip had been an unexpected detour, but for his prize, the delay was worth it. He would wait for his creation to finish evolving. He wondered what sort of creature would emerge. He hadn't thought the seraph would succumb so easily to the darkness. He had expected more of a fight, but then again, the seraph had not expected to find him here in the wilderness. He had taken his prey off guard.

His eyes watched the cocoon sway back and forth in a foul breeze. A regular human would not survive such a transformation. He wasn't sure about regular Harpies, either. But he knew a seraph would survive--pieces of him, fragments--and rise again to serve the Dark God.

An hour later, the cocoon ripped open and a heavy body fell into the marsh. Slow and lumberous, it climbed out of the black tar and stood before him. Cerastes grinned at the sight of the Dark God's new abomination.

With a wave of his hand, he opened a shadow portal. His prize was clumsy, but managed to cross through the opening, into their destination beyond.

They arrived in the basement of his house in The Regency, and the creature crouched close to the floor. Black worms wriggled from the Harpy's nose and mouth. His body looked gray and cold, close to death, perhaps dead already, Cerastes didn't care to know which. The Dark God had the seraph now. He would work His will upon him.

Cerastes climbed the stairs into the house, leaving his new servant in the basement. Now, he had other matters to attend.

Once, the house on Timberlin Lane had been the quaint home of a Second Tier family. The front walk had been shoveled and salted daily, the windows cleared of frost and the garden trimmed.

Now the house appeared forgotten, with wooden shutters over the windows and waist-deep weeds covering the front walk. No one remembered who owned it. Cerastes had made sure of that.

He walked down the hallway, his black robes billowing behind him, to enter a small study at the front of the house with a desk and a bookshelf along the far wall. He closed the door behind him.

He knew *The Book of the Named* was gone. The loss did not trouble him anymore. He had learned everything from the book that he needed.

Tame yourself, he thought. *See clearly.* The fire stuttered momentarily, seeming to speak. Cerastes stared into the flames, seeking his god's voice. He reached out, allowing the fire to lick his fingers. The flame did not burn him, but soothed him like warm water.

He needed the third sacred weapon, and for that, he needed a Cat's Eye, but he couldn't wield such a stone himself. None of the races could. This presented him with a very specific problem: Cerastes didn't just need a Cat's-Eye stone, he needed a bearer as well.

Sora was the one he wanted, the one that Viper protected.

The fire leapt suddenly in the stone hearth, as though seeking his attention. He tilted his head slightly to one side, listening with fervor.

A vacant smile pulled at his lips.

The door to the study opened and two of his savants entered.

"Grandmaster," the first said.

"We are honored by your presence. How can we serve you?"

Cerastes faced them, calm and self-assured.

"The hour has grown late," he said. "Release the wraith."

CHAPTER 8

The streets of The Regency were frothing with anticipation for winter solstice. Foot traffic swirled and foamed at each street corner. People gathered so densely that horse drawn carriages could barely pass. It seemed all the fine ladies and gentlemen were frantic with last minute preparations.

Danica pointed out the window as they entered the Flower District. She pressed one pink, manicured finger to the glass.

"There," she said. "That's Lady Cecil Daniellian. Just look at that peacock feather on her bodice. Downright garish, if you ask me."

Sora glanced around Danica to see out the window, but couldn't tell Lady Cecil from the rest of the feather-adorned women standing before a cottage-like tea shop. She didn't understand the fashion of the First Tier, and she felt more removed from the topic than usual.

"Horrendous," she muttered.

"Never fear. I won't let Lord Seabourne see you in such dire straits!" Danica vowed. "No cousin of mine shall be seen in peacock feathers. They're strictly for Spring. Oh, just look at how crowded it is. We shall have to pull over. Driver!" Danica opened the little window at the front of the coach. "Make your way over, please."

"At once, Milady."

Sora had visited the Flower District only a few days ago with Olivia to buy dresses. She recalled, now, how she had left Olivia to find Lord Seabourne and learn more about the death of her step-father. Somehow, she felt like weeks had passed, instead of just a few days. Her questions surrounding Lord Fallcrest's death remained unresolved, but she remembered that Martin Ebonaire had been heavily implicated. She didn't think Danica would know anything about it.

Decorative masks and wreaths covered each store front in the Flower District. Streamers and banners were strung across the road. Since the parade, it seemed the winter solstice celebration was in full swing. Sora's carriage passed a large park where countless nobility skated about on a frozen pond.

"What are those shoes?" She pointed at one young boy, whose bladed shoes propelled him along the ice.

"They're called *skates*," Danica said disinterestedly. "I'm no good at them. Almost broke my ankle last time."

Their carriage continued around the edge of Diadem Park. The theatre sat, a domed goliath of a building, at the far end of the park. The building was made of countless arches and columns, its roof curved like a great crystal ball. Streamers hung above the entrance, announcing the names of various actors and famous musicians who would be performing in the play. Lanterns illuminated the doors and the long driveway, where a row of carriages waited in line.

Danica tapped on the roof for the driver to pull over. As soon as they had stopped, she opened the door and hopped down onto the snowy sidewalk without a hand to assist her. Then she gave Sora her own gloved hand and helped her down.

"Father said you've never spent winter solstice in the city before," Danica said, ushering her away from the carriage. "You're in for a treat. The theatre is fantastic. You'll forget all about the real world, until you step outside again. Still, it doesn't hold a candle to First Winter's Ball. Every year, the royal palace is transformed into a wonderland of festivities. And oh, my friends will adore you! You must save your very best stories for us alone, promise?"

Sora felt a sudden wave of anxiety. She didn't want to be the center of attention, as flattered as she was by Danica's friendship.

As they walked, Danica continued to gush about what kind of a stir Sora's presence would cause at the masquerade. Slowly, Sora realized that Danica didn't care much about where she came from, or what had brought her to the city. No, Danica wanted to show her off like a shiny new brooch—a glittering new ornament for her towering reputation. Perhaps it was for the best.

Finally, they started up the slippery front steps of the playhouse, gripping each other for balance. When they reached the top, countless colorful skirts blocked Sora's path and she found it impossible to continue forward. Hundreds of lords and ladies inched across the wide pavilion to the theatre's open doors, where they were funneled inside by ushers in black suits and seasonal masks.

Sora could already hear a chorus of voices calling out Danica's name. She released the girl's arm, and Danica turned away from her. The young Ebonaire began waving animatedly through the crowd.

"Yes, I'm here!" she called. "Elward, Travid, this is such a surprise!"

Sora allowed Danica to push away from her, toward her group of friends. Meanwhile, she let the tide of the crowd carry her to the edge of the pavilion, where she sank against a stone wall. She didn't regret losing track of Danica in the sea of faces. Truth be told, the number of people and perfumes was overwhelming. She stripped off one silk glove and touched her face, only to find her skin hot and clammy. She wondered if she wasn't fully recovered from the poison. Perhaps leaving the manor had been a bad idea.

Then a strange chill went down her spine. Sora turned and surveyed the crowd. Her eyes traveled down the wide steps to the carriages and then across the street to the snow-covered park. A cold wind blew up the steps of the theater. It carried a strange, sour odor. The smell unsettled her, and she bristled without thinking.

A threat. The thought came from her gut, instinctive. Something was coming this way. Something wrathful and rancid with the plague.

I will not be prey.

She remembered that she was outside of her cage.

Without a backward glance, Sora picked up her skirts and started down the wide front steps. Her Cat's Eye glowed blue at her neck, its light reflecting off the ice and stone. She crossed the street and entered the snowy park, following the stench on the breeze, her heartbeat growing louder with each step.

Ferran grabbed Burn's shoulder and pointed out the carriage window.

"There," he said. "She left the play, just like we suspected."

"Where is she going?"

Ferran didn't know. Sora was heading determinedly out into the middle of the park where several children skated on a frozen pond.

"She's searching for something on the ground," he guessed, observing her bent posture. Then he noticed the blue light gleaming from her necklace. "See that? The *garrolithe* is active."

"Then we must follow her." Burn was already opening the door of the carriage. His boots crunched in the snow as he stepped down. "Last time, she was trying to get down into the sewers. She might be looking for a hatch."

Ferran knew of several iron hatches on different sides of the park. But which one would Sora find first? The wind was blowing harder now, kicking up swirls of snowy mist, making it difficult to see.

He climbed down after Burn. His friend was unloading a bundle wrapped in coarse linen from the back of the coach.

"What's that?" Ferran asked.

"A picnic."

Burn dumped the contents of the bundle into the snow. Steel flashed in the wintry air. He lifted a long and heavy greatsword from the pile and strapped it to his back.

"In case the Shade decides to attend the theatre."

"Good thinking," Ferran agreed, and buckled a sheathed sword to his belt. Then they started across the snow.

As they walked, Ferran noticed his own Cat's Eye glowing at his wrist. He felt cold at the sight, beyond just the weather. Something was coming.

Sora dug through the snow at the east end of the park where a row of hedges more or less blocked her from view. After a good half-minute, her gloved hands found the cold iron rungs of the sewer hatch, and she pulled upward. The snow and ice were stubborn, but endless strength seemed to fuel her arms, and with a groan, she dragged the hatch open.

Then she faced a new problem: her dress wouldn't allow her to climb down. With a groan, she began unfastening her heavy outer skirts. If she could simply get the panniers off, she would be able to move freely.

"I daresay, that's far from proper!" a voice interrupted her.

Sora turned to see Ferran and Burn approaching through the snow.

"A little help?" she called, unperturbed that they had followed her. In fact, she was somewhat relieved. Whatever was coming, she wouldn't have to face it alone.

Burn glanced at the open porthole before her. He wrinkled his nose.

"It's mighty ripe down there. Sora, is this really...." He paused at her expression.

"Something is coming, Burn," she said, aware that her voice had dropped a notch. "We either fight it here in the park, or we lead it away. But I think it's coming for me."

Burn's gaze darkened.

"It's in the sewers," Ferran said, and held up his hand, displaying his glowing red Cat's Eye. "She's not lying."

"Why would I lie?" Sora didn't have time to be affronted. "Now help me out of this dress so I can get on with the hunt. I'm tired of being prey."

Burn and Ferran shared a look. Then Burn drew a wicked knife from his belt and cut through the ties at the back of her dress. With the knife's assistance, they had the panniers off in no time, and Sora found herself in baggy white drawers and corset. Tall fox-trimmed boots encased her feet up to her knees. Shivering in the cold air, she pulled on the short green jacket that had once covered her dress.

"Follow me," she said, and started down the iron ladder into the sewers.

Darkness enveloped them, but Sora's glowing blue Cat's Eye—accompanied by Ferran's red stone—lit the way. Once underground, the presence of dark magic was strong enough to make her dizzy.

The ring of sleigh bells told her which direction to go. Her Cat's Eye urged her forward, leading her around corners and down dank, moldy tunnels. Ferran and Burn followed in silence.

After several minutes, a strange smell caught Sora's nose.

Primal excitement stirred her blood. She turned and sniffed the air. Rot. Rust. Blood. A memory flashed in front of her eyes, and she put a hand to her head. *You know this smell.*

The scar burned on her ribs. She saw the black wraith in Delbar again, and before that, the spectre on the plains that drove its rapier through her body.

A third wraith, she thought, *here, in the city.*

The roar grew inside of her, pressing against her stomach. *Worthy,* she thought. *A worthy hunt.* Her eyes dilated in anticipation.

The Shade's hideout was nearby. Sora didn't question it. She could smell imprints of many feet weaving paths through the earth.

I can't fight it below ground. It's too enclosed, reason told her.

But the roar didn't agree. *I will devour it whole.*

"I'm sorry," she murmured to herself, or perhaps to Burn and Ferran, though she had all but forgotten their presence. Then she fell headfirst into a red haze. She ran down the tunnel, following the wraith's scent and the need in her bones. She sprinted faster than she ever had before, tipping farther and farther forward, until at times she ran on all fours.

Light pierced the passageway before her, filtering through a metal grate in the street above. Icicles formed along the ceiling. At times, thicker icicles blocked her path like barred gates, and she barreled through them using her shoulders.

She ran through underground chambers where storm water formed streams and rivulets. She cut down passages slick with ice and grime. At times, she crawled.

The trail's scent grew stronger, harsher.

Finally she reached a juncture of many different tunnels, all converging like the heart of a spider web. A circle of dim light spilled through a metal grate overhead. Outside, through the grate, she glimpsed the charcoal sky and swollen clouds.

She tested the air of each passageway. She smelled footsteps, countless dozens, all mixing and overlapping on the floor. She was close now, but which way forward?

The thickest trail, she thought, going to one tunnel and then to the next, opening her mouth to taste the air. *The thickest, where they all go.*

Then she felt it coming toward her in a dark and furious wind. Sora's fingers arched into claws. She turned and faced her prey.

"She's just up ahead," Burn panted, with Ferran just behind. Then his steps faltered at the sudden stench of evil. He drew his sword, anticipating battle.

CHAPTER 9

S ora faced the wraith at the crossroads of the tunnels. A grate in the ceiling cast bars of silver light between them.

The creature regarded her as well. It floated a few feet above the ground, a vague, man-shaped cloud of black mist swathed in a tattered cloak. She could smell Volcrian's magic on the beast: the stench of moist organs and wet blood.

Through her Cat's Eye, the spectre looked different, larger, its power more potent than the wraiths she had faced before. A visible aura surrounded it, glinting like fire off a black pearl. Sora shivered. She could feel its hatred burning through her, and with a glimmer of understanding, she realized the wraith and the *garrolithe* were not so different. The wraith, too, was a mecha-animist, a forbidden war-spell combining Wulven blood magic with the dark power of the underworld.

The monster within Sora rose to the challenge, unafraid. When she looked down at her hands, she saw her body encased in blue light. She gripped her necklace in her left hand and allowed the *garrolithe's* energy to flow freely. She heard the distant sound of bells in her ears. The stone's power washed over her like warm rain.

The stone thirsted. It *craved*.

"Sora, no!" Burn yelled as he and Ferran stumbled into the chamber behind her.

She threw herself upon the wraith with animal ferocity. The creature screamed in fury as they wrestled in the darkness. Her fists flashed with azure fire every time she landed a strike, a scratch, a punch. When her knuckles split, she curled her fingers into claws and tore at the creature's cloaked head. She managed to knock its bow to the ground, winning a screech from its lips. Then it threw her off with a desperate heave.

Sora smashed into the tunnel wall. The impact brought a shower of ice and snow down from the ceiling. She shook herself, crouched on all fours and growled. This underground passageway was too restricting. She needed an open area to run, to outmaneuver her enemy.

She pointed to Burn and Ferran with a glowing sapphire hand.

"Don't follow me," she said, low and guttural.

Their eyes widened with...awe? Terror?

Sora darted down the nearest sewer canal. The wraith followed, its shrill screams chasing her into the dark.

Ferran signaled to Burn that they should follow. However, at that moment, the entire tunnel began to quiver and shake. Too late, he saw a large crack where Sora had struck the wall. It traveled up the mortar and across the ceiling.

"Watch out!" Ferran yelled, and dived away from the collapsing stone. Burn fell back in the opposite direction.

When the dust cleared, Ferran found himself alone. A pile of rubble stood between him and the way back.

"Burn, you alright?"

"Right as can be expected," the Wolfy replied with a cough.

"I'll go on ahead!" Ferran called. "The sewers empty at The Bath. I'm sure that's where they are headed."

"I'll take the streets," Burn agreed.

Without wasting more time, Ferran turned and ran down the same tunnel in which Sora and the wraith had disappeared. His Cat's Eye glowed at his wrist, and the stench of rotten magic clogged his lungs.

Sooner than he expected, a whiff of brisk, fresh water caught his nose. He sensed daylight up ahead. He was eager to reach the end of the stinking, frozen labyrinth. He didn't relish the thought of fighting underground. It was too difficult to see, and too easy to become trapped or cornered.

The exit came upon him suddenly, and for the last few meters, he slid down a frozen pipe onto the hard, flat surface of the lake. The wintry air shocked his lungs, and he struggled to find his footing on the ice. To his right, at a distance, he could see the curve of the southern docks. To his left, dense woodlands gripped the shoreline. He knew a road led through those pine trees to the Healer's seminary, but it was not visible from his location. The leaden clouds were growing lower and thicker by the minute. Another storm was primed to bury the city.

A bone-jarring shriek drew his attention. Ahead of him, across the ice, he saw an animal running on all fours. It turned and skidded to a halt at the center of the lake, and he recognized her blond hair, even if he couldn't believe his eyes. Not an animal—Sora.

Burn had explained, very briefly, how he had followed her from the manor just that morning, and why he suspected the *garrolithe* controlled her Cat's-Eye necklace. Ferran had listened without question, and understood more completely than Burn could know. The treasure hunter hadn't just read about such things—he had seen them firsthand. Sora was in the thrall of a power far greater than her own, and far greater than his.

Several meters beyond Sora, the wraith hovered. Its telltale black cloak whipped about in a sharp wind. Something akin to smoke, dark as soot, peeled off its body, swirling into the air, dissipating into the ethers.

Ferran touched the Cat's Eye at his wrist, and a red light flowed over his skin, creating a protective barrier. Then he walked out onto the frozen lake, keeping balance with his arms. He didn't know what he would do once he reached the wraith. Should he drag Sora away from it, or should they join forces and fight? Would the *garrolithe* allow it? They needed to secure the third and final weapon of the Dark God, but not at the expense of Sora's life.

He cursed her quietly for having brought them onto the lake. The ice offered no advantages, and it was becoming precariously thin underfoot. Ferran reached the point, far too soon, that he could go no farther. Sora was smaller than him, her weight spread out on all fours, so she could travel across the thinner ice.

He wondered what to do next. For now, the fight was at a stand still.

Then, to his surprise, the wraith flickered out of existence. It disappeared, then reappeared directly in front of him.

His mouth opened, silent, agape.

A blast of dark energy struck him in the chest, and he flew backward—arced—fell—*crack*. He landed hard on the ice, and it crumbled beneath him, shattering like glass. Ferran found himself under water, his body paralyzed by the cold, and by the impact of such powerful magic.

The Cat's Eye at his wrist brightened, and the sound of his own heartbeat filled his ears.

He tried to regain control of his limbs. Finally, his body recovered from its shock and he swam up to the surface of the lake, but somehow, he had misplaced the opening in the ice. A filmy, opaque barrier trapped him underwater. He pounded against the ice. Cracks spread. Slowly.

When Sora leapt on the wraith's back, the creature felt solid, real—nothing like the two apparitions she had defeated before.

Her elongated nails sunk deep into the creature's back, deep into its spongy, rotten-wood flesh. She tried to absorb its energy, tried to dissolve it into her Cat's Eye, just like any other spell. The sound of bells filled her ears. The necklace began siphoning the wraith's power.

Then her lungs closed. Her stomach churned. Bile entered her mouth.

The wraith broke her grip and flung her down. She landed hard on the frozen surface of The Bath. She would have crashed through it like Ferran, but the garrolithe's reflexes were too fast. Catlike, nimble, she leapt up and away. She danced backwards across the ice. She found her balance on all fours. She crouched and growled low in her throat.

The wraith pointed its bow at her and took aim. A beam of darkness spread between its hands. Sora braced herself, ready to jump, roll, or dodge, depending on how the bolt flew. She had seen Ferran struck down. She didn't know if the blow had killed him. The thought seemed far away, inconsequential. She had to find the wraith's weakness. She had to win.

Bells chimed in her ears. Bells, and then a new sound, startling: the rhythmic, pounding beat of a drum.

Unexpected light drew her gaze. She looked down. Beneath the ice, a red blaze, much like fire, or the sunset, drew her eyes.

Cr-crack. Spiderwebs crossed the surface of the lake. Sora skipped backward, but the lines tried to catch her like a net. The wraith followed her with its bow, howling, hovering, turning as she changed directions. A bolt of midnight struck the ice near her feet, but missed.

The pounding in her head continued. *Not a drum,* she thought. *A heart.* Her own?

Then the ice broke directly beneath the wraith. Red light blossomed up from the water. Ferran, defying gravity, defying all rationality, flew up and grabbed onto the wraith.

Sora gasped. For a moment, she saw a red winged halo on his back. *Like a phoenix,* she thought.

Ferran dragged the bow from the wraith's hands. He flung it across the ice. When the creature tried to chase after it, the red light from his Cat's Eye engulfed its body, stopping it, *binding it,* Sora thought. The red halo returned, and Sora didn't know if she saw a man, a bird, or living fire.

"Troublesome, aren't you?" Ferran said, grappling with the beast. He slipped his red hand through its robes, searching, grasping. *Blood, filth and shadow,* the Cat's Eye told him. *The heart still beats.*

Firmly entwined with the creature, Ferran understood the source of its power: a human soul tied to this empty, blighted vessel.

"Let's free you now," he said.

His hand reached deep inside the wraith's ribcage, or where a ribcage might be on a living being, and he finally grasped *it,* the source, the spirit's anchor. No larger than an apple. No heavier than a stone. The soiled, putrid heart turned his veins to ice. His bones ached, his hand turned numb, but he did not loosen his grip. His Cat's Eye, mounted on the cuff at his wrist, glowed brightly.

Take it, he thought. *Take it now.*

He ripped the heart from the wraith's body.

Corrupt magic ran from the blistered organ into the stone at Ferran's wrist. He felt as though his very flesh would disintegrate. A cry of agony ripped from his throat.

"Sora!" he yelled. "It's defenseless now. Finish it!"

Then he collapsed into the lake. Steam rose. Ice cracked. He doused the blackened heart underwater, and held it tightly as his Cat's Eye pulsed with light, absorbing its tainted magic.

* * *

Sora didn't understand what Ferran had done, but the drumbeat had stopped, and the wraith was furiously spinning in circles, its aura greatly diminished.

She gripped her Cat's Eye in one hand and thought of Ferran's words. *Finish it.*

She felt a growing pressure in her chest. Blue light flashed. She fell to her hands and knees, her back arching, her breath heaving.

The light brightened. She watched the *garrolithe* fight its way from the Cat's-Eye stone at her throat. It seemed to emerge from her own body: the light rising from her arms and forming into much greater limbs, then a fanged muzzle issuing from her own face, the formation of twisting horns, and a thick mane of quills. Sora felt as though she were expelling it, regurgitating it, from her own body.

The *garrolithe* finally ripped free from the organic confines of its cage and, with a thunderous howl, charged across the ice.

Sora collapsed. She gripped her throat as sweet oxygen returned to her lungs. No longer did she feel the beast's power burning up her limbs. Now, she watched it run.

The *garrolithe* sprang upon the wraith like a lion upon a man. Its cavernous jaw closed around the wraith's hooded head. Bits of shredded cloth and rotten flesh flew through the air as the *garrolithe* devoured its prey. Sora stared, transfixed. How had she contained such a powerful being for so long?

Within minutes, the glowing blue monster stood over the sorry remnants of the wraith's cloak. It raised its majestic head to the sky and howled. The sound shook the forest, snapping branches and sending showers of snow to the earth. It caused waves to ripple across the unfrozen waters of the lake. It broke the ice. Sora thought it would break her teeth.

Then the *garrolithe* fell silent. Like a glowing blue ghost, it crossed the waters back to her side. Sora climbed to her feet to meet it. She could barely stand.

The *garrolithe* paused before her, where it stood, eye to eye, as it had in her dream. Sora reached out a hand and touched its soft muzzle. She stroked between its eyes and down its nose.

The *garrolithe* crouched, and without hesitation, Sora climbed upon its back. The beast carried her across the lake, bounding from one floating patch of ice to the next, until they found the wraith's fallen bow. Sora picked it up. The weapon was colder than the wintry air.

Then the beast carried her into the forest. Beyond the treeline, it began to run. Sora knelt forward across its back, gripping its wide horns. Within seconds, her face grew numb from the wind.

The *garrolithe* carried her through snow-buried meadows and frozen rivers. They emerged on a hill beyond the City of Crowns, where a row of windmills spun lazily in the wind. The beast dashed through the massive wooden blades and carried her down the hill, to the city wall, then leapt that wall in a single bound.

They dashed across rooftops, shattering tiles in their wake. All the while, Sora felt as though they ran through a tunnel of their own making, invisible to the people below, aware only of each other and the endless, open horizon. She felt her heart expand and soar. Her mouth opened to the winter air and she devoured every breath.

The *garrolithe* circled around the city, from the gates of the royal palace to the Temple of the North Wind to the southern docks. There, the beast carried her across The Bath in a single monstrous leap, and for a moment, she thought they flew.

The *garrolithe* came to a halt once again in the woods, in a grove of silent birch trees, and she dismounted. Her pounding blood made her skin hum. She realized her face was stretched in a wide, joyous grin.

There, they regarded one another again. She saw a fierce, familiar fire in its blue eyes.

"I understand now," she said. Her voice was raw. "You're not meant to be controlled or restrained. Go now. Travel where the winds take you. Run free." She touched the creature's soft white fur. "Perhaps someday we'll run together again."

The garrolithe tilted back its head and released a bone-chilling howl. It sniffed her face once more, then turned and dashed into the forest. Within seconds it was gone, leaving behind pawprints that would soon disappear in the snow.

CHAPTER 10

"Help!" Sora called, waving her arms at the squadron of soldiers coming down the road. They were traveling from the Healer's seminary, or so she guessed. Relief filled her.

"Over here! I need help!" she called again.

Riding the *garrolithe* had been a wondrous experience, but with its power gone from her necklace, she now felt the bitter sting of the wind and the bite of snow against her bare feet. She had walked as far as the road, but couldn't continue on her own. She would lose her toes soon. Besides that, she had to find Ferran. Last she remembered, he had fallen into the lake.

"Help!" she yelled again.

The soldiers saw her.

"Up ahead! I see a lass. Blessed bells, she's wearing a shift!"

"Out in this weather?"

"She must be mad."

The soldier in the lead held up his fist, and the squad slowed down.

"Thank the Goddess," she said as they approached. "I thought the roads were abandoned. Please, I'm lost and...."

Her stomach sank. A distinguished man, dressed in a dark blue cloak and black boots, guided his horse around the squadron of twelve soldiers.

Lord Seabourne's expression soured when he saw her.

"My Lady," he said, routinely polite. Then, to his men, "All of you, continue ahead to the city gates. I'll assist this young woman."

His soldiers looked curiously at her. At first no one moved, then Gracen cast them a narrow look. One by one, his men continued past, until they disappeared down the road.

Lord Seabourne dismounted and pushed his cloak back over his shoulders. He looked quite dashing in his indigo uniform, his badges displayed prominently on his breast and a sword at his hip. The ride had tussled his dark hair in a roguish sort of way.

"Lord Gracen," Sora began, but her voice faltered. Strange, that she could ride a garrolithe without fear, yet she lost her voice when facing this man.

"Do I ask now, or do I wait for dinner?" he asked.

"What?"

"Lord Martin invited me to dine at the Ebonaire house tonight. I thought of putting him off, but now I'm intrigued."

"I...this must look very strange...."

"Oh, it does." He held out his hand. "Let's get you out of the snow."

Gracen patiently assisted her onto the back of his horse. If he noticed the unstrung longbow in her hand, he didn't mention it. The warmth of the beast made her legs ache. Then he withdrew a linen shirt from his saddlebags and cut it into long strips with his knife. Sora watched, embarrassed.

"Always carry a change of dry clothes with you," he said, noting her damp shift. He wrapped her feet in the dry linens and then tucked each foot into a stirrup. "Press your feet against the horse to keep warm."

"It hurts," Sora mumbled.

"Be thankful you can feel anything. I'd offer you my boots, but they're a bit damp, and our goal is to save your toes, not lose them."

"Thank you, I...." Sora hesitated, then pushed on. "I need you to help me find Ferran Ebonaire."

"What does Ferran Ebonaire have to do with this? Did he hurt you?"

Sora bit her lip. She couldn't tell if he was angry or just suspicious. His reaction was strong.

"He fell into the lake. Please, I have to find him."

"Where is he?"

She pointed to The Bath.

Gracen started through the trees, leading her on his horse. By the set of his shoulders, she could see that he was a true soldier, trained to take action. He hadn't asked why she was out in the woods, alone, in her undergarments. He didn't ask about the unstrung bow, or how Ferran had fallen into the lake. She was grateful for his silence, but she knew it wouldn't last for long. Either she would have to invent an exceptional lie, or admit to an impossible truth.

They reached the edge of The Bath after twenty minutes or so. To Sora's eyes, the evidence of a battle was obvious. The lake's surface, once covered by a thick layer of ice, looked like a shattered mirror. In some places, trees had toppled over, their trunks snapped like twigs.

Gracen surveyed the lake in silence. *He's Captain of the King's Guard,* Sora thought. Of course he would recognize the signs of battle.

"Where did he fall in?" he asked.

Sora didn't know for sure. In her memory, the battle was a confusing blur of adrenaline. She floundered for a moment, trying to remember, then she realized she had a Cat's Eye at her neck. She touched the stone and asked for a direction, dreading the answer she might receive.

It responded instantly, easily, without delay. The sound of sleigh bells rang softly in her ears.

"This way," she said, pointing to her right.

Gracen led his horse through the icy mud. Sora continued to direct him around the lake, following the pull of the Cat's Eye. Sooner than she expected, they came upon Ferran's body lying in a bed of dry, yellow cattails.

Sora's heart leapt to her throat. She thought, perhaps, that he was....

Then Ferran stirred and groaned at their approach. Lord Gracen left her and crossed to Ferran's side, where he helped roll him onto his back. Only then did Sora notice the black arrow protruding from his shoulder. Blood drenched his coat.

Gracen drew his knife and, with military calm, cut off Ferran's sleeve. The arm beneath it was caked with blood, the wound itself blackened by the Dark God's essence. Sora went cold at the sight. The veins of his shoulder had turned black.

Before she knew it, Sora stumbled down from the horse. She almost collapsed in the snow, but managed to keep her legs under her. She used the Dark God's longbow as a walking stick, and crossed to Ferran's side.

"My lady, please!" Gracen said, but she ignored him and knelt in the snow. When she reached for the arrow in Ferran's shoulder, her hands shook.

"Removing it would be most unwise," Gracen said. "The head might be lodged in his bone. If you pull it out, it will break off. He could lose an arm."

"We can't leave him like this!"

Gracen placed a firm, if surprisingly gentle, arm between her and Ferran's body.

"Let's get him to a healer. The seminary isn't far up the road."

Sora felt numb. Ferran gazed at the sky with glassy, hooded eyes. Despite his initial groan, he seemed unresponsive to their presence. His Cat's Eye seemed dormant as well. Beneath the stone, his skin looked cracked and blistered, as though he had thrust his hand in a furnace

Sora looked from the stone to the black veins spreading down Ferran's arm.

"I can fix this," she muttered. "I know what's wrong."

"What do you mean?"

"He doesn't need a healer. He needs *me*."

She clenched her teeth and set her hands on Ferran's wound. Without the *garrolithe* to interfere, she could feel her Cat's Eye more clearly than ever before. The stone responded instantly to her thoughts. She felt the plague infecting Ferran's body like worms crawling under his skin.

Dispel it, she thought.

The necklace responded with a bright green glow. Sora sucked in a sharp breath. The Cat's Eye absorbed the Dark God's power from the wound.

All the while, Lord Seabourne watched her with an unreadable expression.

A minute passed, but the black veins on Ferran's arm did not recede. Finally, Sora had to sit back. She wrapped her arms around her waist and swallowed a wave of nausea. The plague kept reviving itself. The source was in his body and she couldn't dispel it with the arrow still in his shoulder.

Sora took Ferran's hand in her own. *Please,* she thought, watching the black veins creep up his neck. Tears stung her eyes. *Please....*

She could remove the arrow, but as Gracen had said, part of it might snap off in his shoulder. *What to do?* Sora thought. *What to do?*

Her gaze found the Cat's Eye at Ferran's wrist. A dim red light had awakened inside the stone. It seemed to wink at her.

A sudden idea came to mind. She hesitated, uncertain, but she saw no other choice.

Sora grasped Ferran's burnt hand, ignoring the blood between their palms. She directed her thoughts toward his Cat's Eye, hoping, somehow, that her stone might connect with his. It would have a stronger link to his body. Together, they might be able to dispel the plague.

Bells echoed faintly in her ears, and she waited, trusting it was a good sign.

Then a musty smell, like an old gutter, struck her nose. She wrinkled it.

"Ugh," she muttered.

"What is it?"

"The smell."

Gracen sniffed the air.

"I smell nothing, unless you mean the snow or the forest."

"No," Sora grimaced, "it's a sourness, something rotting. Is there a dead animal nearby?"

Gracen looked around, then he sniffed the air again.

"I smell nothing," he repeated.

Sora's eyes traveled back to the arrow in Ferran's shoulder. She noticed his Cat's Eye glowing brightly at his wrist. Then she blinked. Another absurd idea entered her mind. Could Ferran actually *smell* magic? Was this how his stone communicated?

Perhaps each bond is completely unique, she thought, awed.

Now she knew, with certainty, that his Cat's Eye was responding to her. She wasted no time issuing her command.

Stop the plague, she told it. *Dispel the Dark God's arrow. Eat the sickness.*

Ferran's stone grew bright red. She kept their hands conjoined, their powers blending.

Heavy smoke began to pour from the wound. Lord Seabourne grunted in surprise. The arrow began to dissolve into the air.

Sora's head spun. She clutched Ferran's hand in a death-grip. His blood trickled down her wrist. The black veins began to recede from Ferran's arm and neck as the two stones nullified the dark magic. Eventually, his skin returned to its normal, pinkish color. The arrow was simply a shadow now, a cloud of ash dissipating on the wind.

Finally, after several minutes, the arrow was gone. The stones dimmed, their glow fading.

Sora released Ferran's hand, turned to one side, and promptly threw up.

Ferran groaned. Then he, too, rolled over and vomited, nearly missing Lord Gracen's shoes. He looked up for a moment, wiped his mouth, and muttered, "Pardon."

Then he slumped back to the ground.

Gracen stared at them both, speechless.

Sora straightened and wiped a bead of sweat from her brow.

"Well," she said, "I'd say that was successful."

Gracen didn't respond, but continued to stare.

Sora picked up the longbow from the ground—the last of the Dark God's sacred weapons—and used it to stand up. Then she made her way back to the horse, which had traveled an impressive way up the bank.

Gracen followed her.

"Where is the arrow?" he asked. "And your necklace, and the stone at his wrist, why were they glowing? And that smoke...?"

"Are you sure you want an explanation?" Sora called over her shoulder. She was exhausted and slightly sick from the plague's residue, not to mention the cold and wet, and she didn't have much patience left.

Gracen passed her and caught up to his horse. Leading his steed by the reins, he turned back to face her. He fixed her with a perplexed frown, and Sora thought he looked almost comical, like a child first tasting a lemon.

"It was magic," he said.

"It was," Sora agreed.

"But that's impossible."

"It's not."

He glanced at her necklace again, then at her feet. Sora saw a look of determination come over his face.

"Get on the horse," he ordered. "Your bandages are wet. I told you to keep your feet dry."

He's afraid, she thought. She didn't argue, but allowed him to assist her into the saddle. He didn't mention the unstrung longbow, and he didn't attempt to take it from her.

He led his horse back to Ferran's unconscious body. After a moment of thought, Gracen lifted Ferran and, with a heave of his powerful shoulders, slung the man over the back of the horse. Sora shifted to make room. She tried not to be impressed. Ferran was a grown man, taller than Gracen, yet Gracen had lifted him with relative ease. His horse, as well, was well-trained and strong enough to bear the extra weight.

Then Gracen Seabourne took the reins and led them back to the road. They walked in silence for a good half-hour before he finally spoke.

"That arrow," he said, "it wasn't *really* an arrow, was it?"

Sora thought for a bit. "I suppose not. It wasn't made of wood, if that's what you mean. And it wasn't from this world."

Gracen didn't seem pleased with her answer. "Then where did it come from?" He sounded like he wanted to argue.

"It came from the underworld. This bow," Sora raised it in the air, "is one of the Dark God's sacred weapons, from the old legends, or don't you remember? Each of the gods and goddesses had one."

"I know of the stories, like most people do," Gracen snapped. "Children's stories and legends of a different time. Even my grandfather said they were nonsense. Am I to believe that you hold the weapon of a god in your hands?"

"Yes," Sora said, "and you'll believe a lot more by the time we get to the Ebonaire manor. You're taking us there, aren't you?"

Gracen paused, as though he hadn't considered their destination until now. "Yes."

"Then we have a ways to go. I can tell you the whole story, if you like, but you can't ask any questions or interrupt me until I'm finished."

"And if I don't believe you?"

"Then you can forget you ever laid eyes on this longbow or my Cat's-Eye stone."

Gracen glanced over his shoulder at her. His eyes found her necklace at her throat. When he spoke, he sounded uncertain.

"A Cat's Eye? They don't exist. We destroyed them all long ago, before this kingdom came to be."

"Then explain to me how I'm wearing one."

Lord Gracen came to a halt and faced her fully.

"How do I know this isn't all a hoax?"

"After what you just saw, do you think it's a hoax?"

He hesitated. "No. But I won't be mocked like an ignorant child. I am a grown man, Lady Sora, with quite a few more years under my belt than you."

Sora clenched her jaw. "I understand." She might have been a bit snippy with him, but only because he was so domineering.

He fixed her with a discerning stare. "If I listen to your story, will you tell me the truth of why you're here in the City of Crowns?"

"I will."

"Can I trust your word, Lady Sora?"

His question caught her off guard.

"Yes," she said. "Always."

"Then I will listen, and I won't ask any questions, and I trust you will tell me everything—*everything*—I need to know to keep the royal family safe."

His request surprised her again, and she thought she understood him better now. She placed a solemn fist over her heart.

"I promise I will tell you everything," she swore.

They continued down the road as Sora began her tale.

Unnoticed, two shadows perched upon the city's wall overlooking the southern docks.

"We could have helped," Crash said, his voice bitterly cold.

"They didn't need our help," Natrix replied. It was not an excuse, but a fact.

Crash stood next to her on the city wall overlooking The Bath. Large cracks ran across the surface of the lake. The battle had been stunning to watch, and many times, Crash had almost leapt down to help. But Natrix's presence had kept him on the wall. She didn't move, but watched, riveted, as the wraith and the garrolithe faced off.

"You have powerful allies," she said.

"We've journeyed together for a long time," Crash agreed.

He thought of Ferran and the red fire of his Cat's Eye. He thought of Sora's blue light. He had never witnessed such a battle before. He knew nothing about the vast capabilities of a Cat's-Eye stone. Perhaps Cerastes, as well, was ignorant to their true power.

Now, the battle was finished, the ice silent, and Natrix turned her back to the lake. She surveyed the city's smoke-filled skies.

"So this is where Cerastes hides?" she asked, and folded her arms.

"The Shade have left the city for now. I don't know why, only that winter solstice grows close, and Cerastes seeks the third sacred weapon."

"You say he has *The Book of the Named?* We must read it. I must understand what he wants and where he will be in the coming days."

Crash hesitated. He had been trapped in the desert with The Shade for several days before meeting with Natrix. Cerastes had not spoken openly of his plans, but Crash had discerned, through overheard whispers and rumors, that *something* had been stolen. He thought, perhaps, that Sora or Ferran had recovered the book.

A commotion at the base of the wall drew his attention. Crash looked down at the busy streets of the city. Far below, he saw the figure of a giant man running down the road, pushing aside people and startling horses as he went. He recognized Burn.

"What is it?" Natrix followed his gaze.

"A stroke of good luck. Wait here."

He leapt to a nearby rooftop, then dropped down into a frozen alley. He ran the length of the alley to the main road just in time to intercept the Wolfy. With a lunge, he grabbed Burn's arm.

Burn turned, his fist cocked for a good punch, but Crash ducked his head.

"Friend!" he said. "It's me!"

Burn skidded to a halt on the icy street. He seemed barely winded. His eyes remained narrowed on Crash, his look unwelcoming.

"What do you want?" Burn quickly surveyed the street around them, perhaps looking for members of the Shade.

"Sora and Ferran defeated the wraith. It's over," Crash said. "The fight is done."

Burn's ears drooped slightly. "So soon? What about the third weapon? Did they retrieve it?"

"Sora has it. She's headed back to the Ebonaire manor, I believe. There's nothing more to be done."

Burn cursed loudly and put his hands behind his head. He walked in a slow circle. "Useless. I'm completely useless."

"Far from it. I need your help. Has Ferran found *The Book of the Named?*"

Burn appraised him with a hard eye. "So you've come looking for the book, then? The others won't like it. They think you've joined the Shade." He paused. "Have you?"

Crash considered his response. His training, his upbringing, told him to lie. Told him to say whatever Burn needed to hear—or say nothing at all. But this was different. Burn already knew his reasons. He had been there when Crash surrendered himself to Cerastes.

"I have, in some ways," he admitted. "You know as much. The weapons were exchanged for your life. I take it you were released?"

"Perhaps. Seems more like they forgot about me."

"For the best, then."

Burn nodded.

"I'm not here to help the Shade, if that's what you're worried about," Crash said.

Burn's gaze fastened on someone just over Crash's shoulder. "Then who is that?"

Crash felt Natrix behind him and didn't have to look.

"I've returned to my people, but not in the way you think." Then he stepped aside, and Burn and Natrix assessed each other. "This is Grandmaster Natrix of the Hive. She is on a mission to kill Cerastes, but we don't know where he is hiding. Perhaps you can help us? We must start by reading *The Book of the Named*."

Surprisingly, Natrix bowed her head. "Well met, Wulven. Your kind is rare indeed."

Burn considered her a moment longer. Then he looked back to Crash. "We've had *The Book of the Named* for days now with no way to read it. We need your help, provided we can trust you." His eyes slid to Natrix again.

"Trust is foolish," she said. "*Know* that we want the same thing. Take us to the book and let's learn of my brother's plans."

Burn raised an eyebrow. "No words wasted, hm? Better than the Shade, I suppose. I'll show you back to the manor."

Chapter 11

L orianne reached the city gates in the Ebonaire coach, but could not proceed any further. The gates were closed. A crowd of peasants and merchants swirled along the southern docks. Some threw rocks or rotten vegetables at the wall, screaming in outrage.

"Let us in! My family is inside!" one man roared, hurling a brick at the closed gates.

"You can't close the gates! It's winter solstice!"

"Bad luck. Very bad luck."

An anxious-looking guard force stood in front of the closed gates, their weapons held at ready. Lorianne hoped the crowd of peasants didn't grow any more enraged. A proper battle could break out, and although the commoners outnumbered the soldiers ten to one, the soldiers had armor and spears.

"They've closed the southern gates?" Lily murmured next to her. "So fast? I don't believe it. How do we get in?"

Lorianne stared out the window in thought. The emblem of the Ebonaire family on their coach might win them entry, but it would be dangerous to attempt in front of so many peasants. It could incite a riot. If the soldiers were smart, they'd turn them away to keep the peace, and they didn't have Martin Ebonaire there to persuade them. There must be another way.

Her eyes caught on a frozen metal pipe jutting from the side of the city wall. During warmer months, it likely drained wastewater into the lake. Now, it was ringed with icicles.

Her mind raced. She thought of Ferran and the map he had found in Martin Ebonaire's study. Sewer access tunnels crisscrossed under the city from The Regency to the king's palace, and traveled under the Temple of the North Wind.

A hard rap on the door interrupted her thoughts.

Lily cursed. "Bells, they've seen us! They think we're nobility. They're going to drag us into the street and murder us!"

Lorianne placed a calming hand on her shoulder. "Let's not jump to conclusions."

"Aye!" a voice called from outside, followed by another hard knock on the door. "Aye, Ebonaire! Open up! You can't hide from me, Ferran. Now open the damned door!"

Lorianne frowned. She knew that voice, and it made Lily's fears seem even less realistic. She unlocked the coach door and cracked it open. She met a pair of familiar blue-green eyes.

"Silas?"

"Aye. Where's Ferran?"

"He isn't here."

"Oh."

Lorianne opened the door wider. The pirate captain looked scuffed and ragged, very far from his usual self. By the dirt on his neck, he hadn't bathed in several days. His silky fine hair fell, loose and greasy, around his face. His pristine blue jacket was smudged by soot and torn at the sleeves, and he held his captain's hat in one hand, folded and crumpled in a sad sort of way.

"What happened to you?" Lorianne asked, shocked.

"What happened? *What happened?* Some scary bugger showed up on my ship and burned her to the ground! The *Dawn Seeker's* floatin' in pieces, nice n' spongy, at the bottom of The Bath. You hear me? *My ship is drowned* and I blame that *bastard blowfish* of an Ebonaire! Soon as they open the gates, that weevil-eating freebooter is going to pay up. Ships aren't cheap and neither are teeth for all he's gonna lose!" Silas threw his singed hat on the ground.

Lori stepped down from the coach and picked his hat up, dusting it off.

"Wait a minute. You're talking too fast. The *Dawn Seeker* was attacked?"

"Aye, destroyed, and I would've been on Ferran's doorstep two days ago, but for the blizzard and now the bloody gates are closed. You humans can keep this miserable city. Soon as we get a new rig, me n' my crew are back to the coast."

Lori handed him back his hat. Then she found herself looking up and down the docks. Sure enough, where the *Dawn Seeker* had once been anchored, she saw a vacant space between many large ships. Crews with scaffolds and lumber worked on the schooners and barges to either side, patching their hulls where they had been damaged by fire.

With all the commotion at the southern gates, she hadn't noticed the *Dawn Seeker's* absence. Now she felt a cold, hard knot in her stomach.

"I'm so sorry," she said, turning back to Silas. "I had no idea...is the crew alright? Were there any casualties? Have you need of a Healer?"

Silas waved his hat back and forth, brushing aside her words. "We're right enough, my beauty. No casualties. Most of the crew were at the parade. We've weathered much worse, truth be told, storms n' hidden reefs n' whatnot, but that bastard Ebonaire is going to pay up one way or another. As I said, ships don't come cheap. Now if only they'd open the damned gates!" He roared the last bit into the crowd, and several more peasants hurled rocks at the iron portcullis.

"We can help each other," Lorianne said quickly.

Silas picked up a nearby piece of broken mortar and pitched it at the gate.

"How do you mean?" he asked.

"You need to get to the Ebonaire manor, and I need to get to the Wind Temple. I think we can use the sewer access tunnels to get into the city."

"The sewers? Really? This is my good dress!" Lily spoke up from behind her. She had been listening from the coach, and Lorianne had almost forgotten her presence. Lorianne held up a hand, asking for patience.

"Hear me out. Ferran found this old map of the sewer system in Martin's study. I remember parts of it, and I think I can retrace a path through the city—"

"On memory alone?" Silas asked, sizing her up. "Well, I suppose you're a right bit smarter than the average fish."

"Do you know of any large tunnels nearby?" Lori pressed him.

Silas frowned in thought. Then his eyes flickered. "Aye, there's an outlet up the docks, a ways past where the ships are anchored. Why are you headed to the Wind Temple? Seems a bit late to pray, Healer."

Because the king's life is in danger, she thought, *and because Cerastes can't be allowed to win.*

Instead, she said, "It's never too late to pray."

Silas picked his hat off the ground and smashed it down on his head. "Follow me, then. Best tell your driver to abandon your coach. Sooner or later, some angry citizen is going to come a'knockin."

Lorianne looked at the roiling crowd of peasants. A few were looking in their direction, though none had grown the courage to approach the carriage yet. It was only a matter of time. Taking the pirate's advice, Lorianne told the driver to take shelter where he could, and to return to the manor when the gates were open. The man seemed eager to vacate the area. Then, with Lily in tow, she followed Silas up the docks, away from the southern gate.

He led them past moored ships and barges unloading crates of goods, past pleasure crafts and rows of smaller fishing vessels and even further, up the banks of The Bath, through groves of birch and pine trees. Eventually, the docks and the city gates vanished from sight. Lorianne thought, if they headed in this direction long enough, they would find themselves back at the seminary.

Then Silas took them off the road and into the dormant woods. He led them through snow drifts and bramble to a secluded area of the lake where brown cattails grew in the shallows. There, a blackberry thicket hid the entrance to a sewer tunnel.

Lorianne thought back to Ferran's map and tried to remember how all the tunnels had intersected on that old, wrinkled parchment. She had given the map only a cursory glance, but she remembered the blue ink that had outlined certain junctions through the city. She took a careful look around, memorizing their position and which direction they needed to travel. She hoped she would retain her sense of such things underground.

The tunnel's entrance gaped at her, an unwelcoming black maw with icicles for teeth. A stale, rotten stench gusted into her face, and she imagined a beast panting.

Silas seemed less concerned, and she remembered that he and Ferran had traveled down countless caves and ancient passages during their treasure-hunting years. He hummed low in his throat as he gathered branches from the ground, then bid her to rip several strips of cloth from her skirts. Using the wood and cloth, he fashioned a handful of makeshift torches for their journey.

All the while, Lily gazed back in the direction of the southern docks, her face full of mingled hope and trepidation. Lorianne knew the gates wouldn't open anytime soon, but the girl was obviously wishing she had stayed with the driver. She wasn't an adventurer like Sora. She didn't look ahead, but behind.

"You don't have to accompany us," Lorianne said gently, touching the girl's arm. "If you like, you can go back and wait at the docks. We'll send for you once we reach the manor."

Lily lifted her chin. "Oh, I couldn't do that, Ms. Lorianne. If anything happened to you, Sora would never forgive me."

Lori studied the girl's face. "You and my daughter are close friends, hm?"

"It's improper of me to say," Lily admitted, "but I suppose, you being her mother, you should know Sora was like a sister to me. She was my best friend at the Fallcrest manor. Without her—well, without her father, I suppose, but *without her*—I would've grown up a thief or a beggar or worse. She gave me this life. She doesn't realize that, I think, but even if she did, she would never hold it over me. That's why I love her so." Lily gave her an earnest look. "That's why I'm going with you."

Lorianne was taken aback by the girl's sincerity.

"My daughter is very lucky to have you as a friend. You will always have a place with us, my dear girl." She gripped Lily's hand, and the two women smiled at each other.

"If you're both ready, we shouldn't waste the light," Silas said, brandishing his first torch in hand. Lorianne hadn't seen him light it, but she thought, perhaps, he had used his Fire element to do the work.

Together, they entered the tunnel. The smell of dank sewage hung heavy in the air. Ice encrusted the bottom and sides of the passageway, which made walking difficult, and for the first leg of their journey, they made slow progress.

Lori could tell when they reached the city proper. The sound of foot traffic and the clop of horse hooves echoed through the underground. Occasionally, they passed under metal grates in the road, where silvery daylight filtered down from the streets.

Silas stopped when they reached an intersection of various different tunnels, and held his torch high.

"Which way, Healer?" he asked.

Lori tried to remember the map, but as she had feared, without any view of the sky or the surrounding terrain, she had lost all sense of direction.

"We need to head to the east wall," she said, but that was all she knew.

Silas held the torch up to the mouth of each tunnel. He tried to brush a layer of frost from the stone.

"This one?" he finally asked. "There are markings here."

Lori squinted at the archway above the passage, and finally made out a symbol that might have been an "E" and might have meant "East." They examined the other tunnel openings and she came to the conclusion that her first guess had been right.

"Workers must have carved these here when they were laying the original sewers," she said. "Thank the gods. Let's go."

They followed the tunnel through similar crossroads and intersections. It seemed crews of bricklayers and stoneworkers from long ago had marked each tunnel's direction above its entrance, which Lori found immensely helpful. She became more confident as they passed through a dozen other intersections.

Almost an hour passed before they came across an iron rung ladder leading up to a metal hatch. The symbol next to the ladder was not a letter, but a rough drawing that looked much like a temple. Lori supposed it made sense. Only about half the workers in the lower class would be literate.

"Thank you, Silas. You've been an incredible help. When you reach the manor, make sure to tell Ferran that I couldn't have made it this far without you. Best of luck with your new ship." She set her hands on the ladder.

Silas placed a hand on her shoulder, stopping her.

"I think not," he replied. "I'll accompany you to the temple. We can return to the manor afterwards."

"It's really not necessary...."

"I'm not going to leave you alone with the Shade about. I'm a pirate, not a coward, and tough as you might be, Lorianne, you are just one person. I'm in no rush to get the manor now that we've breached the wall. I will stay with you."

"And I, as well," Lily added. She wore a determined look on her face. "I don't know much about this Shade business, but I do know Sora would want me to keep an eye on you, ma'am. I owe it to her to be here."

Lorianne could tell it was pointless to argue. "Very well, then," she sighed, "but prepare yourself for a boring afternoon. I only intend to speak to the High Priestess about what's been happening in the city. Hardly the place for a pirate, or even a handmaid, no offense."

"I am undeterred," Silas drawled.

The metal ladder was old and rusty, and led them to an equally rusty trap door. With enough force, Lorianne lifted it open. She expected to emerge onto the street, or perhaps somewhere on the temple grounds, but instead she found herself in a cramped, unlit space. She reached behind her for Silas's torch, then peered around curiously.

In the torchlight, she saw stacks of boxes and barrels in the corners, and furniture covered in white sheets. She saw an ancient statue of the Goddess with its face partway crumbled and one arm broken off. Perhaps it had fallen over at one time.

She recalled Ferran's map, and knew an access tunnel ran under the Temple of the North Wind. She just hadn't expected to climb directly into the temple's basement.

She climbed out of the tunnel with Silas and Lily at her back.

"Now what?" Silas asked, brushing dust from his stained coat.

"Now, we find the High Priestess."

Lily turned in a slow circle, looking about the room. "Are you going to tell the Priestess about...tell her about, you know, what the prince said...."

"That, and a fair few other happenings." Lorianne headed for a stone staircase that climbed, in a slow spiral, to the upper floors. The priestesses were guardians of ancient lore. Their order went back thousands of years, before the War of the Races. "Sora tried to come here when we first arrived in the city, but the doors to the temple were closed and she couldn't get in. Well, we should have tried harder. The seminary won't help us with the plague, but maybe, if I can convince the High Priestess to listen, well...." *This kingdom might stand a chance.*

Lily didn't answer. Lorianne didn't think she knew anything about the Shade or the Dark God, but to Lily's credit, she didn't ask a lot of questions. Lori thought her training as a handmaid played a part: *listen sincerely, then forget what you heard, and don't pry into bad business.*

The stairwell deposited them behind a giant statue of the Goddess on the temple's ground floor. With some hesitation, the three travelers stepped warily into the room.

A wavelike pattern of glass tiles covered the floor, mimicking the wind. Across from where she stood, a pair of granite doors, each carved with scenes of Kaelyn the Wanderer on her various journeys, stretched a hundred feet to the ceiling. The sight was grand, and for a long moment, Lorianne could only stand and stare. The doors were carved with immaculate precision. Four wide marble columns supported the ceiling, each engraved with sacred writings from *The Book of the*

Four Winds. Silent statues inhabited each alcove along the wall, circling the room until they reached the grand figure of the Wind Goddess, who knelt at Lori's back like a mother sheltering her children.

At the goddess's feet, a stone table stood where gifts or offerings could be left. Lorianne crossed to it now, and laid her hand against its smooth, polished surface. Usually, the priestesses burned incense here. The table was never left unattended.

Except the temple appeared to be empty.

Lorianne listened. She heard no footsteps, no voices, although the chamber's acoustics made her very breath roar in her ears.

"Where are the acolytes?" Lily asked softly. The question echoed around the room without answer.

"Something is wrong." Lorianne headed for a small door to the right of the Goddess's statue. Silas and Lily followed. Beyond the door, another staircase led them up to a second floor. Lori marched up it, then down a hallway lined with dorm rooms. All of the rooms were empty. Disturbingly, some looked as though they had been abandoned in haste, with candles burned down to their wicks, and plates of fruit left rotting on different window sills.

At the end of the hallway, another set of stairs took them one level higher. There, they entered a round antechamber. A pair of closed doors, carved with patterns of the wind, blocked them from moving forward.

Lori felt the breath leave her. The floor, the walls, the chairs—all was covered in blood.

Her hands began to shake.

Silas stepped past her, his torch held in one hand like a weapon. He tried the mahogany doors. The handles were caked in dried blood, turning them from bronze to black.

"Unlocked," he said.

"I don't want to go in," Lily moaned.

"We must." Lorianne stood up straighter. She joined Silas's side and together, they pushed open the doors.

The stench was overwhelming. Beyond the closed doors, the High Priestess's audience chamber resembled a mass grave. Lori stared in shock. At least a hundred bodies were piled high in the room, their blue robes stained purple.

Lori forced herself to inspect the pile of bodies nearest to her. She saw no signs of bruising or mutilation. One after the other, each acolyte's neck had been slit and their bodies left to drain onto the floor. The cold precision of it all unnerved her.

"This wasn't a massacre," she murmured. "This was an assassination."

She pushed further into the room. A walkway led through the different mounds of corpses. The air grew thick with the smell of decay, becoming almost a physical barrier.

Finally, Lori reached a raised dais at the very end of the room. A chair was mounted upon the dais, and before the chair, a marble pool filled with red water. She halted before the pool. Her entire body trembled.

Healers and priestesses both served the Wind Goddess. Both were sacred orders, surviving since before the War of the Races. She knew, from her time at the Healer's seminary, that this was a scrying pool, used by the High Priestess of the North Wind to communicate with the other wind temples, and perhaps even with worlds and realms beyond.

The West Wind was the Eye of the Goddess, seeing far into the past and the future.

The East Wind was the Grace of the Goddess, giving life to the world.

The South Wind was the Might of the Goddess, defending her realm.

And the North Wind was the Herald of the Goddess, spreading her message far and wide.

Face down in the scrying pool was a woman dressed in black and silver robes. Lorianne bowed her head and knelt before her body. She steeled herself and picked up the woman by her shoulders, and dragged her out of the water. The High Priestess's face was bloated beyond recognition, and she swiftly turned away with her wrist to her mouth. Her knees weakened in shock, and she knelt by the pool before she could fall.

Without thinking, she began to pray. Here lay the High Priestess of the North Wind, sacrificed in her sacred chamber. She had died alongside her acolytes in service to her order. *Goddess, take their spirits,* Lorianne prayed. *Release them to the winds. Set them free of this place.*

Lorianne tried not to be overtaken by despair. Who could she warn about the threat to the king? Who, now, would stand against the plague? Who would shield the Goddess's people from the Dark God's corruption? Lori felt tears sting her eyes. *I tried,* she thought. *I tried.* She had arrived too late.

And what could you have done? a voice seemed to whisper. *We died in service to the Wind.*

"I could have helped. I could have warned them...." Lori murmured, not realizing she spoke aloud.

Your life was spared, Child. Spared, for Her purpose.

A strange wind brushed her hair. At first, Lori thought it gusted through an open window, but all the windows were closed.

"She wouldn't allow this to happen," Lori whispered. "Your deaths were not Her will."

All things move with Her.

"I don't understand...."

In silence, they came. The Wind to our backs, we fell. We are the message.

Filled with a sudden compulsion, Lori lifted her hand and placed it on the water of the scrying pool. It was red with blood. Her fingers tingled when she touched the water, its texture like ink or oil, and ripples began to spread outward from her hand. Rings continued to form across the water long after the surface should have stilled.

Into the crimson depths of the pool, she focused her vision. Compelled, she began to speak. She didn't know if she whispered aloud or if the words simply echoed in her mind, but she spoke of the Dark God and the plague, and the scrying pool seemed to answer back. It showed her images of what she had seen and experienced since setting out on her journey. She didn't know if she was sending a message, or simply surveying a series of memories—it seemed like the same thing. She summoned more recent images of the massacred room and the closed gates to the city. The ripples across the pool increased in frequency. The invisible wind blew stronger.

"Lori," Silas said from behind her.

A frown of annoyance crossed her face.

"We should go," Silas insisted. "*Lori.*"

"What?" she snapped, her trance broken.

She looked over her shoulder, squinting through the shadowed room. It was darker than before. The stench came back to her twofold, dizzying, suffocating. Bile rose in her throat.

Silas stood at the base of the dais, beckoning to her with one hand.

"Lori, take my hand *now.*"

She saw, then, a ring of black shadows forming beneath her.

Lori jumped to her feet and launched from the dais in a single motion, like leaping from a fire, just as the shadow portal stretched to consume her. Silas caught her, or else she would have stumbled across the floor. They turned as one, staring back at the dais in horror.

An oblong shape bulged from the shadow portal. Ribbons of tar stretched into the room, forming black robes, like curtains, and then emerged the face of a man.

"Run," Lorianne cried. "*Run!*"

They turned and sprinted through the room, following the narrow walkway through the piled corpses. *He's here, he's here,* Lori thought, fear pounding in her veins as her feet pounded the floor. *Dear Goddess, protect us!*

Lily stood frozen by the door to the antechamber. The poor girl hadn't taken more than two steps into the room. She gazed past them in horror as Silas and Lorianne reached her side.

Lori grabbed her by the arm. "Come on!" she yelled.

Then the doors to the anteroom slammed shut.

Lori almost barreled into them face first, but Silas stopped her. He beat against the closed door with his fist, then tried the handle. It broke off in his grip. He turned to Lori with a grimace of terror on his face. She could only stare at him in return. Neither knew what to say.

Then all three turned to face the room.

Lori didn't know the name of the Shade's leader, but now she knew his face. His very presence turned the room to night. It seemed, suddenly, that they stood in a very wide cavern, somewhere dank and moist underground, filled with the reek of death. Silas's torch cast a small circle of light, but the light couldn't save them from the monster that waited just beyond its rim, where it hungered, where it *burned*.

Lori drew in a shuddering breath. She forced herself to stand straight up instead of cowering against the wall.

"It's too late," she said. She thought she spoke strongly, but her voice sounded thin and frail. "The message has been sent. The priestesses know what you've done. Soon, they will come. The Wind Goddess twists your own deeds against you. Be gone, demon. You have no power here."

A great hissing sound filled the room, sinister.

"You will find the Dark God has power wherever I step. Power in decay. Power in sickness. Power in despair." With each statement, the man took a step forward, and Lori felt herself flinch. "You belong to His Shadow as well now, as does every corpse in this room. Terrified and mindless, they fell under my blade like sheep to the altar. The Herald of the North Wind flies too late. Your message echoes, Healer, but it falls upon deaf ears."

Lori couldn't explain how, but she knew this was a lie.

She heard something rustle in the far corners of the room. She couldn't imagine anything living that would make that sound.

"Silas!" she yelled, "the torch!" but the Dracian was frozen in terror.

She wrenched the torch from his hand and threw it into the darkness, onto a pile of bloated gray corpses, praying it would ignite. The flames spread in a very small circle. In the flickering light, she saw human-like shapes climbing to their feet at the side of the room, and bloated faces turning toward her. A scream welled in her throat but could not break free.

Then Silas came back to himself and raised his hands.

The torch exploded in a burst of light, and Lorianne remembered that Dracians wielded elemental magic, and both Silas and his son, Tristan, controlled Fire.

"Yes!" she gasped. Hope ignited in her breast. Suddenly, her legs could move again. She grabbed Lily's hand and dragged her across the room to the row of windows on the left wall.

Halfway across the room, she realized Silas wasn't following them. She turned and saw him standing where she had left him, his hands before his chest, his face twisted in concentration.

"Silas!" she yelled. "Silas, to me!"

"The windows! Go!" he yelled hoarsely. He moved his hands like a conductor leading an orchestra, and the flames danced and leapt through the room.

Lori realized he wasn't able to follow her, that to do so, he would have to abandon the fire, and it wouldn't burn on its own. The bodies were not yet dry enough to catch light.

"Tell Ferran," he stammered, "Tell Ferran he owes me a new ship!"

Lorianne bit her lip until it bled. Then she grabbed Lily's hand and the two women rushed to the row of glass windows on the far side of the room. Smoke choked her, and twice they changed direction to avoid the growing flames.

Lorianne reached the first window and dragged aside its heavy curtains to reveal a sharply slanted roof and a dizzying drop to the ground. From this height, the peasants walking on the streets below looked the size of acorns. With shaking hands, she undid the latch and shoved the window open. It creaked on reluctant hinges.

She turned back to Lily, who was pale in shock. Silent tears ran from the girl's eyes.

"Look at me," Lorianne said. "Look at me, Lily. You have to go out onto the roof. Lily, can you hear me? Take my hand. That's right. Look at me. Lily?"

The girl's eyes widened, the tears streaming down her cheeks, and she gazed past Lori, transfixed. Lorianne glanced down at their feet to see a growing shadow darken the floor around them. She turned to find the demon standing directly at her back, so close that his black robes brushed her arm.

Without warning, Lily grabbed her by the shoulders and shoved her through the window.

Lorianne gasped. She reached for the window frame—missed. In painful detail, she watched the room fall away and the gray sky take its place. She struck the roof. Something cracked, perhaps the tiles, perhaps her bones. She rolled uncontrollably down, down, down. Then the roof disappeared, and she plummeted through empty space.

CHAPTER 12

Sora arrived at the Ebonaire manor in a carriage with Ferran next to her and Lord Seabourne riding his steed outside. After getting them through the city gates, which were closed for some reason, Lord Seabourne had flagged down the first coach he found and hired the driver to take them to the Regency.

Thankfully, Ferran's wound was no longer bleeding heavily, and they didn't leave much of a mess on the coach's seat. It also seemed that Ferran had returned to consciousness—or some semblance of it.

"Lori," he muttered in his sleep, "I should have stayed by your side."

Sora sat quietly and thought of her long talk with Lord Seabourne. He had listened to the retelling of her adventures without interruption, just like she had asked. After her tale, however, he hadn't spoken much, which left her uneasy. She didn't like feeling studied, or vulnerable, and since finishing her story, she had felt both.

When they reached the front of the Ebonaire manor, Gracen paid the driver and then assisted Sora from the coach. Then, together, they lifted Ferran out of the carriage.

Donwick the butler appeared at the wide steps to the Ebonaire manor and immediately called for more hands. Servants rushed to their side to help. She could see the Ebonaire staff darting quick, curious glances at her as they carried Ferran indoors. She did her best to hide the Dark God's longbow under her cloak, but it was almost impossible.

Surprisingly, Martin did not make an appearance and she wondered if he was home. Sora gazed up at the facade of the house, allowing the sheer size of the Ebonaire manor to settle over her. It could have been a castle, or a fortress of ancient times. Then she blinked. For a moment, she caught sight of a face peering down at her from one of the windows. When she looked again, it was gone. Perhaps it had been a passing cloud or tree branch reflected in the glass, but she had thought it looked like Crash.

Crash. Where was he?

She had last seen him at the parade....

A streak of pain split her head, and Sora winced. Her hands gripped the bow. She hadn't thought much about the parade, or the poison, or her days spent lying in a coma, since her fight with the wraith. But now the series of events stole her strength, and she wrapped Gracen's cloak more tightly around her, suddenly exhausted.

"Lady Sora," Gracen called her name, and she looked up. Several house servants were hesitating on the front steps of the manor, lifting Ferran's weight between them.

"Take him up to his room," she directed, and followed Lord Seabourne up the front steps and into the house.

Once in the foyer, she stopped to ask Donwick about her mother, but discovered Lorianne was still absent. The news was somewhat troubling. Someone had to properly bandage Ferran's shoulder, and if her mother wasn't here, that left her in charge. She steeled herself against her exhaustion, and sent two maids to bring hot water, bandages, and medical herbs up to Ferran's room. Then she followed the rest of the servants up the staircase.

Her room was just down the hall from Ferran's, and she ran there quickly, where she stashed the Dark God's longbow in the first hiding place she could think of--under her mattress. Then she headed back to Ferran's room, where Gracen waited for her by the door. He didn't ask where she had gone, and although he must have noticed the weapon's absence, he didn't mention it. He seemed deep in thought. Together, they entered Ferran's sprawling bedroom, where the servants had laid the treasure hunter out on a giant four-poster bed. She dismissed them and checked Ferran's vitals. He didn't have a fever, and the wound looked pink and healthy. She didn't anticipate any complications.

The two maids returned with Sora's supplies, and she went to work dressing and bandaging the wound. All the while, Gracen stood patiently next to the bed, so quiet and still that she almost forgot his presence.

"You have many skills," he finally said, disrupting the quiet, dusty air.

"I learned a few things from my mother."

"But the *Cat's Eye*...." He almost whispered the words, *"what you did by the lake...."*

"I was extracting the plague. Otherwise, he would still be infected. But magic won't heal a flesh wound." *At least, not a Cat's Eye,* she thought.

Gracen fell silent once more.

Sora finished her work and turned to him. She was about to explain more about the plague, when the door to the bedroom opened unexpectedly. She turned toward it, annoyed. Usually servants knocked before entering.

She gasped when she saw Burn standing in the doorway.

"By the look on your face, I believe you forgot about me," he said, twitching an ear. "I found a friend of ours who you'll be glad to see."

He stepped aside, and Crash emerged from behind him.

At the sight of the assassin, a rush of memories caused Sora to take a physical step back. She remembered the parade, the fight with Cobra, the poison, and then...*yes*...her night in the Smokestacks, his warmth next to her, his lips on her cheek, her mouth, her neck....

Up until that moment, her memories of that night had been dim and dream-like, laced with fever and delirium. Now, face-to-face, the curtain fell away.

"You've returned," she said, her mouth dry.

"I have."

Seeing him should have been a relief, but Sora couldn't hide her discomfort. She didn't know how to act. She wanted to touch him, *connect* with him, but in front of Burn and Lord Seabourne, she could only stand and stare.

Crash's gaze focused on Seabourne, and his question was obvious.

"This is Lord Gracen," Sora said quickly. "We can trust him."

The two men sized each other up. Burn, as well, looked skeptical about Seabourne, but he didn't voice any complaints. Between Gracen and Crash, however, the tension became palpable.

Sora cleared her throat.

"Gracen, these are the companions I told you about. Perhaps now you'll find it easier to believe my story."

Gracen was obviously put off by the assassin's cold demeanor. He broke eye contact and instead, he studied Burn's enormous height.

"So you're a...a Wulven," Gracen said. "One of the ancient races."

"One of the last of his kind," Sora confirmed. "Crash is also one of the races. A different race."

Gracen didn't spare the assassin another glance. "I see."

"I trust them both with my life," she added.

"They do appear to be formidable warriors."

"And you're a soldier of some kind?" Burn asked, noting the badges on Gracen's uniform.

"Captain of the King's Personal Guard and defender of the throne," Gracen said. He sounded blunt and formal, like an officer. "I am investigating a threat to the king."

"Then it seems that we can help each other." Burn held out a hand, and surprisingly, Gracen took it. They grasped each other firmly by the wrists, and finally, the tension in the room lessened.

Then Crash stepped to one side, clearing the doorway. "I've also brought someone to help us."

Sora's eyes slid to the woman who entered after him. She had a way of standing—silent, perfectly still, like part of the room—that made her almost invisible. She was one of the Sixth Race, as thin and menacing as a wasp. Her face was pinched, her black hair braided tightly against her skull, her eyes slanted and aloe-green. She was not a young woman, perhaps close to Burn in age, both toned and sinewy.

Sora wondered how long Crash and his mysterious companion had been in the city.

"Sora." Burn drew her attention. "This is Grandmaster Natrix. Crash brought her to us from the Hive. She can read *The Book of the Named*."

Sora looked back at the strange woman. She had mixed feelings about trusting any of the Sixth Race after what she had seen of the Shade, but perhaps the Hive was different.

The woman pointed to the unstrung bow in Sora's hand, which Sora had completely forgotten about.

"Is that a sacred weapon of the Dark God?" she asked.

Sora hesitated. "It is."

"May I see it?"

Handing over the bow was more difficult than giving away gold, but Sora managed to do it.

Grandmaster Natrix studied the ancient weapon in the candlelight, her expression unreadable. After some time, she gave it back.

"And Cerastes has the other two?"

"He does."

Natrix said nothing more.

"I take it Ferran still has *The Book of the Named?*" Burn asked, his gaze traveling to the unconscious man on the bed.

"I believe so," Sora said, uncertain. She began to explain the condition of Ferran's wound, but was interrupted by a rapid knock to the bedroom door. She almost sighed in exasperation. What now?

In a flurry of movement, Natrix dissolved into the shadows and Crash sank into a dark corner next to the hearth. Burn stood, bulky and obvious, in the center of the room. He and Sora shared a look.

The knock came again.

"I'll see to it," Lord Seabourne said mildly, and crossed to the door. He opened it a crack and stuck his head out. "Yes? What is it?"

Outside, Sora heard Donwick's voice.

"My Lord, this message came for you. Two soldiers are waiting for you downstairs. They say it's urgent." A letter exchanged hands.

"Thank you, I'll be right down."

Gracen shut the door. A long, slow breath escaped him, echoing Sora's weariness. He opened the folded parchment and scanned the letter. Sora watched his usually-serious face grow even more stern.

"I must go," he said.

"What is it?"

He didn't answer her immediately, so in three steps, Sora crossed to his side and plucked the letter out of his hands. He opened his mouth, perhaps to protest, but the words died on his lips. Instead, he crossed his arms and watched her.

As Sora read the letter, her knees weakened and her stomach sank. She almost sank with it.

"Sora?" Burn asked.

She looked up. "The Temple of the North Wind...has been destroyed."

"What?"

"The High Priestess is dead."

Her words hung in the air for a moment.

"I must go," Lord Gracen repeated, and turned once again to the door.

"I'm going with you."

"I can't allow that, Lady Sora. It might be dangerous...." Gracen stopped, as though realizing the inanity of his own words.

"We are all going," Burn said, ignoring him. "If the Shade is involved in any of this...."

It seemed Crash and Natrix felt the same way, because they both joined Burn's side, their faces determined. Sora turned back to Lord Seabourne and gave him a pointed look.

He sighed, then opened the door and strode from the room.

Two soldiers met them on the floor below, and within half an hour, Sora was back in a carriage and heading into the city proper. Burn, Natrix and Crash all accompanied her. Gracen rode ahead of them with his men.

The city seemed overrun by chaos. Foot traffic bogged down the streets, most unrelated to the calamity at the temple, as groups of winter solstice revelers wandered around in packs, some in costume, some singing off-key songs, some roaring with drunken laughter. She saw scuffles break out on street corners as people pushed and shoved their way to different pubs. The winter solstice festival was in full swing, and the city guard seemed stretched too thin.

They continued through the streets, closer and closer to the temple. Sora smelled the fire before she saw it. Smoke stung her eyes, thick in the air, and the stench of burned wood suffocated the city. The energy of the crowds changed. Here, the peasants looked on the verge of a riot. Outraged people filled the pavilion outside the temple gates. Some carried bludgeons or knives, others threw rocks. They shouted angrily at the top of their lungs. Soldiers lined the street, trying to keep the crowds under control.

"*The Goddess has forsaken us!*"

"*'Tis a sign!*"

"*The king has displeased Her! His people suffer!*"

"*Open the gates! Open the gates!*"

"The king is a traitor to his people!"

"'Tis a sign! Arise! Arise!"

Soon, their carriage couldn't continue through the throngs of people, and Sora and her companions walked the rest of the way on foot. Burn and Crash both walked protectively close to her. Sora worried that the crowd might attack them before they gained entrance to the temple grounds, but a circle of soldiers led by Lord Seabourne enclosed them. The soldiers used long, blunt poles and shields to force the peasants back as Sora and her party slipped through the temple gates. Once the gates were closed, the crowd of peasants rushed forward, roaring in frustration. They reached through the iron bars toward their Goddess, grasping, crying out.

Sora could understand their fear and even their sorrow, but not their anger. Didn't they know the king's guard wasn't to blame for this tragedy? Their eyes rolled like frenzied horses as their temple burned.

Sora stood in the courtyard just inside the temple gates. She imagined, in springtime, it would be filled by magnificent blooms. But now ice covered every surface, from the stone fountains to the cracked flagstones.

Burn paused next to her, his head turned toward the wind. An anguished frown marred his features. He looked like he was listening to some terrible cacophony of sound.

"What is it?" Sora asked, wondering at his expression.

"The wind is *keening*...." His long ears twitched, and Burn's voice faded.

Sora listened. The wind might have been unusually strong, but to her round human ears, it sounded empty and unremarkable.

Burn faced the temple, still entranced by whatever sound he was detecting. Sora followed his gaze. The dead priestesses were laid out in rows in the snow beyond the courtyard. Most of the bodies were charred beyond recognition. Of the temple itself, its main structure, a rotunda and domed oculus built of granite, still stood, yet most of the wood-shingled roof was destroyed. Sora could see the great statue of the Goddess bowing her head to her people through the debris.

The temple's surrounding structures, such as the dorm rooms, audience chambers and prayer houses, were in ruins. In some places, embers of the fire still smoldered. Because of the snow and ice on the ground, the fire hadn't spread to the rest of the city. Sora wished the peasants would take note of that. Perhaps the Goddess had protected them after all.

Sora crossed the courtyard back to Gracen's side. Burn trailed after her in distraction. When she reached Gracen, she overheard one of the guards briefing him.

"Most of it burned out on its own. We're still dragging bodies from the rubble. We don't know what caused it."

"Any survivors?" Gracen asked.

"One, that we know of. Several onlookers saw her fall from the roof."

"One of the priestesses?"

"We think so."

"Let me see her."

Sora followed Gracen back across the courtyard to a small tent. Inside, a Healer in white robes leaned over a woman stretched out on a cot. The Healer had just bandaged the woman's head and was wrapping her in heavy blankets when they entered. She finished her work and backed away, allowing them to approach her patient.

Sora saw the woman's bruised face and grabbed Burn's arm for support.

"You say she fell from the roof?" she asked. Her voice came out in a whisper.

"That's what several peasants witnessed, my Lady," the soldier replied.

Sora stared, dumbfounded.

"Do you know this woman?" Lord Gracen asked.

"She's my mother."

The room quieted. After a pause, Gracen turned to the soldier. "Thank you, lieutenant. You're dismissed."

The man saluted and left the tent.

Then Gracen turned back to her. He took her hand and led her to a chair next to the cot. Sora could barely make her legs work.

"I take it your mother isn't a priestess, then?" Lord Gracen asked.

"No. She's a Healer."

"Do you know why she was at the temple?"

"No."

"When did you last see her?"

"I...I don't...." Tears stung her eyes and Sora's throat closed. The events of the last day—of the last week—suddenly overwhelmed her. "So much has happened...." Her eyes traveled to the Healer, who stood quietly in the corner of the tent. "Will she live?" she heard herself ask.

"Yes. She's in miraculously good health, considering what she's been through. She fell into a deep snowdrift, and I daresay it saved her life. Luck of the Goddess. She has a concussion, but she should recover." The woman bowed her head respectfully. "I believe the Goddess spared her."

Sora nodded. Tears burned her eyes, but she was too shaken to cry. She reached out and touched her mother's hand.

"We need to bring her back to the manor," she said.

Gracen nodded. "It will be done. This Healer can accompany us as well, if she is not required elsewhere."

The woman bowed again. "Of course."

Burn's hand touched Sora's cheek gently. A fatherly note entered his voice. "I think you should return to the manor with Lori. We'll finish up here."

"But, the temple...."

"The fire is almost out, and there are no lives to be spared." Burn's voice saddened. "There's nothing you can do. I'm sorry, Sora."

She wanted to protest, but the words stuck in her throat, and all she could do was hang her head. She felt dizzy with exhaustion. She realized she hadn't eaten a bite of food all day, and ironically, she still wore her ripped and tattered petticoats. The day was finished, and there was nothing more she could do. She knew Burn was right. She needed to return to the manor with Lori, change into a warm nightgown, and sleep.

"I shall have your coach brought around," Gracen said, and left the tent with a quick step, already summoning his soldiers. As much as he wanted to help her, Sora knew his work lay outside, in the cold night, where he and his men would spend the rest of the evening sorting through rubble and stamping out fires. She did not envy him.

"Where is Crash?" she asked.

"Investigating the temple. I'll keep an eye on him. Please," Burn insisted, "you need to rest."

Sora relented. An escort of guards entered the tent with a litter, a stiff cloth stretched between two poles, and carried her mother back to the Ebonaire coach. Sora followed wearily after them, barely able to lift her feet. Together, she and her mother returned to the Ebonaire manor. As they traveled through the city, she watched the burning temple slowly disappear in the distance, her breathing heavy from smoke and tears.

CHAPTER 13

W ithout intending to, Sora slept in late the next morning. She woke up with a pounding headache and, although she wanted to run to her mother's room directly, her body demanded food. She called for the maids instead, and a tray of breakfast was sent up from the kitchens.

When Sora had eaten her fill, she felt calm enough to think clearly. She needed to bathe and dress, and act like a proper noblewoman today, because she knew with certainty she would run into Lord Martin or Lady Danica, and she needed to look presentable. She counted herself lucky that they hadn't seen her yesterday evening, when she had practically devolved into a wild animal. Despite all that had happened, she still needed to keep up appearances, at least until the Shade's threat had passed.

She called for Lily, but was surprised when Olivia appeared.

"My Lady," the servant said, "I'm sorry, but your handmaid is absent from the manor."

Sora frowned at that. "Where has she gone?"

"We don't know. The staff is still looking for her, but I don't think she is on the grounds." A little smirk hovered around Olivia's lips while she spoke. She and Lily did not get along.

Sora didn't like it. "If I find out you're responsible for her absence, there will be consequences."

Olivia wasn't phased by her threat. "Yes, Milady. As I said, we can't find her. May I help you dress this morning?"

Sora sighed and accepted Olivia's assistance with her bodice and panniers. Today, she donned a simple burgundy dress with silk ribbons on her sleeves. At her request, Olivia only pinned back part of her hair, leaving it to cascade down Sora's back.

When Olivia was gone and the breakfast plates cleared, Sora finally allowed herself to walk to her mother's room. The Healer from the temple answered her knock at the door.

"Is she...?" Sora started.

"She's awake," the Healer said.

A relieved smile broke across Sora's face, and she rushed into the room. Lori sat up in bed, supported by a mountain of pillows, and surprisingly, she was not alone. Ferran sat next to her on the mattress, her hand in his own. Lord Gracen Seabourne sat in a chair at the foot of the bed. The three looked like they had been having a deep conversation.

They looked up at her as she entered, and Sora paused, taken aback. She remembered, then, that Lori and Ferran shared the same room, since they were posing as a married couple. Gracen's presence was less explainable. Sora curtsied to him after another awkward moment, then crossed to her mother's bed and pulled Lorianne into a tight hug.

"I'm so very glad you're alright," she said. She felt a knot rise in her throat, and forcefully swallowed it.

Her mother held her for a long time. "Seeing you makes me feel a hundred times better. I'm relieved to see you've recovered as well. Ferran and Lord Seabourne told me something of your adventures yesterday." Her eyes searched Sora's. "You defeated the wraith?"

"I suppose I did," she agreed, though she felt uncomfortable taking full credit. "I couldn't have done it without Ferran." Really, it was the *garrolithe*, but the beast was gone now, and she couldn't quite explain to her mother what had transpired. Half of the battle felt more like a dream.

"Where is the sacred weapon?" her mother asked.

"I've hidden it," Sora assured her.

Her mother looked satisfied. Then she said, "If you can sit with us for a few minutes, I have something to tell you." Lori glanced over at the Healer from the temple. "May we have a moment of privacy?"

The Healer bowed and left the room, closing the door behind her.

When Lori looked back to her, Sora saw a shadow in her eyes. She noticed Ferran's subdued expression as well. Lord Seabourne sat, his hands folded, without interrupting.

Lori took her hand.

"Sora," her mother said, "Lily was in the temple with me when the fire broke out."

"Oh," Sora said, confused. "Where is she now? I called for her this morning...."

Her mother's expression saddened, and Sora suddenly felt cold.

"I'm sorry...." Lorianne murmured.

Her mother didn't need to say anything else, and Sora didn't ask any questions. She dropped her mother's hand without meaning to, and folded her arms as though staving off a chill.

Lori spoke softly. "She saved my life. She was very courageous. She loved you, Sora. She called you her sister. She protected me for you."

Sora expected to feel tears in her eyes, but instead, she couldn't summon any feelings at all.

"I understand," was all she could say. *It's my fault.* If she hadn't reunited with Lily in the Regency...if she had never asked her back to the Ebonaire manor....

"Silas was caught in the fire, too. The Shade is responsible for all of it. Their leader killed the priestesses. He was there, in the temple," her mother said. "Silas and Lily fought very bravely. They saved my life."

"I-I'm sorry. I should have been there...." Sora said brokenly.

"It's tempting to blame ourselves," her mother said, "but we need to remember who's really at fault."

Sora knew her mother was right, but her words didn't ease her sense of guilt. She took a deep breath.

"Now what?" she asked. "How do we stop the Shade?"

"We need to call a meeting," Ferran agreed. "Now that Crash has returned, we can read *The Book of the Named.* He and Natrix are still investigating the temple now, but they will return this evening. It's time we learned what Cerastes is up to. It's time we *stopped him.*"

Sora nodded. It was easier to think about their next task than about Lily's fate. She didn't want to think about her fallen friend. If she did, she feared it would overwhelm her, and she didn't know if she would have the strength to keep fighting. *We can still defeat Cerastes,* she reminded herself. They had the third weapon, and possibly an even greater advantage with *The Book of the Named*. She counted the days leading up to First Winter's Ball. With a start, she realized winter solstice eve was tomorrow night, and the ball, as well. They didn't have much time left to discern Cerastes' plans.

"There is one more thing," Lord Seabourne said unexpectedly. She had almost forgotten his presence. "Lori, you said you overheard something at the seminary. You were about to tell me?"

"Right," Lori said, returning to the conversation she and Lord Seabourne were having before Sora's arrival. In a slow and steady voice, her mother spoke about her trip to the seminary and her encounter with Cedric Daniellian and the prince. Sora listened and tried not to cringe when she heard Lily's name. Ferran looked disgruntled at the mention of Cedric Daniellian, but he didn't interrupt.

Sora gasped when her mother retold the part about Prince Peric.

"But that's treason," she balked. "The prince can't be serious." Despite all that had happened, it was difficult to imagine the royal family turning against each other.

"You're sure of what you overheard?" Gracen asked.

"Yes," Lorianne insisted. "If I'd known you could be trusted, I would have gone to you directly."

"You did what you could and more. On behalf of the crown, I thank you. This is disturbing news, indeed."

Gracen asked a few more questions about Lori's encounter with the prince. Eventually, the conversation slowed and he seemed to make a decision. He bid them farewell. "I intend to investigate this further. I have much to do before the ball. I should take my leave."

"We're grateful for your help," Lori replied.

Gracen gave them a brief nod and turned to leave the room. Sora watched him go. Her mother's story was troubling, to say the least, but Gracen had a certain urgency about his demeanor that piqued her curiosity.

She stood up. "I'll return soon," she said, and excused herself as well.

She went into the hallway and caught sight of Gracen disappearing around the corner. She trotted after him. She expected him to head to the front door, but he ran up a staircase instead and traveled deeper into the house. She hurried to keep up.

"Lord Seabourne, wait," she called. "Where are you going?"

Gracen stopped at the sound of her voice. He glanced around the empty hallway. They were alone.

"Something has upset you, more than this news about the prince," she said once she reached his side. "If you're having difficulty understanding all this business with the plague, I'm not offended—"

"I believe you."

"Oh."

"I've heard a lot of lies in my profession, and quite frankly, your story is too farfetched to be a ruse."

"I see." She wasn't sure she liked that.

Lord Gracen sighed. Weariness touched his face, and in the dim light, she watched him age by a decade at least.

"Yesterday, I saw things beyond explanation. The burning of the temple has shaken me deeply, and the repercussions will be felt throughout the entire city, if not the entire kingdom. In the weeks to come, I don't know what to expect. Terrified people make terrifying decisions."

"I understand," Sora said.

Gracen gave her a look that said, *Do you? Do you really?*

"I believe your story," he said aloud, "but that doesn't give me any clear path forward. I am responsible for the safety of the royal family, but how do I protect them against a power I cannot comprehend? The answer is, I can't. However, what your mother claims she overheard is within my power to investigate, and with winter solstice upon us, I must investigate quickly."

"Is that where you're going now?"

"Yes."

A breath of silence passed between them.

Then Gracen said, "I need to speak with Martin."

Sora tried to read the expression on his face. Suspicion? Anger?

"You mean, about the prince's plan?"

"About that, and a good deal more." Gracen turned on his heel and continued up the hall. "I've hesitated far too long, but now I fear what the king's enemies intend to do. Something is terribly amiss, and I mean to get to the bottom of it—for the kingdom's sake, and for yours, Lady Sora. Today, we will have answers."

She hurried to keep up with his pace, trying to remember everything she had learned from their last conversation about Martin Ebonaire at The Knob.

"You think he knows about the prince's plan?"

"We shall soon find out."

They reached the door to Martin's study. Gracen paused there. Unexpectedly, he took her hand. His gray eyes met hers.

"Lady Sora, I am a practical man. I live by facts. But I am not so bullheaded as to ignore what I've seen with my own eyes. I have no magic stone, no special power, but from now until the kingdom is safe, I will do everything I can to assist you on your quest. Lady Sora, you may count on me as your ally."

She found her cheeks growing pink from the intensity of his gaze. She searched for words that wouldn't come. Finally, she dropped her eyes and fell into a curtsy—a noblewoman's defense.

"Thank you," she murmured.

Gracen released her hand and opened the door to the study.

They found Martin Ebonaire poring over his end-of-year reports. A massive volume had been collected and bound of all the Ebonaire investments. She recalled her stepfather, Lord Fallcrest, doing much the same thing around this time of year, except his book had been significantly smaller.

Martin looked as polished as a portrait. He wore a gray waistcoat and wide-sleeved tunic, a cravat tight about his neck, and reading glasses perched on his nose. One of his forearms was bandaged in white linens, and she wondered if he had been injured during the attack on the parade.

Sora hovered by the door, waiting to be invited in, but a very perturbed Lord Gracen stalked past her.

"Martin, a word."

Lord Ebonaire looked up at them. He had been so deep in concentration, he hadn't heard them enter.

"Gracen, Sora," he said, a look of concern crossing his face. He half stood from behind his desk. "This is an unexpected surprise. I didn't know you both had returned to the manor." Martin frowned doubly at Sora. "My daughter was very worried. She said you became ill at the theatre and left without a word?"

Sora felt guilty about that, but recovered.

"I had a relapse," she said without any real explanation.

"What's all this about, then?"

Gracen took a seat across from Martin and fixed him with a discerning stare.

"I have questions for you, Martin, and I want the truth this time."

Sora settled into a chair as well. A guilty man would have looked nervous, she thought, but Martin looked more resigned. He closed his heavy, leatherbound book.

"My back is against a wall, and now the hounds have come," Martin said. "I will tell you whatever you'd like to know, and I will even let you throw me in jail to rot, if you promise to protect my daughter. And before we begin, I must ask—are you certain Sora should be here? She doesn't need to be involved."

Gracen seemed taken aback. Sora hadn't expected such a straightforward response, either. She darted him a look, which he didn't return.

Then, Gracen said, "It's my wish that she attend our meeting. Please, tell me, what do you know?"

Martin looked back and forth between them, obviously unhappy that Sora was there. Then he began to speak.

"I have been quite disturbed since the attack on the parade, but I wasn't sure what to do. And now the prince finally got his way and the gates to the city are closed. Feels like we're being *caged in*, don't you think?" Martin paused to rub his temples, as though fending off a headache. "I'm glad you came to me, Gracen. I should have come to you a long time ago."

Lord Seabourne leaned forward. He looked as focused as a hawk.

"What does Peric plan?" he asked.

"Exactly what you suspect, I imagine. You wouldn't be here with that look on your face if you were completely ignorant. Let me fill in the gaps for you. The prince wanted to scare the king into closing the city gates, so he gave a stash of weapons to a band of insurgents and had them attack the parade. I happened to be an unanticipated casualty." Martin indicated his bandaged forearm. "I fear Peric plans a similar attack on First Winter's Ball, now that he's distracted the city's guard force and blocked half the upper tier from attending. He means to oust the king from power however he can."

"And you didn't think to mention this sooner?" Gracen asked.

"The water has grown too hot, my friend. I am in danger now no matter what I do. Whatever he and Cedric Daniellian plan against the crown, I believe they mean to pin it on me."

"How could they pin it on you?"

"How else?" Martin smiled without humor. "I've invested almost a quarter of my fortune into the king's clocktower project, but I fear some of those funds have gone to this insurgency against the crown. The insurgents kill the king and ransack the castle, and it all leads back to me, the richest man in the kingdom who obviously must have some agenda against the crown. The prince simply has to point a finger, and I'm done for. Thus my close inspection of these reports." He motioned to the book on his desk.

Gracen sat back. His eyes traveled to the ceiling, and Sora could almost hear the gears churning in his head.

"So Prince Peric is hiring assassins to attack the royal family?" he mused.

"I don't think he's hiring them," Lord Martin said. "I think the insurgents are real enough. Some groups believe King Royce has reigned too long. If Peric is crowned king, they think he will heal the kingdom."

"That's madness," Sora blurted. "No one with any sense would believe that."

Martin looked both sad and amused. "The lower tiers are afraid. They need someone to blame for all this tragedy and misfortune. And now, with the temple burned, we need to tread carefully. Riots can turn into revolutions, and we can't have Prince Peric stoking the flames."

"It's the perfect time for the prince to leverage their fear to gain the crown," Gracen agreed. "Martin, why didn't you come to me sooner?"

"Please believe me, I didn't think they would go this far. Prince Peric may want the crown, but he isn't a killer. You know him as well as I do, Gracen. He swoons at the sight of blood and knows more about wine than swords. Something has changed in him. He and Cedric have become very close. He takes pleasure in violence now, and laughs at inflicting pain. Even his hounds fear him, and my horses shy away from his touch."

Sora raised an eyebrow at that. Gracen, as well, looked troubled.

"There's still time," Gracen said. "Allow me to speak to King Royce about this...."

"Do what you must, but know they have threatened my family should I talk." His gaze traveled to Sora. "I've made arrangements for the estate, in case the worst happens."

Sora nodded. Danica must not know of the danger. Perhaps that was for the best. She mulled Martin's words over in her mind. Why would the prince act so out of character when the kingdom was at its weakest? She had her suspicions, but they might be unfounded.

Still, Cerastes had burned down the temple, and it seemed the Shade were behind every misfortune in the city. Could they have somehow gotten to Prince Peric, too?

"Martin, *uncle*..." she said softly, "Do you know anything about the deaths surrounding the clocktower project?"

A look of shock crossed Martin's face. Then his expression softened.

"I can tell you what I know, but I'm not sure how that relates to any of this."

Sora noticed she had Gracen's attention as well. Unlike Martin, he knew about the Shade now. Perhaps he would follow her logic.

"Have there been any strange happenings or strange people around the clock tower?" she asked.

"I know that Peric befriended a very odd man who was placed in charge of the project. The man claimed to be an architect, though I thought he looked more like a soothsayer. I never asked many questions about him, but on occasion, other workers and investors have expressed their misgivings."

"What did he look like?" Sora asked.

"Sickly and gaunt. His hair was long like a woman's and very black. I don't know where the prince found him. He claimed to be from overseas. Claimed to have built palaces for foreign kings. The prince seemed quite taken with him."

"Do you think this man is somehow involved in the plot against the king?" Gracen asked.

Martin motioned to the volume of reports again. "Impossible to say, but over the course of the project, I've noticed funds being withdrawn with only a few vague words in description. When I asked the prince about them, he said they were special commissions and left it at that. But there have been many peculiar deaths surrounding the clocktower project, as I know you are aware, Gracen."

"Commissions," Sora murmured, thinking of her late stepfather, "or paid assassinations? Perhaps to silence Prince Peric's enemies?"

"Again, I cannot say, though I know that some amount went to these insurgents over the past few months."

"I'll need to examine these reports," Gracen said.

"Be my guest." Martin stood and crossed to the bookshelf behind his desk, where he opened a box and withdrew a cigar. He lit it. "I'm afraid you won't be able to tell much by the entries alone. They don't have descriptions, as I said. They're just...odd."

"I'll need records going back to the beginning of the project," Gracen said. "With luck, I'll find a correlation between the dates of the withdrawals and the obituaries we have recorded." He glanced at Sora. "We shall begin with Lord Fallcrest."

Martin frowned. She watched him search his memory, and she felt a sliver pierce her heart. Her entire life had changed with her stepfather's death, and Lord Martin couldn't even remember his name.

But then, Martin did.

"Ah, yes. I recall you asking after him before."

"He contacted me for a private audience," Gracen said. "He had information too sensitive to put in writing."

"Then he must have overheard something between the prince and Cedric Daniellian, perhaps at the Daniellian manor. The poor fellow should have fled."

"Fleeing didn't save him," Sora said, trying to keep the bitterness from her voice.

Martin looked curious. "Was he a friend of yours?"

"I met his daughter, once."

"My heart goes out to their family. Such a tragedy."

Sora couldn't stand his flat tone of voice, his words so proper, so empty.

"Your funds paid for his death. You should be held responsible."

"We don't know that yet, my lady," Gracen said.

Sora flared in anger. To Martin, she said, "You've known about this for years, and you did nothing. That's as good as committing the murders yourself. And if the prince manages to dethrone the king come winter solstice, you're partially responsible for that as well."

Martin's face had become dangerously stoic. His back and shoulders stiffened.

"Calm yourself, Lady Sora," Gracen said. "Murder is a serious crime. Let's not throw the word around lightly."

"I'm not," she seethed.

"You forget your place, dear niece," Martin said, his words stiletto sharp. "I have generously allowed you to take part in this interview, but only as a favor to Lord Seabourne, not to invite your opinion. I can just as easily dismiss you from this room and, in fact, my house."

"Let her be angry," Gracen said. "She is young, Martin."

Lord Ebonaire glared at her, and Sora realized, dimly, that she was confronting perhaps the most powerful man in the realm. Certainly one of the most influential. She hated the superiority in his tone, in his stance, but she also knew she wouldn't gain anything by insulting him. Her heart twisted in frustration. Was she so utterly powerless? And had her stepfather's death been so inconsequential, so insignificant? *It's done now,* she reminded herself, *it's over with.* That chapter of her life was closed. She needed to clear her head.

She was gripping the arms of her chair, and forced her hands to relax. Finally, she bowed her head.

"My apologies, uncle," she said through gritted teeth.

Martin continued to study her, taking a thoughtful puff on his cigar. Then he turned away.

"So," he said, "what do you suggest we do, Lord Gracen? Despite my niece's outburst, I truly don't want the king harmed."

"I will need to post a much larger guard force around the palace during First Winter's Ball," Gracen said, "and warn the king, of course. I daresay the prince has already proved a disappointment to his father. This won't be easy for King Royce to hear. Perhaps you can accompany me to the royal palace? I think it will take us both to explain what the prince has done."

Lord Martin looked pale at the thought. But she also knew Gracen's request wasn't really a request at all.

Finally, Martin bowed his head. "Happily, my lord."

Sora found herself climbing to her feet.

"I shall return to my rooms, to rest," she said, sensing it was time to leave. "I'm not as fully recovered from my illness as I first thought. Thank you, uncle, for all you've done for our family."

Martin Ebonaire bowed as well. "My pleasure, Lady Sora," he said, so sincerely that Sora almost forgot their brief confrontation. She saw no evidence of displeasure on his face. *The power of propriety,* she thought. He was impossible to read.

Then she took Gracen's arm and he led her back across the room to the door. Before entering the hallway, Gracen paused to speak over his shoulder, "I'll meet you downstairs in an hour, Martin?"

"Yes, I will need time to prepare," Martin agreed.

Then Gracen escorted Sora from the room. She felt cold and lightheaded as she walked down the hallway. Questions circled her mind, unanswerable. Was Cerastes behind the clocktower project? Was he also influencing the prince's coup? Could he—indirectly—have caused Lord Fallcrest's death?

Which meant that, when Crash was hired to kill her stepfather, he was ultimately helping the Shade?

The coin came from Lord Martin's purse, she rationalized. Even if the prince or Lord Daniellian had ordered the assassination, Lord Martin had paid the toll. In some capacity, that placed him at fault. What had her stepfather stumbled upon? A meeting between Cedric, the prince, and Cerastes, perhaps? He had obviously overheard something treasonous.

Did Crash know his part in all this? How could he possibly know? How could he possibly *not know?*

Gracen walked with her down the flight of stairs and long hallway to her bedroom, then came to a halt. Before she entered her room, he took both her hands.

"I will see you tomorrow at nightfall," he said.

Sora remembered, again, that tomorrow was First Winter's Ball.

"I will be waiting," she replied.

Then Gracen took his leave, and she entered her room. She took a seat in a large armchair near the window and relaxed into the soft feather cushions. The day was only halfway over, and her head was already spinning.

CHAPTER 14

S ora spent most of the afternoon sleeping. She awakened only once when a
maid came to her door to deliver a note from Lady Danica, written on her
personal stationery that smelled like lavender.

In the note, Lady Danica expressed her sincerest apologies at Sora's relapse,
and blamed herself for her cousin's frail condition. She prayed for Sora's swift
recovery, and hoped they might attend First Winter's Ball together, *as family,* and,
if Sora felt strong enough, would she join Lady Danica for breakfast tomorrow in
her private quarters, to spend the morning in the way of highborn ladies, dressing
and primping at their leisure, as they prepared for the ball? And please, the letter
finished, might she write a response on the line below?

Sora thought about it. She read the note a few times, then gazed out the
window, wishing the ball could be over, and winter solstice past, and Cerastes
defeated and the Shade annihilated from the earth.

Then she wrote, "*Yes—with delight!*" and sent the invitation back with the
maid.

She took dinner in her room that evening, blaming her poor health, then
napped by the window until the sky had turned dark. Then another knock came
to her door.

"We can begin now," Ferran said, his voice tired but steady.

Sora stood up reluctantly and followed him into the hallway. Ferran took her
to Lori's bedroom. Inside, a low fire burned in the hearth. Crash and Natrix were
waiting. Burn had not yet arrived.

Sora sat down on the bed next to her mother. Lori looked pale and Sora noticed a certain tension around her eyes. A clay mug of tea sat cooling on her nightstand, and Sora recognized the peculiarly pungent odor of willow-bark tonic, a strong potion often used to relieve pain. Her mother must have refused to drink it, trying to keep her head clear. Sora didn't like that.

A few more minutes passed, then the door opened.

"I can't find him," Burn said.

Ferran looked nonplussed. "Well, he could be anywhere, I suppose. I don't think we can wait any longer."

Sora looked around the gathering and realized one person was conspicuously absent.

"Where is Caprion?" she asked.

"I saw him yesterday morning," Ferran said, "but not since we recovered you from the snow."

"Well, he can't be on the *Dawn Seeker* as the ship is sunk," Lori said. "Is he guarding our prisoner in the attic?"

Ferran and Burn exchanged a wary glance.

Sora raised an eyebrow. "Have either of you checked on Krait since yesterday?" she asked.

"I thought Caprion was guarding her...." Ferran's voice trailed off.

For a moment, they all stared at each other in silence.

Then Natrix spoke. "You've captured one of the Shade?"

"For what good it's done," Ferran grumbled.

"Then I should speak with her."

Ferran rubbed a tired hand along his chin. "You can speak to her if you wish. Caprion has been interrogating her for the last few days. She feigns ignorance of Cerastes' plans, but perhaps we simply haven't asked the right questions. You're welcome to try."

Burn appeared to be in agreement. "Shall we take this to the attic, then? Perhaps Caprion is up there. I wasn't sure how to navigate all those staircases. This place is a maze."

"I can lead you upstairs," Ferran said before turning to Lori. "You, however, will have to stay put. Healer's orders."

Lori didn't look pleased. "I can walk just fine."

"Not with that concussion. I don't want you losing your balance and falling down a flight of stairs."

"Mother, he's right," Sora said softly. "You should drink your tonic and sleep. You've been through quite enough already."

Lori opened her mouth in silent indignation. Sora crossed her arms, waiting for her mother to protest, but then Lori sighed and slumped back against her pillows.

"Very well, very well," she muttered. "I suppose it's my turn to take the sickbed, hm?"

"And there's nothing you can do about it," Ferran agreed. He joined Sora's side and took the mug of tea from the table. In passing, he said to Sora, "your mother is a terrible patient. I can attest to that firsthand." He passed the mug of willow-bark tea to Lori, who took it reluctantly and began to drink. The lines of pain around her eyes began to ease.

Sora waited for her mother to finish her tea, then with Ferran's help, she adjusted Lori's quilts and pillows and stoked the fire. It didn't take long for her mother's eyes to begin to close. Then Ferran lit a candelabra and one by one, they filtered out of the room.

Ferran took the lead and, walking in a single line, they started up to the attic. They climbed up a half-dozen flights of stairs in the flickering firelight, then Ferran opened a trapdoor in the ceiling, and they climbed up quite a few more. Sora thought Burn's description from before was quite accurate. The Ebonaire manor truly was a maze, and at night, it turned into a dangerous labyrinth of steep climbs and sudden drops. Sora found herself keeping one hand against the wood-paneled walls.

Finally, they arrived at an oaken door at the very tip-top of a narrow, dusty staircase. Sora had lost all sense of direction and wasn't even sure they were in the same house. The door creaked on its hinges as it opened.

The attic of the Ebonaire manor was sectioned into four quadrants: North, South, East and West. Ferran led them through each of the wide rooms, past boxes covered in dust and furniture hidden by moldy sheets. The light from his candelabra reflected off old portraits in silver frames, and archaic suits of armor. The air was freezing cold, and every now and then, the roof creaked from the force of the wind outside.

At the far end of the attic, they found a girl chained to a chimney pipe. Most assassins would have used their shadow magic to escape, to slip their chains and

run, but Sora remembered Caprion's warning: the girl did not have a demon of
her own. She could not work magic at all. Despite her physical prowess, she was
no more dangerous than a human.

Krait was sleeping, but woke up at their approach. Surprise registered on her
face before a stoic mask replaced her expression.

Sora wondered if the girl had been expecting Caprion. She wondered if Krait
knew where the Harpy had gone. Ferran lit several more candles in the room, then
set down the candelabra. They stood aside as Natrix approached the girl.

"So this is one of the Shade," Natrix murmured. "One of Cerastes' pawns."

Krait spat with sudden venom. "I serve the Dark God. I am *not* a pawn."

Natrix's head tilted to one side, catlike. "Who is your Grandmaster?"

"Cerastes."

"Cerastes has been exiled from the Hive. Do you know why that is?"

"I don't care. He belongs to the Dark God like the rest of us."

Natrix looked at Crash but didn't say anything.

Sora wished they would speak openly. She wanted to know the Grandmaster's
thoughts. What did she think of the Shade?

Crash knew what Natrix was thinking. Krait was another specimen of the brainwashed drones in Cerastes' camp. Now Natrix could observe, up close, the extent
of Cerastes' teachings—how deeply the Grandmaster influenced his followers.
Not long ago, that same influence had almost slipped over his own neck like a
noose.

"I see through your facade, child," Natrix said, bending before Krait to look
into her face. "He covers your scars just as he covers your mind with illusions, but
I can see past that to what lies beneath."

She touched Krait's cheek and the girl flinched back. Still, Crash saw the
skin of Krait's face ripple like water. In waves, in layers, the skin peeled back,
and gruesome scars emerged from underneath. They ran across her cheek and
partway down her neck. Her eyes turned white and sightless. The burns were

unmistakable. *Harpies,* he thought. The girl had been tortured. He found his own hand going to the scar at his neck, where a sunstone had once burned him.

"I know you," Natrix said, her voice like cracking ice.

"You know nothing about me," Krait spat.

Natrix rolled back on her heels, still focused on the girl's blind, scarred face. Rarely did a Grandmaster indulge in emotional displays, but Natrix's surprise, her fascination, filled the room.

"I *do* remember you, savant. My savant. You were very young when they took you from the Hive." Her voice faded, lost in memory. "I remember the day you disappeared."

Krait recoiled again, shrinking into the corner of the room. Her blind eyes probed helplessly at the darkness. Crash resisted the urge to look away. Her vulnerability was hard to watch.

"I remember nothing of you," she said, her voice a thin rasp. "If I was stolen from the Hive, then none of you came for me. You left me to die."

"How were we supposed to follow you? With wings? With maps? You were long gone, child." Natrix considered Krait, her expression unreadable. "If I invited you back to the Hive, would you come?"

"No."

"*Return.* Become my student again. Be with your people—your *true* people—and wear your true face. In the Hive, we do not fear scars. I will teach you to welcome your blindness."

"Cerastes restored my eyes. I will not betray him."

"And you are satisfied?" Natrix quipped. "You see only what he wants you to see, what he allows you to see. Your sight is an illusion. You are still blind, child."

"I am not blind!"

Natrix stood. Her lips twisted. When she spoke, she made no effort to hide her contempt.

"You *are* blind if you put Cerastes before the Hive. He cares nothing about your wellbeing. In the Hive, we make vows to our students. We honor our code, our community. He broke his vows and betrayed his people. He has betrayed you as well."

"And what of your vow, Grandmaster?"

"You are still my student, however long ago, however lost you are."

Crash glanced between them, studying Natrix's stance, her rigid spine, her thinly veiled...*compassion*. He looked again. It was not like human compassion—it was harder, less forgiving—but he couldn't call it by any other name.

Was this the true bond between Grandmaster and student? Cerastes had never shown him this kind of loyalty. How many of his experiences, how much of his understanding, was tainted by his Grandmaster's corruption—by his cold and violent mentorship?

Eventually, Natrix sighed. Her tone changed, cooling.

"I myself have stood in the Dark God's shadow, and I know the true calling of our people. Consider your answer, child. Where hides Cerastes?"

Krait was silent, her scars laid bare, her mouth open and skin stretched.

"So be it."

Natrix stood and walked away from her student. Crash trailed behind her across the attic floor, back to where Sora and Ferran stood in the candlelight.

"She knows something, I can sense it," he murmured. "We can press her...."

"I'm not interested in what she knows, only in what Cerastes has done. How has he convinced so many to believe his lies? She will turn against him. It is only a matter of time."

Crash wondered how Natrix could be so sure, but she sounded confident, as though it had already happened.

They rejoined Sora and her companions in the east quadrant of the attic, where Krait could not see them, and their voices would reach her as mere whispers.

Natrix folded her arms before her. "It is time to read the book."

* * *

"Here?" Ferran asked. "Is that wise?"

"Here, we are hidden. No one will accidentally open the door."

Ferran still looked uncertain. "And if *she* overhears us...."

"She is harmless. A rodent. A moth."

Sora agreed with the Grandmaster. Krait wasn't a threat. She might already know Cerastes' plans, but even if she didn't, overhearing them wouldn't help her or the Shade. Ferran seemed to reach the same conclusion, and with a nod from Burn, he withdrew *The Book of the Named* from the pocket of his greatcoat.

Sora recognized the tattered leather binding of the book. It looked more like a well-traveled journal than an ancient tome holding the secrets of the Sixth Race. Ferran offered it to Grandmaster Natrix, and she took it from his hands with care.

Sora tried not to cringe when the Grandmaster touched the book. She still didn't fully trust her. She didn't really trust any of the Sixth Race anymore, except Crash, and even those feelings left her conflicted.

Natrix seemed to sense her reaction, and fixed her with a hard gaze.

"Do not let your Cat's Eye interfere with the spell I am about to cast," she said. "You and your friends will not be harmed."

Sora found herself touching the stone at her neck. She shared a look with Ferran. Then she nodded.

Natrix cleared a space in the middle of the room by pushing aside boxes and furniture. Then she knelt to the dusty floor. She drew an invisible circle around her by sliding two fingers slowly, intentionally, along the floorboards.

"Let us begin," she said.

Natrix opened the book in one hand and slowly exhaled upon it.

Sora heard a dull ringing in her ears as the Cat's Eye responded, but she touched her necklace to silence it.

Natrix exhaled longer than seemed natural. Her breath turned into a gust of wind that grew in strength until the candles flickered and several went dark. The shadows seemed to grow and stretch along the walls. The roof creaked and popped above them, and Sora felt a certain energy fill the air, like the static before a thunderstorm.

Natrix blew again, and the pages of the book began to turn. They fluttered back and forth like tiny wings. Then the book lay open.

Sora suppressed a gasp. Before her eyes, black script appeared upon the book's blank pages as though written, in that moment, by an invisible hand.

Then Natrix began to read aloud:

"Who has the nerve to light thy fire,
to steal thy blade and risk thine ire....

"Who has the nerve to knock the door,
Unlatch the latch and kneel before
the altar of the crimson sea;

Nameless, who has summoned me?

"*Of my prison stand guardians, three;*
In their hands, a severed key
That if combined, shall then release
the lock that sets the seventh free.

"*Of my power, none shall have it,*
A worthy vessel, I shall inhabit,
To find that vessel, so my shade
Shall plague the world, and invade
The strongest man of every race;
He who survives shall become my face."

Natrix stopped reading, and for a long moment, her silence remained heavy upon the room.

Then Burn spoke up.

"A severed key?"

Sora's mind raced. "Three guardians, and in their hands, a severed key...it must mean the wraiths and the sacred weapons. The three sacred weapons are a key?"

"What's the seventh?" Ferran asked.

They all looked at Natrix, who didn't answer.

"We know your race guards its secrets closely," Sora said, "but this isn't the time to withhold information. Please help us."

Natrix considered her. "I believe it speaks of the seventh gate."

Crash answered more quickly. "The Hive teaches that our bodies have seven gates of power. Each gate unlocks as we reach different levels of mastery in our training."

"What do the gates do?" Sora asked. She tried not to sound suspicious. He had never mentioned this before.

"Some allow us to use greater magic. Others, a deeper connection to our demon. The seventh gate is the final gate. To open it," he continued, "one must sacrifice their own humanity and give complete control over to their demon, which Cerastes no doubt intends to do."

"If he has not done so already," Natrix added with a disturbing lack of alarm.

"So the seventh gate is in the mind, or the body, or what have you," Burn said, "but this book speaks of it as though it is a place."

"With a key, no less," Ferran mused.

Natrix glanced down at the book. "It could be that there is more to the seventh gate than the Hive teaches."

Another contemplative silence fell upon the group.

Sora thought of the sacred bow hidden beneath her mattress in her bedroom. It was their one advantage against Cerastes.

"Well, let's start with what we know," she pondered aloud. "Cerastes wants the sacred weapons because together, they form a key. Is there a...a spell of some kind that combines them?"

"It appears so," Natrix said, turning a page in the book. Then she paused. "It's missing."

"So he still has the spell?"

"Yes."

"Then we know what he's doing," Sora said, trying not to sound excited.

Ferran added, "Winter solstice is a time when the barrier between this world and the Dark God's realm is weakened. If Cerastes plans to combine the three sacred weapons, he'll do it then."

"Such a spell can only be worked on sacred ground," Natrix said, "even on winter solstice. That much is known by any race that works magic."

Sora looked around at the grim faces of her friends. Her eyes widened.

"The Temple of the North Wind," she gasped. "Of course! It's built on sacred ground, is it not?" All of the pieces seemed to be falling into place.

Then Ferran put a damper on her idea. "The ground is sacred to humans, perhaps, but humans do not wield magic, and the place itself holds no power. It wouldn't be significant."

"Oh," Sora said, crestfallen.

"What Cerastes seeks would be an ancient place known only to our race," Crash agreed.

"What does the book say?" Ferran asked.

Natrix blew on the pages once again. Candles flickered. Pages turned. After another minute, the book lay open to a new page, and she began reading. This time, she did not read out loud.

"There are coordinates here, of a sort, but they relate to star charts," she finally said. "These are thousands of years old and the stars have long since changed...not even I have heard of these constellations. *Cerastes*...." She said the name like a curse, "You've spent years calculating the right location, haven't you?"

"What if," Ferran interrupted, "this ancient place was buried beneath the city?"

"What do you mean?" Sora asked.

"I mean, what if humans built the City of Crowns over sacred ground, without intending to? What if," his eyes met hers, "Cerastes had to dig beneath the city to reach that sacred ground?"

Sora blinked. "The clocktower."

Then, instantly, she realized the connection between Prince Peric and Cerastes. She realized, as well, how Martin Ebonaire and Cedric Daniellian had become unknowing pawns of The Shade.

She began to pace.

"This is all a game to him," she muttered. "The city gates, the royal family... He's just using us to get the key, then he's going to topple the kingdom. Humans aren't even a threat to him, but he's still going to destroy us."

"You are beginning to see your enemy," Natrix said.

Sora found the Grandmaster's eyes. "Why is he doing this?"

Natrix clasped her hands behind her back. She considered her words before replying.

"Because some of our race value death over life. They believe our sacred purpose is to return all living things back to dust, back to darkness. But they forget our highest calling—we must keep the world in balance. Life decays, but new seeds must grow. Cerastes has stumbled across a doctrine from a time long ago that once led to the near-destruction of this world. We cannot allow him to proceed with his plans."

Ferran ran a weary hand over his face. "So the sacred ground is beneath the clocktower. Why didn't we see it before?"

"It explains why the Shade have left the city," Crash said. "If the excavation is complete, and winter solstice is upon us, they have no more reason to be here."

Burn nodded in agreement. "It's true. The Shade as good as released me. I wasn't even enough of a threat to kill."

"And they burned down the temple as a parting gift," Ferran said bitterly, "the city's last hope against the plague, destroyed."

"How do we stop him?" Sora asked. "Can the Hive help?"

"Our elders think they can deal with Cerastes from afar," Natrix said.

Sora waited for an explanation, but then she felt a glimmer of understanding. "They sent you to kill him."

Natrix neither confirmed nor denied her statement, just fixed her with another hard stare.

Crash spoke next. "We have to consider that he released the wraith on purpose, not to destroy the city, but to *be destroyed* so he can collect the third weapon. He will come for it eventually. We are all pawns in a game to him, and his plans are coming into alignment."

"We must keep the third weapon from him at all cost," Ferran agreed.

"Or better, we can use it to our advantage," Natrix continued. "We can lure him into the open, into a trap, and end him. If you give it to me...."

"No," Sora said.

The entire room looked at her in surprise.

"I'm sorry, but no. Crash went to Cerastes with the last two weapons without consulting us. I'm not giving away the third."

Crash's face hardened.

Sora met his stare. "Ferran is injured, and Burn has no defense against Cerastes' magic, so if someone is going to be used as bait, it will be me."

Sora expected her friends to argue with her as they always did—to protect her, to shield her—but instead, she saw Ferran and Burn nod in mutual agreement.

"You've defeated three wraiths," Ferran said. "I think you're ready for whatever lies ahead. But don't tell your mother I said so."

"Your skills have grown since we first met," Burn added. "You've become a much more capable fighter, far stronger than I can compete with."

Sora felt her face crack into a smile. She hadn't realized her own expression was so solemn.

"Does that mean we have a plan?"

"The beginning of one," Burn said.

Crash remained silent, but Sora could tell he was furious.

"We should reconvene in Ferran's compartments," Burn said, his eyes traveling to the back of the room where Krait was chained in the shadows. "No sense speaking up here anymore. It's cold, and the hour grows late."

"Agreed," Sora said. She knew Krait couldn't hear them very well, but she still didn't want to take the chance.

It seemed that the rest of their party felt the same way, because Ferran picked up his candelabra and motioned toward the door. Natrix slipped *The Book of the Named* into a pouch at her belt, and no one argued. In single file, they exited the room.

CHAPTER 15

S ora wasn't sleeping, but waiting.

She knew he would come to her, and he did.

After reading *The Book of the Named*, and after meeting in Ferran's room to discuss their plan for winter solstice eve, their party went their separate ways. Sora noticed how Crash's eyes lingered on her, and she felt the unspoken tension between them. When she returned to her room in the wee hours of the morning, she sat and waited, expecting to hear a knock on her door.

The knock came, and the door opened. He entered without her invitation. She knew the width and height of him, even if the shadows obscured his face. He came to stand at the foot of her bed, and for a moment he stood over her, studying her, like a beast in the night.

She didn't know how to feel about him, but she knew she wasn't angry. She remembered their intimate night in the Smokeshafts and the trust she had felt then. Infected by poison, tainted by delirium, even then, she had understood him.

"Sit with me," she said softy.

He joined her on the bed. His weight pressed down the mattress, and she leaned into him. She found the nook of his shoulder easily. It seemed natural to touch him, and this time he didn't pull away.

"I keep thinking of the night after the parade," she said.

He rested his chin against her head, listening.

"I can't remember, Crash. Did we....?"

He snorted. "No."

"Oh. I thought, perhaps, we did...."

"You were poisoned, Sora. We certainly embraced...." His voice faltered. "But I wouldn't take advantage of you in such a state."

"Of course, I didn't mean to imply...." But she had implied, hadn't she? The question had lingered in the back of her mind since she had remembered their embrace. She relaxed into his arms, his warmth burning against her like a furnace. She felt sheltered and secure.

"In the Smokestacks, I remember you said you would be gone for a while. I'm glad you are here with Natrix, but how long do you plan to stay?"

"I didn't expect to return so soon," Crash said slowly, reluctantly, as though dragging up the words from the bottom of a well. "I can't stay long. I'm sorry."

Sora held him in silence.

"After Natrix completes the task she was sent to complete, and Cerastes is dead, I must return with her to the Hive."

"But why? You said you were exiled...."

"I was. And now I must return."

She pulled away so she could look at his face. She searched the sharp line of his jaw up to his brooding eyes. She looked for any expression, any hint that he was lying, or evading her, but as always, he revealed nothing.

"What I feel for you..." she began slowly. "It hurts so much, this endless reaching and grasping for one another, then separating."

He stared at her. His mouth twitched.

"This isn't love, Sora."

"Then what is?" She held his hand. "I know you better than anyone else. And *none of them*—not my mother, or Burn, or Ferran—know me better than you."

He denied her with the smallest shake of his head.

"That isn't true."

"I know it's true."

His mouth tightened. Then, finally, his voice hoarse, he said, "I would kill to protect you, Sora. When you're near me," he touched her hair, "when you're near me, I don't think of anything but your safety. I can't tolerate the fact that I brought all this upon you."

"Isn't that love?"

He didn't answer.

"Then, is it trust, Crash? Because I trust you with my life. Is it a shared experience? Is it friendship? Tell me why *this thing* between us is so flawed, so impossible, that you can't possibly call it love. If you tell me, I promise I won't speak of it again."

"You're asking the wrong man."

"I've seen what you are," she insisted, peering into his face. "Look at me, Crash—*I know you.*"

"Sora...."

"I know you feel the same need inside of you. It draws us together. No matter where you go, no matter how far you run, you will always return to me."

He pulled his hand away—his whole body away—disturbed by her words, perhaps because of their truth.

He spoke to the shadows, as though addressing someone else in the room. "Don't you see, if I could let myself have *this*, I would destroy it. I can't look at you without feeling the guilt of a hundred stolen lives. Your stepfather, and Dorian, and your own life as well, I count among them. What I feel for you doesn't save me from the darkness of my own race."

"No, but you have Fire within you," she said softly, "and if the Elements have any say in this, then Fire is passion incarnate."

"And destruction."

She touched his face. She felt the walls falling between them, and suddenly he melted against her, wrapping himself around her body, pressing his head against her breast. She sensed his indescribable frustration, his hopelessness.

"This is a different world," she said. "We're taught stories and histories of a war long past, but that's all we know. Maybe the truths you learned about your race were wrong. Why can't we change the way things are?"

"And if it all ends as I say it will? If my demon escapes, and you are devoured? At my own hand?" He turned to her, a flash of anger on his face. "Have you thought of that, Sora? Have you considered *all* of me?"

She didn't allow the fear to show in her eyes. "I have a Cat's Eye," she said. "Have you considered that?"

He didn't reply.

"This is my choice to make as much as yours, Crash."

He stood up, tearing away.

"As long as Cerastes lives, this bond between us will only be exploited. I must protect you from him and the others of my race. In part, that's why I'm here. He will come for the third weapon. I need you to give it to me."

"I can't do that."

His demeanor grew cold.

Sora stood up. "I'm sorry, Crash. The last time I gave you the weapons, you took them to Cerastes."

"I wouldn't do that again. You said you trusted me—"

"I trust you to act like yourself." An ironic smile pulled at her lips. "I will keep the bow, and when Cerastes comes for it, Natrix will put an arrow between his eyes."

"And if she misses?"

"She's a Grandmaster. She's the most capable of us all. Do you think she will miss?"

Crash ran a hand through his dark hair. "I don't know what to think anymore, but I don't like you putting yourself in danger...."

"Who else?" Sora snapped. "Ferran is wounded. Burn has no defense against magic. Caprion is missing and you...."

"You can say it."

"You're too unpredictable." She cocked her head. Was that the right word? "I trust you to fight alongside me, Crash. But I don't trust your judgment around Cerastes. You told me you lost yourself for a while among the Shade. Correct me if I'm wrong. Please." He wasn't evil for being drawn to his own kind, but this was their best chance at stopping the Shade and she wouldn't let him foul it up.

"You don't know who you're dealing with," Crash said.

She appraised him. "I know better than you do, I think."

"She's right."

Crash and Sora both looked up, surprised. Natrix unfolded from the corner of the room, where she had been standing in the shadows. Sora wondered how long the Grandmaster had stood there, and if she had witnessed their entire encounter.

Natrix crossed to the bed and stood before them, gazing at Sora.

"The girl is right," she repeated. "Cerastes was your Grandmaster once, Viper, and that history can make you blind. I've seen the power he wields over Krait and others of the Shade. The third weapon will be much safer in the hands of a human with a Cat's Eye." Her eyes flickered to Sora's necklace. "I don't think Cerastes knows all the secrets of that stone."

"Thank you," Sora said, taken aback by the show of support.

Crash didn't seem pleased by Natrix's interruption, but he didn't argue with her. Sora found that curious. He could be quite bullheaded, but around the Grandmaster, he obeyed without question. Did he truly respect Natrix that much? Or did she have some sort of power over him, some hold Sora couldn't see? Crash hadn't said much about his trip to the Hive. She knew he had been exiled before. *Is there something he's not telling me?* she wondered. She looked back and forth between them, trying to read their body language, but it was impossible.

Of course he's hiding something, she thought, both saddened and frustrated. *When has he ever been entirely honest?*

"We have much to prepare for," Natrix said briefly. "We should go."

Crash looked reluctant, but he didn't argue. Sora watched with discerning eyes how he dropped his head.

"Until tomorrow," Crash murmured, and touched her hand in farewell.

"I trust you," she felt the need to say.

He searched her eyes one more time, then turned away.

Sora felt a horrible sense of yearning overcome her as Crash followed Grandmaster Natrix into the shadows. Her Cat's Eye chimed softly as they disappeared into a darkened corner.

"Please stay," she whispered to the vast emptiness of the room.

The shadow portal transported Crash and Natrix to the roof of the Ebonaire manor, where they stood, gazing out over the city. Tonight, the air was crisp and clear, the wind strong and cutting, and the moon visible through breaks in the clouds. Crash imagined, as he caught a glimpse of lunar light, that he was trapped under a frozen lake, gazing up through cracks in the ice—as sharp-edged as the clouds in the sky—at some unknown world above.

Natrix stood with him in silence for several minutes, contemplating the night. He wondered why she had brought him here. Despite her excuse to Sora, they didn't have much to prepare. Natrix had her weapons already prepped and ready, and besides learning the lay of the palace grounds, all they could do was wait until Cerastes showed himself.

She spoke after several minutes, and when she did, he found himself taken off guard.

"You would not be the first of our kind to love."

Crash gave her a sideways glance. Did she mean to make him confess to yet another trespass against the Hive's law?

"I wouldn't call it love," he said, guarded.

She half-smirked, but didn't reply. Instead, she waited for him to speak, and over time, Crash grew curious.

"If others of our kind have loved," he began, "why doesn't the Hive keep any record of it?"

"Because those who fell in love all left the Hive."

"Exiled, you mean," Crash said. "The Hive exiled them."

"Some left by their own will."

Natrix folded her arms and gazed out over the flickering city lights. "Some were savants not worth mentioning. Some were Named when their hearts led them astray. Some remain, living on the fringes of the colonies, perhaps drawn to what they once called home, perhaps waiting for others to follow in their footsteps."

"Lachesis," Crash murmured. He hadn't said that Name in a long time: the hermit Grandmaster that traveled between different colonies of the Hive, disappearing for months at a time, then reappearing unannounced, unanticipated. Years ago, Crash had studied with him after Cerastes had abandoned the Hive. Still, he and Lachesis had only interacted for a matter of months, for a handful of training sessions. The hermit Grandmaster remained shrouded in mystery.

"Is that why Lachesis left the Hive?" he repeated.

"I would not speculate." Natrix paused. "You could leave the Hive, if this girl is so important to you. You are already in exile. Why return with me, when you know they will take your life?"

Crash shifted uneasily on his feet. "I no longer wish to run."

"Run from what?"

"What I did. What I've done. I caused all of this." Crash's gaze traveled to the half-built clocktower, its length protruding from the city like a steel pike. It reminded him of the red plateau in the desert of Ester. "Volcrian summoned the wraiths to avenge his brother. Without me, the plague never would have leaked into this world."

"I see." Natrix clasped her hands behind her back. "You feel guilt, then."

"I feel fear."

She glanced at him sharply.

"I am afraid I cannot stop Cerastes," he said, "and I am afraid I cannot protect the one who is most important to me."

"And you say it isn't love."

Natrix mocked him, but Crash would never use that word in front of a member of his own race. He didn't trust Natrix fully. She was more his warden than his friend. Anything he said, she could use against him before the Elders.

Though it's a bit late for that, isn't it? he thought.

"I don't fully believe your reasons," Natrix said. "I think some part of you wants to return to the Hive to continue your training. I think, when Cerastes abandoned the Hive, your future was cut short as well. Your plans and destiny were severed, cut adrift. I remember you. You were always a good student. You thirsted for knowledge and progression. He took that from you. I think you want it back."

Crash considered her words and tried not to feel his heart quicken. She had struck upon a truth that he had long since buried and kept hidden from himself. He had thought, after leaving the Hive, that he had given up any hope of continuing his training. But that was a lie. His exposure to the Shade had brought back his desires full force. He wanted to open the fifth gate and even the sixth gate, if he could. He wanted to become a Grandmaster. He had never spoken those words aloud, but after seeing Cerastes again, and now standing next to Natrix, he could feel the need burning in his blood.

"You were there that night," he said, summoning memories from a lifetime ago. "When the fire broke out, and we fought the Sandsorrow Hive. The night of my exile. I remember you were there."

"I was," Natrix agreed.

"I did not intend to betray the Hive's law." Perhaps it was useless to explain himself now, but he felt the need to try. He had been young and arrogant before the Elders when they had put him to trial, and they had been eager to punish him. "I tried to open the fifth gate before I was ready, and I lost control. The Elders made their decision, but sometimes I question their judgment."

Natrix looked thoughtful.

"It was against the Hive's law to use powers beyond your control, unsupervised, and in battle with our allies," she admitted. "Do you remember why you tried to use the fifth gate?"

Crash frowned. In fact, now that she asked, he found it hard to pinpoint the specific reason. All he remembered was the fire that broke out afterwards. Or had the fire happened first?

"I was threatened," was all he could say. He had been so young, with hardly any knowledge of his demon. Cerastes had just abandoned him. He had been angry and desperate to prove himself. Once he had transformed, he had lost all sense of time. He recalled the fire, but had he caused it, or was he trying to escape it?

Natrix spoke.

"The Elders didn't know what to do with you. They couldn't assign you to another Grandmaster because of Cerastes' reputation. The other Named assassins were questioning your presence. They were constantly provoking you."

Crash remembered several incidents. Despite his aggressors, he had always been the one punished by the Hive's law.

"It's long been my belief that they wanted to get rid of you," Natrix said.

"They sentenced me to death."

"It was easiest. The Sandsorrow Hive was calling for blood after what happened. I've long wondered if Cerastes orchestrated the incident in some way. The battle was so strange, and escalated so quickly, and there you were in the middle of it. They attacked first. I know it's true, even if Sandsorrow denies it. Perhaps Cerastes got into their heads. I think he manipulated their savants into ambushing you. Don't you agree?"

Crash recalled the mission. He and two other Named assassins had been sent to meet with emissaries from the Sandsorrow Hive, to exchange gifts and offerings of respect, as was custom between different colonies. Except something had gone wrong. Crash remembered a skirmish in the woods. He remembered flames and smoke. Then a battle, and then the demon's red heat in his mind....

"You arrived after the fire broke out," he said, remembering Natrix's face.

She nodded briefly. "I don't think you or the Sandsorrow Hive was at fault. Cerastes intended to take you down. You had already become displaced within the Hive, and this was his final nudge to get you out. He feared what you would become if you continued your training."

Crash considered her words. "He thought I would be his undoing."

"He did."

"But *you* will be his undoing."

Natrix smiled at that. "We shall see."

"It's no use speaking of what happened," Crash said, gazing out over the city. "The Elders made their decision, and I have made mine. After you kill Cerastes, I will return to the Hive to meet my fate. It is time."

"It is time," Natrix echoed, and the two stared out over the darkened streets of the city, the knifing moonlight and the clocktower, needle-like, piercing the sky.

CHAPTER 16

The next morning, Sora awoke to Olivia's knock at her door. The handmaid bustled in with several lower servants in tow, who quickly wrapped Sora in a fur-lined robe and slippers.

"If you are quite ready," Olivia said, "Lady Danica is expecting you."

Half-asleep, Sora remembered her promise to have breakfast with Danica that morning. She wondered if she could cancel, blaming her health, but then decided against it. This might be her last night in The Regency, and besides that, she was hungry.

She followed Olivia out of the room and into the hallway. Olivia's flock of housemaids accompanied them, and Sora tried not to think of Lily, even though her heart ached at her friend's absence.

"I've already brought your dress to the room," Olivia said, hardly glancing at Sora. "I do hope your handmaid shows herself soon. We don't tolerate such behavior among our own staff. In her absence, I have my best assistants to help you dress."

Sora bit her lip. She wanted to smack Olivia across her pale, high-boned cheek. Instead, she muttered, "That will be fine."

Olivia opened the door to Danica's room, and Sora entered somewhat hesitantly. She had last seen her cousin on the steps to the theater. She hoped Danica had moved past the incident. Her note had been promising, but Sora couldn't be sure.

Danica's room was divided into four quadrants, and Sora thought the term "apartment" might be more appropriate. Olivia led her through a sitting room full of small, overstuffed chairs and chaises, then through a set of double doors into a bedroom. Rays of morning light flowed through a wide bay window. Outside, Sora saw a snow-covered garden and a view of the stables.

Danica's bedroom had been transformed into a lady's paradise, filled with decorative hat boxes, streams of silk and chiffon ribbons, and a vanity covered in powder pots and face paints. Full-length mirrors lined the room, and several stands displayed feather-studded headdresses and bejeweled wands. Sora counted over a dozen dress designs, all of varying colors and fabrics--from satin and velvet to silk--pinned to different mannequins for Danica. Her own humble dress of blue and white was pinned off to one side.

Danica lay across her bed in a corset and drawers, her hair freshly brushed and falling to her waist. When she saw Sora, she leapt up and floated across the room, graceful as a swan.

"My dear cousin!" she said, grasping Sora in a tight hug and kissing her cheek, "You look so much healthier today. I am relieved. I swear, I thought you were right behind me at the theater. I didn't realize you fell ill. Your uncle says you had to return to the manor?"

Sora lowered her eyes demurely.

"It was my fault," she admitted. At least that much was true. "I shouldn't have been in such a rush to go out. I wasn't as recovered as I thought."

"But you're recovered enough for the masquerade tonight, I hope?"

Sora didn't reassure her immediately, and Danica gave her a reproachful look.

"I do pray you're recovered enough to attend," she said. "I was hoping to spend the evening with my new cousin."

Sora realized she was being rude. Danica wasn't at fault for any of this, and the poor girl seemed so sincere.

"I feel much better today," she said. "Just a bit overwhelmed, I suppose. I grew up in the country, you see. We didn't have any of this." She motioned to the row of dresses.

Danica laughed and floated back to her bed, beckoning Sora to follow. Sora saw a lavish breakfast laid out at the bedside.

"It's certainly indulgent, but then again, tonight is winter solstice eve! Don't be intimidated, dear cousin. Despite my family's wealth, you'll find our hearts just as generous and compassionate as any commoner. Perhaps even more so. I mean, how generous can a peasant possibly be, if they have nothing to give away?"

Sora raised an eyebrow. She was tempted to explain to Danica that generosity didn't always mean giving out gold coins. Sometimes, it meant listening with patience, or painting a barn door, or teaching a farmhand to read. But she didn't think Danica cared to listen. Instead, the girl passed Sora a silver platter of breakfast pastries, each barely the size of a mouthful. Sora tried one and found herself overwhelmed by the rich flavors of strawberry syrup and cream.

"Now," Danica said, "we have the whole day ahead of us, and that might not be enough! Shall we begin?" She clapped her hands. "Minstrel, a song, please?"

Only then did Sora notice the young girl with a lute sitting in the corner of the room. She couldn't have been older than ten years old. When her fingers lit upon the strings, a beautiful melody flowed forth.

"You hired a minstrel?" Sora gasped.

"Of course. I love music in the morning."

Sora didn't know what to say.

"I've had Olivia bring your dress," Danica said, and pointed to one of the mannequins. "I've yet to decide on a design for this year, so I had my seamstress make a few different options. Perhaps you can help me choose?"

"Ah," Sora muttered. "Of course."

At Danica's nod, Olivia rounded up the maids, and an hour later, Sora found herself standing upon a stool in a shift and corset as two maids pinned her dress in place.

As the maids worked, Danica talked. She told Sora stories of prior years and other winter festivals. She talked about the different families and who was engaged to whom. She talked about her Blooming next year and how many people she thought would attend. She wondered if her father would ever buy her a "proper ship" so she could sail off after her uncle, Simeon, Ferran's youngest brother, who was spending the winter season on the coast.

"Pirates and treasure and foreign cities!" she gushed. "Can you imagine?"

Despite the frivolity of their conversation, Sora found herself slowly warming to her cousin. For all that Danica had lived a privileged life, she was full of stories, laughter and snatches of song. She had a love of adventure tales and they discussed the stories of Kaelyn the Wanderer at length. Danica didn't have a shy bone in her body, and often blurted out her opinions with little regard for who might be listening. She spoke like someone used to being seen, used to being heard, and who rather liked the attention. Sora found it unexpectedly refreshing.

Their conversation led them, inevitably, back to the topic of First Winter's Ball.

"Why, you've never been to Elysium before, have you? Oh, how I wish it were my first time all over again. You're in for quite an evening."

"Elysium?"

"The royal palace's ballroom. The royal family named it so. They host First Winter's Ball every year. The queen and her festival committee always manage to outdo themselves. Do you dance?"

"Yes." Sora thought of her Blooming and winced inwardly.

"I'll have to teach you the Wanderer's Waltz. They always play it. 'Tis tradition."

"I'll gladly learn."

Danica took a sip of tea and studied her.

"You don't seem all that excited."

Sora was preoccupied, but she couldn't possibly tell Danica about Lily's fate, which weighed heavily on her heart, or the threat of Cerastes and the Dark God. So she stuck with the obvious.

"I've never attended such an extravagant affair. I already feel out of place."

"You can't worry yourself about that, my sweet." Danica placed her hand lovingly on Sora's arm. "Of course you'll be out of place—you're new—but don't be afraid. You've traveled with my uncle all over the world. Tell us stories of your adventures. You'll steal all the attention!"

Sora wondered about that. "Ferran—my father—left the city in disgrace," she said. "Perhaps the other families won't be very accepting."

"My dear, this is the city, not the country. Life carries on. Ferran left our family decades ago. He was spoken about when I was a young child, but not anymore. Most of my friends are too young to remember. They will flock to your side. Why, your mysterious allure has already caught the attention of Lord Seabourne!" She grinned conspiratorially. "No one has managed to do that in, well, *years*."

"Gracen?" Sora asked, scrunching up her nose.

"He must be very intrigued by you. He's never brought a partner to winter solstice before, not since I can remember. I've seen many ladies try to land him, but never successfully."

"Oh."

Danica carried on. "I'm surprised—and pleased—that he asked you to the ball. You know our current queen is a Seabourne *and* his eldest sister. They're a good family, loyal to a fault, but Gracen has always been very solitary. They say his job keeps him too busy for a wife and family."

"Understandably," Sora felt the need to defend him. "He's Captain of the King's Guard and defender of the throne, after all."

"Of course, of course, I'm just stating facts. The truth remains that he is somewhat solitary and eccentric in the eyes of The Regency. But very handsome, no doubt! Perhaps he would make a perfect match for you."

Sora blushed. "I haven't given it much thought...."

"As though any girl in The Regency would turn down a Seabourne!" Danica laughed. "No need to act coy, my sweet. Not around me. I fully approve of the match."

Thankfully, one of Danica's maids interrupted their conversation at that moment. Sora was politely escorted over to a bedpost, where she braced herself as the maid went about tightening the strings on her corset. Across from her, Olivia and Danica assumed much the same position.

When Sora was able to speak again, she asked Danica with genuine curiosity, "Why hasn't Lord Gracen married for heirs? He could hire a governess and continue with his job."

Danica shrugged. "No heirs necessary, I suppose, with so many siblings. He's the youngest of seven, and he's never been rushed to marry like his older brothers. He's not due to inherit anything impressive, beyond whatever gifts the king bestows upon him for his service to the throne."

"But for alliances...or adding to his family's wealth...."

Danica snorted. "His sister married the king, what other alliance do you need? He's in the rare position where he can *marry for love,* and I think that's holding him up. Love is a complicated business." Danica spoke with a teasing sort of irony, and Sora couldn't tell if she was being serious or not. "Whatever the case, after King Royce passes, I don't think Gracen will continue serving under Prince Peric. Perhaps he will retire and marry then."

"Why wouldn't Gracen serve Peric?"

"Because the prince is a twit."

Sora snorted with laughter. "I haven't met him personally."

"Spare yourself the agony." Danica sighed. "He's pompous and vindictive and keen to inherit the throne. Most of us--the upper tier I mean--is holding its breath, dreading King Royce's final day. Still, there are those who would rather see the king step down. 'Tis well known who's on whose side," Danica said gleefully, "or rather, in whose pocket."

Sora wondered if Danica *really* knew who was in whose pocket.

She ventured an opinion. "A lot of peasants will suffer now that they've closed the gates to the city."

"It's regrettable," Danica said simply. "But what if this cursed affliction spreads to the royal family? To the whole First Tier? What would the kingdom do without a ruler? Nobility doesn't grant us immortality, sad to say."

Sora caught a note of bitterness in Danica's voice, and remembered that the girl had faced this reality very recently with her mother's death. She put a comforting hand on Danica's shoulder. Beneath all of her bravado, she was still a young girl.

"They'll find a cure," Sora said. "I promise. The kingdom won't fall to this."

"I believed that once." Danica pulled away from Sora. She straightened her spine and raised her head, suddenly untouchable. "Let's not waste time on such sad thoughts. What do you think of your dress?"

Sora searched Danica's face, but all hint of sadness was gone. *The Sixth Race aren't the only ones who wear masks,* she thought.

Then she acquiesced. She stood up and crossed the room to a tall standing mirror, and for the first time, she gazed upon herself in her winter solstice gown. She hardly recognized herself. Her wide skirts, boosted up and out by her panniers, fell in royal blue satin layers. A light blue jacket covered her bodice. Her sleeves and the hem of her skirts were trimmed in black lace.

Danica handed her a porcelain mask that went with the dress. It was made to rest above her upper lip, painted white and studded with sapphires and crystals.

The dress was breathtaking, but as Sora thought about the evening to come, she found herself growing less enthusiastic. She would need some way to carry a weapon. Perhaps, if she wrapped a few silk ribbons around the Dark God's longbow, she could match it to the dress and carry it like a prop. *These skirts are thick enough to catch an ax,* she thought. At least they would provide some protection.

"You don't like it?" Danica asked, misinterpreting her expression.

Sora realized her eyebrows had knitted into a tight frown. She forced herself to smile.

"I adore it. Truly. I've never worn a dress so lovely." *Blood will turn it purple.* "Thank you, Danica. You and your father have been so welcoming to me. This is a priceless gift."

Sora focused on the mirror again. "I do have a question...what am I supposed to be?"

Danica lifted a card from the table, next to the brown paper packaging that had once wrapped Sora's dress. She read it with a flourish, "*A blue jay sits in a nest above the Crown's Rush as starlight illuminates the forest.*"

Sora blinked. "So I'm a blue jay?"

"That, or a starlit forest. Or perhaps the Crown's Rush?"

Sora realized Danica was teasing her, and started to laugh.

"It's a bit over-the-top," Sora said.

"Absurdly so, and we wouldn't have it any other way."

Morning slid into afternoon unnoticed. Olivia spent three hours on her hair, braiding Sora's golden locks and pinning them under an elaborate headdress. The headdress was the crowning glory of her costume. It contained a nest, five hand-painted quail eggs, bluejay feathers, pinecones and white stars crafted from paper mache.

Finally, as daylight waned outside the bay windows, the two girls stood before the mirror and assessed their costumes.

"Well done, Olivia," Danica praised. "The dress is perfect in every way."

Olivia bowed. Sora didn't miss the subdued smile on her lips. Her heart twisted again for Lily, and for a moment, she thought she might cry.

Then she recovered herself. "Your dress is beautiful, cousin," she said to Danica, who twirled in a graceful circle. Danica's black gown was gloriously cut and layered to show off the canyon of her chest and the small of her back. Sora would never have been allowed to dress like that before her Blooming, but, she reminded herself, this was the city.

Danica held up a mask to her face. It, too, was black and painted with shiny silver moons and stars. Her dark hair was twisted and twirled atop her head, and held in place with a hundred diamond pins. She looked like a goddess.

"I have a competition with Princess Elyssa this year, and I plan to win," she said.

Sora gawked at her. A competition with the princess? *Ebonaire, indeed.*

"Do you truly like it?" Danica prompted. "I'm the *night sky*."

"You look beautiful," Sora repeated, and for a brief moment, she felt a flare of jealousy.

Then the maids began clearing the room.

"Your escort will be here soon," Lady Danica said. "If you need anything from your room, you should get it now. Lord Seabourne will arrive at dusk."

Sora said her farewells. She couldn't believe an entire day had passed in Danica's company, simply dressing for the ball. As she left the room, she realized that she had enjoyed most of it, even if she hadn't expected to.

She started back to her room, where she made a brief stop, then she continued down the hallway to Ferran and Lori's compartments. Her mother was a fine seamstress, and Sora needed a few practical adjustments made to her dress.

* * *

"You can't go to the ball dressed like that," Lori said, though she wasn't sure why she cared. Didn't they have greater matters to worry about?

Ferran stood before her in his leather, travel-worn greatcoat. At best, he looked like a swarthy adventurer, with high-buckled boots and a red vest and tunic under his coat. At worst, he looked like a common thief. He was armed to the teeth with more daggers than Lori could count. She couldn't imagine what he would look like in the royal ballroom standing next to his brother, Lord Martin, who would doubtlessly be dressed in the latest fashion.

Burn, who would be accompanying the Ebonaires as their carriage driver, had just left the room sporting a two-handed longsword across his back. Both men looked like they were going to war, not a frivolous affair like a ball.

Lori fidgeted in bed. "I should be going with you," she said in annoyance. "What if the Shade attack, or those thugs hired by the prince? You might need a Healer!"

"I'm sure there will be other Healers at the ball," Ferran assured her. "Headmaster Duncan will be there, at least. I'm sorry, my dear, but you are firmly anchored to that bed." He gave her a roguish wink. "Keep it warm for me, will you?"

Lori fumed at him. "I don't see why Martin wants you as his guest. If he means to make you a spectacle, or humiliate you over your disownment...."

"Martin intends to do no such thing," Ferran said. He was quiet as he hooked yet another knife onto his belt. Then he said, "In fact, after my conversation with him and Lord Seabourne this morning, I do believe he has a *legitimate* use for me."

"As a bodyguard," Lori huffed. Again, she didn't know why she cared. Ferran and Martin's relationship was none of her business.

"I'll be an extra man to defend the throne, should the need arise. Martin has other reasons for me to attend, but we will see how the night plays out." Ferran sat on the bed and took her hand. "Knowing you will be safe here in the manor eases my mind. I will keep an eye on Sora for you. We all will."

Lori slumped back against her pillows in defeat. "I can't stand lying here while you risk your life."

"I know, but as Gracen said, you've already done more than enough. Now the king is personally involved with the investigation of the Wind Temple, and Prince Peric might soon be under question for the attack on the parade, all because of you...." Ferran squeezed her hand. He sat awkwardly for a moment, and Lori searched his face. "When I return from the ball, there's a question I've been meaning to ask you," he continued. "It may seem a bit soon, and a bit out of place, but it's been on my mind for some time...."

Lori gazed at him. She thought she knew what he was going to ask. Surprisingly, she wasn't as adverse to the idea as she had expected to be.

"Best to wait until after the ball, then," she said. "As you said, see how the night plays out."

"And you're to stay here. You're wounded, Lori. Let's not push our luck."

Lori knew that, with her concussion, she should take it easy for the next few days. She *knew* that, yet she also couldn't stand the thought of lying in bed while her daughter and Ferran risked their lives. Her eyes traveled to the window, where she could barely see the roof of the Ebonaire stables. She wouldn't be able to change Ferran's mind, but perhaps, after they left, she could find some other way to the ball.

A knock came to the door, interrupting their conversation. Lori suppressed a groan, imagining yet another maid coming to fluff her pillows, or force a sleeping potion down her throat.

"Send them away," she said. "I don't want any visitors."

"Of course," Ferran said, and started for the door.

However, it opened before he could reach it, and Sora walked into the room.

Lori's breath caught. She had never known her daughter as a noblewoman; all of their time together had been spent on Lori's farm, or on the road, covered in dust and sweat. Even since coming to The Regency, they had spent most of their time apart. Embarrassingly, Lori felt tears sting her eyes. Having Sora float into her room like a blue satin cloud made her heart ache unexpectedly. Sora was now a woman, and she looked like royalty. She thought she understood, now, why Lord Seabourne had asked her to the dance.

Lori glanced at Ferran, and he must have seen the uncertainty in her eyes, because he nodded ever so slightly.

"You look beautiful," he said to Sora, who blushed. Her fashionable dress and styled hair all fell away, and Lori saw her daughter's innocence, her self-consciousness. She wanted to enfold her in a giant hug.

"The dress suits you," Lori said.

Sora smiled. "Thank you, but it's not quite perfect. There are a few small adjustments I was hoping you could make. They won't take long." From behind her back, Sora withdrew the Dark God's unstrung longbow. "I just need to figure out what to do with this, and where I can hide a few other things."

Ferran and Lori shared another look, this one a bit more humorous.

"I'm sure we can make something work," Lori said, and reached for the sewing kit at her bedside.

CHAPTER 17

S ora stood on the manor steps, her cloak gripped tight, awaiting the battle—or rather, the ball—to come. With her mother's help, she had made a few adjustments to her outfit. Two daggers had been secured in the folds of her dress, and another in her bodice. She had strung the Dark God's bow with silver thread and held it in one hand. If anyone asked, she would say it was part of her costume.

A cold breeze brushed Sora's bare arms, and she drew her fur-lined cloak tighter. Her porcelain mask covered the upper half of her face. A black ribbon, hidden by her hair, secured the mask. She felt like a doll on display, but perhaps that was the point. Layers of blue satin spilled off her hips and flirted with the wind. The dress wasn't well-suited for outside wear, particularly in the snow, particularly at night...but Danica had assured her, with a wink, that she would soon be trying to cut it off. She referred to all the exertion of dancing and wine-drinking, of course.

Lord Seabourne's carriage of black walnut wood appeared down the front drive, pulled by four majestic bay stallions. It rolled to a stop just before the front steps. An Ebonaire servant opened the carriage door for Lord Gracen, who stepped down into the snow. Sora thought the whole ordeal a bit impractical in such bad weather, but the First Tier had their decorum.

For a moment, Gracen stood at the bottom of the steps and gazed up at her. Sora resisted the urge to squirm. She hadn't expected him to dress in his military uniform. He looked both formal and formidable. An intimidating row of badges and medals covered his left breast. His black, unadorned mask shielded only his eyes, emphasizing his strong jaw and solemn lips. Sora hadn't quite noticed his lips before—sculpted, with a shade of dark stubble on his chin and around his mouth.

"My lady, you are resplendent."

She opened her mouth to reply. Closed it. Tried again. "It's very cold tonight."

Unexpectedly, he smiled. She hadn't paid attention to his smile before, but the mask forced her to focus on his lips, on the dimple in his chin, on his straight white teeth.

He offered his hand, she took it, and the magic of winter solstice descended upon them. She forgot, for a blessed minute, where the night would end. She was a young girl again, her mind and heart rich with wonder, and he was a handsome stranger, both entrancing and mysterious. She could almost feel the story unfolding between them.

Sora leaned on Gracen as he escorted her down the icy steps, and blushed when he helped her wide skirts through the door of his coach. His dark eyes never left hers. With masks in place, they were no longer themselves, but different people, the old year erased, and this night a blank slate on which she could draw anew. She could borrow this other life for just a few hours.

Crash, she thought, guilty for the moment. She could sense the assassin's eyes on her, though she didn't know where he hid himself. According to their plan, he and Grandmaster Natrix would hide themselves in the eaves of the ballroom, watching for Cerastes, prepared for the killing blow. She wondered what he thought of her dancing with Lord Seabourne. She wondered if he cared. If he might even be jealous. *Gracen is a man worthy of jealousy,* she thought before she could stop herself.

Lord Seabourne's footman shut the door, and a minute later, they were off.

Face to face inside the carriage, Sora met Gracen's eyes through his mask.

"Truth be told, I considered cancelling our arrangement," he murmured.

"So you could focus on the king's safety?"

He nodded.

"Why didn't you?"

"Because I wanted to dance with a beautiful woman."

Sora shifted beneath her mountain of skirts. She wasn't very good at taking compliments, and now she had to wonder, was he being serious, or just playing his part?

"There will be hundreds of beautiful women at the ball," she said.

"Yes, but you are quite different from the typical heiress, wouldn't you agree?"

Sora didn't know how to respond. Gracen had warmed to her considerably since their encounter by the lake, but she hadn't seen this side of him before.

"The king's safety is important," she said awkwardly. "His life might be in danger tonight. You really shouldn't be dancing with me."

"My soldiers will be ready. I've made arrangements." His tone changed, becoming more businesslike. "I only wish to make you comfortable, Lady Sora. If you're concerned that I might neglect my duties to the king, you needn't worry. In all honesty, we probably won't have time for more than a few dances. I intend to make them count."

Sora felt pleased by his little speech, though she didn't want to admit it to herself. She felt flattered. A man like Gracen Seabourne, taking time away from his vigil to dance with her at the ball? What girl wouldn't be at least a little swayed?

Sora wondered how Lord Gracen had spent his day prior to this. She imagined him, a solitary bachelor, spending breakfast alone in his study, then heading to the palace to confer with his sister, the queen. After, she imagined him gathering his lieutenants at the barracks and assigning extra guards to patrols. She wondered if he had slept at all since their meeting with Martin Ebonaire. She bet, if he removed his mask, she would see dark circles under his eyes.

He could have cancelled their arrangement, yet he hadn't. Despite everything else, he had wanted to be here. With her.

Sora shook her head. *It's folly to think like this*, she thought. She didn't want to dwell on the countless paths her life might have taken, if she had never worn the Cat's Eye, if she hadn't abandoned the Fallcrest estate. What if Crash had never taken her from her manor? What if Volcrian had never summoned his wraiths?

She didn't know if she truly liked Gracen, or if the spell of winter solstice had stolen her common sense. The First Tier held a certain magnetism. He was the king's shield and the queen's youngest brother. And he was here, in this carriage, with her, because he wanted to be.

Sora realized she had been silent for some time. She forced herself to look out the window. It had stopped snowing, and to her surprise, a sliver of winter moonlight had broken through the clouds.

"I've heard many strange rumors about this night," she said thoughtfully. "Some say, on winter solstice, the dead come back to life. Others say you can commune with the spirits. If you're owed bad luck, it will find you. It's a night of celebration...but it is also a night of dark energies. I hope no bad luck befalls the dance."

Lord Seabourne followed her gaze. "It won't, if I can help it."

Sora watched the darkened streets of The Regency pass by outside the window. Before them, she glimpsed the spiraling towers of the royal palace. Their carriage followed a winding cobblestone drive through The Regency and up a slight hill, their way lit by lanterns hung from wooden posts.

A long row of carriages waited before the palace gates. A soldier checked the inside and outside of each coach before allowing them to pass through.

"Is this one of your precautions?" Sora asked.

"It is."

When they reached the gates, their coach was waved through without inspection. Lord Gracen nodded to the soldier outside the window.

Beyond the palace gates, yet another long stretch of parkway led to the ballroom. They passed a hedged maze covered in snow. She could recognize the outlines of topiary animals, rabbits, wolves and deer, cut from the bushes. Beyond that, they passed rows of statues and fountains caked in ice.

"And now, you may gaze upon Elysium, the queen's royal ballroom," Gracen said as their coach rounded a corner and cleared the final grove of snow-dusted hedges.

A dome of pure light dazzled Sora's eyes. The royal ballroom was ringed by immensely tall windows. Its apex was at least four stories high. It reminded her of the white marble buildings she had seen on the Lost Isles. The palace carried all the majesty of Asterion, the Harpy city.

She could see clearly into the ballroom through the glass. She saw musicians on a stage at the center of a wide dance floor, already plucking the first song of the night. At the north end of the rotunda, she saw a raised dais where four throne chairs stood—for the royal family, no doubt. She could see long banquet tables laden with food and ice sculptures; from the walls and ceiling, she saw streaming silk ribbons and wreaths of winter flowers, and faceted glass crystals dangled like snowflakes.

"Beautiful," Sora breathed as their carriage turned toward the front steps.

"The king had it built as a wedding gift for his bride. The queen's festival committee spends all year on it," Lord Seabourne explained. "They've probably already begun planning for next year's ball."

A long line of guests stood outside the ballroom, waiting to enter through the wide glass doors. Sora spied several soldiers checking under masks and inspecting costumes for hidden weapons.

"It seems your precautions are causing a bit of a stir," she said, indicating one richly dressed lord who was scolding a guard for upsetting his wife.

"Ah yes, old Lord LeCroy. He's always one to complain."

The withered fellow shook his cane, blustering, then trailed after his wife into the ballroom.

"Do you think the nobility will cause a problem for you?"

"We have the royal family's support," Gracen said. "That's all that matters."

Their carriage rolled to a stop. Sora tried not to feel nervous. Tonight, they would dance in the same room as the king and queen. Anyone who was *anyone* would be there. It was starting to sink in. Her stomach twisted as she watched the ladies before them leave their carriages and walk across the pavilion. Each one looked twice as beautiful as the last.

"It's been so long since...." she started, then stopped.

"Since?"

After a tense moment, Sora allowed herself to speak freely. Lord Gracen knew her true identity and her past.

"It's been years since I attended such an affair, and never of this magnitude." She realized she was gripping her skirts in her fists. "I imagine I will make a fool of myself."

Gracen snorted. "After what you've told me, I don't think you have anything to fear."

"You seem to think very highly of me."

"That, and not very highly of them." Gracen smiled dryly. "Women can be cruel to each other, but you seem quite above all that, Lady Sora."

She didn't respond immediately, so he continued to speak.

"You have nothing to fear from a flock of chittering birds. If they wish to ridicule you, let them. They have nothing better to do."

Sora hesitated, then allowed herself to speak openly again.

"It's very freeing, *not* being one of the upper class. I've enjoyed my time on the road very much. You don't have to impress anyone, or worry about what society thinks of you. Growing up in the Fallcrest manor, all I learned were rules and limitations. Being a noblewoman was like being in a cage. I may have lost my fortune, but in some ways, I've gained my freedom, and I am much happier than I was before."

Gracen didn't jump to agree with her, but instead looked out the window and considered her words.

"I understand your sentiment. Being a nobleman, as well, comes with its burdens and responsibilities. I often wish to run away, but some of us cannot."

"Why not?" Sora asked with more challenge in her tone than she intended. At his look, she rushed to say, "I realize you carry a lot of responsibility. You've sacrificed a lot for the royal family."

Gracen studied her, perhaps trying to read through her words.

"I've sacrificed more than some, but not as much as others. Despite it all, I do not regret the life I've chosen, perhaps *because* I chose it." He looked out the window then. His profile was strong and angular against the golden light of the ballroom. "To answer your question, I stay here despite my burdens because...well, I suppose love holds me bound."

Sora didn't expect him to say those words.

"King Royce is a man worth defending. He is a brilliant engineer and a compassionate ruler...and Queen Vanessa, my sister, well, she's the strongest of all of us. We used to call her the Tigress when we were little. She always knew she would marry the king. He fell in love with her the day she first pushed him into the mud. They were twelve."

"That's a perfect story," Sora said.

"Yes, and I intend to keep it as perfect as possible. Not many understand my job, Lady Sora, but they are my family and I will protect them."

She took his hand. "You will, Gracen. I know it."

"Your help has made that possible."

At his words, sudden warmth rushed through her.

"I think I've misjudged you," she said.

He raised an eyebrow. "And I, you," he agreed. "From the very beginning, I misjudged you. You're not a victim, Lady Sora, and you're not a criminal. You are...so very unexpected."

Sora's cheeks flushed beneath her mask. His words were flattering, but she held herself back. He could only see her facade: a highborn Lady dressed in expensive finery, with all the subtle graces of the upper tier. He had never seen her barefoot, sunburnt, running in the sand with her hair full of wind. She wondered if he would have said the same pretty words on the Lost Isles, or on her mother's farm.

She missed it suddenly—the road, the wilderness. The sense of limitless possibilities and endless terrain. She missed the warm rain upon the fields near her mother's cabin. She missed the salty, crashing waves of the coast, and the humid citrus scent of the Lost Isles.

Here, in the City of Crowns, all was ice-locked, dull and gray. In all directions, she knew she would find nothing but streets packed between countless streets. Madness, betrayal and intrigue all closed behind painted doors and garden walls. The city's parks were tame and disappointing. She could never be happy here.

The driver opened the carriage door, disrupting Sora's thoughts. Lord Gracen stepped down first and then offered her his hand.

Sora wanted to run the moment her feet touched the ground. She didn't care which direction. She had years left to live, to rebuild, to abandon this fight and find a new destiny for herself. She could go.....

She gazed longingly into the darkness beyond the coach, remembering another darkness outside a different ballroom, when she once fled with a mysterious stranger into the night.

Then she turned and took Lord Gracen's arm.

Together, they climbed the salted steps to Elysium.

In the attic of the Ebonaire manor, shadows stirred. Draining down the walls like muddy water, they flowed across the room and pooled in the center of the floor.

Then they rose up to form the figure of a man. His robes became distinct from his hair, distinct from his ashen skin. Lastly, his eyes opened and glinted in his skull-like face.

Krait thought, at first, that she was dreaming. She sat up, her chains dragging on the dusty floorboards.

"Master."

Cerastes was dressed differently than she had last seen him. Gone were his robes of black and purple, and he no longer wore the boar's head medallion around his neck. He looked dressed for a party, and that confused her, because parties were human things.

The shadows began to form a second figure: broad, masculine, powerful. At first, she didn't recognize the stranger who emerged from the portal. A tar-like substance covered his clothes, and filled the attic with a putrid stench. His skin was the color of a drowned corpse. Thick black veins ran along his neck and forearms. His nails were also black. Gray bandages covered his mouth and eyes. Like a fallen star, his body carried a dim halo of light. White feathers dusted the ground around him, bleeding from invisible wings.

"Is he not beautiful?" Cerastes asked.

Krait tried not to feel the lurch of recognition.

Caprion.

Cerastes crossed to her side. With a touch of his hand, the metal chains rotted and dissolved from her wrists. They fell with a heavy clunk to the floor. Her master had come to save her, and now there was no Harpy to interfere. She should feel triumphant and vindicated...but instead, she felt empty.

She stood on uncertain legs and stared at the fallen Harpy. His body stank of corruption.

"He suffers," she said.

The thinnest smile crossed Cerastes' face.

"Yes, he does."

"Why not kill him?"

Her master's smile grew. "Because I have plans for you both. Tell me, Krait—how willing are you to serve our god?"

She found herself dropping automatically to one knee.

"My life is His." Somehow, the words didn't come as easily as they had before.

Cerastes' hand appeared before her. In surprise, she took it. He raised her back to her feet.

"Come. We are late for the ball."

* * *

Ferran stood next to Martin under the twinkling crystal lights of Elysium. His brother raised a goblet of wine to his lips.

"This is quite impressive, Martin," Ferran said, gazing at the decorations. Even in his youth, he didn't remember First Winter's Ball being this extravagant. He noticed, however, a sour look upon his brother's face. "Is the wine not to your taste?"

"It's not the wine."

Ferran considered his next words, then said, "I'm sorry your late wife could not be here with us."

Martin looked up at him, surprised. "And I'm sorry Lorianne couldn't make it as well." Then his tone turned self-deprecating. "Look at us, a couple of sad saps in the midst of all this beauty. I suppose we should enjoy the night while we can."

Ferran scanned the room again. "While we can," he echoed.

"I see there are plenty of lovely dance partners in the room. We shouldn't be shy," his brother pointed out. Somehow, the words seemed hollow, and Ferran doubted either of them would be dancing at the ball. Martin was still in mourning, and Ferran, well....His thoughts traveled to Lorianne. She treated him differently now, keeping him at a distance where before she greeted him openly. Over the past few days, he had wished many times over that he had never brought up Sora's possible heritage. It had needlessly complicated things, and in some ways, driven an awkward wedge between them. Now she broke eye contact too often, and hesitated before speaking. He could feel her pulling away.

Which, in some ways, made him even more eager to win her back. He wanted to reassure her. He was not a young rogue anymore, reckless and untroubled by his mistakes. He was ready to take on the burdens of the Ebonaire estate, and start a new life for himself—for both of them, if she would have him. He felt certain that, beneath her cautious demeanor, she yearned for the connection they once shared. If he let her push him away, he would be failing them both.

Martin glanced over Ferran's worn jacket. "I should have ordered something made for you. Sorry, brother. Since all this madness with the prince, I forgot."

"I don't mind at all," Ferran said, and placed a cinnamon stick in his mouth. He had donned his leather coat as a form of protest, he supposed. Tonight, Martin planned to legitimize him before the royal family. He didn't want Martin to mistake his *legitimization* as a form of *castration*. He would never be a follower. Wearing the leather greatcoat was a not-so-subtle reminder of his last twenty years on the road. He wanted Martin to see that and accept that.

He also thought it looked better on him than anything with lace and frills.

"Let's introduce you around," Martin said.

The two Ebonaires started through the room. Martin glided from one group of revelers to the next, greeting the lords he knew—which seemed to be all of them—and introducing Ferran. At first, the masked nobility were formal, but as the wine flowed and conversation eased, many approached Ferran with questions about his life as a treasure hunter. The coat, it seemed, lent him an air of authenticity that the nobility found intoxicating. Soon, a group of twenty surrounded him, hanging on his every word as he began an embellished retelling of his journey to the dunes of Ester.

If Silas had been there, the Dracian captain might have corrected a few details; he might have convinced Ferran to wear something other than a tired greatcoat, too. But the pirate captain would not share in Ferran's stories ever again.

As Ferran finished the tale, he found his heart growing heavy, and he raised his glass in a toast.

"To those who perished on the road," he said, and he thought of Silas and drank. The rest of the nobility seemed happy to drink with him, echoing the phrase like some age-old expression.

After his tale was finished, much of the group dispersed, some drawn to the dance, others drifting toward the banquet tables. Ferran scanned the room again, this time searching for Gracen and Sora. They should have arrived by now, though he hadn't seen them in the crowd.

Then he heard Martin say, "Cedric Daniellian! There you are, old fellow. Have you met my brother? I really must introduce you."

"Has Simeon returned already? I thought he wasn't due back until spring. Well, if you insist but only for a moment. The prince is expecting me...."

"No, not Simeon, he's still traveling the coast. But surely you recall Ferran, don't you? We grew up together."

Ferran looked up. He and Cedric caught sight of each other at the same time. He grinned at the bastard, and watched Cedric's eyes ignite with recognition and contempt.

"You," Cedric said. "I know you."

"Well of course you know him," Martin laughed. "Recognized him far faster than I did! He hasn't shown his face around here in twenty years."

Cedric smiled tightly, but Ferran knew he was referring to another incident: a fistfight on the docks of the Healer's seminary when Ferran and Lori first arrived in the city. Ferran had landed a stunning blow to Cedric's nose. He wondered if the man's face was still bruised beneath his mask. Cedric had lost the scuffle, and Lori had been wounded by his footman. Many threats had been exchanged. At the time, Cedric had mistaken him for a common brute or vagabond, but now Ferran watched all the little gears turn behind his eyes.

"I remember your reputation," Cedric said. "Disowned for theft, was it? And how shall I address you now? Not a lord and hardly an Ebonaire, by the make of your coat." He turned back to Martin, dismissing Ferran's presence as he would a lowly peasant. "Martin, I hear you and Lord Seabourne visited the king yesterday afternoon. I hope the matter was settled. All of this cloak-and-daggery is very off-putting."

"It was nothing," his brother said, his expression bland. "Your investments are safe, I assure you."

"Good. Should any other problems arise, do notify me. Now excuse my hasty departure, but the prince is waiting for me."

"Of course."

Cedric walked away. When he was out of earshot, Martin glanced at Ferran.

"I guess Cedric hasn't forgotten you," he said. "Sometimes a grudge is remembered far longer than a friendship."

"I've never liked him much." Ferran watched Cedric disappear through the crowd. Seeing the man's smug face—even wearing a mask—was enough to make his blood boil. He thought of what Cedric had done to Lorianne and wanted to plunge a knife in his back.

With any luck, the guard would have them arrested by the end of the night, or so Ferran consoled himself. He had only to wait for the uprising Cedric had supposedly orchestrated; he and the prince were obviously up to something devious. It appeared that Lord Seabourne had equipped the ballroom for an attack. He saw more guards than seemed necessary lurking in the corners of Elysium, and half were stationed near the royal family. The sight should have been comforting, but Ferran still felt uneasy.

Martin didn't seem as concerned.

"Let up, Ferran. Enjoy yourself. Don't forget, part of my meeting with the king was to restore your title. The king shall announce tonight that you've returned to the upper tier with full rights reinstated. Let us toast to that."

Ferran tore his eyes away from the ballroom and raised his glass to his brother.

"To the dawning of a new year," he said.

"And the beginning of a new life," his brother agreed.

They drank as one.

"Now," Ferran said, "I think we should stand closer to the royal family, just in case."

Martin sighed. "If you insist. The dance has barely begun. Whatever the prince plans, I'm sure he will wait until later in the evening, when everyone is well into their cups."

"Then I suggest we are doubly prepared," Ferran said, and set down his wine glass on a passing tray.

The two brothers started through the crowd to where the king and queen sat on their raised thrones.

CHAPTER 18

A steward announced Lord Gracen at the door. Sora wondered if their arrival would cause a stir, but only a few people turned to hail him. No one seemed eager to approach the Captain of the King's Guard. Perhaps he didn't have such a fun reputation.

She and Gracen passed through the foyer into a spacious anteroom. The nobility all wore decorative masks, but in truth, Sora didn't think anyone was trying to hide their identity. The men, in particular, wore bands of leather or silk over their eyes with holes cut to see by, leaving their faces mostly exposed. The women were more extravagant by far, with dresses of every matter and make. Even then, everyone seemed to recognize each other.

A goblet of wine found its way into Sora's hand from a passing tray. She and Gracen paused at the entrance of the ballroom and surveyed the landscape. She had to admire the decor; the entire room held a mysterious, twilight beauty. Soft golden light, cast from countless crystalline stars along the ceiling, illuminated the dance floor. The orchestra sat on a raised platform at the heart of the room above a sea of dancers. Sora heard flutes, cellos, violins and lutes, and the occasional rattle of a tambourine. Her senses were overwhelmed, and she felt momentarily suspended above her body, like one of the stars from the ceiling.

"Would you honor me with a dance?" Gracen asked.

Somehow, she hadn't quite expected to reach this part of the night. *Could* she dance? Would her feet remember?

"Yes, of course," she said, and set down her cup.

The melody dipped, and so did the dancers, and so did Gracen Seabourne as he led her onto the floor. He danced as she had imagined—perfect, punctual, his motions like clockwork. She felt inadequate next to him, and found her steps faltering and hesitating. She had to sling the Dark God's longbow over one shoulder, and with each turn, it slipped a little down her arm.

She caught Gracen's smile as she misplaced her foot, and his hand moved from her arm to her waist.

"You are perfect," he said softly.

A bit of the tension left her shoulders, and Sora began to enjoy herself more. She danced two more songs with him and refused the third. Her restrictive corset made it difficult to breathe, and she wanted to scan the room for any sign of the Shade.

Gracen understood and, with an elegant bow, escorted her from the dance floor. He led her through the crowd of people in search of a place to sit down. Sora was more preoccupied looking for Cerastes. With so many people in masks, it was impossible to tell a normal human apart from the Sixth Race.

"Ah, dear cousin! Over here!"

At first Sora didn't see Danica—another mask among many—but her cousin vigorously waved a lace-gloved hand in the air. Then the girl pushed her way to Sora's side.

"I saw you both dancing. Marvelous, just marvelous. Such a beautiful couple." She curtsied to Gracen. "Are you enjoying your evening, Lord Seabourne?"

"I am," he replied.

"Good, I am very glad. I hate to interrupt, but may I steal my cousin away for a minute? My friends are simply dying to meet her. You musn't keep her to yourself all evening, Gracen. It would be criminal."

Sora wondered if Danica had used the word *criminal* intentionally, because Gracen winced. Sora maintained her grip on his arm. She didn't want to spend time around Danica's friends, and she hoped Gracen would refuse to give her up, but he relented far too easily.

"I should make my rounds as well." Then, to Sora, he said, "I will find you after I'm finished?"

"Of course," she said.

He left, and Danica took Gracen's place, wrapping Sora's arm in hers.

"So?" Danica asked, leaning in close as they walked. "How is Gracen? Is he charming? Has he kissed you?"

"He's very nice," Sora muttered.

"I'll say. He looks very dashing in his uniform! You seem a bit flustered. Did he compliment your dress?"

"Yes, he did."

"Lovely!"

Danica continued to tell Sora all about her arrival at the ball and her evening thus far: the clumsiness of her footman, the excellent wine, and how she had already received at least thirty offers to dance, including old Lord LeCroy, which was laughable. As they walked, even more hopeful dance partners approached Danica, and Sora watched her cousin flirt and laugh and turn them away. As Danica's cousin, she received almost as much attention, and Danica seemed to delight in introducing her and even flaunting her before different suitors. Sora thought, finally, that she understood the appeal of such a ball. She had never imagined that flirting could be so much fun.

Finally, the two girls arrived on the opposite end of the ballroom, where Danica's group stood in front of a tall window.

Danica introduced her around, again, with enthusiasm.

"This is Marcella LeCroy and Travid Montague and Fauna Seabourne. Fauna—Sora is accompanying your uncle tonight."

Fauna was the youngest of them all, possibly thirteen. The girl politely greeted her.

"Danica says you've been to the coast," Travid said. His voice was hoarse and crackly, and Sora placed him around fifteen.

"Was it very exciting?" Marcella asked. Her hair fell in tight blond curls around her shoulders, and with her small lips and wide eyes, she looked like a porcelain doll. Sora guessed her costume was a swan—or a mountain with snow on it—or something to that effect.

"It was exciting, yes," Sora admitted.

"So? Where have you been thus far? Do tell us of your travels!" Travid begged.

Sora found herself fidgeting, searching for something to say.

"Tell us about the coast," Fauna echoed in a very small, high-pitched voice.

Sora started slowly. "Have you...have you heard of the pirate city of Sonora? Or Barcella, home of the West Wind?"

Crash passed through the revelers like a ghost.

Sixty feet above him, Natrix perched on a shallow ledge close to the ceiling, a poison-tipped crossbow held at ready. She was invisible from below, but he could sense her gaze pass over him by the chill on his neck.

Over the past hour, he had patrolled the room once, twice, thrice, each loop wider than the first. His eyes had probed each mask, searching for members of the Shade, or perhaps Cerastes himself. So far, he had only encountered regular humans.

He watched the nobility become drunker, louder and more obnoxious as the night wore on. The room grew hotter as one dance followed the next. Heavy incense thickened the air, meant to disguise the smell of sweat. Perhaps it worked for human senses, but he had to suppress the urge to gag.

On his fourth pass around the room, his eyes found Sora on the dance floor. He couldn't see her face and her headdress was unfamiliar, but he recognized the way she moved. He recognized the longbow she wore around her torso like part of her costume. Worse, he recognized the man who held her in his arms.

Gracen Seabourne guided Sora across the dance floor. Crash saw how their eyes connected, how their hands touched. Gracen wanted her—and he was seducing her, claiming her, in his own human way.

The demon uncoiled beneath his skin, and Crash found himself standing still, watching her, as tension throbbed at his temples.

Eat him alive, the demon snarled.

No. Sora deserved this—a partner to dance with, a ballroom, a dress. *Normal. Human.* She was born to this world. As much as he hated to admit it, she fit here. She knew the steps. He remembered the first time he had ever seen her, dancing before a crowd of silent spectators, alone. Now she had a partner. *This is how it should be.*

The demon writhed in his gut. He could smell her sweat. *Remember*, the demon hissed. *Remember.*

Gracen and Sora passed by him again, step-step, again. Crash tried to suppress his envy, even as it crawled up his throat. He wondered if Natrix watched him, if she saw his weakness from her perch near the ceiling. His desires were clear and overwhelmingly simple. He wanted to turn Sora in his arms, lead her with his hands. He wanted to stand next to her, a part of her world, even if he couldn't be, even if he was lying to himself.

Sora and Gracen left the dance floor after the next song. They appeared to be looking for a place to sit down and rest. He knew he should continue his patrol and circle the room again, but instead, he followed them through the crowd at a distance.

Telling stories was much easier than Sora had first imagined. She didn't have to go into great detail. Danica's friends seemed satisfied with descriptions of the various cities and the people she had met. She talked about the Priestess of the West Wind and the City of Barcella with its countless bells. She talked about the rows of ships along the shoreline in Delbar, and the hotel on the docks, and her voyage overseas.

"Who's that?" Fauna asked, interrupting Sora's description of the ocean.

Their group peered curiously behind her, and Sora turned around as well. At first she only saw a confusing montage of colorful skirts and towering headdresses. Then the crowd parted, and Sora tried not to gasp.

He stood only a few paces away from her, dressed completely in black. A somber wooden mask covered his face above his upper lip, but displayed his sharp jawline. His dark greatcoat, his black vest, and the high collar around his neck were all impeccably designed.

People passed him by without noticing him. He was a shadow come to life, and she felt helplessly drawn to his side. *Crash.* He knew better than to approach her, yet here he was, holding out his hand to her, a slight smile on his lips.

She glanced around, looking for Lord Seabourne, who had yet to reappear. Ten minutes or so had passed since they had parted ways, perhaps not enough time for him to finish his rounds. A new waltz was beginning, this one slower, with notes that reminded her of a misty, hidden meadow in a spellbound forest.

Crash simply stood, silent and still, with his gloved hand outstretched.

"Oh, such romance! Such *mystique!*" Danica whispered excitedly. "Go, Sora. That could be the prince himself and you'd never know."

"I know him," Sora said. Her voice sounded soft and dreamlike in her own ears. Crash was supposed to be patrolling the room with Natrix. Why would he come to her side? Dare she even question it?

She couldn't hesitate any longer.

She crossed to him, three steps, and took his hand, and allowed him to draw her onto the dance floor. His eyes shone emerald through the holes in his mask, his lashes dark, his gaze unfathomable. She wanted to reach up and touch his face, but she couldn't bring herself to dislodge his mask. Hidden from each other, hidden from themselves, she could pretend, for just one night, that they were perfect strangers. That he would not pull away. That he would welcome her for the rest of his life.

He came to me. I knew he would, she thought. She found herself free of doubt, free of inhibition. Perhaps this very night, he would realize they were meant to be together.

He pulled her into the dance. She recognized the motions of his body from hours of sparring. Together, they moved across the dance floor like water, soft and fluid. This time, each step was natural. She knew the grip of his hands as he turned her, as he touched her waist, her shoulder, her arm. His fingers grazed her cheek.

As she stared into his eyes, she felt herself becoming blind to the rest of the room—blind to the entire world.

Crash relished the feel of her in his arms. They communicated purely through touch. Her scent was a drug—not her perfume, but the hot sweetness beneath it.

He gripped her narrow waist through her corset. The waltz was easy. After an hour of studying it, he had mastered the steps. He led her across the floor—*turn, step-step, turn*—around and around. She followed him without resisting.

Could he truly be this man for her? Could he truly live in the human world, surrounded by crystalline lanterns and tiled floors, each day ordinary and mundane? Perhaps he could grow used to it. Perhaps he could even live behind The Regency walls and become fat and complacent. Surely, that would be easier than returning to the Hive? He could still escape his fate.

Bitterness rose in the back of his throat. He was a fool to entertain such thoughts. Once Cerastes was dead, he would be dead as well. The Hive would come for him. The black mark on his neck ensured as much.

Only one thing was simple—his desire for her. He didn't need to lie to himself about that. He wanted to protect her. He had never felt anything so fiercely in his life.

He dipped her backward in his arms. And, in heated inspiration, he pressed his mouth to hers—roughly, passionately. He let her feel his need, his urgency, and hoped she understood.

They broke apart when he pulled her back up, and she stared at him, her lips red and parted. She looked shocked. He kept waiting for the expression to pass, but it didn't. He began to doubt himself, and to wonder if he had upset her somehow. Perhaps she preferred Gracen? Perhaps he had lost her already?

Sora saw his eyes change behind his mask, focusing on some invisible thought. She could sense his discomfort, his turmoil.

"What's wrong?" she asked.

He turned her again in his arms.

"I have...regrets."

"Do you want to talk?" she asked. "We can find a quiet place."

He studied her, assessing, then nodded.

With a few quick steps, they gracefully maneuvered across the dance floor, then into the crowd. She found herself scanning the half-lit room, worried that she would run across Lord Seabourne, that she would have to explain her strange new suitor. Finally, she caught sight of him. Gracen stood near the raised thrones of the royal family. He was speaking to the queen. He looked like he would be preoccupied for a little longer.

She allowed Crash to lead her toward the opposite end of the ballroom, where a series of glass doors exited out onto a white marble balcony. The balcony appeared empty due to the cold weather. Crossing the crowded ballroom was no easy task, but they made it to the doors. She tried to open one of them, but it was frozen shut.

Crash reached past her and pushed the door open with a firm shove.

Sora immediately regretted stepping out into the cold night. A thin layer of perspiration covered her arms and neck from the dance, which only made the wind more biting. She hesitated near the doors, where the curve of the building somewhat blocked the wind.

"Perhaps this wasn't the best idea," she said.

"It will do," he replied, allowing the door to shut behind them.

Sora scanned the balcony for any sign of the Shade, but it was empty. Then she crossed her arms, shivering.

"Well? What did you want to talk about?" she asked.

Crash's gloved hand stroked down her cheek. "I can't allow you to endanger yourself any longer. Please, give me the weapon. I will face Cerastes for you."

"We discussed this. It's a risk I've chosen to take," she replied.

"You're just a young girl," he insisted, and took a step forward, crowding her into a corner. "You can't possibly stand against a Grandmaster as skilled as Cerastes. I will shield you from him. Give me the weapon."

Sora realized his hand had moved from her cheek to the bow. She wore it slung over her shoulder. The thought crossed her mind that he might try to rip it away from her. In the distance, she heard the vague jingle of a tambourine, except it wasn't in time to the music from the ballroom. She realized, belatedly, that the sound of bells was coming from her own head.

Her skin turned colder than the snow.

"Remove your mask," she said.

Crash turned Sora in his arms again. The shocked expression had finally left her face, and she gazed at him through hooded eyes. He knew what that look meant, and felt the heat of his own body rise in response.

She slid her hand down the front of her bodice enticingly, seductively. He inhaled, unable to look away.

He almost didn't see the knife.

The blade flashed as she drew it from her wide skirts. She tried to stab him in the torso.

Crash responded without thinking. He twisted her arm to the side and kicked her feet out from under her.

The dancers around them stumbled, recovered, and continued moving counterclockwise around the floor. No one stopped.

Sora hissed at him, her hairpiece askew. Her mask fell off and clattered to the ground. Then the air shimmered. The headdress became a brown scarf. Her extravagant dress turned into a pile of rags.

Malice twisted Krait's blind, scarred face. She raised the knife again, ready to lunge.

Thwup!

An arrow landed at her feet. Krait looked up at the ceiling.

Crash didn't have time to deal with her. He shoved her into the dancers, then plunged in the opposite direction, wading through the tide of people in desperate search of Sora. If Krait had been sent to distract him, that meant Cerastes was here at the ball, and if Sora was alone....

Flashes of green light caught his attention. His head turned. Far across the dance floor, beyond the wreaths of hanging ribbons, the crystalline lanterns and ice sculptures, he saw a wall of glass doors leading outside.

He saw another flicker of colored light beyond the doors, out in the darkness. *Damn.*

At that moment, the dancers came to a slow and delicate halt as the song ended. They held their different poses until the music completely faded, then they all broke into applause, some laughing, some cheering. Crash found himself blocked by a wall of dresses.

The ensemble of musicians stood and bowed to the guests. Then, in a loud voice, a steward announced, "The musicians shall take an hour of rest! Meanwhile, please give your attention to our beloved royal family as the king welcomes us into the new year!"

Everyone cheered again and began to shuffle toward the raised dais at the other end of the room. Crash found himself heading opposite the tide of people. He braced himself against the bulky skirts, towering hats and wigs, his eyes set on the distant glass doors to the balcony. He didn't know where Krait had disappeared to, if she had followed him or gone elsewhere. Natrix, as well, had yet to show herself.

He didn't care if an entire army of the Shade waited for him outside those doors. He could only think of reaching Sora.

CHAPTER 19

With a growing sense of dismay, Sora wrenched away from the assassin and dislodged his mask. It clattered to the ground.

As she had suspected, the man before her only vaguely resembled Crash. Pronounced veins stood out upon his neck and forehead. His skin looked like parchment, thin and creased, and he wore his inky black hair in a knot at the base of his neck.

Sora continued to back away, putting distance between them. He didn't follow her across the stone pavilion, but stood as still, as marblesque, as a statue.

"Do you know who I am?" he asked.

"Yes."

"Then you know what I want."

Sora shielded the bow from him, knowing it was too late to run.

"Give me the weapon and I won't kill you."

She had expected to feel fear—but she only felt red hatred for the man before her, for the suffering he had wrought upon her kingdom. *Yes, my kingdom,* she thought: the human court she had once loathed, the nobility she had once mocked, the peasants she now pitied. She would protect all of them.

"I, too, know who you are, stone-bearer," Cerastes spoke, snakelike. "You've cost the Viper his life. You must know that. I would have made him a general, a prince, but you stole away his destiny. You don't even know the crime you've committed."

He's provoking me, Sora thought. *Stay focused.*

Cerastes' grin showed his gray gums and elongated teeth.

"I have your attention now, do I? Viper can't be like you. Not when he is like me. That is love's meaning to our kind—to be at war with ourselves—to hate what we are, what we cannot be." Cerastes spread his hands. "I would accept him as he is—train him to be better, to reach the pinnacle of our kind's power. I would show him, but he is blind to me. You are his teacher now. You can teach him to be human, but you can't undo his nature. He is a demon. He will return to the chaos from which he was formed."

Sora realized she was clutching the Dark God's bow with shaking hands.

"Viper—Crash—can be whoever he wants to be," she said.

Cerastes laughed. "So, by that logic, whoever I desire to be, I shall become? Such revelation!" Then his laugh turned cruel. "What we are born as, we cannot change."

Then, without warning, he was directly in front of her. He struck her torso with a fist that felt more like a hammer. Her corset crunched as whalebone shattered, and then she flew back across the pavilion, her feet off the ground, until she slammed into an icy stone pillar.

She slid to the floor of the pavilion, her head spinning. She tasted blood in her mouth.

The sacred weapon prodded her in the back, pinned under her body.

"My spies tell me Viper has been training you," Cerastes said. He watched her from where she had once stood, almost thirty feet away. "Let's see it, then, *savant*. Are you ready to take a Name?"

Sora struggled to her feet, her head ringing, and grabbed the sacred longbow in one hand. She held it across her body as she would her staff—it was almost the same length.

With a thought, she summoned her Cat's Eye.

This time, she heard subtle warning bells before Grandmaster Cerastes vanished. This time, she raised the bow to defend herself.

He appeared behind her and struck her between the shoulder blades, hard enough to knock the wind from her lungs. She fell to her knees, her skirts twisting. She heard fabric rip as her hoops tangled and broke. Fumbling, Sora undid the clasps that held the panniers in place, and detangled herself. She crawled from her dress like a bug from a cocoon, shivering in the snow in her undergarments.

On all fours, Sora felt her skin prickle. The Cat's Eye's light flickered blue, then back to green. Some part of the *garrolithe's* power, its fearless strength, remained within her. She sniffed the air, picking out Cerastes' toxic scent. The night became sharper.

This time, she attacked. She swung the bow. He vanished, and when he reappeared, she lunged at him, changing direction fluidly. She struck him across the face with the end of the bow. A spatter of blood graced the snow.

When he looked at her, she almost lost her stomach. Her blow had ripped the skin from his cheek like tearing through paper. Part of his nose was gone. In its place, she did not see a skull, but black, swirling smoke and sticky, shiny blood.

Cerastes raised a skeletal finger to his lips. *Shhh.* Then, as though slicking back his hair, he ran his hand across his cheek and smoothed his skin back in place, restoring his facade.

Sora touched her necklace, drawing upon the knowledge of her ancestors, of past stone-bearers, asking for their skill and strength. Now that the *garrolithe* was gone from her necklace, she felt a new ease of control. Green light encased her body like a suit of armor.

This time, when she struck Cerastes, her hands moved faster, guided by the bearers that had come before her. Each time she landed a blow, or blocked one of his, her hands flashed with green light.

With some satisfaction, she could tell he was taken off guard. For a time, she was able to push him back across the pavilion, but she still sensed he was toying with her, biding his time, waiting for *something*. His gaze returned to her necklace over and over again. He didn't hide his fascination.

Only her continuous motion kept her from collapsing, heavy, in the snow. Dare she run back inside the ballroom, back into the warmth and firelight, to seek help? Should she risk bringing the battle closer to the nobility? She didn't want to endanger any lives. Cerastes wouldn't hesitate to kill anyone in his path...and yet he seemed to hesitate when it came to her. Occasionally, he reminded her of his speed, his ferocity, but then he stepped back, pacing himself. *Is he testing me? Or studying the Cat's Eye?* she wondered. Perhaps he was simply waiting for her to drop from exhaustion.

Then his hand slipped through her defenses, and Cerastes reached for her necklace. Sora gasped, stumbling backward.

Snap!

His hand drew too close to the stone, and a flash of green electricity crackled between them. He recoiled, burned. A strange sound emitted from his throat as he clutched his hand: a strangled laugh, or a stifled groan of pain?

Sora regained her footing and stood her ground. She watched him cautiously.

"I wondered what would happen if I tore it from your neck," he said. "Not quite as easy as I had thought."

"The races can't touch the stone," Sora said, her voice hoarse from the cold air. "It will draw the magic right out of you. Even kill you, if you like."

"And that is how the war was won, and the world ended," he mused.

"The world didn't end."

"It did, for us."

They faced each other. Flecks of snow began to fall from the sky. Sora felt the cold night drag at her body, trying to pull her to the ground. She was shaking uncontrollably now, down to her knickers and broken corset, with the Dark God's weapon clutched in one hand. Why hadn't he tried to take it from her yet?

Suddenly a door to her left swung open, forced by a powerful arm. Three figures spilled onto the snowbound terrace.

Cerastes turned calmly to face them.

"Ah, Viper. Did you enjoy the dance?"

Crash was wearing a black suit identical to Cerastes. Krait stood next to him and slightly behind. The girl's hair was in disarray, half-hiding her face. Her eyes looked wild, seeing without seeing. She clutched a dagger in one hand and looked ready for blood.

Crash's eyes darted back and forth between Sora and Cerastes.

"Get away from her," he said.

"I will in time," Cerastes assured him.

Then his attention was drawn by the third figure that emerged behind Crash and Krait.

Natrix released the crossbow bolt without warning.

Cerastes raised his hand and caught it in his flesh. The arrow pierced through his palm.

Two chakrams followed the arrow, and Cerastes threw himself to one side. The first bladed ring flew past his head, just missing his neck, while the second embedded itself in his leg.

With a cry, Cerastes fell, but his magic saved him. He flickered out of existence, and reappeared directly behind Sora.

For a moment, she didn't realize why the entire party had turned to her. Then Cerastes took her upper arm in a steel grip. He dragged the sacred weapon from her grasp.

"No!" Sora gasped and struggled, but he slammed the bow into the side of her head, and the world spun. He didn't release her, but pinned her to his side.

"Natrix," Cerastes said through gritted teeth, "how *surprising* to see you."

"It has been many years, my brother."

"Brother, indeed. I had plans for the Viper, but now I see you have plans as well. Shall I tell him why you're here?"

Natrix arched one of her eyebrows. "He knows his fate in the Hive. He came to us on his own. I am here to stop you, Cerastes."

Natrix's words seemed to enrage him.

"Why?" Cerastes snapped. "Why defend the Hive? You doubt the sanctity of their ways; you always have. Join the Shade and you can have the freedom you crave."

"Assuming that is what I crave." Natrix twirled a chakram around her wrist. "You and I differ greatly from each other, Cerastes, but you already know that. Give me the girl and the sacred weapon. End this madness. The Dark God has no love for you or any other living thing."

Alarm bells went off in Sora's head as Cerastes opened a shadow portal. She met Crash's eyes across the snowy pavilion. She saw the turmoil in his gaze.

"I have many surprises planned for the Hive," Cerastes said. "One of them lies beyond this portal. Follow me, if you are ready."

Sora could have stopped the shadow portal with her Cat's Eye, but she knew that wherever Cerastes intended to take her, she would find the other sacred weapons. She had to go with him. She couldn't allow him to win. In taking her to sacred ground, he would seal his own fate.

And she, in turn, would seal her fate as well. She would sacrifice her life for the world. She was surprised by her own clarity, and her determination.

She met Crash's eyes one last time.

Then Cerastes plunged through the portal.

Crash watched, a shout caught in his throat, as Cerastes stepped through the shadow portal with Sora in his arms.

Natrix ran past him, drawing symbols in the air with her hands, muttering words of power. Her own shadow flew up from the ground to stop Cerastes, but too late. The Grandmaster had vanished.

Natrix skidded to a halt before the portal, which Cerastes had left open to taunt them. She cursed under her breath.

"We must follow," she said.

"Death awaits you on the other side," Krait sneered.

Crash grabbed Krait by the nape of her neck. She thrust her blade at him, but he wrenched it from her hand. He shook her like a kitten.

"When will you learn that I am stronger than you?" he hissed. "If you hope to ever see your master again, you'll do exactly as we say." Then he dragged her across the snow to Natrix's side. He flung Krait between them and she landed on her knees, her head bowed. She seemed content to rest there, submissive for the moment.

"Is it wise to plunge through the portal headlong?" Crash asked. Every bone in his body yearned to rush through the portal and reach Sora's side, but if it meant losing his head, he would wait.

"We're not plunging through blind," Natrix said, her hands still held out before her, her shadow stretched into the darkness. "This portal leads to the clocktower. I can see the path Cerastes has taken. I don't sense his presence on the other side." Concern flickered across her face. "This is most assuredly a trap."

"Aren't you curious?" Krait breathed.

"I know you are," Crash said, and dragged her back to her feet. Then he shoved her through the portal.

He unsheathed his Named dagger from his belt. "Let's go."

He entered the darkness. Icy wind howled past him. He emerged on the other side slightly off balance. Slick cobblestones met his feet. Above him, a few street lamps glimmered through the thickening snow.

Natrix exited the portal behind him with a chakram held in each hand. The circular steel blades glinted orange in the dying streetlamps. Before them, the height of the clocktower stretched into the sky like an iron-gray plateau. They stood in the frozen courtyard at its base. Crash turned in a slow circle, looking for Cerastes. The shadow portal had closed behind them. They stood in an abandoned construction yard ringed by a stone wall. On every side, piles of broken rocks, discarded dirt or old lumber lay beneath a growing layer of snow.

Across the yard, another dim light caught his attention. Crash hardly noticed it at first, but his eyes returned to it again and again. It seemed to be growing brighter. Or closer.

A manlike shape emerged through the falling snow. Like some disfigured aberration, it struggled forward in short, uneven steps. Wet rags enwrapped its being; a black and putrid substance dripped to the ground. The creature stank of death and rot. Crash found himself recoiling.

"What is this abomination?" he heard Natrix murmur at his side.

Crash had seen corpses reanimated by the plague, or by Volcrian's magic, but this was different. As the thing grew closer, a queer sensation traveled over his skin, like music with no sound.

"Is that...a Harpy?" Natrix asked, and took the slightest step back.

A Harpy. Crash felt that strange, muted vibration cross over his skin again. Realization dawned, and his skin crawled. Somehow, Cerastes had gotten hold of Caprion. *But how?* It didn't seem possible. Crash doubted himself until the figure drew closer and he saw the skeletal framework of wings protruding from its back.

"Multiple sets of wings," Natrix said. "A seraph? Is that possible?"

"It is," Crash said grimly.

Seraphim were the greatest threats to the Sixth Race. They were created to hunt demons, and only Caprion carried six wings, tripling his power.

Except now the six-winged seraph had been infested by the plague. *Is that even possible?* Crash wondered, but the scent of the underworld clung to the Harpy's clothes.

"Look there," Natrix said softly from his side, and pointed.

Behind Caprion, far to the left of the compound, Crash saw a wooden staircase protruding from a hole in the ground. The snow around it was indented by footprints. Cerastes must have taken Sora down there, into the underground tunnels beneath the city. They had to reach Cerastes before he could enact the ritual from *The Book of the Named*.

Crash turned back to the abomination before him. Caprion halted a few meters away. Now, he could see the Harpy's gray, colorless skin and the black veins coiling down his neck and arms. A dirty gray bandage covered his mouth. He couldn't use his voice. He stared at Crash with white, hollow eyes. For all intents and purposes, he looked dead, except for his upright position.

A second figure joined Caprion's side—Krait. Of course. Crash had almost forgotten about her. *So this is Cerastes' trap.* It suited his Grandmaster's sadistic sense of humor.

"Well? Is your curiosity satisfied?" Krait mocked. She held her bullwhip in one hand.

Natrix answered. "Savant, can't you see this vileness and corruption? This is not the purpose of our race. You've been deceived. Return to me. Return to the Hive. Until your last breath, you still have a choice."

Crash noticed Krait's hesitation. She didn't seem quite as confident as before. She didn't answer, but cracked her whip, striking the stones at Natrix's feet.

The Grandmaster released a slow hiss of air. Then she bent into a fighting stance.

"Come, Viper," she said softly. "Let's see if you've kept up with your practice."

Crash sank into a fighting stance as well, but he couldn't shake his sense of unease. He had never liked Caprion, but the Harpy had been a staunch ally to Sora since their time on the Lost Isles. He did not deserve this fate. Crash hoped Sora hadn't seen the Harpy like this. He imagined how much it would hurt her, and in imagining her pain, he could feel it.

Caprion drew his sword—a blade that once burned with the fire of the heavens, but was now extinguished.

Crash drew his Named dagger and rushed at the Harpy. Natrix followed on his heels.

CHAPTER 20

Ferran bowed low after his brother handed the sealed scroll into the king's hands.

Lord Gracen, who stood at the queen's elbow, was listening.

Behind them, the entire ballroom full of hundreds of nobles stood still and quiet, watching. They knew the protocol, though it hadn't been enacted in over a decade, to reinstate a disowned brother.

When Martin spoke, he projected his voice over the audience like an actor in a play.

"It is my desire, your royal highness, that Ferran be reinstated as an heir to the Ebonaire fortune, with all of his titles in tact. I have written my wishes in this contract that, with your signature, will make official his return to the Ebonaire line."

King Royce was a well-built man who, despite his wizened age, didn't look a day over fifty. His hair was still thick, if shock-white, and his skin was smooth and unblemished, except for a spattering of dark freckles above his left eyebrow. He wore a stately gold vest under his boar-skin mantle. A heavy gold crown weighed down his brow.

The queen sat next to him. She wore a mask that looked like a golden sun, and a dress of many blues and russet reds and yellows. Her costume was the same every year: the first day of winter.

The king took Martin's sealed scroll with a solemn frown about his lips, broke the seal, and read the contract therein.

Ferran stood patiently and waited. This was, of course, just protocol. Martin and the king had already reviewed the scroll that morning.

King Royce finished reading and rolled the scroll back up in his hands.

"I approve this proclamation of legitimacy and shall have it sent immediately to the royal registry where it will be officialized. Ferran Ebonaire, take your knee."

Ferran did so, kneeling down on one knee and bowing his head. The king touched him upon both shoulders with his scepter.

"You may rise Lord Ferran Ebonaire, heir to the Ebonaire estate, with all the rights and titles provided for therein."

"Thank you, my liege," he murmured.

Behind him the crowd broke into uproarious applause.

"My blessings to the Ebonaire family," the queen said to Martin, "and may your health remain strong for many more years. My deepest sympathy again, Lord Ebonaire, for the passing of your wife."

Martin bowed. "You honor her memory, my queen."

Ferran turned to face the ballroom and bowed again, then stepped down from the dais with Martin at his side. He shook Martin's hand as they entered the crowd. Ferran found himself surrounded by many more handshakes and claps on the shoulder as lords and ladies from different estates approached him. He didn't recognize any of their faces, particularly behind their masks.

The full weight of the evening settled on his shoulders, and he released a long breath. Now that he was an Ebonaire again, officialized before the entire First Tier, he had a lot of names to learn. *Am I truly ready for this?* he wondered. *Do I truly want it?* He would always be a treasure hunter at heart, but he supposed, deep down, he did want to return to his roots. It was time.

Then the king stood up and raised his arms in the air. The room quieted again. Every face turned expectantly toward the royal family.

Martin took Ferran by the elbow and drew him to the side of the dais, between two tall marble pillars. There, they waited as the king prepared to make his formal speech for winter solstice.

"This year has been challenging for all of us. Uncertainty and illness plague our kingdom. But on this night, we celebrate what makes our kingdom strong: our loyalty to each other, our generosity, and our courage...."

As the king spoke, Ferran kept glancing to his left where Burn waited for him at the servant's hall. He could see the Wolfy's giant shadow flickering against the wall at the mouth of the corridor. Burn had been waiting there, watching over the royal family and guarding the hallway, since the dance had commenced. He wondered when the prince's so-called uprising would begin.

Lord Gracen stood at the queen's side looking equally alert. Ferran recalled that Sora had accompanied Gracen to the dance, and he scanned the nearby crowd for her blue dress, but didn't recognize it among the sea of masked faces. Of course, she would be difficult to spot in such a large room. He trusted that she was safe with Crash and Natrix watching over her. Surely, if the Shade were present, there would have been a sign by now. In the meantime, he had to guard the royal family.

The king finished his speech to the applause of hundreds of adoring nobility. Then Prince Peric stood from his seat next to the king and took his father's place at the front of the room. Ferran shared a suspicious glance with his brother.

The prince began speaking.

"My loyal subjects," he said, "neighbors and countrymen; young heirs and blooming daughters; fat dowagers and bent patriarchs; I welcome you to First Winter's Ball."

The nobility applauded, though Ferran didn't miss the mutters that ran through the crowd.

"Once, far back in our history, our primitive kind believed that winter solstice was a time of renewal and rebirth; a time when the barrier between the underworld and our own weakened; a time when the soul, ever changing as the wind, could don a new face. Well isn't that appropriate, considering the new face of our kingdom that frowns in discontent?

"This past year, rot and disease have befallen our kingdom. Our livestock are dying; our crops are rotting; our temple has been burned to the ground. The common people are crying out for help. If not for the upper tiers, this kingdom would have dissolved into chaos long ago. We are its strength--its living, beating heart. For that reason, the gates to the city were closed to protect us. To protect every single one of you in this room. *I did that.*"

The audience seemed tense and uncertain.

"The true strength of our kingdom does not lie in such vague concepts as courage or generosity, but in our willingness to *act*, our willingness to sacrifice for *self preservation*. This is not the time to cater to a mass of frightened cattle. I do not consider myself bold in proclaiming that my father—our beloved king—should either address the kingdom's concerns, or step down, and leave the kingdom in more efficient hands."

"What is this?" the king grunted, but the queen's hand stayed him.

Angry voices sounded throughout the room.

"What is this heresy?"

"Is he asking for the king to step down?"

"He isn't wrong...."

"Perhaps the rumors are true...."

Ferran found himself reaching for the sword concealed beneath his brown greatcoat.

The prince turned to his father, a sickly smile on his face. In his hands, he held out a gold box, which he opened to reveal a bejeweled pocket watch. It glimmered in the lantern light. The guests standing close enough to see it gasped.

"For my father," the prince announced, "in honor of the completion of his clocktower project, I present him with this pocket watch, a treasure I hope he will wear proudly upon his breast until his final days. It is *time*, father, to step down, and allow a younger generation to reign."

The prince twisted his words with dry humor, and an uncertain bout of laughter trickled across the room. He presented the watch to his father, who stood up from his throne and took it in hand.

An odd smell teased Ferran's nose, and he found himself stepping forward. Martin grabbed at his arm, but Ferran shrugged him off.

In a few long strides, Ferran crossed to the king's side. He grabbed the king's wrist. They stood there, the three of them, staring at one another, their hands united over the watch.

"What is the meaning of this?" Prince Peric hissed.

"Release the watch, my liege," Ferran said, his skin already crawling. "It's tainted with the plague."

The king frowned. He looked down at his hand where he gripped the watch, and all three men saw the black veins beginning to form down his fingers. With a gasp, the king let go and shoved the prince away from him. Ferran stood with the watch in hand.

Peric stumbled backward, teetering at the edge of the dais.

"How dare you!" the prince and the king roared at the same time, for entirely different reasons.

Then Cedric Daniellian, from somewhere in the masked audience, shouted, "To arms! To arms! To arms!"

Guests began to scream. Ferran realized, too late, that the prince's insurgents were actually in the audience, disguised as servants or even noblemen wearing masks. He saw a member of the nobility fall under the swing of a blade, and another man raise a cane to defend himself.

Within seconds, the entire ballroom dissolved into chaos. Ferran couldn't respond immediately. Instead, he focused on the pocketwatch in his hand. His Cat's Eye glowed red. He cleared the plague from the item, rendering it harmless, and he dropped it to the ground.

When he looked up, the prince was staring at him, his face twisted into a spiteful snarl. He appeared frozen in shock and rage.

Then Lord Gracen leapt from the podium and tackled the prince to the floor. Ferran joined him, and together, they dragged the struggling prince back to the king's throne. There, Gracen chained him to the heavy gilded chair.

The queen stood over her wayward son, a string of epithets and reprimands on her lips. An arrow struck the ground nearby, bouncing from the marble tile, and Gracen took the queen by the arm and dragged her bodily away. At his signal, Burn stepped onto the dais to escort the queen and princess to safety. With some amount of urging, he took the royal women back to the servant's corridor where they disappeared down the hall, presumably back to the royal chambers, where they would be safer.

As the princess and queen left the ball, the royal guard flooded the room, their plated armor glinting. Gracen greeted them with more orders. He directed his men to different pockets of the room where the insurgents were terrorizing the nobility. The thickest ring of soldiers remained around the king, who had drawn the sword at his hip.

"Protect the king!" Gracen bellowed, and Ferran heard the cry taken up in separate parts of the room.

Protect the king, indeed, he thought. It seemed that Gracen was more than prepared to defend the royal family. The insurgents didn't seem to have strong leadership, and several groups had already surrendered. They had relied on the prince to lead them against an unprotected king, but Gracen had nipped their plan in the bud.

"Ferran, look there!"

Ferran turned at the sound of his brother's voice. Martin stood a few dozen feet away, pointing desperately. Ferran followed his arm in time to see a masked figure, in the colors of the Daniellian house, creeping behind the royal dais to the servant's hall.

"Go!" Martin called, even as the crowd carried him in the opposite direction. "Stop him!"

Ferran struggled through the current of panicked people, then finally broke clear and dashed after Cedric down the servants' corridor. At first Cedric walked, but then he heard Ferran's pounding footsteps behind him and took off at a run. He held his mask over his face with one hand and didn't look back.

Ferran sprinted after him. The servants' corridor split off into many different hallways that doubtlessly led to separate areas of the royal palace. Ferran had no idea where they were going, and he didn't think Cedric had much of an idea, either. He saw no sign of Burn or the queen, and could only assume they were somewhere safe and far away.

Ahead of them, the corridor turned sharply to the left. Ferran could smell the heavy scent of spices and roasting meat. He barreled after Cedric around the corner, and immediately plunged into a hallway filled with panicked servants and kitchen staff. He caught a glimpse of Cedric up ahead, shoving people out of his way.

"Stop that man!" he roared, pointing. The staff did the opposite, falling away from Cedric as though a wolf ran past them. "Stop him! Dammit! Are you deaf?"

Someone listened. A short blond boy sprung from a conjoining hallway and tackled Cedric to the ground. The boy grappled with Cedric, who was almost twice his size, and managed to twist the nobleman's arm behind him. Cedric let out a piercing squeal, and Ferran thought his arm might be broken.

Then the boy rolled Cedric over, sat on his chest and started pummeling his face. Blood spattered the plush green rug beneath them.

The boy's green velvet hat fell off, revealing a swath of white linen bandages wrapped around his head. As Ferran reached their side, he realized the short boy was most definitely a woman, and for better or worse, it was Lorianne.

He grabbed her and wrenched her from Cedric's body. Cedric's swollen, black-and-blue face was nigh unrecognizable.

"He's done," he said, dragging her into his arms. "He's finished."

Lori fought him for an instant, then collapsed into his chest with a sob.

"I was going to kill him," she mumbled, "I was going to kill him." She muttered the words over and over between her tears, and Ferran realized, as a Healer, she would have broken her vows to the goddess.

He cradled her, shielding her from the eyes of curious servants.

"Have you lost your bloody mind?" he murmured into her hair. "Your concussion...how did you get here...."

"I took a horse and followed you. I'm sorry," she sobbed. "I'm sorry. I was wrong. Please don't let me go. The room is spinning."

He held her and watched Cedric on the ground, who eventually groaned and tried to sit up. Then, without losing his grip on Lori, he placed his heavy boot over Cedric's right hand.

"Move, and I'll break your fingers," he said.

Cedric might have scowled at him, but his face looked like raw meat, so Ferran wasn't sure. Eventually, Cedric returned to his sprawled position on the ground, his eyes closed, perhaps losing consciousness. Ferran didn't care. He tightened his hold on Lorianne and promised himself he wouldn't let go.

It felt like hours passed, but it couldn't have been more than thirty minutes before Lord Seabourne appeared down the hallway, running with two soldiers at his back. He reached Ferran, winded, and surveyed the bloody Lord Daniellian.

"I did it," Ferran said, releasing Lori from his arms. He offered his hands up for arrest. "I got a bit carried away, but he's still alive. He let the insurgents into the palace. He was trying to escape."

Lord Gracen glanced at Ferran's clean hands, then to Lori's bloody knuckles, but he didn't say anything. He nodded, and a guard grabbed Ferran from behind. Cedric, as well, was lifted off the ground and restrained.

"Lord Ebonaire...it is *Lord* now, isn't it?" Gracen said with a slight grin. "You are under arrest for attacking a fellow nobleman."

"Gladly," Ferran muttered.

Gracen ignored him. "And you, Cedric Daniellian, are under arrest for treason. We shall hold you both in the royal dungeons until we come to a conclusion on this matter."

They began marching Ferran away. They carried Cedric, who only seemed half-conscious and hardly aware of what had transpired, down the hall.

Ferran glanced over his shoulder and gave Lori a roguish smile.

Lori clutched Gracen's arm. "You can't," she whispered. "I did it. I attacked Lord Daniellian. Please let Ferran go."

"Hush, not so loud." Gracen pulled her to a quiet corner of the hall. "Ferran just saved the king's life. I can't imagine anyone more likely to receive a royal pardon. You, however, are a commoner, and if I arrest you for attacking a noble, the punishment will be quite severe."

Lori hardly heard the second half of Gracen's explanation.

"Ferran saved the king?"

"Yes. Quite heroically, I might add." Gracen stepped away from her. "Now, if you will follow me, I will take you to your friend Burn and he can escort you home. You should be resting, Healer, not gallivanting about the royal palace with your bandages half undone. For Ferran's sake, go home."

Lori flushed, only slightly embarrassed. She watched Gracen turn away, his cloak swirling, and march back down the hall. A small smile pulled at her lips. Then she followed him.

CHAPTER 21

The battle against Caprion was not going well. If Cerastes had meant to stall them, then he had succeeded. Caprion's rotted wings carried him effortlessly through the air, and his sword moved as fast as Crash's own. He hardly flinched when Natrix's chakrams struck his thighs and torso, and his wounds didn't bleed.

Krait's whip, though a mere annoyance in comparison, entangled their legs whenever either assassin dropped their guard. She landed several strikes on Crash's forearms and even dealt a few blows to Natrix. Any time they seemed to gain the upper hand on Caprion, Krait was there to knock them back.

Finally, he and Natrix came to a halt in the snow. Crash knelt to one knee, catching his breath. Blood dripped from a dozen stinging wounds on his arms and legs, caused by Krait's bullwhip. Natrix had taken a much stronger blow to her right arm from Caprion's sword, and kept the limb tucked protectively against her side.

Caprion landed atop a crumbling wall at the edge of the construction yard, several meters away. Krait stood below him, in his shadow.

"This is a waste of energy," Crash panted. He spoke under his breath, for Natrix's ears alone.

"Cerastes intends to tire us out," she agreed.

Crash knew the inevitable. One or both of them would have to take on their demon form to defeat the seraph. They had tried everything else.

He fixed Natrix with a weary look and she read his expression clearly.

"No," she said, placing a hand on his shoulder. "He's a seraph. Perhaps he will be stronger against our demons. We don't know."

Crash spat a bit of blood in the snow. "I'm willing to find out."

"We should save our energy for Cerastes," Natrix repeated.

"I have energy to burn."

With that, Crash allowed the gates to fall and his limbs to swell with power. He grew taller, stronger, his skin darkening and hardening as long blades erupted from his shoulders and elbows, down the ridge of his spine, across his skull. His leathery wings emerged. His heat melted the snow on the ground.

Natrix darted ahead of him to engage Caprion. Crash roared, but Natrix didn't allow him to enter the fight. For a moment, the Harpy and the Grandmaster fought, blade screaming against blade as sword and chakram struck. Then Caprion spread his wings and, with a mighty stroke, sent a jarring vibration through the air. It picked up Natrix like an ocean wave and carried her across the construction site. She slammed into a pile of wooden beams and did not get up.

Crash threw himself upon the Harpy, ready to finish the fight.

Krait watched Viper pummel Caprion backwards, one vicious blow after another, until Caprion was slammed back against a stone wall. The gray bandages came loose around the Harpy's mouth. With a horrible retching sound, Caprion curled over and vomited.

The sunstone struck the ground with a ringing vibration. Viper stepped back, away from it.

Krait stared. The sunstone was covered in a black, tarlike substance. She didn't know what made her pick it up, but she did, and wiped the tar off on her leather jerkin.

White light dazzled her eyes, but more so, a stream of unexpected sound issued from the stone. It was a song. Pain split down the middle of her forehead. She dropped the sunstone and clutched her skull with a sudden cry. The light grew blinding, and she fell to her knees. The song resonated through her thoughts, a melody she remembered. She couldn't stop it, couldn't block it out.

And then she saw his face, clear as day. *Cool hands.* She remembered him.

Her vision dimmed, yet in her thoughts, a fog lifted. She smelled it now, the orange breeze of the Lost Isles. She saw a golden sunset beyond the empty white towers of Asterion. The memories flooded her as the sunstone's music stroked her skin. She remembered the abandoned areas of the city where he would take her, entire buildings and parkways submerged in water, and they would spend their time far away from the prying eyes of his people. She remembered the dark prison where he had found her. She remembered that once, they had both been children.

She began to breathe again. She could see his light before her and little else. The shapes of the construction yard were dim shadows against deeper blackness. She was not completely blind, though she had very little sight left.

She heard Natrix's voice. "Kill him!"

She turned toward the Grandmaster and held up her arms.

"Please!" she yelled. "Stop! Please!"

They didn't listen. She saw a blur of movement, though she didn't know who or what moved past her, save for the dim white glow that was Caprion.

"Please," she kept speaking, "please stop fighting. I remember. I remember all of it. Caprion, they're not the enemy. Viper, Grandmaster Natrix, please, listen, I remember now...."

The blur of movement continued, dizzying, frightening. She heard Viper bellow in pain. She thought, perhaps, that Caprion had thrown him to the ground.

She took a sightless step forward.

"Please Caprion...my light, my hope...do you remember? Do you remember our song?" Her voice grew steadier as she walked. Her eyes hurt from straining to see. "Grandmaster Natrix, I remember the Hive. So many years ago, I was merely a child...." She didn't know if she was making any sense. "Grandmaster, I will return with you. Please allow me to undo what Cerastes has done."

Still no one answered her. She slipped on a patch of ice and fell to the ground, where she crawled forward, her fingers scraping along the stone. She must save Caprion; he had fought so hard to save her. She must undo Cerastes' evil. She dragged her body close to where she knew Viper lay, seething, on the ground.

Caprion hovered over his body, and she found his sword pointed at the Viper's chest. She pushed herself between them without fear.

"Caprion, they're not your enemy," she repeated. "Caprion, stop this. You're not yourself."

She climbed back to her feet between the shining light and the smoldering shadow—between Caprion and Viper. She faced the Harpy, relying on her newly recovered memories. She knew him. She felt more certain now in her purpose than she ever had before.

"Long ago, when I was a child, you found me. You saved me from the most horrible fate. You gave me my name: Moss. You fought against your people to free me, and you guarded me from their hatred. Your wings were a shield at my back; your light, always, my guide. Caprion, you are my *beautiful warrior.* Please remember your star." She choked, wondering if he could hear her, or if the Caprion she had known was already dead. "The One Star gave you a great destiny, a destiny I could not follow. Your people tried to kill me, but I survived. They left me on the shore, lost, far away from you. I was saved by an evil man, and I followed him, and I betrayed you. I forgot your face...but I remember now. My sorrow. Gods. Caprion. Answer me! Remember who you are. Answer me, Caprion!"

Briefly his light grew before her, magnanimous, swelling. Her blindness lifted, if only for a moment. She held out her hands, grasping, aching. She reached up and found his face. Felt the planes of his cheeks, the ridge of his jaw. Found his lips.

Viper had kissed her accidentally at the masquerade. That kiss still burned—the truth of it, the conviction. She had experienced so little affection in her short life, but through that kiss, she had known all of love and more.

She gave that gift now to Caprion, praying it would be enough. His lips were cold against hers. *Remember.*

Then something struck her in the stomach, and the wind left her lungs.

* * *

Caprion met Crash's eyes across Krait's body, impaled on his sword. He listened to the last breath of life wheeze from her lungs. Then he dropped his sword—and her body—to the ground.

"No," he murmured, still feeling the imprint of her kiss. He was sick and weak from the plague, but he was himself again, and she was...she was....

He curled around her body, keening the words that wouldn't come. Only sounds issued from his throat, primitive, animalistic. *She's dead. She's gone. I killed her.*

The assassin watched him warily. The second one, Grandmaster Natrix, joined his side. She was limping heavily. Blood streamed down her arm. They stood for a moment over Krait's body, then, as one, they turned toward the wooden scaffolding and the hole that led underground.

Caprion kissed Krait's forehead, her lips, her nose, her mouth. Her body was still warm, and he held her for a long moment, urging her to open her eyes, though he knew she never would again. His hands trailed over her scarred face, her tangled hair. He allowed her blood to spill over him, a baptism, a sacrament.

Then he released her into the snow. He picked up her sunstone, and her song, a lullaby, still sang through the night. He clutched the stone in one hand and felt a new vibration ignite his wings. The light returned to his body, and he lifted up from the ground. He knew, in his heart, what he must do.

"Wait," he said, turning to the two assassins.

They stopped and looked back at him.

"Take her," he said, nodding to Krait's body. "Please, give her a proper burial, one befitting to your kind. Get as far from here as you can go."

Crash stared at him, then said, "Cerastes took Sora. She is down there with him."

"I know. But you cannot be, if you want to live."

Understanding flickered in Crash's gaze. Then he turned and picked up Krait's silent form. Natrix turned to the Harpy and bowed low.

"I have failed in my task to my people," she said, "I am not proud of that, but I am grateful for your presence here, Harpy. It appears, on this holiest of nights, that we are allies. I shall tell my people of your bravery and sacrifice."

"And her," Caprion said, nodding to Krait. "Without her, all would have been lost."

Natrix nodded. "It shall be done."

Then the Grandmaster opened a shadow portal, and Crash lifted Krait in his arms. The three assassins, one dead, two living, disappeared into the darkness.

Caprion focused his power, allowing two, then four bright wings to unfurl from his back. As a seraph, he wielded six wings altogether. His final set, he would save for just a few minutes more. Then he would allow himself to fully ignite. He would channel all the power of the One Star through his body, becoming light itself. And then his song would end.

He descended down the stairwell with Krait's stone in hand. Their songs would end together.

Chapter 22

Sora clutched her bruised shoulder and wondered if she had dislocated it. Half-built granite walls and exposed iron rebar surrounded her on every side. The clocktower was a haunting place, partway constructed, partway decayed, like the exoskeleton of some terrifying corpse.

After transporting her away from the royal palace, Cerastes had taken her down several collapsing corridors to the ground floor of the clocktower. There, he had wrested the Dark God's longbow from her hand. In a short and violent tussle, he had thrown her to the ground amidst a pile of rubble. She had lain still, feigning unconsciousness, hoping he was too impatient to finish her off. And he was. Cerastes had left her behind, the third weapon in hand, and plunged down a black stairwell into the underbelly of the clocktower.

She had activated her Cat's Eye the moment he was gone. Now she stood at the top of the stairwell, surrounded by a protective dome of green light, and looked down. She couldn't hesitate any longer. Cerastes was about to combine the three sacred weapons. She didn't know how to stop him, only that she must.

She wished then, fervently, that she still had the garrolithe's power, but when she touched her necklace, she sensed the beast was very far away. Still, the memory of its courage was enough to fuel her own. She started down the stairwell, using the light of her stone to see by. The stairwell was surprisingly short and led her to a hallway paved with flagstone. At the end of the hallway was a wooden ladder leading even deeper underground.

Down the wooden ladder, she found herself in an ancient stone corridor that looked much older than the clocktower's construction, or even the city's sewer system. She traced the stone wall with her hand as she walked, and noticed the sharp stab of frost under her fingertips. The tunnel was frozen, and the thin stream of water at her feet hardened by ice. Her boots crunched softly with each step.

Several minutes passed. Then Sora came across an intersection of tunnels. A pile of abandoned rubble and mortar blocked two of the corridors. A third continued to her right, angled downward through earth and clay. She saw no footsteps, but instinct told her Cerastes had passed this way.

Down the earthen tunnel, the air changed, growing thicker and hotter. Static filled her clothes and made locks of hair lift from her shoulders. The dim jingle of bells accompanied her steps—a soft warning. Through her Cat's Eye, Sora sensed the pressure mounting in the air, until her ears popped. Sacred ground on winter solstice night—the very earth seemed alive.

Finally, ahead of her, she saw a dim red light. A hole appeared in the wall to her left, and belatedly, she realized she had come upon the sacred chamber.

She stood at the narrow opening and peered beyond. Moody, crimson light from several torches illuminated the interior of the temple. Marble pylons supported the chamber's domed ceiling, and ancient stone paved the floor. It was strikingly tall and wide, a much bigger space than she had envisioned. To one side of the chamber stood a heavy iron door. She guessed it was inaccessible from the outside, since Cerastes had tunneled through the wall. Where she stood was not level with the sacred ground; she would need to drop down about six feet to enter the chamber.

Perhaps the most striking, and terrifying, image in the room was of a malevolent, glowering face carved into the far wall. It spanned the chamber from floor to ceiling. As Sora stared at it, the cruel, narrow holes of its eyes seemed to find her. Its nostrils flared. Its mouth twisted into a contemptuous snarl. Did it move, or did the firelight trick her eyes?

At the middle of the circular chamber was a slab of uncut stone. The Dark God's three sacred weapons had been laid upon it in a perfect triangle: the sword hilt, the unstrung bow and the spearhead. From her angle near the ceiling, she could almost see how the three objects would form a key, when placed together in the right order.

A black figure danced between the malevolent stone face and the unhewn altar. Sora's eyes were drawn to Cerastes. He swept his arms slowly from one side to the other, his shadow twisting around him like a serpent. Then he knelt, scraping invisible symbols into the floor, then stood, drawing more symbols in the air. She heard his voice, like a whisper of sand, frantically muttering words in a language she didn't recognize. As he spoke, another red torch flared to life in the room, this one at the base of the statue. It seemed, then, that the statue moved, its mouth curling into a leer. The ground rumbled, and black smoke began to pour forth from its great stone nostrils to cover the altar in a blanket of mist.

We're out of time, Sora realized.

She tried to slip through the hole into the room, but an invisible barrier stopped her. She tested the barrier with her hands; it seemed both fragile and strong, like a spider's web. At her touch, several black strands glittered into existence, like strings of tar, so thin they were nearly invisible. She sent a command to her Cat's Eye, and with a resounding chime, the stone disarmed the spell. The barrier fell away. Then she dropped into the room.

The air of the chamber was stiflingly hot and humid. Within seconds, sweat beaded her skin and soaked the back of her neck. Sora felt her lungs grow heavy. It was difficult to breathe through the oppressive energy of Cerastes' spell.

The Grandmaster either didn't hear her or ignored her and continued his incantations. The black mist grew thicker. Sora fought her body's discomfort and forced herself closer to the altar. She touched her necklace and reached out the other hand toward the sacred weapons.

"Shield," she murmured.

Green light flowed from her hand to form a dome around the altar, blocking the mist.

Silence filled the room as Cerastes stopped muttering. He turned to face her.

She met his eyes and almost screamed. The skin had melted from his face like candle wax, and in its place was something she couldn't describe, something inhuman and horrible and empty—something like the contorted monster on the wall.

"I was going to let you live," he said simply. Then he raised his hand and his own shadow rose with it. Then his shadow darted across the ground toward her, melting the stone where it passed.

Before Sora could react, the shadow was upon her, engulfing her with stifling heat. She couldn't breathe—it was choking her. Her Cat's Eye responded without her prompting; it abandoned the sacred weapons and came to her defense, absorbing the shadow into itself, draining Cerastes' power.

He cursed and tried to pull back, but the Cat's Eye had a grip on him now, and wouldn't release his shadow. The sacred ground made the stone much more powerful, like a center of gravity in a vacuum. His voice filled the room with echoes.

"Such a nuisance! Such an ungodly abomination, an insult to the Elements, you are a sniveling child, you are *grotesque....*" Another string of curses fell from his lips. Then, suddenly, Cerastes was at her back. "I guess I will have to dismantle you by hand."

Sora turned in time to block his strike, but one blow sent her crashing to the ground. He kicked her in the ribs, hard enough to send her tumbling into one of the marble columns. She hit it hard enough to leave cracks in the stone. A shower of dust fell upon her head, and Sora curled into a ball. She struggled to pull in a breath of air. She thought she might have broken a rib.

Cerastes tried to use his magic to lift her into the air, but again, the Cat's Eye counteracted him. With a cry of outrage, he appeared before her and lifted her by the throat. His touch burned her skin like hot coals. His other hand hovered near her stone, unable to touch it, yet his fingers curled in yearning.

Sora stared into his face, horrified. She would have screamed, but she couldn't breathe. The power of his demon bled through his physical body, rotting it. Flesh dripped from his face, skin unraveling in ribbons, exposing the evil beneath.

"I don't have time to play with you," he said through dry lips. A flake of dead skin landed on her cheek. "Will you have me punish the Viper more than I already have? Will you have me kill you?"

Through his mocking, acidic tone, Sora thought she heard a whisper of regret. But it meant nothing. Even locked together in this suffocating room under the earth, he toyed with her.

She forced herself to stare into the ruins of his face. Beneath the mask, Cerastes did not exist—only the demon, and even then, beneath the demon, something far worse.

Struggling to control her limbs, she managed to grab his wrist. Her grip was pathetic, weak as a child's, her fingers difficult to move. Then she opened herself to the magic saturating the ancient chamber. An ineffable groan escaped her lips. With fierce concentration, she bid the Cat's Eye to move. She felt it pull upon Cerastes' magic, and she sought out a deeper current, attempting to draw upon his life force the way she had Volcrian. *Drain him,* she thought. *End him.*

With a roar of outrage, Cerastes cast her away. She tumbled across the floor to the base of the altar, where black mist encircled the sacred weapons. She saw threads of darkness weaving between the sword hilt and the bow, the bow and the spearhead. *Too late,* she thought. *I'm too late.* The weapons were beginning to transform into the key. She looked up at the angry stone face on the wall, and for a moment, it was as though a god stared down at her, its seething mouth agape, prepared to devour her soul.

Then white light entered her vision. She looked up and found Caprion standing over her. He looked different. Black rings circled his eyes and a sickly pallor tainted his skin.

"Caprion," she gasped, "the weapons...."

He lifted her into his arms. In two seconds, she was suddenly at the heavy iron door of the chamber. Caprion sang a few words under his breath, and the symbols on the door glowed to life. She heard gears churn, and slowly, the door opened.

"This is a song-spell laid by the Harpies to seal this chamber for eternity," he said. "Cerastes has released a powerful and malevolent energy from the earth. I must stop him."

Sora could barely arrange her thoughts. "Let me help you...."

"No." He said the word gently and touched her face. "Go in strength and courage, Lady Sora. Your destiny is not to die here. The Wind Goddess isn't finished with you yet. But my God of Light, the One Star...." He turned back to the seething furnace of the room. "My Song is calling me."

She saw a look on his face that she couldn't explain. A lion's look. And she knew, even at the end of her days, when time had turned her bones to glass and her spirit had outgrown her body, she would still remember it.

"When I shut this door, use your Cat's Eye to summon your strongest shield. And pray."

Caprion didn't give her a chance to reply. He closed the iron door and she was left in the dark.

She curled herself into a ball, holding her Cat's Eye tightly in her left hand, and buried herself in its green light.

Caprion faced Cerastes.

This was not the first Grandmaster he had fought. Cerastes was powerful only because he drew upon the Dark God's essence. But Caprion, too, had been called upon by a god. Caprion, too, had been blessed with the sacred power of his race.

The smoke had stopped pouring from the statue's nostrils and now surrounded the three sacred weapons in a dark curtain. Beyond that curtain, sparks of red energy ignited the air. Pressure in the chamber continued to increase.

Cerastes no longer looked like a man, though what replaced him was something so far removed from the mortal plane, it defied description.

"The regal star returns. Where is Krait? Did you kill my little servant?" his voice sneered, seeping through the statue's snarling mouth. "She was such a diligent puppet."

The sound of her name amplified his Song. He could hear it now as a symphony playing in the dark, the drum his heartbeat, the chorus his blood, pounding, surging, a stampede of music.

"She betrayed you in the end," Caprion said. "I wouldn't be here without her sacrifice."

The Grandmaster laughed.

"Sacrifice. Sacrilege. Most die in greed or a poverty of wealth, starving for youth, starving for lust or bread or honor, but men like you and I, we die for our convictions. We die for our *corruptions*. Which do you intend to die for, Harpy? For your god, or for *her?*"

"For my Song," Caprion said, his voice ringing like a bell. Around his body, his aura intensified, shedding bright light throughout the room. "Music is as immaterial as the soul. It may not fill a rich man's pockets, and it may not lend power to your hands, but its vibration, the true evidence of life, resonates throughout the world and once issued, *it is immortal*. Long after I am gone, Dark One, my Song will resound in the hearts of my people, and so I shall live on in my purest state, in the form the One Star has given me. I am not here to die, but to assume a new body beyond the grasp of your infernal intellect, and *you shall be silenced.*"

Cerastes snarled.

"Die in corruption, Harpy."

The Grandmaster's body expanded, deforming, contorting, and a wave of pure darkness swelled toward him, filling the chamber, smothering the air, but Caprion focused on his wings. His Song swelled in his chest. His body pulsed with light as piercing vibrations rocked the room, making stone jump and marble crack, and dust crumble from the ceiling. Light flooded the chamber as his final set of wings appeared. He found himself lifting from the ground to hover in the center of the room. His jaw opened, and sound poured forth, a terrifying and incoherent cacophony—the holy song of a god that outstretched any mortal voice. Searing pain filled his body as his final set of wings materialized, formed as if from light itself, upon his back.

Six wings, and every nerve was on fire. Six wings, and his bones were melting, his skin splitting. Six wings: the burning power of a star.

In those final seconds, he saw the demon laid out before him, bare and monstrous, paralyzed in the white light. He saw archaic symbols on the wall and floor burn away under the force of his magic. He saw the statue's vile mouth open to expel a gust of rancid air, like the breath of a coffin, which became a thousand voices of a thousand tortured souls, screaming.

And then his light overtook them all, and the world was lost to a blinding, pervasive silence.

When the great light overtook the city, thunderous vibrations shook the ground, sending ripples of destructive energy through the earth. In an instant, snow melted from the streets and icicles dissolved from the gutters, and a torrential flood swept down the Royal Road, toppling buildings and crushing bridges already weakened by the earthquake.

The entirety of the First Tier fell to their knees, some screaming, others quivering in fear, as the royal palace rocked and groaned.

Far beyond the city's eastern wall, among the frozen windmills, Crash and Natrix stood with Krait's body. They watched the explosion of light envelope the city. Later, Crash wondered how they didn't go blind.

Chapter 23

Lorianne stood up from her kneeling position and stretched her back. Then she gave her wounded patient a tired smile.

"The ankle should mend in time, but you won't be growing any of your toes back, sad to say."

"Just lucky to be alive, mistress," the old woman said, then looked down at her bandaged foot. "I have no way to pay you...."

Lori waved her off. "The seminary set up these medical tents around the city to help all of the survivors. That's what Healers do. You're free to go, but use your crutch and stay off that foot for a few weeks."

The woman nodded and kissed her hand in gratitude, then hobbled out of the tent on a wooden crutch. Lori tossed a pile of bloody rags into a boiling cauldron of hot water, then she left the tent.

Outside, a brisk, damp wind had her wishing for a cup of hot tea. She wrapped her wool cloak a bit tighter around her shoulders. To her left, more blue robed Healers were ducking in and out of similar tents. The crowd of injured peasants seeking medical treatment seemed endless.

It was the day after the Great Light. Lori and the rest of the upper tier had awakened that morning to a city in ruins. Almost half the City of Crowns, from the river to the windmills, had toppled to the ground.

The city was a roiling mass of barely contained chaos.

The nobility blamed Prince Peric and his group of anarchists for the explosion, though Lorianne knew the prince was not at fault. He was being held in the castle dungeons for a public trial, which meant his fate would be decided before all of the city's inhabitants, rich and poor. Peric could hire a lawyer, but the king alone would mete out justice to his wayward son.

Lorianne had listened to her share of gossip from the common folk since arriving at the medical tents. Because the Temple of the North Wind had been utterly decimated, the peasants called the explosion an act of the Wind Goddess. Many believed the goddess was angry with them, and cited at least a hundred reasons why: the upper tiers were corrupted; the king was too old; taxes were too high; the prince had committed treason; the priestesses were not chaste enough; certain rituals were no longer being followed, and on and on. No one mentioned the king's clocktower, which had been destroyed in the explosion.

Ferran, Lord Seabourne, Crash, Burn, and dozens of soldiers were excavating the clocktower site, looking for Sora's body.

The thought of that made her feel ill.

Initially, Lori had gone to help with the search, but when she had approached the epicenter of the explosion, the decimation was so horrific, she had collapsed. Ferran had banished her to the medical tents, where Headmaster Duncan put her to work. Treating victims of the blast helped her stave off her strong emotions. Some of the peasants had been blinded by the explosion. She applied poultices to their eyes and warned them not to remove their bandages for a week at least, hoping the blindness was temporary. Others suffered from broken bones or nasty cuts from broken glass. Many had ringing ears and reddened skin that looked like severe sunburns. Lori didn't see any new victims of the plague. She held out hope that perhaps Caprion's sacrifice had been worth the cost.

As she worked, she tried not to betray the weakness in her hands, the dark spots at the corners of her vision. Her concussion was not much better than it had been the night before. Truly, she should be resting back at the Ebonaire manor, but she could not stay in bed on a day like this. She had to stay busy, or else she would lose her mind with worry. She had to trust that Sora was safe somewhere, and that Ferran would find her daughter and bring her home.

Headmaster Duncan had established a tent city at the southern docks for the Healers to work: a safe haven where survivors could gather. With the city half-toppled, not only were the tents completely full, but the docks were overflowing with displaced families. It was a nightmare, and the king's soldiers were only just responding to the traffic.

As Lori pushed her way through the muddy, crowded banks of The Bath, her mind wandered back to the night before. She blushed, remembering Ferran's hand on the small of her back as they arrived at the Ebonaire manor from the royal palace. She remembered the protective way he had ushered her upstairs, into their shared bedchamber. He had closed the doors behind them and built a fire in the hearth to warm the room. She watched his broad shoulders as he worked. How many times had he built her a fire?

Once he finished, knowing full well what was coming, she leaned up on her tiptoes and kissed his cheek. SHis face turned, and Ferran captured her mouth with his own.

She remembered his intensely focused expression as he kissed her; how his brown eyes had gazed into her own, silently asking for permission. His title and reputation might have been restored, yet she still saw the dashing rogue from her youth, with his halfcocked smile and keen, mischievous eyes. She had stopped resisting the pull of her heart, and crumbled into his arms.

Finally, finally, yes, I know what I want.

She saw him clearly now: a man of courage and honor. She had found him washed up on his houseboat in a small fishing village, and now, he was a nobleman again, his reputation and lands restored. She knew that he had done all of this for her.

Lori had awakened that morning in a state of bliss, completely ignorant of the Great Light or the decimation of the city, even forgetful of Cerastes and the Shade. Miracle of miracles, she and Ferran had slept through the explosion. The Ebonaire manor only suffered a few cracked windows and a half-toppled brick chimney; it stood far enough away from the clocktower project.

Their bubble of peace dissipated when Martin Ebonaire burst into their bedroom, Lord Gracen on his heels.

Lorianne shrieked and pulled the bed sheets up to her chin.

Ferran, far less modest, half-mooned their audience as he rolled over in bed. "What is the meaning of this?" he demanded, stifling a yawn.

"Where is Sora?" Lord Gracen's voice shook. "Did she come home last night? *Lorianne, where is your daughter?*"

Lori's heart stopped. It was the worst question anyone could ask a mother.

She and Ferran had dressed and joined Gracen downstairs. There, Crash and Natrix were also waiting. They told the story of the battle with Krait, Caprion and

Cerastes, in as much detail as Lori could tolerate. Then Lord Gracen explained with military precision what had transpired the night before, and the plan to erect medical tents by the lake to treat survivors. By the dark circles under his eyes, he hadn't slept at all, but had spent the night managing the king's emergency response to the explosion. Or was it an earthquake? No one could decide.

A terrible mantle of guilt had weighed down her shoulders all morning. How could she have spent the night in Ferran's arms, when Sora was fighting for her life?

How could she call herself a mother?

Returning to the present moment, Lorianne stood behind the medical supply tent, where she pumped water into the empty bucket. The city might not know the source of the explosion, but she knew the full story. How could Caprion justify hurting so many innocent people? There must have been some other way to stop Cerastes, surely? Lori couldn't think of one—she didn't know much about magic or the Races—but seeing all the displaced peasants around the southern docks left her sick with anger.

She also didn't like that Crash had left Sora alone, underground, with Cerastes. She didn't recall that being part of their plan. Couldn't he have done something, *anything*, to get Sora out before the explosion? Lord Seabourne, Ferran, and even Burn seemed to share her sentiment, and Crash had been unable to argue with them. To his credit, he looked like he blamed himself, too.

Such thoughts tortured her all morning into the afternoon. If not for her work, Lorianne would have pulled out her hair from worry.

Then, just past the noonday meal, she heard a familiar voice calling her name.

She was stitching up a rather nasty cut along the head of a man whose ear had almost been torn off by a flying bit of wood. She paused when she recognized Ferran's voice. She tried to suppress her sense of dread.

"Lori!" Ferran called, pushing aside the tent flap. "Lori! Come quickly!"

"Is it Sora?" she croaked, her voice dry.

"She's alive! Natrix found her. She's breathing. Come quickly. She needs you."

Another Healer approached Lori's side to take the needle from her hand. Lori didn't remember washing her hands or stumbling out of the tent. Then she was on a horse, galloping behind Ferran down alleyways and sidestreets, as they navigated the ruined city to the epicenter of the explosion.

Sora was in a tomb, deep underground.

No, that didn't seem right.

She was covered in moss, asleep in a cave. She had grown into the roots of a massive tree. She could hear water trickling, feel the cool clay against her cheek, smell the moist earth. She was caked in mud. Something white, shining. She looked toward the mouth of the cave. Still too bright to see. *Too bright. Shield your eyes. Don't look.* The light hurt. It was deadly. *Back...go back.* The moss, the earth, the sweet darkness called to her. She buried her face in it. She was small and safe, an animal splashing in a stream of green water, hiding between the rocks.

"She's awake."

"No, she's dreaming."

Sora tried to open her eyes but she couldn't see anything. She closed her left hand in distress, and felt the smooth texture of silken sheets. She tried to inhale through her nose, but she couldn't, so she took a deep, shuddering breath through her mouth. The air was cold. Her lips were chapped.

The sound of trickling water in her dream was actually the snap of wood in a fireplace. She could hear it but not see it. She thought she must be in the Ebonaire manor from the feel of the mattress beneath her. It was soft and lumpy, like a bed of moss.

"Am I alive?" she asked. She didn't know if her voice carried. Her words were parched.

Her mother answered, "Yes, and you'll be staying that way."

"You're safe and in good hands," Burn's voice agreed. His heavy, warm hand found hers on the blanket.

"Why can't I see anything?" Sora tried to keep the tremble of fear from her voice.

Her mother hesitated. "Your eyes were damaged. Headmaster Duncan treated them himself. Your vision should return eventually, but you can't remove the bandages for a few days."

"We hoped you would sleep until then," Burn said. "We moved you yesterday from the seminary back to the manor. The city has been in quite a disarray since...well...."

"What of Cerastes?" Sora asked, thinking back to the battle. "Did we stop him? Caprion was there. I don't remember...."

No one answered her at first. Then, a new voice spoke—Crash.

"Caprion is dead," he said. "He activated his six wings. He used his power to stop Cerastes."

Sora felt a slight drop in her stomach. She struggled to sit up, but sharp pain moved through her torso, and she went still.

"He took out most of the city with him," Burn added. "I had no idea the seraphim were so powerful."

"He paid the price of his magic with his life," Crash said, his words practical, logical. "The battle is won."

Sora felt a weight upon her chest. The news of Caprion's death was difficult to accept. She had considered him a friend, no matter how little she understood him, or how distant he seemed.

"Lily, Silas, Dorian, Caprion...we've lost so many," she murmured.

"We will have a proper memorial for them all," her mother said softly. "This is a day for funerals. I'm sorry, Sora, but we need to leave for a time. Another Healer is here to watch over you. We will be back in a few hours."

"Where are you going?"

"King Royce is holding a public address. Many people were caught in the explosion when Caprion...when he...." Lori's voice grew thicker. "They are still recovering bodies from the wreckage. Today, the king will speak before the city, or what's left of it."

"I'm sorry," Sora said. She searched for her mother's hand briefly across the covers, but the pain in her ribs stopped her. Even the slightest movement was agonizing.

"Here," her mother said, "drink this. I will check on you when we return. I won't be long from your side."

"You're leaving me?" Sora couldn't keep the sudden fear from her voice. The thought of being blind, too weak to climb out of bed, filled her with terror. A skilled assassin could change his appearance, and easily infiltrate the Ebonaire manor. What if the Shade came for revenge? What if they were watching her right now? She couldn't defend herself. Could she trust the maids in the room?

"I will stay with you," Crash said. "I am here, and Natrix. No one will enter this room who we do not know."

Sora felt the tension leave her body. Her momentary panic left her exhausted and sore. Someone helped lean her head up, and she was able to take a sip of warm tea. She recognized the taste of a sleeping draught her mother often brewed. She sipped on it without resisting, knowing she needed to rest. She hadn't truly *rested* in a long time.

Then she was back in the cave, embraced by the moss and the good earth and the quiet.

Days passed. Sora spent most of her time sleeping. During brief periods of wakefulness, she ate broth and sipped herbal tea. She otherwise lay still.

When she woke up, though she didn't always speak, she felt Crash's hand cover her own, a silent reassurance that he was still with her. She was grateful for his presence. Without him, she would not have been able to rest. When she was awake, she jumped every time the door opened, or she started if she heard footsteps around her bed. Crash would reassure her with a touch, and sometimes, a word. She knew it was him, because she recognized his warm palm and his quiet energy.

The threat is gone, the Shade is defeated, she tried to reassure herself, but in her blind and helpless state, she could only pass the hours in cold expectation. Crash's presence kept her sane. She expected him to leave her side, to withdraw as he always did. But he remained, keeping a long and silent vigil at her bedside.

She awoke one night to the sound of a storm outside. She recognized the creak of wood and settling of the house. She could tell it was late in the night by the stillness of the room and the chill in the air. She wondered if she was alone. She reached out her hand, and a warm, calloused palm covered her cold fingers.

"What do you need?" Crash asked, his voice a low murmur.

"I wasn't sure if you were there," she said.

"You're in pain."

"A little."

In truth, she was relieved to feel her wounds, as her mother's sleeping draught kept her head cloudy and her body numb. Now the potion had worn off and she was clear-headed. Her ribs ached with each breath. She didn't know the extent of her injuries, but it felt like every inch of her was wrapped in bandages.

She raised a hand and touched the wrappings around her eyes. It frightened her, not being able to see. Headmaster Duncan was adamant that not even a sliver of light leaked through her bandages. She tried not to wonder when her vision would return. She disliked feeling so helpless and weak.

She tried to sit up, but stopped when her ribs groaned.

Wordlessly, Crash shifted onto the bed. She felt the mattress dip under his weight. He placed his shoulder behind her and helped her into a sitting position, guiding her by touch. He was so gentle. She rested against his chest. His warmth was like a furnace against the cold night.

"Please," she said softly, "I would like to get out of this bed. So many days have passed, I should try to stand."

He paused, but he didn't argue. "*Slowly*, then," he finally said, and pulled the blankets off of her. She slid her legs to the side of the bed. She felt utterly helpless, unable to see the mattress, the floor, or the room. She stood up with his help. He supported her with his arm.

Leaning heavily on him, she took a few steps. Her knees trembled, but she felt better standing.

"I want to walk around the room."

"I will lead you," he said.

She walked in darkness, his strength her support, his hands leading her in a slow circle. He was patient and waited for her to take each step. An eternity passed before she reached the window, where she touched the cold glass.

"It sounds like a storm outside," she said. "I can hear the rain."

They stood by the window, listening to the rain against the glass and the wind howling through the chimneys on the rooftop. It was a haunting sound, but soothing.

Then she asked, "Crash, how long has it been since...?"

"Ten days."

"Then tomorrow they will check my eyes." Sora tried not to sound worried. How had so much time passed? Had she really slept for so long?

"I will not leave your side. They know that by now," he reassured her.

"Why do you stay with me?" she asked softly. *Surely, he has somewhere more important to be.*

"To protect you," he said after a pause, "as I couldn't against Cerastes."

Sora felt her throat close. "This is not your fault, Crash."

"It is. If I hadn't left your side on winter solstice eve...."

"You followed the plan. We knew the risk." Sora's voice wavered. "My mother and Headmaster Duncan are confident my vision will return."

Crash's silence spoke volumes. He didn't reply immediately, but she felt his hand touch her cheek.

"Until it does, and you are strong enough to stand on your own, I will remain here, next to you. I will keep you safe."

Sora fought the urge to collapse against him. She turned toward the sound of his voice. Without warning, she felt something brush her lips. His mouth was warm, gentle. His hand cupped her jaw. His breath warmed her.

He kissed her next to the window for a long time. His lips caressed her mouth, her chin, her nose. His touch was careful and slow. She felt his apology through his touch. *I'm sorry. Don't be afraid. You are safe now. I'm here.*

Tears welled up in her eyes and slid down her cheeks.

"It was terrible," she whispered, choking. "It was terrible in that dark place underground. Then Caprion's light burned the world. I thought I would die."

His arms wrapped around her, gently clasping her against him. "But you lived, Sora. *You lived.*"

His tenderness shocked her. She hadn't thought him capable of such passion. She almost doubted this could be the Crash she knew, but his scent, his warmth and his very aura reassured her. They embraced each other for a time. The storm raged on outside, oblivious to the lovers in the window, who held each other as though for the last time.

He noticed when her strength began to wane. With a final soft kiss to her nose, he scooped her into his arms and carried her back to the bed. There, he lay down next to her, and wrapped her in a gentle embrace. She fell asleep with her head on his chest, listening to his heartbeat.

A few days later, Headmaster Duncan removed the bandages from her eyes. Blurry halos of light surrounded the windows and the fireplace, but Duncan assured her such things would fade with time. Otherwise, she could see clearly, and she felt an immense sense of relief.

Shortly after her bandages were removed, her mother visited her bedside and told Sora the full story of winter solstice night. Sora could scarcely believe how the prince had attacked the king, and how Cedric Daniellian had been arrested for treason.

Her cousin, Danica, visited her bedside as well, to tell her the latest gossip circulating around the Regency. Prince Peric and Cedric were both on trial, and the hearing had been ongoing for over a week. Ferran, Martin and Gracen were all involved as witnesses. They had arrested many ranking soldiers and local businessmen in the conspiracy, with more names being added to the list each day.

"The papers publish the latest news every morning, so I don't know why I should continue to attend the trial. I'd much rather hear the latest development from my father, or Uncle Gracen, or Uncle Ferran, since they were witness to it all," Danica lamented, "but they will be busy at court until the prince's fate is decided. The king was going to hang him with the rest of the traitors, but the queen interceded. That's a mother's love, I suppose. Still, the prince is a brute and everyone knows it. They can't let him run free, don't you think? He'll just plot against the king and try again."

Lady Danica sat at Sora's bedside with the afternoon light shining over her shoulder. Her hair was plated down her back with a blue ribbon, and a single feather hung on a little silver chain behind her ear. In her hands, she worked on a piece of embroidery. Sora watched her hands move with short, elegant stitches.

"Well?" Danica prompted. "Don't you think they should behead the prince and be done with it? Or is that too bold of me to say?"

The two maids in the room paused their dusting and cleaning. They looked shocked by Danica's outburst. Even if Prince Peric had committed an unforgivable offense by turning against his own father, he was still a prince. Speaking of his death would be considered treason under any other circumstances.

In truth, Sora couldn't bring herself to have an opinion. After the battle with Cerastes and the leveling of the City of Crowns, the failed coup seemed like a small matter.

Danica waited for the maids to leave the room. Once she and Sora were alone, she asked, "So? Tell me about First Winter's Ball. How did it go with my uncle?"

In truth, Sora hadn't thought much of that, either. "You mean, Gracen?"

"Yes, you two danced several rounds before it all went pear-shaped. The whole First Tier witnessed Gracen and his soldiers defending the throne. The ladies of The Regency are all aflutter over his bravery. But, that's nothing new. That's why I ask, how did the evening turn out? Did he propose?"

Sora, who was taking a sip of tea, almost choked. "Propose? That seems fast."

"I thought he might do so at the dance."

Sora studied Danica's face until the girl's cheeks turned pink and she dropped her gaze. It seemed that Danica had a sense of propriety after all. Despite her bravado, she was still just a fifteen year old girl.

"Even if he did, that would be Gracen's private business," Sora said softly. "But no. He didn't propose. I don't expect him to."

Danica sighed; she seemed relieved. "Well, I suppose it would be strange if you were to marry my uncle. You would become my aunt, but you are only a few years older than me. I'd much rather we remain cousins."

They finished their tea in silence. After the maids returned, Lady Danica excused herself. She placed a hand over Sora's own and wished her a swift recovery.

Sora wondered why Gracen or Ferran hadn't visited her since winter solstice, but now she knew they were both at the trial. They were likely staying at the palace until the proceedings were over. She had received a large display of flowers a few days after her bandages were removed, with a very simple note that read, *"For a dance I will not soon forget."* The flowers were unsigned, but she knew they must be from Gracen.

Perhaps it was just as well that Lord Seabourne was unable to visit her. He had no knowledge of the true battle that had occurred under the clocktower on winter solstice eve. Still, Sora found herself remembering their turn around the dance floor, his confidence and magnetism, and feeling a little flustered all the same.

Not long after, Sora felt strong enough to climb out of bed and dress herself. It was around that time that Crash began to leave her room more often, since she was receiving more visitors. He always returned after the maids had gone, usually without a word, to sit in his chair near her bed and wait through the long nights. If the manor's staff noticed a mysterious chair pushed to the side of her bed in the mornings, they did not mention it. Sora was grateful for his presence, because she did not yet feel brave enough to sleep alone, although she knew the threat of the Shade had passed.

She awoke in the early morning on a clear winter day, with sunlight streaming through her window. Crash's chair was already empty next to her bed. She moved carefully around her room so as not to draw the attention of the maids next door. She pulled on a loose fitting wool gown, and tied it at the waist with a length of ribbon. For a while now she had felt the desire to go outside. Perhaps today she was strong enough to take a walk in the gardens. The sun was out, and it hadn't snowed in a few days. She slowly pulled on a pair of fur boots, then wrapped herself in a woolen robe. Then she pulled on a tassel that hung next to the door, and somewhere deep behind the walls, a bell rang.

A maid appeared at her door a minute later. She curtsied and asked, "Good morrow, my lady. You are looking much recovered. May I bring you breakfast?"

"Not yet," Sora said. "Can you get my mother for me? I wish to go for a walk this morning. Please ask if she would like to accompany me."

After a half-hour or so, Lorianne met her downstairs near the back door that led to the stableyard. Sora brought her staff with her as a walking stick; her ribs were still sore and bruised. Her mother insisted they walk slowly, even though Sora was eager to move about.

First they walked through the stables, where they stopped to greet a few horses in passing. Then they walked to the rear gardens, which were covered in winter frost. The sky was full of hazy, pastel pinks and blues. Slumbering rose bushes and clusters of dormant hydrangeas made statuesque shapes in the winter garden.

They crossed over a little bridge to where a willow tree cast its branches into a half-frozen lake.

Then, her mother said, "I have something important I'd like to speak to you about."

Sora thought of Lady Danica, and wondered if it might be about the prince's trial. It seemed like everyone was full of important news.

"I was waiting until you were somewhat recovered. But I see now you are strong enough."

"What is it?" Sora asked, searching her mother's face.

Lorianne looked perplexed. She also seemed nervous. Sora tried not to worry. "Is it Ferran? Is he alright? Did something happen in the trial?"

"No, no. This is different. Ferran and I, we've been...well...." Lori stopped, looking perplexed again. "You see, Martin Ebonaire petitioned the king to re-instate Ferran's title as heir to the Ebonaire estate. It's an unusual request, but the king agreed to it. Martin will keep the manor in town and two-thirds of the Ebonaire estate, which he will pass to his daughter Danica when he is gone. But Ferran will be granted one-third of the Ebonaire estate and holdings, to replace the inheritance he lost before his exile. Do you follow?"

"Yes, I think so," Sora said, though she wasn't very interested in the details of the Ebonaire family fortune. She wondered what all of this had to do with her and her mother.

"The king legitimized Ferran before the First Tier at the ball. Perhaps you missed it, so much transpired that night. But you should know, we no longer have to lie to Martin or the rest of the family. Ferran's title as Lord Ebonaire has been restored, and he is once again accepted among the ranks of First Tier. Martin just deeded Ferran his summer manor, which I hear is a small castle located a few miles outside the city, past the windmills. It's used as a hunting retreat, but hasn't been utilized since the plague began to spread. Now it will belong to Ferran. Martin has been very generous to his brother."

"That's excellent news. I'm happy for Ferran," Sora said. She waited, sensing there was more news her mother wanted to share.

"Also, you should know that Ferran proposed to me, and I accepted. We are now engaged to be married."

Sora blinked. "Engaged?"

The news struck her. She tried to think of something thoughtful to say. In truth, she was shocked.

"But why? I thought you hated him," Sora blurted out. "You always seemed so annoyed by him! Is this because he is an Ebonaire once again?"

"That's a bold thing to say," her mother balked.

"I'm sorry. This is so sudden. But are you sure...?"

"Sora, you know I don't care about noble titles or wealth. I am happy with my farm in the south."

"Then why accept his proposal?"

Sora didn't know why she was upset. Ferran had some good qualities, and he seemed like a loyal man. He had mentored her for a time, sharing his knowledge of the Cat's-Eye stone, and he had helped her defeat the third wraith. He was a skilled fighter and courageous. They were almost friends. But the thought of him marrying her mother felt almost like a betrayal. When had they fallen in love? Were they in love? It was hard for Sora to imagine. Lorianne and Ferran were such opposites. He was reckless where her mother was cautious. He was thoughtless and lazy where she was methodical and productive.

"Are you sure? He might have regained his title, but remember how you found him... He was a mess before we came here."

Lorianne winced. "I realize that this news is a bit of a shock for you. Truly, he is a good man, and we knew each other in our youth. Ferran has... many layers."

Sora thought of how her mother and Ferran spent time together, how he looked at her, how happy she seemed in his presence. It all made her squeamish and uncomfortable.

But, she resented the idea. She wanted her mother all to herself. It felt like they had only just reconnected after a lifetime apart. She wasn't ready to share her mother with a man, even if that man was Ferran.

"I thought we would return to your farm after this," Sora said, trying not to sound petulant. "I thought we would return to that small village and help the local people, just like we did before the plague. I was happy there. It felt like home."

Lorianne's face twisted in anguish. "I thought so too, Sora. We can still go back to visit the farm. I haven't thought of selling it. Cameron is still waiting for us. Nothing has changed."

"Everything has changed, if you are engaged to Ferran Ebonaire, and if he is now a lord of the First Tier." Then Sora's eyes widened. "Does Martin know about the engagement? Doesn't he believe you are already married? A wedding would not make sense, and cast an odd light on you both."

Lorianne shrugged. She looked uncomfortable. "I thought the same thing when Ferran proposed to me. I thought we might elope quietly together. But Ferran wants us to be married in front of the First Tier families to make sure we are legitimized. He promised to smooth things over with Martin. And..." Lorianne searched her face. "He wants you to be recognized as his heir."

"What?" Sora sputtered.

"I knew I should have waited until you were stronger. Do you need to sit down?"

Sora was leaning heavily on her staff. She thought she might swoon, but caught herself.

"No, no, I am just surprised. Mother, I don't want to be Ferran's heir. Danica is heir to the Ebonaire state, not me. I was a Fallcrest, and the Fallcrest estate is long gone."

"It is Ferran's decision. If we are to be married, then he will become family to you, as well. You will be his daughter...."

"He is not my father, and marriage will not make him so."

Lorianne bit her lip. She glanced down at the ground.

Sora stared at her mother's face. Her eyes widened. As the silence stretched, she thought her mother was about to say something that would completely change her world.

Then Lorianne said, "Perhaps in time, you may see him as a father. But that is between you and him. I hope our marriage doesn't affect your friendship with him."

Sora sighed. *For a moment, I thought she was about to say that Ferran was my father. But that's silly! This roleplay has gotten to her head.*

"Your mind is set on this, then?" Sora asked. The more she thought about it, she knew it would be a relief to leave their costumes behind, and settle into The Regency without needing to hide their identities. Sora was tired of pretending, and she knew her mother felt the same way.

"I wanted to speak to you first." Her mother clasped her hands before her and gazed at Sora, looking hopeful and vulnerable all at once.

Sora felt suddenly guilty for her reaction. This wasn't about her. This was about Lorianne's happiness, and who was she to stand in the way of love?

She took a deep breath.

"You have my approval, if that is what you're asking," Sora said. Her head was still reeling from the news.

"You don't sound pleased. I know this is sudden, but I hope you can be happy for me. For us."

"I'm sorry, mother. I...." Sora paused. Then, without warning, she drew her mother into a fierce hug. "Of course I'm happy for you. You deserve to be happy. You deserve someone who loves you the way Ferran loves you. I know he will make you a good husband." Sora hoped her words proved true. *If he betrays you, I will castrate him myself.*

Then she asked, with some difficulty, "Do you think you will have children with him?"

Her mother blushed, appearing suddenly girlish. "Well, I haven't put a lot of thought into it, I've been mostly worried about you," she admitted. "And I'm no longer a young maiden. Children would be hard on me at this age."

"Maybe you should put some thought into it then," Sora suggested. "But... I wouldn't mind a little sister or brother."

"Really?"

"Really. In fact, I think I'd be quite taken with them."

Her mother smiled at her–a true smile, which lit up her face and made the winter day warm. Sora wondered, perhaps, if love made everyone look younger. Her mother's eyes sparkled, and her face glowed. The two women clasped hands. With an unexpected laugh, Lori began telling her about Ferran's proposal: how he had proposed in the carriage on the way to the prince's trial, and tied a leather string about her finger in promise of a ring.

Sora found herself grinning over the whole story, imagining Ferran's awkward attempt to get on one knee while the carriage rocked back and forth.

"Is the wedding soon, then?" Sora asked.

"I'd like to wait until spring, when this business with Prince Peric has passed, and the snow thaws," Lorianne said. "And of course, I will need your help planning the event, because I haven't been to a wedding in a very long time. I was thinking we could say our vows here, in the garden, beneath this willow tree. What do you think?"

"I think it's perfect," Sora said, and for the first time, she felt excitement at the prospect of a wedding.

CHAPTER 24

Two days later, an unexpected visitor came to the Ebonaire manor.

The wind was brisk and cold on this particular afternoon, and the clouds moved overhead with uncharacteristic speed. Thin beams of winter sunlight broke through the cloud cover, but they weren't quite strong enough to melt the snow.

Although the apple trees in the garden were bare of leaves, and the rose bushes covered in frost, Sora still heard birdsong. She walked through the Ebonaire gardens at a slow, meditative pace.

She wished to be alone on these afternoon walks, but she knew her companions kept a close watch over her. Even now, she could sense someone's eyes on her back. She often suspected Crash or Burn, but she never saw them.

Little stone walls separated the garden into private alcoves where one could sit undisturbed and feel secluded from the world. Sora sat in one such alcove now, her hands clasped in her lap, her thoughts heavy and distant.

Just that morning, the prince's trial had come to a close. It appeared the prince would be punished for treason and sent to some faraway location on the coast. Cedric would be imprisoned for life. She knew, now, that Cedric Daniellian had ordered the assassination of Lord Fallcrest and most of the murders surrounding the clocktower project. However, beyond the misuse of funds against the crown, the clocktower project appeared to be inconsequential. No one seemed aware of Cerastes' involvement, or the Shade, or the Dark God's underground chamber beneath the city. The kingdom's population, including the upper tiers, were still completely ignorant.

It disturbed her to think that she had almost died for a cause that would never be known or understood. The plague was still infecting victims, which led her to believe that, whether or not Cerastes had been killed, the Dark God's curse upon the land had not been lifted.

But the weapons were gone, and half the city leveled, and she couldn't comprehend what else they could do. Perhaps the plague would simply fade away over time. Perhaps not. For now, she could only knit her brow in worry, and try not to sulk.

Considering her dreary thoughts, Sora didn't immediately notice the beams of sunlight intensifying around her. Then her skin grew unexpectedly warm, and she finally looked up, squinting at the passing clouds overhead. There, she saw a bright shape descend from the sky, and for a heart-swelling moment, she thought it was Caprion.

However, the Harpy who landed before her was not Caprion, and Sora's look of shock turned into a pinched frown.

"Sora," the Matriarch said, her voice echoing ever so slightly, "I have been searching for you across the mainland."

Sora reflexively crossed her arms. The Matriarch had wanted to kill Crash and imprison her friends. She glanced around the dormant gardens, wondering if she should call for help, but they were alone.

"I see," she said, guarded.

The two women studied one another. The Matriarch's eyes and hair were as pale as moonbeams, and her face held an ethereal beauty. Her long, silver robes appeared to be made of light. Sora noticed the Matriarch bore no weapons.

Finally she asked, because she couldn't help but ask, "How is Laina? Does she still live with you on the island?"

"She is happy, from what I know," the Matriarch said, and held up one gentle, long-boned hand. "Please," she said, "let us not tarry. I have come on behalf of my people to honor Caprion's sacrifice. His Song has been silenced. My people have been praying for days for a sign from the One Star. Finally, I could pray no more, and I came to find you. Am I right in assuming that he has vanquished the evil one, and his light has returned balance to the world?"

Sora thought of Caprion's last words to her. She wrapped her arms tighter around her torso. She also thought of all of the lives lost in the blast.

"He did what he needed to do," she said, her voice harsh in her own ears. "He stopped the Dark God from awakening. He saved all of us."

"Then he fulfilled his purpose. Do not mourn his death, young one. It was his destiny, and a great honor, that he was chosen to become a seraph. His name will forever be remembered in Asterion."

Sora nodded.

"Tell me of his death, that I might tell my people," the Matriarch asked.

Haltingly, Sora relayed the story, and as she spoke, she realized she hadn't truly spoken of it yet, only at night to herself as she tried to fall asleep. She found herself pausing as memories overwhelmed her and her throat closed. She pushed herself to continue.

The Matriarch listened patiently to her tale.

When Sora finished, the Matriarch held out a silver chain from her pocket. A circular amulet, etched with strange and archaic markings, hung from it. A small white sunstone was embedded at the center of the amulet.

"If you are ever in need, you may contact me with this medallion. It marks you as an ally to our people. If you rub the surface like this," she ran her fingers along the edge of the amulet. A few seconds of silence passed, then the metal began to emit a low, dull hum. It *sang*. "As you can see, it's now activated. Only use it in times of great need. Give it to no one."

Sora took the medallion and bowed in gratitude. "Thank you, I will keep it safe," she said, and draped it around her neck. The chain was surprisingly heavy.

The Matriarch briefly touched her hand. "This gift has never before been bestowed upon a human. Cherish it. Use it wisely."

Sora nodded again. "I will. I promise."

The Matriarch gazed past her. "You may show yourself now, Dark One."

Sora turned. There, standing just beyond the garden wall in a splash of shadows, was Crash. She wasn't entirely surprised. She knew he often trailed her outside the manor, though they hadn't spoken much since she had recovered her vision. She knew a very serious, and very permanent, decision lay between them, and she was putting it off. For now, she simply wanted him by her side.

"Tell your people of what has transpired here," the Matriarch said, her voice becoming sharp as steel. "Tell the Hive that, should the Dark God threaten this world again, I shall summon every shining warrior at my command and extinguish your kind like a fire doused."

Crash, as was his habit, said nothing.

The Matriarch looked again at Sora. "Your bravery will not be forgotten." Then, with a flash of light, she lifted into the sky. Sora watched as the Matriarch spread her grand wings, a diameter of twenty feet, and rose to the heavens. Soon, she disappeared among the clouds.

Sora turned back to Crash, an eyebrow raised and words on her tongue, but the assassin had disappeared as well.

It was a day of many meetings.

Later that afternoon, Sora left the manor in an Ebonaire carriage and traveled into the city, to the refugee camp where the Healers cared for the city's wounded and displaced people. She wanted to help her mother tend to the survivors. She had had enough sitting and waiting and thinking. She needed to make herself busy.

Their carriage entered the refugee camp as one might enter a forest. White canvas tents sprawled across the encampment with only the vaguest pretense of roads. Both outside and within the camp, laymen and workers were already beginning to rebuild the decimated streets of the city. The king and the upper tier families—Ebonaires, Danillians, Seabournes and others—were bearing the full expense.

Sora had to admit, the air was full of unexpected enthusiasm—a sense of community and gratitude, of bustle and busyness—that she had to admire. Humans, when faced with unparalleled disaster, seemed to forget their differences. She saw wealthy merchants passing out meat and bread to the poor. She saw serfs and nobility alike distributing blankets to the refugees who had lost their homes. Excited voices hailed one another, sharing uplifting news and information about work or jobs. Everyone seemed saturated with *purpose*. Without realizing it, she began to smile.

Sora hunted down her mother at one of the medical tents. Lorianne was assisting several patients whose wounds were infected, and she greeted Sora with a tired smile. Sora washed her hands, tied back her hair and joined her mother's side, assisting with each patient as best she could.

Several hours passed without Sora noticing, until she finally stretched her back, wiped a bead of sweat from her brow, and looked around the tent. Surprised, she saw that Ferran had arrived with Martin and Gracen at his side. They stood, hovering with uncertainty, at the entrance to the tent.

Sora waved to them, attracting their attention, then Ferran left Martin and Gracen to cross to her side. He maneuvered his way awkwardly through the many rows of cots.

"Sora, Lori." A current of tension ran through his voice. "You need to accompany me to the city gates."

Lori straightened from washing her equipment.

"Is it really necessary?" she asked Ferran. "There are so many more waiting...."

"It's quite urgent. I'm sorry. I wouldn't ask otherwise. But we must leave now." Ferran touched her shoulder.

Sora observed their casual contact. Then she looked away uncomfortably and cleared her throat.

"I'll accompany you, if my mother wants to stay."

"Thank you, Sora," Ferran said, "but Lori, it's really important that you come."

Lorianne nodded and wiped her hands dry. Then the two women followed Ferran out of the tent. Ferran mounted his horse and pulled Lori up behind him. Sora found herself riding behind Gracen Seabourne, who she hadn't spoken to since winter solstice. She felt a little awkward leaning against his back as they rode through the crowded streets. She remembered, at a distance, how the magic of winter solstice had descended upon them on that one fateful night, and how for a few precious hours, she had been innocent again.

They reached the western gates of the city, which Sora hadn't visited often. The western gates led to a drawbridge that crossed the Crown's Rush. Two watchtowers stood to either side of the iron gates, which were closed and barred.

A defensive wall stretched along the riverbank, away from the iron gates, creating a ring around the eastern half of the city. Burn had told her that, far back in history, the city had sprung up around the king's palace and grown outward until it crossed the river. The western half of the city, beyond the wall and the drawbridge, was widely unplanned and practically lawless. The drawbridge that connected the two banks was another of King Royce's technological marvels, and the only one of its kind.

They dismounted at the foot of the first watchtower. A quiet and somber group, they followed Gracen inside the tower, then through an oak door and up a set of stairs. They exited the staircase to the top of the wall and stood on the battlements. A cold, harsh wind ruffled Sora's cloak. She was surprised to find Headmaster Duncan and several other city officials already gathered there.

"Have you sent word to the queen?" she overheard one ask.

"Yes. This is quite unexpected. We must await her reply."

"How did they know to come...?"

"Another mystery of the Goddess."

"The Wind tells all."

Sora looked out over the Crown's Rush at the western half of the city, its endless chimneys spewing black smoke into the sky, then her eyes traveled to the drawbridge below. She gasped.

There, a gathering of several hundred men and women stood. Their robes were a colorful mix of red, purple, and yellow. Some wore veils over their hair, while others wore armor and carried spears or swords.

Directly below them, at the very gates of the city, three women waited. Sora recognized the Priestess of the West Wind, who sat low and hunched on a short, stocky mare, her white hair falling in a thick braid down her back. Her robes were purple, trimmed in gold, and a gauzy veil covered the lower half of her face.

Sora could only assume the other two women were also High Priestesses. One wore yellow robes tied at a sash at the waist with a white cloak.

"The East Wind," her mother murmured, pointing. Sora knew the Temple of the East Wind worked closely with the Healer's seminary and followed similar tenants.

Lorianne crossed to where Headmaster Duncan stood. "Did you send word to their temple?"

The Headmaster shook his head. "We received news of their arrival by hawk this morning. They traveled almost as fast as their messenger."

The third priestess wore plated armor over a red tunic and pants. She rode upon a tall black charger that snorted and pawed the ground aggressively. A red plume of feathers decorated the top of her helmet. It billowed like a flame in the wind.

"The Strength of the Goddess," Sora murmured, mesmerized by the red woman atop the black horse. She represented the South Wind, the Wanderer's Wind, the warrior priestesses who served the goddess.

As though prompted by Sora's words, the South Wind approached the gates and spoke.

"One week ago, a storm visited my city in the southern plains. The wind howled so fiercely it ripped trees from the ground and toppled wagons from the road. I knew, then, that a great catastrophe had angered the Goddess." She paused, her words ringing significantly on the air. "Each of us has received a vision of unimaginable violence. A vision of death and fire. A vision of wicked works and the fall of our northern temple. The North Wind screams with the spirits of the dead. Is it true? Has the North Wind fallen?"

The entourage gathered on the wall looked at one another and mumbled, uncertain.

"Well?" Headmaster Duncan hissed, looking about. "The queen and king are not here. Who shall speak?"

Shockingly, Lorianne stepped up to the ramparts. Sora watched her mother with a dry throat.

"I was there when the temple fell," Lorianne said. "I was the only survivor of the slaughter. An evil man came to this city and burned the Temple of the North Wind to the ground. It is true, the North Wind has fallen."

A horrible, static silence followed her words, disrupted only by a hollow gust of wind.

"You are a Healer?" the South Wind asked.

"I am."

The warrior priestess removed her helm. Sora found herself fascinated once again. The woman wore her dark brown hair shorter than most men. She gazed up at Lorianne on the wall.

"We have traveled far from our respective temples to rebuild your fallen temple and recover what's been lost. We request a meeting with the royal family, and anyone else who can give us insight into this horrible tragedy. We hope you will accompany us, Healer. The time for secrets and silence is over. Please. Give us entry into the city. Let us help you."

Lorianne looked from Headmaster Duncan to Ferran and then Seabourne.

"Go on," she said. "Why wouldn't you let them in?"

Headmaster Duncan interrupted Seabourne. "The king has ordered the gates to remain closed. We must await his royal command."

Seabourne gave Duncan a scornful look. "This is an exceptional circumstance. As the queen's youngest brother, I'll assume command." He signaled to his men on the cobbles below. "Lower the gates!" he called. "Guard the bridge. Barricade the streets. Only the priestesses may enter." Then Seabourne entered the watchtower and started down the stairs.

Sora exchanged a glance with her mother. The two women linked arms and followed Seabourne with the rest of the officials in tow.

"The priestesses wish to speak to you," Sora said in a low tone. "Perhaps now, the truth of the plague can come to light."

"It has to," Lorianne agreed. "We must gather everyone—Burn, Crash, even Natrix if we can—to prove our story. The priestesses will listen to us. The West Wind already knows about your vision and will recognize your face. Oh, if only we still had the sacred weapons...." Lori paused, grimacing. The Dark God's chamber was buried by several stories of wreckage, including the entirety of the ruined clocktower. Recovering the weapons might prove impossible, but to simply leave them there, under the earth....

They exited the watchtower. Outside, on the cobblestone street in the gray weather, Seabourne's men had created a barricade to keep the road clear. More soldiers guided a long procession of priestesses through the city gates, led by the three High Priestesses on their magnificent steeds.

Sora couldn't look away from the warriors of the South Wind. They marched past, rank after rank, row after row, in shining armor and crimson robes. They looked exotic, tan-skinned and muscular in their uniforms. They had different features, some blue-eyed and blond-haired, others dark-eyed with black curls, but they all looked earthy and strong.

Lori leaned close to her again. "I don't trust Headmaster Duncan alone with the priestesses. I don't want him placating their fears. I intend to go with him to the royal palace, but I'd like you to accompany Ferran and Martin back to the Ebonaire manor."

Sora's face twisted. "But, the procession...."

"Gather your friends. I will summon you in time, when the priestesses are ready to speak to us. Be forewarned, you might have to be patient. They will want to rest before our meeting, I'm certain."

Sora watched the long line of acolytes in reluctance, wishing she could follow her mother to the palace. "Are you sure you don't need any help?"

Lori gave her a determined look. "I have the Goddess's help," she said. "I believe I was the one who called for them, when the temple was on fire. This task was given to me. I'll be fine. *But I need your help*. Will you do this for me?"

Sora searched her mother's eyes. "Of course." She wasn't sure what her mother's words meant, but she sounded grave. Lorianne was the sole survivor of the Temple of the North Wind, and perhaps she felt tasked by the Goddess to help. Sora didn't see any point in stopping her. With a nod, she went to find Ferran.

They returned to the manor on horseback. Once they reached the stables, Sora left Ferran and sought out Burn in the downstairs library. He spent much of his time there, and today was no exception. When she found him, he was reading a large tome called *The City of Crowns: A History*. He put down the book when she approached his chair.

Sora took the armchair across from him and told him all that had transpired.

"Now my mother wants Crash and Natrix to speak to the priestesses," she finished with a long sigh. "Have you seen either of them around the manor? I saw Crash in the garden earlier, but he didn't stay long."

She thought of the Matriarch's visit, and reached for the medallion that hung around her neck. If Burn noticed her new piece of jewelry, he didn't mention it.

"He and Natrix have been very mysterious of late," Burn said. "I know they have been helping the excavation of the clocktower looking for any sign of the Dark God's weapons, but I believe they are growing discouraged." He looked at her with candid eyes. "I do not believe they will be spending much longer in the city."

Sora tried to look unaffected. "He told me he needs to return to the Hive. Better than the Shade, I suppose. I'm surprised he's stayed this long after winter solstice." Her tone was brief and insincere, and she stared hard at the book in Burn's hands.

Then, she voiced the fear that had been lingering in her mind. "What if...what if Cerastes isn't defeated, and he managed to get away with the sacred weapons, and at this very moment he is awakening the Dark God?"

Burn seemed to be waiting for her words. In fact, by the way he spoke, she thought he had been rehearsing this moment for some time.

"That's simply not the case, Sora," he said calmly.

She sat forward in her chair, eager to argue now that the words were out. "But we haven't recovered anything from the blast, not the weapons or Cerastes' body—"

"Nothing could have survived that explosion," Burn said, and placed his hand over hers. "You did, because of your necklace, but that is a rare exception. Caprion was a seraph. His purpose was to kill demons, and he leveled half the city in the process. Cerastes was at the epicenter of that explosion. He could not have survived."

Sora searched Burn's steady golden eyes. "But..."

"Natrix hasn't found his body yet because, somewhere under all that rubble, a pile of dust that used to be Cerastes and the Dark God's weapons is buried. They are no more, Sora." Then his voice gentled. "You've been fighting a long time. We all have. Sometimes, when we've been struggling to survive, we don't know when the battle is over. We keep fighting on, day after day, year after year, convinced we are under attack long after the threat has passed. You learned this way of life, Sora. Now, we need to remember how to be at peace."

Sora clutched the armrests of the chair where she sat. *Be at peace.* The thought seemed more daunting, somehow, than taming a *garrolithe* or fighting a wraith.

"It doesn't feel right," Sora said, unable to meet his eyes. She stared, instead, at the rug on the floor. She wished she could express her restlessness, or the queasy sensation in her stomach. Her anxiety plagued her day and night, warning her of an imminent attack that never came.

Burn watched her and didn't speak.

Finally, she said, "You really think the threat has passed?"

"I do."

"Then what of the plague? Why are people still infected?"

"Nature takes time to rebalance itself. The plague is widespread; it won't disappear in a few days, or even a few months. But eventually, it will fade back into the earth like melting snow. It also takes time to readjust to a new way of living." He gave her a pointed look. "Your work is done, Sora. You saved us. Believe in that. Let it fill you. You're safe now, at home, and the battle is won."

Sora nodded. She took a deep breath and tried to feel a sense of completion. It was fleeting, but the desire for peace was there, buried deep in her heart.

Then she said, because she felt like she needed to confess, "I wish Crash didn't have to leave."

"I'm not so fond of the idea, either," Burn admitted. "Strange as it is, for better or worse, he has become my oldest friend. I wonder if he feels the same toward us."

Sora played with a loose thread on the armchair where she sat. "I think he does. I don't think he would ever tell us how much we mean to him."

"I think you're right. I'll see if I can hunt him down. I believe he and Natrix have been using the attic as their quarters."

"Really? Have you seen them up there?"

"Not specifically, but I've seen them on the roof a handful of occasions."

Somehow, that made sense. With a sigh, Sora sat back in the armchair. *Be at peace,* she thought. She found herself searching for the next thing to do, the next task to complete, but the thought came to her quite shockingly: *there's nothing that needs to be done.*

So, with timid hands, she reached for another book on the table beside her chair. *Be at peace,* she thought again. She opened to the first page—*The Song of the Four Winds*—and tried to relax. The adventures of Kaelyn the Wanderer should have grown old by now, but instead, after all she had experienced, she found them even more engrossing. In this particular tale, Kaelyn had to master four songs to control the wind. Each song had a special power over nature. Sora found herself turning page after page, her mind filled with a different kind of escape. Before she knew it, hours had passed and the sun had bowed low in the sky.

That evening, while she and Ferran and the rest of the Ebonaires sat down to dinner, her summons arrived from the royal palace. The letter requested her presence in the East Wing, *The Gilded Lilac Room,* at midmorning the following day.

"That's one of the smaller conference chambers," Martin said helpfully. "Seems like the discussion will be informal."

"So the king and queen won't be there?" Sora asked.

"I didn't say that. They might be. But I wouldn't expect more than the royal council to attend, and the priestesses, of course. The entire court won't be present, and it's far from a public hearing."

Sora read the summons again nervously. That meant she would be giving her testimony before a dozen or so people, which still seemed like a large crowd. She didn't enjoy public speaking. She hoped that Burn found Crash and that she wouldn't be alone when it came time to tell her story. She tucked the summons away in her pocket and went back to her meal, finding it suddenly difficult to eat.

CHAPTER 25

After dinner, Sora retired to her room. A servant helped her undress and bathe, and then brushed and braided her thick, blond hair. Another maid stoked the fire and placed a bed warmer under her covers. Then the maids left, and Sora was alone in her four poster bed. She lay, adrift in an ocean of blankets, her mind restless, her thoughts full of dread for the day to come. Disturbing memories of the battle with Cerastes interrupted her thoughts, and left her heart pounding.

She tossed and turned, but she couldn't fall asleep. Eventually, she left the bed and stood before one of the wide bedroom windows, looking out upon the night. The moon was a silver lantern in the sky. She watched a flurry of snowflakes drift down from the sky and stick to the glass.

Although she couldn't see much of anything through the snow and darkness, she could still imagine the wasteland of the city before her mind's eye, from the decimated Royal Road to the southern docks. She could almost hear the coughs and groans of the homeless, and see the fires and tents spread across the streets. The City of Crowns—and perhaps the entire kingdom—would never be the same. The human populace didn't even know why. The refugees would never learn Cerastes' name. They would never know of Caprion's wings or his destiny, fulfilled.

Sora decided she would speak to the priestesses on the morrow, and tell them everything that she knew–the full version of events. She didn't know if her story would ever leave that room. But someone should hear it.

Cerastes is dead now, the threat has passed, she told herself. Yet why did she feel so hollow? Where was her sense of victory? There would be no parade, no celebration. She had been fighting, surviving, for years, with little reward. Burn's words came back to her, and she wondered...was it possible to become addicted to the heat of battle, the adrenaline, the continual conflict? What was life without a great struggle to overcome?

The thoughts troubled her, and the night held no answers. Still, the questions circled through her mind, torturous, keeping her awake. Time passed. Snowflakes accumulated on the windowpane, forming veins of frost.

Sora didn't know how long Crash stood beside her, before she noticed his presence. Silent as a ghost, his reflection in the glass pane appeared to her right. He stood half in shadow.

She spoke without looking at him.

"Tomorrow morning, I'll meet with the High Priestesses and the royal council. I intend to tell them about the Dark God." She paused. "My story would be much more believable if you and Natrix were there. Will you come?"

"I cannot," he said.

"Why not?"

"Natrix and I must return to the Hive. I wanted to make sure you were safe and well-recovered before leaving. I see now that both are true."

He sounded so formal, but his words tore her in half.

She reached for his hand, but he avoided her touch.

"The conference will be in the morning," she said, trying not to choke with sadness. "Just for a few hours. Please stay to explain all the things I cannot. Your presence would change everything."

Crash considered his words before he spoke.

"I want to help you, but humans can't know about the Sixth Race. Imagine the consequences for my people. Your kind outnumber us a thousand to one. Our Race does not want to enter back into this world. We want to be left alone to deal with our own business without human intervention."

Sora stayed her tongue, because she couldn't argue with him. She didn't believe humans were ready to accept the Races again. Magic would terrify them. Many would live in fear.

Crash added, "I would ask that you leave as much out about the Sixth Race as you can."

Sora's hands curled into fists. The muscles on her forearms grew tight. How could he ask such a thing of her? After she had risked death—how many times—to save the kingdom and the world?

"The Races caused this mess. We need your knowledge to survive the plague. You owe us your help," she said.

"The human kingdom has the Cat's-Eye stones. You will survive."

"Are these your words, or Natrix's?" Sora asked with some heat.

"They're mine."

"Then you're being very selfish."

"Please try to understand," Crash said, "it's not my choice. I can't interfere without the Hive's permission. They would never allow that."

"The Hive? You mean, the Hive that you *don't* belong to? The Hive that exiled you?"

Crash bowed his head and didn't argue.

"So they're not Natrix's words, but they're the Hive's words," Sora said. "The Hive that betrayed you and cut you off. That's even worse."

"That's how it must be."

Sora inhaled deeply, trying to control her anger. She pressed her forehead against the icy window, feeling the cold moisture against her warm brow.

"Don't go," she said softly.

"I have to."

She swung at him wildly, fist curled to strike, but he caught her and pulled her into a tight embrace. She released a sob of anger.

"It's not fair!" she cried out, petulant. The childish plea ripped from her throat, from some terrible place deep in her chest. "I don't want you to leave. I don't understand where you're going or why. *You can stay here. You can stay.* I need you. I don't know how to live without...this...*us*...." Her eyes widened, burning. "When will I see you again?"

Crash gazed down at her with glowing green eyes. "Evil is vanquished. You've found a home, a family. You can live here, Sora. Time will pass, and you will forget my face. I want you to forget me."

"*Don't go*," she repeated through clenched teeth.

"I have no choice."

Sora heard the finality in his words. She wanted to beat her hands against his chest. She didn't know what the Hive held over him, but she knew its chains were strong. She couldn't break them. She wanted to, but she felt them binding her as well.

"Will I see you again?"

He hesitated. "No."

"I hate you," she seethed. "I hate you. I hate this. *It's not fair.*"

She struggled, lashing out at him with her hands, her arms, and he caught her wrists again, trying to control her. She fought, but his strength overwhelmed her. In the darkness, their limbs entangled. Suddenly, she found his lips pressed against hers. He pulled her against him with a strength almost brutal in its desire, as though he would pull her body into himself. His arms locked around her. She clutched him in turn, holding on as tightly as she could.

Their kiss deepened. His eyes remained open, and she saw their color flicker from green to black, then green again. She sensed his shadow lift from the ground, enveloping her, and she knew the demon wanted to possess her as badly as the man. She would take them both.

"I want all of you," she breathed against his hot mouth. "*All of you.*"

Her Cat's Eye glowed green, its power crackling between them, biting at him, but he did not shy away. He picked her up, her legs wrapped around his waist. He carried her to the bed and laid her down. He threw off his tunic and bent over her, resting his body across hers. She saw the silver scar that ran from his jaw down his chest. She wrapped her arms around his torso and ran her hands over his bare back, where another terrain of scars unfolded: rivers, mountains and valleys.

His fingers, hardened by callouses, brushed her face and sank into her hair, then traveled downward. He undid the buttons along the front of her nightgown, exposing her smooth body. She trembled beneath his gaze—he had never beheld her like this before. She felt fully exposed. Vulnerable. His eyes roved over her, possessive and full of heat. His hand went to the scar on her ribs where the first wraith had plunged its spear through her torso. His thumb feathered over her scar.

"You're so small," he breathed. He cupped one breast, then leaned in close. He captured her mouth in a kiss that made her shiver down to her toes. He spent some time caressing her, adoring her with his mouth, until she forgot to be shy, and she no longer tried to hide from his gaze.

"*Mine,*" he breathed into her ear as they pressed together. The Cat's Eye glowed dimly, its green light illuminating their bodies. "Other men can try to claim you, but after tonight, *you are mine*. Always. No one will have you like this."

Sora let the heat of the moment cloud her thoughts. She didn't want to think about tomorrow, or what his words really meant: someday, she would be in the arms of another man. He accepted that, even if she couldn't imagine it. No other man would ever have her like this—her first awakening to passion. She would never forget the peppery scent of woodsmoke in his hair, or the ridges of scars and coiled muscles beneath her hands.

Joined together as one, she felt no pain. By the dark intensity of his gaze, she knew that Crash had gone away somewhere, and it was the demon who possessed them both, who moved in waves through her body, who made her limbs burn with a fire that was pleasure and possession and weakness and strength combined.

His demon marked her—she didn't know how, for it was not a physical bruising—and yet, she felt him claim her as one might brand a slave. This was the Viper who loved her with all the fire and darkness of his Race; not a human joining, but a bonding beyond the physical. Although he kept the shape of a man, his shadow surrounded them in a cloud, and she knew now, in a way she had not perceived before, that he could never be human.

The Cat's Eye did not react to Viper's magic, but accepted him. The necklace did not react as his shadow embraced her, seeping into her pores, into her lungs, filling her with his essence. She felt his energy penetrate her. The Cat's-Eye stone accepted his possession, until she no longer felt like they were two separate flames, but one ongoing fire.

His teeth sank into her shoulder, and he took her deep into that primal heat.

Many hours later, after their energy was spent, Sora and Crash lay entwined in the four-poster bed. She nestled her head against his chest, his skin warm beneath her cheek. His heartbeat filled her thoughts. She dozed, on the verge of sleep, while his lips rested against her hair.

His voice was hoarse when he spoke. She almost didn't catch his words.

"I'm sorry."

Sora turned her face toward him and kissed his jaw lazily. "Why?"

"For hurting you. For leaving. I'm sorry, Sora." He paused, and his hand stroked meditatively through her hair. "I want you to promise me something."

"Yes?"

"Find a better man than me. Promise me, you will find a better man."

Sora kissed his chest over his heart and laid her cheek against him. Their conversation brought a painful twist to her stomach, and she curled into a ball.

"I can't promise I will find someone else, Crash."

He wrapped his arms around her.

"I'm sorry," he said again.

"We always find each other. I know I will see you again."

"The Hive does not forgive easily, Sora. I go to meet my fate. I expect to be gone for a long time." His words held a dire note. She wasn't sure what he was implying. But she knew if she asked, he wouldn't say.

"Whatever your fate with the Hive, you will survive, and you will return to me. I know it." She kissed him again, then rested her head on his shoulder, her thoughts cloudy and soft with sleep. "You've taught me to move with the river, Viper, and not fight the current," she mumbled. "Even if this is our last and only night together, I have no regrets."

He held her against him, cradling her like a child.

Deeply at peace, she fell asleep.

The next day, Sora woke up alone in her giant bed. Her body was pleasantly sore. She lay for a time, watching the sunrise through the frosty windows.

Despite her passionate memories of the night before, a bittersweet heaviness lay over her heart. Crash was gone.

Would she ever see him again?

Last night, she had felt so confident. This morning, she was full of doubt.

Her hand slid down her body to rest on her abdomen. She was a maiden no longer. As the thought settled over her, she recalled the demon's shadow embracing her from the night before. Viper was not just a man, and their lovemaking had been far from standard. She feasted on her memories, lingering on every touch, trailing her hands across her stomach. She remembered his relentless passion—his *possession.* Although he was gone, she still felt some piece of him with her.

"Other men can try to claim you, but after tonight, you are mine. Always."

She recalled the darkness in his gaze, the intensity of his face. She couldn't explain it fully in words, but on a deep level, she felt like the demon had claimed her. She checked her body, looking for some subtle bite mark or branding, but she found none. Still, she felt in her heart that he had marked her as his own.

She basked in the afterglow for a time. Then a soft knock soon came to her door, and a maid entered with a breakfast tray. Soon, other maids were building a fire in the fireplace and pouring hot water for her bath. A green silk dress, courtesy of Lady Danica, was delivered to her bedroom for her audience at the royal palace. Her hair was unbraided, brushed, then plaited down her back with ribbons and flowers.

As soon as she was clean and dressed, Sora was escorted out the door, through the Ebonaire manor, and down to the front courtyard. There, a carriage awaited with the Ebonaire coat of arms painted upon its shiny walnut doors. Four towering black draft horses were harnessed to the front of the decorative wagon.

Ferran and Burn were waiting for her in the courtyard. Burn was dressed in a white tunic, a large vest and a fawn colored greatcoat that fell to his knees. His hair was neatly brushed and tied at the nape of his neck. Ferran wore a dashing brocade vest over a linen tunic. His entire outfit was solid black. He wore a gold ring upon each finger, the largest resting on his left index finger with the Ebonaire seal in prominent view. He looked very far from the weathered rogue she had encountered on the Dawn Seeker.

The three companions climbed into the carriage together. A footman assisted Sora with her skirts as she took her seat across from the two men. Then the driver cracked his whip, and the carriage rolled forward.

"Have you thought about what you're going to say in front of the royal council?" Ferran asked.

Sora had been trying very hard *not* to think about her coming speech. Now, as her mind wandered to the audience chamber, she felt numb. She remembered Crash's warning from the night before. The Sixth Race did not want their secrets revealed. Would she respect his wishes?

"I will stick to the facts," she said. "But only the facts they will easily accept."

"That might be wise." Ferran looked her over, his eyebrow cocked. "You seem calm and composed. I expected you to be more nervous."

"Just tired. I didn't sleep well," Sora mumbled.

Burn glanced at her with a swift, piercing look. Then his eyes returned to the window. That look alone was enough to make Sora blush. *He knows.* How could he know? She wondered if he could smell Crash's scent on her with his Wulven nose, even after her long bath with scented soaps and oils. Self-conscious, she took a quick sniff of her dress, but all she could smell was lilac and roses.

They crossed the Regency in silence, then up the long driveway to the palace gates, then through the maze of hedges and gardens to the palace's main entrance. Their carriage rolled to a leisurely stop, and a footman in gold livery opened the carriage door. Ferran stepped out first, and Burn followed him. The Wolfy turned to offer her a hand from the carriage.

As she stepped down, Burn said softly into her ear, "The Viper's mark is on you. It is in your hair. Even in your breath."

Sora stepped away in surprise. "Is that such a bad thing?"

Burn's gaze was solemn. "No," he admitted, "not in human company. Your kind cannot sense such things. But another of the Sixth Race will notice it clearly. Others might perceive a . . . lingering aura."

"An aura?"

Burn shrugged. "A shadow? Whatever it is, it's noticeable to me, at least."

Sora ran an awkward hand over her skirts. "How long will it last? Is it permanent?"

"I can't say. One of his kind would know better. Perhaps you can ask him when you see him next."

Sora bit her lip. She looked down at the pattern of tiles that led to the palace's front steps.

"He left," she admitted. "He's gone back to the Hive. I don't think he will return."

She couldn't meet Burn's gaze because she didn't want to see his pity. She picked up her skirts and walked quickly up the palace steps, following Ferran to the front entrance. Whatever "dark aura" the demon had left on her body was insignificant, if humans couldn't detect it. She didn't think she would meet another one of the Sixth Race for a long time. She tried not to think of Crash's absence, or of his last request—that she find a better man.

He's not coming back. Sora silenced the thought. She couldn't imagine a lifetime spent in his absence, never seeing him again, never hearing his voice, never seeing his face. If she imagined it, she thought she would drown. So she focused instead on the moment, on the palace walls, on the gilded doors, the white marble floors, and the murals painted upon the vaulted ceilings. She didn't regret her choice, but it made their parting that much harder, to think of the life they could have shared.

But it was not to be.

The royal palace was a grand distraction, and far from empty. Courtiers strode back and forth in grand dresses and expensive cloaks. Servants followed at their heels. The halls were full of echoing voices and conversation. It seemed everyone had urgent business of some kind.

A footman in gold livery met them just beyond the palace's front doors. Ferran, Burn and Sora were escorted down several hallways to a chamber shaped like a hexagon. Tall windows that looked out upon a garden framed half the room. A table shaped like a crescent moon stood before the windows, where the royal council sat.

Sora entered the hexagonal room and stood before the gathering. Midday light fell around her feet and made a halo around her blond hair. The king and queen sat at the apex of the table, their royal crowns agleam. Sora had never stood this close to the royal family, and she felt a quiver in her stomach. *Am I... awestruck?* she wondered. She felt at once shy yet captivated. How was she to speak in the royal family's presence, when she was overcome by such awe? She gazed at each of their faces: the king was getting on in years, though he still looked healthy and robust. He had long gray hair that blended with his beard. The queen, a redhead, wore a bright yellow dress with big puffy sleeves. She was younger than the king, though her curly hair was turning white around her face. Sora thought that Prince Peric took more after the queen than the king, though after so much had transpired, she could hardly remember the prince's face.

Fanning outward from the royal couple, five council members sat to their left, including Headmaster Duncan and Lord Gracen Seabourne, who Sora was surprised to see. He hadn't mentioned he would be on the council. To the queen's right sat the three High Priestesses. The South Wind had relinquished her plated armor from the day before, and wore a dyed leather suit of deep crimson, with a black cloak of jaguar fur around her shoulders. The East Wind wore a shapeless yellow smock with lantern sleeves that sparkled when she moved. Her neckline and cuffs were embroidered with floral brocade. The West Wind wore a purple dress of loose, hanging silk with silver bands around her arms. Her face was covered by a gauzy purple veil.

"Welcome, Lord Ferran and Lady Sora of the Ebonaire family," the queen spoke. "I am told we owe you a debt of gratitude for your service on Winter Solstice Eve. Lord Ferran, I believe it was your brother who stumbled upon the conspiracy to assassinate the king. This will not be forgotten."

Ferran knelt on one knee. Sora followed suit with a deep curtsy.

"You may rise," the king said. "Please understand you are not here under threat of persecution, but only because we want a written, detailed account of what transpired on Winter Solstice Eve, in your own words, for our royal archives. First, we would like your account, Lord Ferran, of the events leading up to the attack on the royal family at First Winter's Ball. Secondly, we would like your account, Lady Sora, of what transpired after the ball, leading up to the unfortunate disaster that has wrought such chaos upon our city."

That's a fancy way of describing an explosion, Sora thought. She could tell by the way he spoke that King Royce was not a fool.

A scribe with a tall stack of parchment, a quill, and a pot of ink, sat at a small desk in the corner of the room. His quill made a scratching sound whenever someone spoke.

Accompanied by Burn and Ferran, she described what she had witnessed at her mother's farm in the lower plains, and relayed what she knew of the Dark God's plague. She was so focused on the details of her story, she forgot to feel nervous. Her audience was so quiet, she felt like she was speaking to an empty room. They watched her with frowning expressions, and at times, raised eyebrows.

The only time she lost her train of thought was when the Priestess of the South Wind interrupted her, and asked—perhaps more obtusely than intended—how she had discerned the plague's supernatural nature.

Sora showed them her Cat's-Eye necklace and relayed how it could counteract the plague. She recalled parts of her vision, at least the parts that mattered, and left out what she could about the Races. When she was finished, the Priestess of the West Wind agreed with her story and described her visit to Barcella. Ferran and Burn spoke as well, and Ferran displayed his Cat's Eye on his wrist.

Once they were finished, the king and queen thanked them for their testimony. Sora saw varying looks of doubt and trepidation on their faces. The council looked skeptical, perhaps even upset, and the three priestesses all looked grim.

"Lady Sora, this information is invaluable," the Priestess of the East Wind said in a high, clear voice. "We thank you and Lord Ferran for your testimony. We have much to deliberate, as I'm sure you understand. Our scribe has taken down a record of your account. We will refer to that account as we decide how to proceed."

Then the queen spoke: "We may summon you again if we have questions, so please remain at the Ebonaire manor for a few weeks, and leave word if you make any travel plans. Your service to the kingdom will not be forgotten."

Sora curtsied. "Thank you, Your Grace."

She bowed to the rest of the room, as did Ferran and Burn, then their party of four left the conference chamber. The door shut behind them. No one spoke as they traveled down several hallways to the exit. Outside, the Ebonaire coach awaited them in a small courtyard, and somberly, they took their seats.

"What now?" Sora asked, as their carriage left the royal grounds and started back through The Regency.

"Now, we wait to see where things land," Burn said. "They have a lot of work to do to rebuild the city and the Wind Temple. I expect they will want a demonstration of how the Cat's Eye works against the plague. I wouldn't be surprised if we hear from them again."

"Martin will keep us informed," Ferran said, "and Lord Gracen, I expect."

Sora sat back, her gaze returning to the window as the carriage continued through The Regency.

True to Burn's words, Sora and Ferran were summoned back to the palace the next morning, where the council bid them to use their Cat's-Eye stones to cure the plague. The council brought in a wide variety of patients, all of them commoners. The priestesses and council members, and the king and queen, observed Sora and Ferran closely as they worked. More than once, she heard someone gasp, or someone else mutter, "Amazing!" or "Impossible!"

Sora noticed that the plague seemed weaker than before. Her Cat's Eye dealt with it much more efficiently, and she began to put faith in Burn's words.

The Dark God's essence was fading after all. Perhaps the threat had passed and Cerastes truly was defeated.

After their demonstration, Sora and Ferran were dismissed. A servant came to lead them back through the palace to their carriage. As she followed Ferran down the long hallway, her boots echoing on the marble tile, and was surprised to hear a voice call her name.

"Lady Sora," she heard, and turned.

The Priestess of the South Wind approached down the hall at a swift pace. Sora stopped, suddenly nervous. Ferran looked back as well, then came to a halt a respectful distance away, so as not to intrude on their conversation.

Today, the South Wind wore a red tunic and black riding pants with tall black boots. A sword hung at her hip. Her short brown hair was slicked back against her head in a military style. She had a strong jaw and a straight nose and keen, dark eyes.

Sora curtsied, unsure of what else to do.

"Your dress hampers your steps," the priestess said, pausing before her. "Still, you carry yourself like someone skilled in battle."

Sora blinked. "I do?"

The priestess smiled. The expression looked uncomfortable on her hard face.

"I'm very impressed by the demonstration you gave us today. May I ask, do you have a husband or children?"

Sora was taken aback. "No, not yet...I mean, there's no one...."

"Then I would like to invite you to join our order."

Sora's eyes widened, and her face must have betrayed her awe, because the priestess adopted a cautionary tone.

"The Wanderers of the Goddess practice strict martial discipline. We adhere to a challenging regime that many cannot follow. Our warriors do not marry or raise children while they are in service to the Goddess, so if you have any such plans in the near future, you will not find our order to your liking. I ask that you consider my offer with care. Do not accept my offer lightly."

Sora nodded and shut her mouth, realizing it was gaping open.

"I'm honored that you would even consider me...."

The priestess waved a dismissive hand. "But of course. Why wouldn't I, after all you've told the council? I believe the Goddess has her eye on you. My Wanderers and I will remain in the city for the next few months to help rebuild the temple.

Please take your time deciding. If you choose to join us, then you will leave the city and accompany us back to the southern desert. Several years might pass before you see your family again, so as I said, do not make this decision lightly."

Then the priestess turned as abruptly as she had arrived and walked away.

Sora stared after her, breathless, and managed to stutter, "Thank you!"

The priestess waved casually over her shoulder, her sword swinging at her hip, and disappeared down another hallway.

Sora stared after her, her heart racing. She had never been more intimidated or impressed by a woman. Then she turned to Ferran. "Did you hear that?"

"All of it," he said. He didn't sound as pleased as she had expected.

"Can you imagine," she said, as they continued walking, "that I might train with the Wanderers of the Goddess? Following Kaelyn's very footsteps? *Can you imagine?*"

"I can, more easily than you might," Ferran said, "but you should make your decision before telling your mother. Otherwise she will fret up to the day you decide."

Sora nodded in agreement. She didn't think she would tell anyone else until she had made up her mind. Perhaps Burn, if she needed advice, but certainly not Danica or Martin or Gracen, and certainly not her mother.

CHAPTER 26

Crash and Natrix arrived in the Mistmire Hive in the middle of a torrential storm. A mixture of hail and sleet pelted down from the sky, and the wind howled like a wolf at their heels.

They spent the night in a seaside cavern, waiting out the storm rather than risking the ferocious ocean waves that threatened to smash them into the rocks. Tomorrow, they would travel inland to the colony. They crouched around a small fire, two shadows amongst shadows, eating boiled shellfish. Neither spoke.

Crash contemplated the storm, wondering if the gods had sent him this gift—once last night to dwell on his sins before tomorrow's execution. He wondered if Natrix felt pity for him, and if she had stalled their arrival on purpose. She could have transported him directly to the circle of the Elders. His trial could have begun immediately.

But perhaps that was too hopeful. Perhaps the storm also raged above the other colonies, and the Elders couldn't meet until tomorrow. Either way, he was lucky, if one could call this luck.

The next morning, driftwood and debris covered the rocky beach. Natrix and Crash picked their way slowly up to the dunes, where the rain had turned the sandy soil to clumps of mud and crabgrass. They walked through the grass to a line of twisting trees that rose in a tangle of thorns and bracken against the foggy horizon.

Inside the trees, they followed a different path to the circle of the Elders. Their path circumvented the Hive. Crash wasn't sure how he felt about that. He might have liked to see his colony one last time, if only to remember his reasons for coming here.

Natrix led him up steep sand banks and through narrow crevices of rock, and through overgrown thickets where spindly branches caught his cloak like beggaring hands, and he almost heard the wind say *don't go*.

Deep in the woods, before reaching the circle of the Elders, Natrix paused and turned to him.

"Today, you will pay the Hive's price," she said. "You will be killed, but your Name will be returned to our people's records. Is that truly what you want?"

Crash hadn't expected a single word to pass between them until reaching the Elders. Natrix was his warden, not his ally, and his kind did not lend comfort through words. He searched her face suspiciously, her narrow mouth and wide cheeks, her slanting eyes and arched brows.

"I returned to the Hive to warn them of Cerastes, and I will not run again from my fate," he said.

She stared at him intensely, as though trying to see beneath his skin. "You mean to die for the Hive, who turned their back on you. Doesn't that seem foolish? Bullheaded, even?"

Crash flexed his wrists. "Why are you asking me this?"

Natrix considered him. "It would be a waste of potential." Then she turned abruptly and continued down the forested path. "I think you are doing this to prove something to someone important, but have you considered, if you are dead, then you've proven nothing? She will forget you in time. Your great lesson will be lost and your mistakes repeated by someone else."

"You think I'm doing this for love," Crash said. "I'm not."

"Then why?"

"I've spent years running from the Hive, running from my enemies, running from myself. There is no place for me in this world, not the way it stands now. I can't live that life any longer. I came back to the Hive to warn you and stop Cerastes. If this is the consequence, so be it. I am done running from my fate."

"If you mean to gain honor through death, then you assume a lot about the afterlife."

"And you assume a lot about me."

They both fell silent. Natrix didn't continue her argument, but her displeasure was obvious. They passed through a curtain of willow trees and came upon the circle of faceless statues around the pit of sand. Natrix led him to the center of the circle, where she stood with him, side by side. They both bowed.

"Elders," she said, "you are present."

"True," a woman's voice answered. "We have been waiting."

"I have returned with the assassin, Viper, from our mission. Grandmaster Cerastes is dead. He was killed by the seraph, Caprion, who was born on the broken isle of Aerobourne. On winter solstice night—"

"Where are the Dark God's weapons?" a child's voice asked, cutting her off. The tone was very un-childish, and sounded both severe and aggressive.

Natrix paused. The question broke their code of speech. Traditionally, they were supposed to speak in statements.

"We could not recover the weapons. We believe they were destroyed."

A gust of dry wind traveled through the clearing.

"Impossible," the woman's voice intoned.

"The seraph unleashed the energy of his star. His sacrifice leveled half the city. Every wood fixture was turned to dust in the heat—only stone survived. We searched the area thoroughly and found no remnants of the weapons."

"A god's weapons can neither be created or destroyed," a man's voice intoned from yet another statue. "Fools. You left them behind in the human city."

"They can't be destroyed, but they can be changed," the woman's voice contradicted him. "Seraphim are beings imbued with godlike powers. What Grandmaster Natrix proposes is not so farfetched."

"Changed to what, then?" the unknown man asked. "Dust? Aether?"

"Perhaps transported to some other realm," the child's voice mused. "Perhaps returned to the underworld, whence they belong. It is no secret that Cerastes' work tipped the world far out of balance. We've felt the shifting energies in our bones. Our own dreams have been restless, and we have spoken of them at length. A seraph only appears when the Elements attempt to right that balance. Perhaps the weapons were returned to the underworld by their will. Even for our kind, much knowledge has been lost."

Another period of silence stretched between the statues. Crash gazed at face after empty face. Anonymous. Unmarked. On one statue, a vine of red ivy curled around its weathered feet like a spatter of blood on white robes.

He knew the Elders spoke among each other without his knowledge, their voices drifting between colonies through private campfires and burning incense.

They conferred about the weapons and perhaps Natrix's reputation, and perhaps his own. The suspense left him wary and tense.

Finally, the woman's voice spoke again from the faceless statues.

"We trust your judgement and concede that the Dark God's weapons may have been transported to another realm, or otherwise transformed, by the seraph's power. We acknowledge this may be the will of the gods or an act of the Elements, and otherwise uninterpretable. Grandmaster Natrix, we will require your word to be tested."

"I submit," Natrix said with a slight nod.

Crash knew what the Elders meant. Natrix would be required to drink a truth syrem, and retell the events as they unfolded. It was the only way for the Hive to be certain that they didn't take the weapons for themselves, or some other mishap. Crash understood their decision.

The man's voice spoke next: "Until more time has passed, and further events take place, we cannot discern the location of the weapons. For now, we agree the matter has been resolved. Once we have tested your words, Grandmaster, your mission will be complete." After a pause, he added, "Our respective colonies will not forget how you have aided us. Should you need aid, you may call on us."

The woman spoke again. "If you have nothing more to add, Grandmaster, we shall turn to matters of the Viper."

Crash stood a little straighter.

"True," Natrix said curtly. "I shall speak on behalf of the Viper."

"He is not your student."

"Dissonance," Natrix repeated. "He was my student once. I shall lay claim to my rights as his master."

Crash stared at Grandmaster Natrix, wondering at her game. They had never trained together. In fact, her strongest student, The Adder, had been one of his greatest rivals.

Natrix placed her hands, palms together, before her face. He thought, at first, that she was praying. Then her shadow lifted from the ground like a billow of smoke. The shadow-cloud stretched and contorted, hiding her momentarily from sight.

When the shadow returned to the ground, and flattened into its natural shape, the Grandmaster's silhouette had changed drastically.

The face gazing at him now was round and pale like the moon, with eyes slanted almost vertical. An owl's face, both wise and quizzical. His stature was smaller than most of their kind, but his shoulders were unusually wide. He stood with an easy grace.

"Grandmaster Lachesis," Crash murmured, and knelt in reflex, his head bowed. His heart hammered in his chest. Every conversation between him and Natrix repeated in his mind, taking on new meaning.

Grandmaster Lachesis, the forest hermit and elusive teacher, and unknowingly, his companion for the last several days.

"But," he stammered, "what of Grandmaster Natrix?"

"The honorable Grandmaster Natrix died in the same fire that ended our peace with the Sandsorrow Hive. You wouldn't have known, because you left the Hive before we learned of her death. However, the blame was still placed on your shoulders."

Crash turned to the circle of statues, winded. He felt as though he stood amidst a living, breathing jury. "You knew," he said, his voice hoarse and low. "You all knew."

Then he faced Lachesis again. "Why did you trick me?"

"I wanted to observe Cerastes' protege," Lachesis said. "Should I have been disappointed in your performance, I would have let the Elders decide your fate."

Crash stared at him, his heart still thundering in his ears. The blood had drained from his face.

"And what is my fate?"

"You may still die, should you wish, and seek honor in the afterlife, whatever that will gain you." Lachesis' words were as dry as autumn. "But I will train you as my student, should you wish to continue your practice."

Crash glanced around the stone circle. The Elders did not speak. Despite the flat, empty faces of the statues, he knew they watched. In the distance, a crow released a mocking, choking cry.

He turned back to Lachesis.

"With respect, Grandmaster, you do not belong to any of the colonies within the Hive."

"And that means I cannot teach?"

"No, but...." Crash hesitated, uncertain. "You helped me long ago, when Cerastes first left the Hive, but you've never been known to take a traditional student. Your methods...."

"My methods are very different than what you experienced with Cerastes, but they still fall within the traditions of the Hive. Perhaps you hesitate for other reasons. Do you fear you have lost your edge?"

Crash hardened, regaining himself. "No. Of course not."

"Then become my student, and ascend to Grandmastery."

This was more than Crash had anticipated. Admittedly, he had harbored a vague hope that, after defeating Cerastes, the Hive might pardon him and accept his return. But he hadn't banked on it. He certainly hadn't expected *this*. That morning, he had been prepared to meet death. To his knowledge, Lachesis did not take students. Their encounters before had been irregular and, Crash suspected, granted out of pity.

Of course, he still yearned to continue his practice. He had always yearned for that. Even on the road, alone, he had trained from memory, repeating every exercise, every lesson, until he drove himself mad. Taking Sora under his wing had only intensified his desire to progress, to ascend....

Occasionally, he had heard of Grandmasters seeking out Lachesis in the mountains to hone their skills. *Grandmasters.*

"I will be honored to become your student," he said, and bowed his head to his knees.

"Then it is done." Lachesis turned back to the circle of statues. "The Viper's transgressions against the Mistmire Hive are absolved. His life belongs to me. The Elders find this acceptable."

Many voices responded, all echoing the same word: "True."

"Then arise, Viper, *he who hides in the grass*. Arise a Named assassin in service to the Hive. Your trespasses are forgiven." Lachesis laid his hand along the back of Crash's neck, and with a slight burning sensation, removed the deathmark on his skin.

Crash remained on his knees and forced himself to breathe steadily. He would train with Lachesis, perhaps in the mountains, perhaps in the woods, ever traveling between the different colonies and perhaps to other lands beyond. He would be free of this oppressive place, and free of his past, and free to pursue the future he wanted.

Finally, he stood. Words could not express his feelings, and in the Hive, they were unnecessary. Instead, he faced the circle of Elders and bowed again.

The child's voice spoke: "The Mistmire Hive offers Grandmaster Lachesis provisions from our winter stores. Gather what you and your student need before continuing on your travels. We are ever in your debt for your service to the Hive."

"Go in shadow," the others murmured.

There was no visible indication when the Elders left the circle, but Crash sensed when they were gone. Where once the statues had seemed intimidating and imbued with awareness, they were now just faceless stones. The wind blew hollowly through the trees, and a crow cawed again. The smaller sounds of the forest, the ambience of rustling branches and bird calls, came back into focus.

Lachesis turned in the sand and walked back into the woods. Crash hesitated before following him. Then they passed through the curtain of willow trees and found the path leading back to Mistmire Hive.

The forest swallowed the circle of statues behind them.

They reached the colony as the sun was setting. Overhead, the crimson sky bled through swaths of gray clouds. Savants and Named assassins alike walked quietly back and forth to their different huts, some carrying the day's hunt slung over their shoulders, others scuffed and dirty from practice. None of them met his eyes or even seemed to notice his presence. He knew, once full night had set in and the fires were low, that they would speak of Lachesis and his unknown companion. A few might even remember his face and the story of the Viper. But for now, all was quiet.

Lachesis led him past the silent huts to a square building at the far side of the colony. The building's foundation had been sunk low in the ground, so that they had to climb down a set of stairs to reach the door. Crash didn't recognize the storehouse from his younger days in the Hive and, by the quality of the wooden beams and stone walls, he decided it was new.

Inside, the floor was dirt. Smoked animal carcasses hung from the rafters. Boxes of oats and grain stood along the far wall. By the looks of things, last year's harvest had been thin, much of Mistmire's stores were depleted.

Lachesis took a rucksack from the wall and passed a second one to Crash. Then he began filling it.

Crash opened the sack and looked around, taking inventory of what he might need.

"How long will we be traveling?" he asked.

"Many months. Bring enough to see you through to the spring."

Crash began sorting through the different shelves and crates. He packed away dried meat wrapped in parchment, pouches of nuts, and sacks of uncooked legumes.

As he worked, his mind traveled, inevitably, to Sora. Since leaving The City of Crowns, he had tried not to think of her, and had focused instead on preparing his mind and body for his execution. But he could no longer keep the memories at bay. He saw her face again, her body beneath his, their limbs entwined. A protective surge of heat moved through him. The need to touch her, to feel her next to him, became overwhelming. Memories--scents and murmurs, the light from her Cat's Eye--played before his eyes. He couldn't stop the images and he didn't want to.

The demon uncoiled in his stomach. *Mine,* it seemed to groan.

He wished, fleetingly, that he could tell her of his fate. He thought of writing her a letter, or sending her a farewell gift of some kind, perhaps something sentimentally human, like a pressed flower or a vial of scented oil. But those were gifts for courtship. What had they shared? Stone and steel, campfires and road dust and horse hooves galloping on shale. As a partner, as a warrior, he knew every method she used to attack or defend, each hidden strength, each weakness. But as a woman, he didn't know her at all.

Strange, how his ignorance seemed so loud, so blatant, in that moment, as he gathered matchwood and whetstones into his bag. He knew, so well, the way she caught her tongue behind her teeth when she smiled, and what her hands did when she was nervous. But he didn't know her mind. He could never know that.

But, was knowing even necessary?

It isn't love, he told himself, though he knew that was a lie. He wasn't the first of his kind to love, and he wouldn't be the last. But he had a new road to follow, and he couldn't go back for her now. She would find a better man, a human, to be her husband, and he would put her from his mind.

Perhaps, in the years to come, when the winters grew too cold and the days too dim, he would hold her memory up to the firelight. He would feel her in his arms again, and remember.

He looked up, realizing he had been standing immobile, gazing at the bag in his hands, for some time. He closed the drawstring tight and slung it over his shoulder.

Lachesis stood in the doorway, gazing out at the frosty night. Crash joined him.

"Do you have everything you need?" the Grandmaster asked.

"Yes."

Then the two assassins vanished into the dark.

CHAPTER 27

Weeks turned into months. Like the snow melting in the Ebonaire gardens, Sora warmed to her new life. By springtime, when the birds had returned to their nests and the fawns to the forest, she felt almost at home. In the mornings, she rode her horse across acres of wooded hunting grounds, from the Ebonaire stables to the very wall of the royal palace. She spent her afternoons with Danica sewing, reading, or out on the town. She accompanied Ferran and Lorianne to dinner parties and luncheons, and despite her subtle contempt for her new life, she realized it was a good one.

Ferran became more involved with matters of the Ebonaire estate, and Lorianne assisted Headmaster Duncan at the seminary. Burn found a place as Lord Gracen's assistant, and helped the Captain of the King's Guard on various missions around the city.

Lord Gracen found many opportunities to visit the Ebonaire manor, and Sora enjoyed his company. They walked through the rose gardens leisurely, and at times, she took his arm. He spoke to her of military tactics and his training as a soldier; of the kingdom's progress and the city's new construction; of the king's plans and the occasional frustrations of his position. Sometimes, they didn't speak at all, but sat in various walled-off sections of the garden and read books or letters.

Each day bled into the next, until she opened her eyes one morning to the sound of bells and laughter. It was her mother's wedding day.

She roused herself to bathe and dress.

A new handmaid assisted her into a lavender dress with chiffon skirts and silk bows. Brilliant yellow sunlight spilled through her open bedroom window, and the wind carried the scent of jasmine and thyme. Outside, servants were decorating the manor gardens with wreaths of flowers in preparation for the ceremony.

As Sora gazed at herself in the mirror, running her hands down her beaded corset, she thought again of the South Wind's offer. In the city, the Temple of the North Wind was almost rebuilt. Soon they would elect a new High Priestess, and then the other orders would leave back to their respective temples. She had to choose—did she want to join the South Wind and become a Wanderer, or did she want to stay and see what more The Regency could offer?

Every time she began to imagine her future in the city, her thoughts led her back to her battle with Cerastes, and then to the man who had changed her life.

She thought of Crash often, and wondered if she was a sadist at heart, because his memory caused her such pain and yet she couldn't stand to forget him. Mourning his absence was like grieving a death. The loss was unlike any she had felt before, for it wasn't his death she mourned, but the life she had dreamed of and fought for. She had lost, in many ways, a far greater battle than the one against Cerastes. In her naive and innocent heart, she had held onto the belief that Crash would succumb to the unquestionable bond they shared, and they would be together. She had always believed in that ending, no matter how many times he had refused her, and all the excuses he gave. Worst of all, she didn't want to stop believing. How could she imagine a new life for herself, when she was still so in love with her dreams?

Yet as the months stretched on and his presence drew further away, she began to realize the truth: their story had ended, and she was left unhappy. She couldn't shake her general malaise. In many ways, she was exactly where she had started, living the same life among the same nobility she had once despised. Part of her still yearned to escape, to adventure into the unknown, yet now she knew what awaited her down that road, and she wasn't so certain she would find happiness there.

She could join the Order of the South Wind, but what if Crash returned for her? She could marry a lord and start a family, but would he one day appear on her doorstep? How could she make any decision with the ever-lingering chance that they might still be together?

She had tried to speak to her mother of such things, but Lorianne pushed her to forget about Crash and focus, if she wished, on other eligible suitors in The Regency. Sora suspected that Lorianne would rather she join the Wanderers than pursue the assassin. Her mother meant well. They all did. But none of them really understood what she and Crash had shared.

She had spoken to Burn about it once, but his sad eyes had been worse than her mother's advice. His gentle wisdom had only confirmed her deepest fears—Crash was gone forever, lost to the Hive, and he would never return.

And so, somewhat gray-spirited on this day of celebration, she joined her mother in the lower quadrants of the Ebonaire estate. Lorianne stood in an atrium framed by glass doors that opened into the rose garden. Her robes were conservative: a plain white smock with a square-cut neckline fell to her ankles, tied by a gold sash at her waist. Yellow flowers adorned her hair. In the midmorning light, Sora thought her mother glowed like the sun.

"I am so glad to share this day with you," Lorianne said, and kissed Sora upon her brow.

Sora squeezed her mother's hands and felt tears in her eyes. She wiped at them awkwardly.

"I didn't think I would cry," she said.

"Today is a day for tears and laughter." Lori took her daughter's hand. "Now, I know we've spoken about this at length, but I cannot walk into that garden without asking you one more time. Do I have your blessing?"

Sora felt a rush of love for the woman. "Always," she said.

"Then let us walk."

Sora followed her mother out of the atrium and through the gardens. As she walked, her mind turned to Ferran. It had taken her some time to adjust to the idea of their wedding. She hadn't yet accepted that she would have a new stepfather, and she didn't think that would happen quickly. Still, she wouldn't jeopardize her mother's happiness over her own discomfort. Perhaps in time, as their family became closer, she would look to him as a father, but for now, his friendship was more than enough.

At the center of the garden was a gazebo where Ferran stood in a brown great-coat over a burgundy vest and white tunic. His hair was trimmed and brushed, his shoes polished, and Sora thought he looked very different from the rapscallion adventurer she had once known. His brother Martin and the entire Ebonaire family stood behind him, all dressed in various shades of purple, gold or yellow.

She was the only family member present on her mother's side, but Burn and Headmaster Duncan had joined them at her mother's request, so it wasn't quite so lonely on her side of the pedestal. No one else attended the ceremony. Weddings were strictly family affairs, even in the city. The rest of their friends would celebrate that night at a dance hosted at the Ebonaire manor. Danica had told her the royal family would attend, and most of the First Tier.

Lori and Ferran stood to either side of a basin of water, and between them stood a priestess from the Temple of the East Wind. She wore a golden headdress upon her brow, covered in crystals and dried flowers and little bells, and white paint covered her face with blue markings on her cheeks. In this role, she was to represent the Wind Goddess.

The priestess bid them to kneel and dip their hands in the water. Then, she opened a silk scroll in her dainty hands and read:

The Wind that split our souls atwain
Shall bind us, ne'er to part again.
Tree and vine, we grow together,
Through famine, feast and stormy weather,
Until the day our souls depart,
We shall forever share one heart.

The priestess took two bracelets made of gold, carved and fashioned with intricate detail, and clasped the smaller one on Lorianne's wrist, and the larger one on Ferran's wrist above his Cat's-Eye stone. The two raised their hands from the water, their fingers locked together in a tight grip. Sora felt wetness against her cheeks, and brushed away a stream of tears again.

The two newlyweds left the garden together, and after the ceremony was over, Sora chatted a bit with the Ebonaire family. It was the first wedding she had attended, and she was surprised by its brevity. One by one, they retired to prepare for the evening's festivities.

That night, the same rose garden was transformed into an aethereal place. Colorful paper lanterns hung from fruit trees and pergolas, and jars of fireflies decorated the terrace. Long banquet tables trembled beneath the weight of so much food. Sora saw plates of duck, rabbit and chicken, and an entire roasted pig glazed in honey. She saw fruit bowls of cucumber and melon; green salads with walnuts, dried apricots, goat's cheese and strawberries; steamed buns stuffed with minced meat; loaves of rye bread, oat or pumpernickel seasoned with nuts and herbs; vats of rich vegetable soup and creamy fish stew. The desserts rivaled the main course. Besides the towering wedding cake, there were lemon and cherry hand pies, honey biscuits, pink wedding cookies with butter frosting, chocolate truffles, rice pudding with cinnamon, and bars of peanut brittle. She ate to her heart's content and still hadn't sampled half the food on the table.

Danica walked with her across the wide terrace that framed the back of the Ebonaire manor, spanning from the library to the rose gardens, and introduced her to all the families she didn't recognize. Soon, Sora's head was buzzing with names she would never remember and faces she would soon forget.

The king and queen attended the party briefly, but left early in the evening. The princess, however, remained behind to dance and enjoy the festivities. Much to Sora's dismay, Danica took it upon herself to introduce them. Sora managed to curtsy to the princess, who was Danica's same age and a childhood friend, but then she found herself stuttering and staring at her feet. She couldn't think of anything to say, and all she could think of was Prince Peric's betrayal.

Lady Danica cheerfully made up for Sora's awkwardness with a nudge and a laugh. Then she dived into an intense conversation with the princess, and Sora was left to stand awkwardly as the two girls caught up on news and gossip.

Sora managed to excuse herself after a time. She walked away rapidly, wondering if she would be remembered as Danica's rude cousin.

Her footsteps hurried toward the deeper indigo shade of the gardens, beyond the rose bushes and the fruit trees, but her flight was interrupted by a hand catching her elbow. Sora turned on her heel, annoyed, only to find Lord Gracen at her side. She sucked in a quick breath. He wore his black military uniform, as he had on winter solstice, with his dark hair slicked back against his head, revealing only a few strands of gray around his temples. His eyes, obsidian in the candlelight, flickered to her dress.

He released her elbow.

"Lady Fallcrest, you are stunning, as always," he said, his words flat and droll. Sora knew his sense of humor by now. "I must congratulate you on your rise to power."

Sora blinked. "As an Ebonaire, you mean?"

"Yes. Sincerely, I do mean it. For a dead woman, you are quite accomplished. And I wish your mother happiness in her new marriage."

Sora felt a smile flirting with her lips. She tried to suppress it, but couldn't, so she turned away to hide it. Her eyes found the dance floor. Four stately maple trees, their branches covered in little starlike leaves, encircled a pavilion of paved flagstones. Lorianne and Ferran were at the center of the floor, surrounded by many dancing couples, turning lazily in each others arms to the gentle lull of a ballad.

Gracen spoke again. "If you will walk with me a moment, Lady Sora, I have many thoughts I've been wanting to share with you."

"Of course," she agreed, and took his arm as he led her into the rose gardens. They stayed close to the golden light of the festivities, though far enough away to speak in private. Eventually, they came upon a gurgling fountain, where Gracen paused and faced her.

"My Lady, although we haven't known each other long, over these past few months I feel we have grown close. You've shown me truths about the world I never before conceived of, and for that, I must thank you."

Sora nodded, trying to understand what lay behind his words. Was he concerned about the plague? Although Cerastes had been defeated, infected patients were still arriving at the seminary, and Sora still felt uneasy about that.

"Ah, well, you're welcome," she said, realizing he was waiting for her reply. "Truly, we couldn't have saved the kingdom without your help. So much happened during winter solstice, I can't even recount all of the events. The parade and the prince's treason, the clocktower falling, and the Wind Temple....I agree it feels like we've known each other longer than we have."

"Yes, I'm glad you feel the same." He cleared his throat. "I suppose I should say that I am a serious man, my lady, and I care little for shallow acquaintances. I want to surround myself with people I trust. Do you trust me, Lady Sora?"

Something about his words reminded her of Crash.

"I do," she said with uncertainty.

"Then believe me when I say, what I am about to ask of you, I do not ask lightly. I have put much thought into it, yet my feelings remain steadfast."

Suddenly, Sora gleaned where this conversation was leading, and her stomach twisted.

"My lady, I have shunned marriage for a long time, absorbing myself in my duty to the royal family. Although I do not regret doing so in service to the kingdom, it is a lonely life. However, since meeting someone of your strength and character, I feel my loneliness much more keenly. Please, I would like to propose that we join our two families in marriage."

"Marriage?" She could barely say the word.

"Yes. I thought, as it is your mother's wedding, perhaps now would be the time to reveal my own affections."

They stared at one another. Sora forgot to breathe, but not for the right reasons.

"I see," she said, suspicion coloring her thoughts. "You waited, then, for me to become an Ebonaire?"

Gracen studied her. "My feelings have grown over time, and have nothing to do with your name or title. But I will admit, for me to extend a formal offer of marriage, you needed to be *on the books*, so to speak." His voice turned dry. "I am the one who pronounced you dead so long ago. That creates a problem with our family tree."

Sora didn't respond immediately, but stood very still, her hands clasped before her. She understood, reasonably, that Lord Gracen came from a wealthy family and was not trying to poach the Ebonaire fortune. In many ways, she was at fault for indulging him and encouraging his attention. If she were truly honest with herself, she would admit to flirting with him on occasion, and certainly she had felt a special pull between them. She could see why, and how, a marriage would make sense, and if she were ten years older, she might have agreed to it.

But she was not ten years older, and her heart was full of knots and holes, and when she lay her head down at night and wrapped her arms around herself, she dreamed of another man.

"I'm sorry, but I can't accept your proposal," she said, her voice hollow.

Gracen didn't seem surprised. He took it in stride, as he did everything else.

"Then I'm truly sorry for inflicting such a heavy request upon you. Please, enjoy the celebration, and we won't speak of it further."

She wondered if she had offended him, or hurt him, but his face revealed nothing. He was a soldier, his jaw firm, his eyes steady.

"I'm very flattered...." she tried to say, but he hushed her.

"Please, my lady, I am not a boy new to the field. You don't need to assuage my ego. I knew you were far out of my reach, but I had to try."

Sora hesitated, her hands gripping her skirts, drawn once again to his patience, his acceptance. Then she picked up her skirts and turned away from the fountain.

"I'm sorry," she said again. "Truly, I am."

Sora left Gracen's side and walked deeper into the gardens, beyond the reach of the lantern light. Eventually, she found her favorite place, where stone walls segmented the garden into little private pavilions, each one unique from the last. She walked down a flagstone path between the different garden rooms, her lip caught between her teeth. Gracen's proposal had caught her off guard, and conflicting emotions warred within her, demanding a release. Twice, she swallowed back tears.

In a private alcove overgrown with ivy and jasmine, Sora found a secluded garden bench against the wall. She sat there for a time in the darkness, listening to the music and watching the dancers from afar. There, she allowed her uncertainty to overwhelm her, and let the tears fall openly down her cheeks.

After a time, she heard heavy footsteps along the garden path and knew that she had been found out.

"I've been looking for you," Burn said, approaching her. He joined her on the bench. He was dressed in a linen tunic and black leggings, his clothes new and properly fitted, his hair groomed and tied at the base of his neck. If he noticed her tears, he didn't mention them. They sat for a time, considering the distant noise of the party and the many glinting lights.

Then Burn spoke. "Perhaps you are thinking of Ferran and Lori, and how this has all come about. It must be very strange. You lost a father at the beginning of this journey, and now you've gained a new father at the end. You lost your nobility and, ironically, seemed to have recovered it as well. But I'm wrong, aren't I? You're not concerned with Ferran or your mother, or your title at all." Burn gave her a kindly grin, showing his lion-like teeth.

Sora sighed. "You're not wrong," she admitted, "but it's more than that."

"Caprion, then? I do miss his lofty visits. Or...are you missing a certain assassin?"

"Yes, and no," she said, and wiped her eyes. She studied the dancers beneath the maple trees. The song changed and partners switched, and then they all picked up again. "I suppose I'm thinking about the future."

"Indeed."

Sora considered her next words. "Lord Gracen proposed to me."

"Ah. And that made you unhappy?"

"Not exactly. I know he's a good man and we would make a good match, but I don't think that's what I want. The future is so different from what I imagined at my Blooming, but one thing remains the same: I don't think I want to get married." She sighed and ran a hand over her face, trying to arrange her thoughts. "The Priestess of the South Wind asked me to join her order. I've been considering it for a while. Ferran knows, but not my mother. I didn't want to tell her until I was certain."

Burn studied her face. "And are you?"

"I wasn't, but then Lord Gracen proposed, and now...I know I don't want to marry. I think I want to go with the Wanderers."

Burn sat thoughtfully for a moment, drawing in a great, ruminative breath. "That seems reasonable, if it's what you want."

Sora felt lighter. Some of her tension eased from her shoulders.

"When would you leave?" he asked.

"When the priestesses leave, I suppose. I don't know how long it will take them to appoint a new High Priestess of the North Wind, but once they have, I would travel with them back to their temple in the South."

"For how long?"

"I don't know."

"And Lord Gracen's proposal?"

"I...." Sora wondered if she was running away again, but his marriage proposal had forced upon her a higher truth—she didn't want this life. "I'm sure he will find someone else. But my mother...I don't know if she will understand."

Burn stood up from the garden bench and stretched his back.

"You might be surprised. She was a young woman once, and not that long ago. She might bite a few nails and worry about you, but she will support your decision. She knows she can't dissuade you, if it's what your heart desires. That said, I think she will be proud of you."

"Truly, you think so?"

"I do. And I think you will feel quite at home with the Wanderers."

Sora found herself smiling. She had spent too many hours thinking, doubting, and questioning herself. Speaking the words aloud felt like an invisible wall collapsing, and suddenly, she was excited about the future. She took Burn's hand and let him escort her back to the party. *Life is good,* she told herself, *and the battle is won.* She was free to pursue the life she wanted.

She entered the firelight, surrounded by her family and friends, and joined the dance.

CERASTES' CURSE

Chapter 1

"**F**or the past seven years, we have suffered a drought, but now the desert is in full bloom."

Sora shifted on the hard wooden bench. She feigned interest in the High Priestess's sermon. Her thoughts drifted to the dinner hour, to fresh-baked barley bread and cactus curry.

"Three Elements come together in harmony in the desert: Water, Earth and Wind. From their union, life is sprung. The rains pour down, the plants produce pollen, and the wind carries this pollen across the countryside. From this unity, the desert blooms."

High Priestess Morrigan Karr paused before adding a bit of humor to her sermon: "Of course, it's not a blessing for everyone. Priestess Somana's allergies are more of a curse to her, wouldn't you say?"

The youngest acolytes, who sat cross-legged on the floor closest to the High Priestess, giggled.

"Aye, that's enough," Priestess Somana said from the back of the chamber.

The acolytes tittered into silence.

The congregation sat in a half-moon formation in the low-lit chamber, arranged by order of age. The youngest few acolytes were piled at the High Priestess's feet, aged eleven to thirteen summers. The second row, the grand majority, were fourteen through seventeen. The rest of the priestesses sat at the back of the room, on long wooden benches with no cushions or backing.

Sora didn't sit with the other acolytes. She perched on a bench near the back of the stone chamber with the rest of the priestesses who came to listen. Morrighan Karr did not only teach the acolytes, but all of the priestesses who lived at the temple.

Sora, who had just reached her twenty-first year, was the eldest of the acolytes and the same age as several priestesses. When she had first arrived at the temple two years ago, she had found the age difference between herself and the other acolytes a bit embarrassing. She was no longer a child, but a young woman, and sitting in classes with a wiggly group of thirteen year olds wasn't what she had imagined when coming to the temple. She still hadn't fully adjusted. Her sense of being in-between ranks remained. On the one hand, she had survived more battles and undergone more physical challenges than any of the priestesses in the room. She knew more about the lore of the Races and the Cat's-Eye stones than anyone she had met in the temple so far. But, she was unschooled in the ways of the South Wind, and still considered a complete novice by her peers. Her closest friend, Trylee, was a girl seven years her junior.

The High Priestess Morrighan Karr stood at the head of the room before six vertical stained-glass windows. Each window's mosaic depicted one of the Elements: Wind, Earth, Fire, Water, Light and Darkness. An easel next to her displayed parchments and scrolls. The most prominent scroll, highlighted by a well-placed lantern, showed a diagram of the desert cycles. Little black arrows drawn by an elegant hand illustrated the lifecycle of a seed, and how the wind carried seeds for the next year's blooming: *from dirt to flower to sky.*

"Now, I would like you all to imagine that you are somewhere in this cycle," Priestess Morrighan Karr continued. "Remember the lore of the Wind Goddess. All of life is a cycle. The Wind harmonizes all of the Elements, creating the world of Wind and Light in which we dwell. Other realms exist besides this one. The underworld of legend is a realm of Fire and Shadow, uninhabitable, a burning land where evil dwells. Remember, also, the Realm of the Gods, where the Wind Goddess reigns next to the gods of Fire, Water, Earth, and Light. These three realms, although separate from our perspective, also harmonize together in a great cycle. Darkness and Light ebb and flow. Water, Fire and Earth create the natural world. All of the Elements synthesize to One, and none of this is possible without the Wind."

One of the acolytes in the front row raised a hand. The High Priestess paused, acknowledging the girl with a nod of her head.

"Is there a God of Shadow?" the girl asked. "Isn't 'Shadow' also one of the Six Elements?"

Morrighan Karr nodded sagely. "Indeed, there is a Dark God who is locked away in the underworld. From Shadow, evil men are born. This ancient lore is not taught in the Kingdom of Err, because the Wind Goddess locked away the Dark God many eons ago. But as warriors of the Wind Goddess, we must be prepared for Her call, to take up arms against the Darkness should it arise."

Morrighan Karr turned back to her sermon, indicating the easel. Her hand followed the arrows around the drawing in a circular motion. Her brown eyes traveled over the youngest acolytes in the front row, all the way to the shadowy back of the room where Sora and the other priestesses sat.

"Remember that the Wind harmonizes all Six Elements into One," she repeated. "And that is why the world has order."

Even at a distance, Morrighan Karr struck an imposing figure. The High Priestess of the South Wind stood as tall as a man, with all the swagger and confidence of a warrior. Her choice in uniform was also masculine. Unlike the lower priestesses, who dressed in soft linen robes, Morrighan Karr wore exquisite red hunting leathers and knee-high boots. She had the intense features of a hawk, with a long nose and pointed chin, and short brown hair slicked back from her face.

"Meditate upon the cycle of Spring," she continued her sermon. "Perhaps you are at the beginning, a seed lying dormant in the earth, waiting for the rain to awaken you.

"Or perhaps you have bloomed already, but you are like pollen, flowing aimlessly across the desert plains, seeking your purpose.

"Or perhaps you know your purpose, and you are ready to grow, to work, and to bear the fruits of Summer.

"Life is a grand cycle. Our growth is never finished. We are all constantly turning into something else, at any age, in any season. We bear many seeds and much fruit over a lifetime.

"We shall meditate on this until the great bell summons us for the evening meal."

A gentle rustling filled the room as priestesses and acolytes settled for a long and quiet meditation. It was easy to do in the Sunset Chambers. The stained glass windows did not allow much light into the room. Although the full force of sunset shone through them, casting red-and-blue light across the floor, the chamber itself was dusklike, the air cool. The stone walls of the South Wind's temple were thick enough to block out all extraneous noise, except for the familiar rustle of Sora's benchmates.

A windcatcher funneled fresh air into the Sunset Chamber, cooling the room. Dozens of windcatchers, all shapes, styles and designs, helped regulate the microclimate of the temple. Built like reverse chimneys, they faced the wind outside, funneling cool air through a network of ducts and channels that ran like blood veins through the main pyramid and its surrounding buildings. Without the windscoops, the stone buildings would be uninhabitable in the oppressive summer heat, which soared to deadly temperatures during the day. During her first year, Sora had fainted from heat exhaustion several times before she learned to stay hydrated and walk in the shade.

One such windcatcher emptied directly into the Sunset Chamber, creating a gentle crossbreeze through the room. It was quite pleasant.

Sora closed her eyes and allowed her breathing to slow, to deepen, until she found her breath in sync with the women on either side of her. *From seed to flower to sky.* She allowed her mind to relax and her thoughts to empty. She let the High Priestess's question flow inside of her like the wind, questing for an answer.

Where was she, in this season of growth? Dormant? Blooming? Ready to bear fruit?

Her vision was dark, until it wasn't.

Sora sat beside the window in her private chambers in the Fallcrest manor, surrounded by hand-carved furniture and velvet drapery. Sheet music rested on a stand nearby. She held her flute in her hands and blew softly over the notes, practicing.

Behind her, on the wall, hung an oil painting of First Winter's Ball, practically the height and width of her room. The figures in the painting were to real-life scale: men and women dressed in elaborate masks and costumes, dancing in dizzying circles, with snow pelting from the sky, and clouds half-covering the moon. If she gazed at the painting long enough, she could almost hear the orchestra, almost smell the perfume of that night.

But that painting was behind her, and a window stood open before her, with the sunlight warm and beckoning upon her face. Lace curtains fluttered in the wind, and brought the smell of honeysuckle and rose into her bedroom.

She set the flute down and gazed outside, her eyes drawn to the ocean of treetops behind the manor house. The wind moved through the woodland. The leaves rippled in shimmering waves, green and silver.

Then, she was not in her bedroom anymore. She stood outside, on the grass, on top of a hill, somewhere far out in that woodland. If she looked over her shoulder, she could almost see the rooftop where her manor stood.

She stood in the shade of a white tree at the very apex of the hill. The tree's bark was unusual, as smooth as whalebone, its branches thin and weaving. They made shapes in the wind, like a deaf man's fingers forming symbols to speak. The leaves flashed and rippled around her, falling through the air like silver coins.

Then she was not alone. Someone emerged from behind the tree. Someone she did not expect to see. Someone who made her recoil in horror.

Volcrian stood beyond the white trunk. The swaying branches cast his face in dappled shade. His eyes were a metallic blue, sharp and manic in their bloodlust.

Her body turned cold. Her palms grew moist. She wanted to run like a deer through the forest, as fast as the wind through the trees, but her feet remained stuck to the ground.

Volcrian rested one hand against the white tree trunk. She felt his touch as though his hand were at her torso. He stroked the bark gently, like one might smooth a wrinkled coat.

"He bound a ribbon to the tree," Volcrian said.

His mouth never moved. Blood trickled from his ears, and the corners of his lips, and his manic eyes. He was not a pretty ghost.

Sora looked at the white tree, where a black ribbon had appeared beneath Volcrian's hand. Layers and layers of complicated knots secured the black ribbon around the white trunk.

Despite Volcrian's repulsive presence, Sora found herself approaching the tree, drawn to the black ribbon.

When she touched the dark silk, her fingers turned to ice.

"The tree is inside of you," Volcrian whispered.

Sora's eyes snapped open.

A variety of concerned faces swam into focus above her.

Then a mighty throb began in her head. She tried to sit up, but a friendly hand--Sister Somana--pinned her down by the shoulder.

"You fell a bit hard. Bumped your head there. Easy now," the sister wheezed.

Trylee, one of the youngest acolytes, whimpered softly nearby.

"Is she alright? Is she hurt?" the girl asked.

"What happened?" Sora asked as the world slowly spun to a halt.

"You screamed, child, and fell right off the bench. Almost took us with you," Sister Somana said, and nodded to another priestess whose name Sora couldn't quite remember at the moment. They all looked gravely serious.

"Can you tell us what happened?" Somana asked.

"I...."

Sora searched for the memory. She felt like she had dozed off. Only the fringes of the dream remained. Her head pulsed again.

"Let me sit up," she said.

They helped her into an upright position.

"Stand aside. Give her time to collect herself." High Priestess Morrighan Karr's voice reached them, calm and cool as water. The fuss and hubbub subsided, and the women broke their circle. The High Priestess entered their midst, and then it seemed like nothing was the matter at all.

Morrighan Karr looked her over with compassion.

"It seems Sora is in good health. Why don't you all head to dinner?" she said to the rest of the group. "I will speak to her alone, in privacy."

The priestesses were quick to comply, and ushered the young acolytes out of the room, though Sora saw their curious glances. Some of the acolytes whispered amongst each other, giggling as they left. Sora tried not to cringe. *They are young,* she reminded herself. The oldest few were still three or four years younger than her. They didn't bully Sora outright, but she was never invited to their table on game nights, and among their clique, she was treated like an outsider. Trylee was the only girl so far who had embraced her with open arms.

Many of the acolytes were skittish around Sora, having heard rumors about her Cat's-Eye necklace and the great battle in the City of Crowns. When Sora first arrived at the temple, Morrighan Karr had given her special access to the Wanderer's training grounds, which also set her apart from the rest of the acolytes. Whether it was because of the special treatment, or because of the rumors, Sora had yet to make many friends among her peers. She tried not to take it personally, but it didn't make life at the temple very comfortable.

The girls left the Sunset Chambers, vanishing into the limestone hallway beyond.

Morrigan Karr helped her onto the wooden bench. She sat next to Sora as though they were equals. Despite this, Sora felt a shiver of apprehension. Morrighan Karr kept close relationships with her disciples; she hand-picked them, after all. But she was still a woman who wielded an immense amount of power across the Southlands and the Kingdom of Err. She answered to no one but the king himself.

"Do you feel well?" Morrigan Karr asked, once the chamber had emptied and the doors were closed.

"Just a slight headache," Sora said, and touched the back of her head where she hit the floor.

"Sometimes, when we meditate, hidden fears and terrors can surface to the forefront of our mind," the High Priestess began. "We might see frightening things from our past. We might remember events that were deeply disturbing to our spirit. The past lives inside of us. We are never truly free from it." Morrighan Karr searched her face. "Is this why you cried out?"

Sora frowned. She rubbed her forehead in thought.

"I...I don't remember. It feels like I fell asleep. I dreamed of...." She reached for the images, but they were fading. "A tree?"

"What kind of tree?"

"It was unusual. It was white and smooth as bone."

Even as Sora described it, the image faded from her mind.

"Perhaps I am misremembering," Sora muttered.

The High Priestess studied her for a moment, then said, "You will remember when the time is right." Then Morrighan continued thoughtfully, "You've told me much of your travels with the Cat's-Eye necklace. I imagine it is quite a burden to carry, especially for one so young. I wouldn't be surprised if some visage of the past still haunts you. Have you had many of these moments, where you fall asleep and can't remember your dreams?"

Sora frowned at the question. "How would I know if I can't remember?"

The High Priestess let out a barking laugh. "True point."

"Is there something wrong with me?" Sora asked suddenly. In truth, she may have experienced such blackouts since arriving at the temple, but she always woke up snoozing somewhere inconspicuous, like on a garden bench or in one of the alcoves near the dorms. She had explained it away as weariness from the heat and dry weather.

"No," Morrighan said, "But I fear your soul is heavy. Perhaps we can work to unburden it together. It's partly why I brought you here. I see in you a young woman called by the Goddess in an extraordinary sense, who has been left on her own to shoulder the burden. But you are not alone anymore, Sora. You have friends here. We can shoulder this burden together, whatever it may be."

Sora looked down at her hands. *We can shoulder this burden together.* Yet the burden of a Cat's-Eye necklace went beyond what even Morrighan Karr could understand. She thought of the garrolithe and her battle with the wraith in the City of Crowns. She thought of her final confrontation with Cerastes. She thought of the seraph, Caprion: his unflinching courage, his certainty of purpose, and his rigid backbone as he turned to greet his death. Caprion had known his purpose, and it made him fearless. But what of her own?

She thought of her dysphoria since Winter Solstice Night. Nothing seemed to lift the fog. Not her mother's wedding to Ferran Ebonaire; not the well-wishes from the Harpy Matriarch; not her studies at the Temple of the South Wind, or the life that still waited for her, back in the City of Crowns.

She had thought life at the temple would give her some sort of reprieve. Here, she could serve her kingdom as a Wanderer. She could find a new purpose. She expected to find a certain amount of joy.... Perhaps not the same joy she had known as an innocent girl on the Fallcrest estate, or as a free spirit on her mother's farm, but some sort of happiness in the face of what she had witnessed that terrible night when Caprion died.

But the fog stayed heavy over her thoughts, and she often found herself dwelling on her darkest memories. She wasn't ready to share those memories with anyone, despite the support she had received from the temple.

"You're right, I haven't been myself," Sora admitted. "I've been meditating, but I haven't found any answers yet." She felt guilty, like she should be better, somehow. "I feel like that dormant seed from your lesson, waiting underground for something to awaken me. The pleasure I take in things--riding horseback, practicing in the training yard, reading--is gone. I feel lost, Priestess."

Morrigan Karr leaned forward. When she spoke, Sora was touched by the sincerity of the High Priestess's concern.

"After a great battle, we must retreat for a time of healing. What you feel, all soldiers, all warriors, feel. You must rest for a time after a great Wind has tumbled you about. Do you see?"

"I do."

"Since coming to our temple, you have been in winter, Sora. But I do believe you will soon find your spring again."

"If the Goddess wills it. Thank you, Priestess."

"Does Lord Gracen still write to you?" Morrigan Karr asked.

The question caught Sora off guard. Before leaving for the South Wind's temple, Lord Gracen Seabourne, captain of the King's personal guard, proposed to her in the City of Crowns. She refused his proposal of marriage, so she hadn't expected his continued letters to the temple, inquiring about her health and happiness. She wasn't sure how it made her feel.

Recently, such correspondence had stopped. She wasn't sure how she felt about that, either.

"It's been some time," Sora admitted.

"Does that disappoint you?"

"I can't say. A bit, I suppose."

Morrighan Karr was thoughtful.

"You keep a wall around your heart, Acolyte Sora."

Sora felt a bit defensive. "How do you mean?"

"It would seem you have been deeply hurt, but you are unwilling to admit it, either to yourself or others."

Sora looked down at her hands. She tried not to think of the City of Crowns, of a night of passion she could not erase. *He left soon after*, she thought. *He warned me he would leave. I shouldn't still carry this disappointment.* But it was there, deep in her heart, hidden away.

"It's easy to dwell on the past as a habit," Morrighan said. "But despite our dwelling, we don't understand the significance of what we've experienced. We can't appreciate it. Sometimes, we must fall in love with something new to love something old."

Sora stared at her mentor, puzzled by her words.

The High Priestess patted her knee.

"Be patient. These dreams will run their course, and you will fall in love with the world again, and then perhaps the past won't seem like such a burden. But first, you should head to dinner. I think they made cactus curry tonight, with flatbread and lentils. A favorite of yours, I believe?"

Sora grinned despite herself, and the High Priestess seemed satisfied. They stood from the bench together. Sora turned to leave the room. She walked around the benches on her way to the mess hall, and she shut the heavy door to the Sunset Chamber behind her.

ABOUT THE AUTHOR

Meet the Author

T. L. Shreffler is a noblewoman living in the misty forests of Snohomish County, Washington. She enjoys long hikes through the wilderness, drinking strong coffee or teas, exploring the unknown reaches of her homeland and unearthing rare artifacts in thrift stores. She holds a Bachelors in Eloquence (English) and writes Fantasy and poetry. She is the author of *The Cat's Eye Chronicles,* *Skydust Kingdoms* and *The Dragon Pearl* series.

FOLLOW T. L. SHREFFLER

Follow
T. L. Shreffler
on Social Media!

Email
therunawaypen@gmail.com

Join the mailing list!
www.catseyechronicles.com

Instagram
@catseyeauthor

Tiktok
@catseyeauthor

Pinterest
www.pinterest.com/catseyeauthor

Facebook
www.facebook.com/tlshreffler

BUY A SIGNED COPY!

www.ingramcontent.com/pod-product-compliance
Lightning Source LLC
Chambersburg PA
CBHW030650020726
47493CB00006B/1958